Eater of Hearts

THE BOOK OF COMING FORTH BY DAY
Part Three

LIBBIE HAWKER

The Book of Coming Forth by Day:
Part 3: Eater of Hearts

Copyright 2015, 2016
Libbie Hawker

Running Rabbit Press
San Juan County, WA

Second Print Edition

Cover design and formatting by Running Rabbit Press.
Original cover illustration copyright Lane Brown.

290 ½

MORE BOOKS BY LIBBIE HAWKER

The Book of Coming Forth by Day:
House of Rejoicing
Storm in the Sky

Baptism for the Dead
Tidewater
Daughter of Sand and Stone
Mercer Girls
The Sekhmet Bed
The Crook and Flail
Sovereign of Stars
The Bull of Min

For Paul.

The names of the sacred cattle are:
House of *Kas*, Mistress of All;
Silent One who dwells in her place;
She of Chemmis, whom the god ennobled;
The Much Beloved, red of hair;
She who protects in life, the particolored;
She whose name has power in her craft;
Storm in the Sky, who holds the god aloft;
The Bull, the husband of the cows.

-*The Book of the Dead*, Spell 148.

Ankhesenamun

Year 1 of Horemheb,
Holy Are the Manifestations,
Chosen of Re

TIY'S LIMP BODY was the first thing Akhenaten saw when he entered the temple for the morning ceremony. There she lay, face turned up as if in defiance of the rising sun, but all her haughty power diminished by the stillness of death.

There before his cadre of guards and his ranks of white-kilted priests, Akhenaten fell into the sand beside his mother's body. He wailed up at his lone god, but I am certain his cries were not born of grief. By that time, having been so thoroughly consumed by the singular power any Pharaoh enjoyed, I believe Akhenaten could feel neither affection nor sympathy for any living being. Grief, desolation, the totality of loss—these emotions were as foreign to his heart as the thoughts of a cat or a bird are to human comprehension.

But Akhenaten did have the capacity to feel terror. Fear of his god—of its judgment and punishment—had settled deep into his heart, and like an animal harried by a jackal's jaws, he leaped and turned and dodged with his every word and decision, hoping to save himself from the Aten's disfavor and brutal condemnation.

Tiy's death struck the king an especially devastating blow. I believe that in the loss of his mother, Akhenaten foreglimpsed the inevitable decline of his own strength, the draining away of his creative power—for now that Tiy had joined Akhenaten's father in the afterlife, the original fertile field from which his dynasty sprang had finally dried up and blown away.

The Pharaoh lavished extravagant care on Tiy during all the long rites of her funeral. When the seventy days of her ritual embalming came to a close, he summoned the whole of Akhet-Aten to join the procession to her tomb. The stream of mourners climbed into the high cliffs behind the City of the Sun, seeming as long and broad as the Iteru River. The faces and clothing of the Pharaoh's subjects were darkened with soot and ash, and each strove to cry louder than the others so that they might gain more of Akhenaten's favor.

I remember riding in the royal litter. It was as wide as an ox hide, and was carried by at least two dozen strong soldiers. My sister Meritaten was the last King's Wife remaining, so she sat beside the Pharaoh on a huge, gilded throne. As the only King's Daughter left—the only one who was not bound to Akhenaten in marriage, at any rate—I held a special place at court. I sat on a silk cushion between the feet of my sister and the king. It was a place of ostentatious display. I was the last living proof to the City of the Sun that my father was great in fertility, the very master of creation.

Because Akhenaten wished to be seen—worshiped, one might say—there was no canopy to shelter the litter. I sat straight-backed and unmoving, but I can still recall the heat of the sun, the sweat trickling down my neck to dampen my linen—green, to symbolize rebirth. I remember how the litter tilted sharply and swayed as the procession climbed a steep, red trail that snaked up the face of the cliff. I remember the beaded sweat sparkling on the bearers' backs like cut stones set in gold.

From my place at Akhenaten's feet, I watched as the priests of the Aten bore Tiy's huge, ornate coffin up to her rock-cut tomb. They walked ahead of us, eight men on each side of my grandmother's sarcophagus, which was shaped like a young woman in repose, ornamented with inset jewels and bands of lapis lazuli. The carved face of the coffin was smooth, where Tiy's had been deeply lined; it was bright with gold, though Tiy's true face had been as dark as aged ebony. It smiled gently, serenely—but I could have counted on the fingers of one hand all the times I had seen my grandmother smile. The funeral seemed one great falsehood to me—especially the wails of Akhenaten's people, whose clamor was only intended to gratify the king, not to fortify Tiy's *ka* and *ba* as she trekked down into the Duat.

But the screams and sobs of the people seemed to have the desired effect on Akhenaten. Now and again I glanced up at him and saw him nod, his eyes shining with a light I knew well—a hard, certain spark that said he felt himself cloaked in *maat*, and therefore incapable of doing wrong. It was an expression he wore often in those strange and dangerous latter years, and the longer he wore it, the more fixed it seemed to become.

But when we were deep inside Tiy's final resting place, I saw the king's belief in his own infallibility crumble.

When the procession reached its destination, the sixteen priests lowered my grandmother's coffin outside the maze of chambers, the long corridors and treasure-rooms that were her royal tomb. There, in those shadow-cold halls, Tiy would begin the ordeal of the underworld. The procession fell silent and we all listened, wiping sweat from our brows, as one of the foremost priests of the Great Aten Temple recited a long, poetic litany to the god. My father had written and perfected the piece during the seventy days of Tiy's embalming, and though I am not an Aten-worshiper now, even I must admit it was moving, in a strange and mystical way. When the priest fell silent, Tiy's remaining family—the king, Meritaten, my grandfather, and I—gathered around her coffin and followed it into the blue-dark depths of its resting place.

As we descended into the stone heart of the cliffs, I stared around me in frank amazement. By that time, I had seen every one of my sisters, save for Meritaten, consigned to the realm of the dead. I had witnessed Baketaten's burial, too. But no matter how many funerals I attended, the spells and incantations that covered all of a tomb's surfaces—walls, ceiling, and floor—never ceased to astonish me. My skin prickled as we followed Tiy to her sleeping chamber. It seemed I could feel the sacred writing—and the ethereal, bright-painted images that accompanied those words—coming to life all around me. They whispered their secrets in my ears. They told me, just as they told the dead, all the mysteries of the underworld. What words must be spoken to the guardians of the twelve hours of the night; how I must comport myself when I stood for each phase of my judgment; what magics I must work to pass from the Duat and into the West where the Field of Reeds awaited. There, amid water and rich, black soil—amid flocks of fat, lively birds and herds of gazelle—the happy dead live on forever.

Bless you, Waser the green-skinned, god of rebirth, for granting me that knowledge. For if tonight I meet my death, I cannot be sure of a tomb of my own. I cannot trust to spells and directions incised into cool, dark stone. My body may be discarded without ceremony in a sand pit at the edge of the Red Land. Worse, it may be thrown into the river so that the crocodiles tear and scatter me, as you, Waser, were torn and scattered by that envious god-killer, Set. If I am not granted a tomb to lead me safely through the Duat, then I must rely on memory alone—and I must hope I can recall every detail of Tiy's final, lightless home. If memory fails me, my poor *ba* shall wander lost and hopeless until chaos swallows the world and the gods remake it anew.

I was not the only one who stared around the dark,

narrow passages, wide-eyed and transfixed. By the time we reached Tiy's sleeping chamber, Akhenaten trembled and his skin ran with streams of sweat, even though the air so far below the ground was as cold as the river in winter.

The priests began their last song of respect to a great woman: A King's Mother and King's Great Wife, one who had handled Egypt well, even after she fell from the Pharaoh's graces. But Akhenaten seemed not to hear their song. His shaking intensified; he moaned and sagged forward, bracing his weight with rigid arms against Tiy's coffin, staring fearfully into her smiling, golden face.

The song of praise and farewell trailed off into uncertain silence.

Meritaten was at our father's side at once. She shook him gently by the shoulder, and when he did not respond she spoke sharply in his ear. But Akhenaten did not hear her, nor did he feel her touch. Meritaten shook him harder and raised her voice until the tomb echoed with her concern. She was on the verge of slapping his cheek to bring back his senses, but all at once the king coughed and heaved as if wrestling with nausea. In the flickering light of a few small lamps I could see the eerie paleness of his face.

"She is here!" Akhenaten cried suddenly. His voice was everywhere within the confines of the chamber, redoubling itself against the walls, so piercing I nearly forgot propriety and clapped my hands to my ears. "I see her—my sister, beautiful Sitamun, shrouded in the wrappings of death!"

Meritaten gasped, glancing around as if she might see the specter, too. But there was nothing, of course—no one at all in the chamber save for these last few members of the royal family and the priests whom Akhenaten held in thrall.

"She has come," the king babbled on. His eyes were wide,

their whites showing like clear, pure cuts of alabaster. "She has come to greet our mother. She has come to bar my way. For the sake of dear Baketaten—for poor lost Nebetah!"

Akhenaten lurched away from the coffin and staggered back toward the tomb's long hall. Ay moved to stop him—it was an ill thing, to leave a tomb before the rites were finished—but Ay was an aging man and Akhenaten was still strong, in body if not in *ka*. The king knocked my grandfather aside, as if he were as small and light as a gnat. Then he rushed from Tiy's resting place, his panicked cries echoing loud in the belly of the tomb.

"Finish the rites," Ay barked at the priests. One by one, they picked up the song where they had dropped it.

"If he wasn't mad enough before," Ay said quietly to Meritaten, so low I could barely hear his words, "he surely is now. It's time you brought the king under control, girl, and the sooner the better."

I heard Meritaten's ragged breath, soft as the murmur of the river. "But how? I don't know how—"

Ay jerked his head impatiently toward the coffin. "Tiy was your grandmother. You have her blood in your veins. Live up to her legacy, or we will all perish."

In the dimness of the tomb, Meritaten's hand slipped into mine. She clung to me with cold, trembling fingers. I squeezed her hand for reassurance, but there was little else I could offer. Though she had ruled from the shadows and never stepped into the light, our grandmother Tiy had been the greatest sovereign Egypt had ever known. How could my sister govern half so well... and how could she ever hope to bring a mad king back to his senses?

Another of Akhenaten's cries carried faintly down through the darkness. It made a dreadful tightness in my throat, and in the priests' small ring of lamplight the magic etched into stone seemed to melt, flowing down the walls like spilled wine—like blood.

Meritaten

Year 17 of Akhenaten
Beautiful Are the Manifestations,
Exalting the Name,
Beloved of the Sun

MERITATEN LAY BACK on the down-soft slope of her mattress. She had sent all her maids away; the huge, lavish apartments of the King's Great Wife were empty save for Meritaten herself. The sound of her gentle breath, barely stirring her chest, seemed to fill the whole world. She closed her eyes, delighting in the stillness. There was no rustle of maids' linen dresses as they went about their work, no low hum of their quiet gossip. The strings of her harps and skins of her drums did not vibrate with music, but stood silent and untouched in the alcove where she entertained ladies of the court when the mood for entertainment was upon her.

That mood had not visited Meritaten often over the past two years. Since that fateful day when she and the dregs of her family had sealed Tiy up in her tomb, Meritaten had known precious few moments of joy, or even of simple peace. On that ill-omened day, the fissure in the king's heart had finally broken open, just as heavy rains sometimes open pits in the earth. The hole inside his *ka* yawned wide to reveal a vista of unsettling darkness, its edges crumbling inward, bits of his personality slipping down to vanish forever in the sinkhole of his madness.

Every day since had been a struggle for Meritaten. Every day she had fought her father to remain on her own two feet, to avoid the force of his insanity—that terrible weight that pulled at her like thick, sliding sand, seeking to drag her down into the dark. Every day she had begged the god for mercy, for strength. But her strength was fading away—she could feel it in the trembling weakness of her limbs and back, in the way she sank heavily into her mattress and had no energy to move, not even to flick a fly from her skin. She begged the Aten for succor, but the god, as ever, did not answer.

In the merciful peace of her chamber, Meritaten heard the whisper of a small, rhythmic padding. Smiling despite the effort it cost her weary body, she stretched out her hand, and in a moment the cat sprang lightly up to her bed with an inquisitive, purring meow. Meritaten did not open her eyes, but when the cat placed himself under her hand she stroked his fine, soft fur.

"I'm only seventeen years old," she told Miu-Miu, "but I feel as tired and used-up as the most withered old grandmother."

The cat butted his head against Meritaten's hand, demanding more affection.

"The god will grant me no respite from my work—no one to aid me, to share my burden."

And what a heavy burden it was. One never knew when Akhenaten might break into terrified yelps, shouting about the spirits that followed him through the palace halls or crying out to the god to protect him from curses, from evil eyes, from the ill thoughts of all those who conspired against him, in the living realm and in the world of the dead. He was susceptible to these fits at any time of the day or night, and without regard to his surroundings. Sometimes, while hearing the petitions of his subjects, he trailed off in the midst of a pronouncement and stared down the length of the throne room, his eyes unfocused yet terrified. Or, while leading chants and prayers in either of the two Aten temples, his hymns of praise would rise suddenly as a harsh wail, and turn to cries of dread.

In the months just after Tiy's funeral, Meritaten had been utterly helpless to cope with the Pharaoh's sudden swings. Ay had pressured her relentlessly in those days, issuing nonspecific threats that only cost her sleep and often wracked her heart with palpitations. But as time wore on, she began to notice subtle shifts in the king's behavior—the beading of sweat along the band of his red-and-white crown, the darting of his bloodshot eyes, the flick of his tongue over dry, fleshy lips. When his hands trembled in a particular, persistent way, or when his voice caught and sounded faintly strangled, Meritaten knew she must act quickly, for a turn of mood was coming. In those moments, she was quick to dismiss the court, to hurry the temple ceremonies along, to lead the king off to his bedchamber where she could distract him from his fears. But all too often, she missed Akhenaten's cryptic signs until it was too late to act. And every time the king wept before his court, calling out for Baketaten—every time he shook with fear and threw up his hands to fend off the attacks of an invisible assailant—Meritaten felt Ay's displeasure boring into her heart like a dagger through her flesh.

A loud, wordless cry pealed through the garden. Birds, startled from their evening roost, erupted from the branches of a sycamore with a clatter of wings. Meritaten lurched up and stared out her bedchamber door into the sunset glow of the garden, but she saw no one—nothing save a scattering of leaves falling from the sycamore, knocked from the branches by the birds' hasty departure.

Miu-Miu had leaped to his feet. His body arched like a white bow; his fur bristled with fear as he hissed toward the garden door.

"Sitamun!" The king's voice called mournfully across the garden grounds. "Sitamun, forgive me!"

Meritaten sighed, soothing Miu-Miu with a trembling hand. "It's only the Pharaoh. Isn't it always? Haunted yet again by the spirits of the dead." *It's only my father—my husband. The king of Egypt, master of the Iteru, with a* ka *as useless as a child's broken toy.*

"How I wish we were back in our own northern palace," she whispered to the cat. There she had been able to enjoy peace and beauty, and all the fine, expensive things she desired. There she had lived well apart from Akhenaten— and Ay. There she had been able to shed the demands of court life. But as the king slid further into madness, Meritaten had been obliged to leave her bright, beautiful sanctuary and take up with Akhenaten at his great palace beside the river.

Exhaustion dragged at her, body and *ka*, urging her to sleep—to sleep for a hundred years until Akhenaten was nothing but a dark memory. She wished to sleep until even her memories were dust, trodden underfoot and washed away by the river's deep, eternal current. Then she could wake to a world made fresh and new. Then she could be happy.

Meritaten picked up the cat, cuddling him close. She buried her face against his softness and breathed in his smell, an animal sharpness softened by the clinging notes of myrrh and spice and lazy warmth of garden sunshine. Miu-Miu was her only friend now, the only being in whom she dared confide. She was King's Great Wife—by default, having outlived much better women, women more aptly suited to the rigors of the throne and the stresses of Akhenaten's madness. But even so, she *was* the Great Wife, and a Great Wife could never reveal her weaknesses to any woman or man.

To think there was a time when I envied the King's Wives, and coveted their thrones. Now marriage to the Pharaoh felt like a punishment, not a reward—not a birthright fit for a woman born of royal blood, the glorious half-divine.

Meritaten nearly asked herself what she had done to deserve such a harsh penalty. But before the thought could fully form, she bit her lip to stifle it—as she had done for the past two years. Nearly every day since Tiy's death, those dark musings had haunted Meritaten's heart. And always she pushed stark truth away, afraid to examine too closely the ugliness she knew she would find there.

In that very moment, as if to mock her fears, Akhenaten's hoarse shout filled the garden. "Baketaten! My golden one, my *ka!*"

Meritaten shuddered.

Miu-Miu twisted in her grip and sprang from her arms. The cat bounded off the bed and raced across her chamber, tail puffed as if demons pursued him.

She swallowed hard. Tears stung her eyes, and she nearly cried out for help—called to her nurse or her mother. But Nefertiti was long gone. She had vanished from the City of the Sun the same night Meketaten died. Like the rest of the court, Meritaten presumed Nefertiti had long since died, by her own hand or by another's.

Nefertiti left this mess on my hands. She left me alone with this creature we must call the king. What was I to do, if I wished to keep my place in the world? I was only a young girl, and I had no mother to guide me, no one to consult before I acted.

She bit her knuckle hard until her thoughts stilled. This was the closest she had ever come to admitting the part she had played in that bloody mess, the tragedy that had whisked Baketaten from the Pharaoh's life. Her heart raced, pounding painfully in her chest, the beats ringing like temple gongs in her ears. For a long moment she struggled with herself, gasping in the chamber's silence. She clutched at her throat to soothe its tight burning, and squeezed her eyes shut to banish her tears. But finally she calmed, and when she could breathe easily again she found that her thoughts were startlingly clear.

Akhenaten never had learned the truth of his little favorite's death. Meritaten had lived in terror for several days after Baketaten was killed, certain Mahu would be suspected simply due to his brute strength, if not his reputation for swift and merciless violence. Then the cold-eyed guard would be questioned and the Pharaoh would realize Meritaten was behind the attack. Meritaten had known that once Akhenaten suspected her, her royal blood wouldn't save her—nor would all the hours she had toiled in the king's bed. She would be staked out in the Great Aten Temple to suffer under the god's fiery glare.

But Akhenaten, shattered by grief, had refused to listen to any person who implicated his trusted bodyguard. Instead, he had set his priests to work, conjuring and casting spells, consulting the omens of the god. Within days, the priests had whispered a name into Akhenaten's ear—some poor, hapless *rekhet*, a filthy, staring man without a home, whose heart was as blasted by madness as the king's. Mahu executed the *rekhet* on the Pharaoh's orders, that very day. Meritaten was grateful that she had never learned the method of the man's death. That the king had not required Meritaten to watch the execution was one of the few small mercies the Aten had ever granted her.

All this madness, all this suffering, thanks to Baketaten and her mother. How strange, that I never learned the reason for Baketaten's death. Perhaps it is time I found out just what went wrong that night.

The moment Meritaten thought those words, a blissful peace descended on her *ka*, soothing her under a blanket of warmth. Yes—surely *that* was what the god required! She must confront her past sins, then make whatever amends she could. Then perhaps the Aten would release the king from these hauntings—this long, terrible plague of madness. Then the Pharaoh's *ka* as well as Meritaten's would be easy once more. With the dead appeased—with proper atonement and contrition—life could be beautiful and free again, as it was in the days when she dwelt at the northern palace.

But Meritaten couldn't make amends to the god until she knew how Baketaten had died—and why. She drew a long, steady breath to firm her resolve. Then Meritaten dragged herself from her bed and prepared to stand in the god's eye.

By the time she changed her wig and finished freshening her eye paints, the sun had set, and a slow, gentle twilight had descended on the palace. Dusky, violet shadows hung in the corners of her room like wisps of old spider webs. She wrapped a thick shawl tightly about her shoulders and slipped out of her lavish apartments before the maids could return with supper and fresh oil for her lamps. She did not want her women interfering with her plans or insisting that they accompany her. A trail of flighty, gossipy women would only distract and annoy her. Worse, they would certainly prevent Mahu from speaking plainly once she found him. And tonight, at long last, Meritaten must have the truth.

She had not seen the Pharaoh's personal guardsman for several days, yet she had no doubt that Mahu could be found somewhere in the palace. From the moment his visions of Sitamun had begun, Akhenaten had hardly allowed his bodyguard out of his sight. Even in those rare moments when the Pharaoh relaxed his grip on Mahu, the guard was still not permitted to leave the palace grounds. Akhenaten's fear of shadows—of vague, half-seen threats—had grown steadily stronger since Tiy's death. Tiy's departure was clearly a suicide: the priests of the Aten had found an empty vial in the sand beside her body, and a court magician had confirmed that the small bottle had held a powerful, fast-acting poison. Even so, Akhenaten was convinced that some veiled assassin had struck Tiy down, and might come for him, too—and thus Mahu was needed close by the king's side. The burly man

19

never patrolled the city anymore, nor did he lurk in the cliffs that held the City of the Sun in their red, stony grip. Mahu was tethered to the king by duty, but if he resented his restricted life, he was careful never to show it.

Meritaten slipped quietly down pillared halls. She skirted patches of new-risen moonlight that lent an eerie silver luminosity to courtyards and fountains. Silent and swift as a stream of water, she flowed from one pool of shadow to the next, examining every alcove and portico she passed, staring into its deep pockets of shadow for any sign of Mahu's presence.

But she found no hint of him—no towering slab of darkness to outline his form, no prickle on her skin to warn of his cold, detached gaze.

Voices moved like drifts of smoke into the confluence of two umber-dark hallways. Meritaten paused, trembling with sudden anxiety. She did not recognize the voices, nor could she make out any of their words. She could not even say whether they were male or female, nor whether they belonged to the living or the dead. She only knew that she did not wish to be found by anyone—servant, noble, priest or guardsman—unless that guard was Mahu. She pressed herself back into the shadows of a recessed doorway and held her breath, waiting for the unseen murmurers to pass her by. But after a long moment, she realized the voices came no closer, and Meritaten sighed in relief, slipping off into the colonnades to continue her search of the palace.

She walked that way for more than an hour, dodging any potential watcher, cloaking herself in darkness whenever she heard the whisper of distant voices. But she found no hint of Mahu's presence. Finally, on the edge of another moonlit courtyard, Meritaten pressed herself against a pillar and gazed around the open space in helpless defeat. The moon paled the mudbrick pavers of the courtyard; they looked almost as smooth and bright as electrum.

A single, raised lily pond, small and round, stood in the center of the courtyard. Starlight glinted in the gaps between lotus leaves, gleaming on the still water. There was nothing else in the courtyard—no potted fig trees, no vine-covered bower. And certainly no guardsman.

Mahu is nowhere to be found, Meritaten told herself sensibly, but not without disappointment. *He must be closeted with the king tonight—standing guard inside his chamber.*

Briefly, she considered searching for Mahu in Akhenaten's chamber. But so close beside the king's ear, Meritaten knew she could never speak freely to Mahu about the night Baketaten died.

I shall have to give it up. I may try again tomorrow, if the god permits.

In that moment a faint chirping caught her attention. The noise was like a chorus of sparrows, if the birds were no bigger than mustard seeds. Meritaten glanced up and saw several small black bats tumble across the sky, their little bodies flitting over the field of stars. She followed the bats' direction with her eyes—then gasped. There on the palace wall, silhouetted against the slim curve of the moon, stood the unmistakable, broad-shouldered tower that was Mahu.

Meritaten's stomach lurched with a sudden swell of nausea. But before she could talk herself out of this mad mission, she hurried across the courtyard and up a long, narrow stairway that led to the walkway at the wall's pinnacle. She was out of breath by the time she reached that vantage high above the palace grounds. She stared out at the city and the river beyond. Both glittered with small lights—the city from its many lamps and the fires of rooftop braziers, the river with its reflection of stars.

Mahu did not seem the least bit surprised to find Meritaten here, staring up at him in the blue dimness of night. She supposed the ever-watchful man had been aware of her scampering through the courtyard, and aware of her headlong rush up the stairs, too. Meritaten drew herself up to her full height and faced him squarely, determined to confront him as a self-possessed Great Wife, and not as a girl slinking through night-time shadows.

He said nothing, but raised his eyebrow in a silent question when Meritaten met and held his eye. Meritaten altered her expression to a harsh glare, one that might have done Tiy proud—or so she hoped. It must have been fierce enough; Mahu bowed, albeit much too lazily. He barely hid the frank amusement in his eyes.

"Great Wife," Mahu said smoothly. "How may I be of service?"

She had planned this encounter all evening long, but now that she was faced with its reality, she could find no words. She only stared up at Mahu, feeling foolish and small.

Then, from somewhere far below, from a dark corridor or a moon-silvered garden, Akhenaten cried out against his imagined attackers. Meritaten and Mahu both turned their heads the sound. But soon the murmur of night insects rose up again, and the Pharaoh remained silent.

When Mahu looked at her again, Meritaten found she had a voice after all. "I've come to speak to you about... *that incident*. Two years ago."

Mahu tipped his head, an impudent show of curiosity. "Incident?"

"I want to know what happened to King's Wife Baketaten."

"She died."

His dry, smug demeanor sent hot fury racing down Meritaten's veins. "I *know* she died. Now you must tell me *why*."

Meritaten held his hard stare for a moment, then turned abruptly away. She drifted to the edge of the wall and peered down into the courtyard, but she could see no one below. Their conversation was as private as could be.

She turned back to Mahu with a cross frown. "I specifically told you not to kill her. I told you to *frighten* her. Why did you disobey me?"

"I don't know what you're talking about," Mahu said shortly.

Meritaten knew full well that most of the king's court did not take her seriously. She was young, and woefully unfit for life on the throne—even she was ready to admit that much. But over the past two years, she had grown in confidence and power, and she was not quite the fool she had once been. She drew herself up sharply and leveled a hard stare at the man, so hard he blinked and glanced guiltily away.

"Don't play the simpleton with me, Mahu. An innocent man suffered and died in your place, but *I* know the truth. I know who killed Baketaten. And I have the king's ear, as well as his heart. Explain yourself to me, or Akhenaten will hear the truth. And he will not be pleased."

Mahu's sandals hissed against mudbrick as he took one menacing step toward her. Meritaten's stomach clenched. In a flash, she was painfully aware that she stood high above the earth, at the top of a soaring palace wall. One shove from Mahu, and she would plummet to her death. She forced herself to stand her ground, silently begging the god to still her trembling.

To her immeasurable relief, Mahu shrugged, expelling a huff of surrender. "What happened was... an accident, Great Wife. It's as simple as that. I intended to do just as you bade me. I watched Baketaten for some time, learned her routines and the habits of her attending maids. When I could be sure she and her women were gone from her chambers, I entered them myself. I only planned to set her things in disarray—to break or soil her belongings, make a mess of the place so she would feel unsafe... so she would know, as you wished, that she was not beyond the reach of your anger.

"But she returned to her chamber unexpectedly. I've no idea why. She found me in the act of destroying her property—came upon me so suddenly that I'm afraid it was I who was startled, not she. Baketaten opened her mouth to shout for help, to bring witnesses... and before I could think, before I could stop myself, I lashed out with my club. She was a small woman, and I am... well, I am what you see before you. One blow of my club was all it took to end her life."

Chilled and stricken, Meritaten nodded. Yet even as she shuddered at the thought of Mahu swinging his club, she also felt strangely soothed. All this time she had wondered what had happened on that terrible night— what Mahu had been thinking when he had lashed out with such breathtaking violence at Baketaten. Knowing at last—picturing Baketaten's final moments, however gruesome—brought her a grim sort of peace.

Finally she asked, "But how did you avoid being caught? Baketaten's women found her so fast... almost while her blood was still flowing."

"I leaped out her bed-chamber window. It was a risky move—anyone at all might have been in her garden, and might have seen me do it. But the garden was empty. I've often wondered why the god arranged it so. I can only assume that the Aten wished me to live. The god is not yet done with me. There is more work I must do in the Aten's service."

Meritaten wrapped her arms around her body, hoping the gesture hid her shiver. "Perhaps that is so."

"By cutting through the garden, I was able to circle back around and arrive at Baketaten's chamber door just as the other guards did. In that manner, I removed myself from suspicion."

"Clever," she said dully. Then her stare sharpened on him once more. "But still, you disobeyed my command. And now you can see what your blunder wrought for us all—the Pharaoh believes himself harassed by Baketaten's spirit, as well as her mother's. If his favorite wife hadn't died, his heart would have remained untroubled."

"Great Wife, it is all one to me, whether a mad king or a sober king rules Egypt. The god doesn't seem to care, one way or the other. The Iteru has risen and fallen in its due course for all the years of Akhenaten's reign. The Aten seems well pleased with our king, even as he loses his wits. Who am I to question the will of the god?"

"You have no idea the strain this has placed on Egypt," Meritaten said sharply. "I wouldn't expect one such as you to understand. In truth, I ought to have you killed as punishment for your blunder. Perhaps that will appease the Aten enough that he will free the king from his madness!"

Mahu laughed indulgently. The sound of it gripped Meritaten's heart in a cold fist. She knew in a moment that she had dared too far.

"Try it, little King's Wife, and I'll tell the Pharaoh, the court, the whole damned world that it was *you* who hired me to kill Baketaten."

She swallowed hard. Mahu had her caught, like a goose in a fowler's net. He knew it, too—she could see it in his eyes, in their sudden, hot flare of greed and triumph.

"By the way," Mahu said casually, "you never paid me for the job. You promised me many fine goods in exchange for—"

"You filthy creature! Here, take your payment!"

Meritaten clawed one golden bracelet from her wrist. She pulled back her arm, taut as an archer's bow, and threw the bauble as hard as she could at Mahu's grinning face. One of his huge hands flashed up; he caught the bracelet easily, then held it up to the starlight to examine it.

"That's all you'll ever get from me," Meritaten hissed. "Be glad I don't give you a spear in your guts, too. That would be a more suitable payment, by far!"

She spun away from Mahu and hurried back down the stairs. Laughter as harsh as a stoneworker's rasp trailed after her, grating on her nerves and filling her gut with fear until she lost herself in the shadows of the palace corridors.

Meritaten ran all the way back to her apartments, holding the fine linen of her skirt so tightly in her fists that by the time she reached her door the fabric was hopelessly creased where she had gripped it. She cursed under her breath, trying to smooth away the evidence of her unseemly, panicked state.

I ran like a rabbit from a hawk. Tiy never would have shown such fear. And my mother Nefertiti never would have allowed a man like Mahu to laugh at her, to mock her...

When her breathing steadied—as much as she could hope for, at any rate—Meritaten pushed open her chamber door. A handful of maids flitted about the receiving room and the living quarters beyond, lighting cheery lamps, murmuring in quiet conversation as they readied her rooms for the night. Their familiar presence was a comfort to Meritaten, as was the smell of her supper, which wafted from a tray on her low ebony table.

Meritaten sank down on her couch and stared at her supper. The maids had brought her beef broth with onions, and fresh-baked bread. A wisp of pale steam rose from the bowl. The onions were plump and translucent, the bread soft and fragrant—but her stomach twisted, and she found she had no appetite.

"Is anything amiss, Great Wife?" Meha'a, the most

senior of Meritaten's personal staff, leaned over the table and examined the tray of food with concern.

"No, nothing is wrong," Meritaten reassured her. "I... I simply have small appetite. We had a difficult day at court; the king was affected worse than he normally is."

"A little broth will keep your strength up," Meha'a said. The older woman's dark eyes shone with sympathy. "I will pray to the Aten to fortify you, my lady."

Much good may it do me, Meritaten thought wryly. *If the god doesn't listen to my prayers, I see no reason why he would listen to yours.*

Meritaten tried to oblige her maid by dunking a bit of bread in her soup. But when she tried to swallow the morsel, her throat tightened. She nearly choked. The lamps in her chambers did little to beat back the surrounding night. She could feel darkness closing all around her, waiting just on the other side of her walls. Darkness—shadow—a fitting disguise for Mahu, whose heart was as black as ash.

He will find me in the night and wrap his hands around my throat. Or hit me in the face, as he did to Baketaten.

Meritaten dropped the bread back onto the tray and stood impatiently. "All of you leave me, save for Meha'a and two others. You may choose who will stay, Meha'a. But when the rest of my women are gone, bar my doors—all of them."

"Bar your doors, Great Wife?"

"You heard me. I am going to bed now, Meha'a. You and your women may sleep on mats in my room."

Their nearness might bring some comfort, though Meritaten would have preferred strong, alert soldiers to watch over her sleep. No chance of finding any soldiers now—not without rousing Mahu's suspicion.

Silent and pensive, Meritaten allowed her women to dress her for bed. They turned back the sheets and coverlets of her bed, and she crawled beneath those warm linens and curled herself tightly, trying to ignore the night that blackened her narrow chamber window. Miu-Miu leaped onto the bed, announcing his presence with a loud meow. Meritaten lifted an edge of her bedding so the cat could slide underneath. Miu-Miu settled in a ball of warmth against Meritaten's chest. His soft fur and gentle purring calmed her a little, and ordered her thoughts so that she could examine her predicament with greater clarity.

The night's encounter with Mahu had brought her no closer to righting past wrongs, nor to appeasing the god and holding together the king's unraveling sanity. While her women prepared their sleeping mats, Meritaten stared at the nearest lamp, captivated by the slow, irregular dance of its amber-red flame. She could see Ay's disapproving stare, his hard, unforgiving eyes, flickering in the lamp's light. In her heart she could hear her grandfather's voice, chastising her, insisting she find a way to bring the king under control.

Ay—he has haunted me since Tiy's funeral, just as Sitamun haunts the Pharaoh.

Meritaten had tried to avoid the old man as much as possible over the past two years; his judgment and anger made her nervous—made her feel like a useless little fool. But now, as Meritaten lay stroking Miu-Miu's fur, she realized that her grandfather might be the answer to her predicament. The old man was exceedingly shrewd. Was it possible that Ay knew some obscure way to bring Akhenaten to heel? For Meritaten, the situation had become dire. Mahu was a threat to her now—and the Pharaoh was the only man in all the world who could control Mahu.

"I must go to Ay in the morning," she whispered to the cat. Miu-Miu yawned, taking no interest in her words. "Perhaps it is time my grandfather and I worked together."

Ay

Year 17 of Akhenaten
Beautiful Are the Manifestations,
Exalting the Name,
Beloved of the Sun

AY ROSE BEFORE THE SUN, as he did every day. It was his custom to stand alert and ready on the roof of his apartments, to fix the first bright beams of the morning with his stern, observant eye. He liked to watch light spill over the crest of Akhet-Aten's cliffs, liked to watch it pool and creep along the narrow alleys and grand, broad roads of the city. It gave him a sensation of surety, of knowing all that was to come.

He sipped from a bowl of thoroughly watered wine, training his attention on the place where the cliffs dipped inward like a northman's saddle. There the sun would make its first appearance—there he would see the vision that had first inspired Akhenaten to build the City of the Sun. A thread of bright-red light traced the lower edge of the dip. Then the rim of the sun-disc rose ponderously into view. Brilliant orange fire flared across the cliffs, but Ay did not squint as he watched the god awaken, nor did he shield his eyes. The Aten did not yet burn so brightly that an old man couldn't stare the god down.

Ay's mouth twisted wryly as he watched the sun rise. The Aten—a faceless, uncaring god, whose only attributes were heat and light. The Aten was possessed of no fury, no love, no passions of any kind. Therefore, it had no reason to care about the mortals who worshiped it as it moved across the sky, intent on its inscrutable business. The god had no concern for the City of the Sun—nor the mad king at its heart, who grew madder by the day. And if it did not care for Akhet-Aten, then the god had no reason to trouble itself about Egypt as a whole. It seemed to Ay that he was the only being left—mortal or divine—who cared at all for Egypt's fate.

The sun blazed, pulling itself higher over the hills, surging with its own hot power. More of its grand, golden disc showed, and the light became painful to look at. Ay blinked water from his eyes and finally turned his gaze away. The Aten had won again—as it always did. The outcome of this game was predictable, but somehow Ay never tired of playing it.

What is it about the Aten that so provokes me? Why this scorn? He questioned himself with casual curiosity, like a child examining pebbles in a stream. The Aten was a god like any other, though a good deal less personable than Egypt's older gods. Ay had never been a devotee of any god in particular. He attended the temple whenever such duties were required, but he had never been rocked by religious spasms of either fear or bliss. Even so, Ay was not fool enough to actually incite the wrath of *any* divine being, if he could help it.

It was the world of men—of power—that truly interested Ay, not the world of the gods. This realm, which he could see and touch and taste, was a world Ay could observe now, affect now, while he was still alive and potent. Like any sensible Egyptian of means, he had built for himself a lavish tomb. One day its spells would guide him to his final reward. But even then, he would be loath to leave this thrilling realm of power behind.

Who will look after you, poor, broken Egypt, when I am gone?

Distantly, Ay wondered what the other gods thought of the mess Egypt was in—the old gods, the ones the Aten had displaced. Did they still care for this land at all? Were they shut out while the Aten remained supreme, and would they return one day when the Aten fell—when the sun finally set on its strange power?

The first rays reached over the cliffs like grasping hands and fell upon the Great Aten Temple, which stood not far from Ay's secluded wing of the palace. He watched as the mudbrick walls, painted a bright, searing white, flared with sudden luminosity. The shadows inside the roofless sanctuary fled. Ay watched as the upper edges of the interior walls turned golden in the new dawn. From his vantage he could just make out the peaks of Akhenaten's crowns—the colossal statues that lined the inside of the sand-floored temple, staring down in silent amusement at worshipers below.

Was this the last thing you saw, Tiy—the new sun rising? Or did you make your exit before the god could look down on you?

The thought of his sister sent an unexpected pang through Ay's chest. How Tiy would laugh at him now! How she would mock his melancholy mood! Regret clouded Ay's thoughts—not for the first time since Tiy's death—and sat like a dull stone in his gut. He missed his sister. He still hadn't recovered from the sheer *surprise* of it all—of knowing that he would probably always mourn her death. He and Tiy had spent so much time as enemies, bitter rivals for influence and power, that Ay had never realized how much he *liked* her. Now that she was gone forever, he wished fervently that Tiy were there beside him, and that he had made better use of her while she lived. He should have treated her more kindly, given her greater respect, for she was a powerful player of the world's best and most inspiring game. If she were there with him now, Ay could seek her counsel, learn how to control her son Akhenaten—even though he knew full well that Tiy would be as much at her wits' end as Ay was himself.

He stared down at the temple sanctuary, his mood

turning morose. Suicide. Of all the ways Tiy might have ended, death by her own hand was the last Ay would have predicted. What had brought her to such an extreme? Guilt? Perhaps so. Akhenaten was her son, after all, born of her own body and nurtured at her breast, insofar as Tiy ever nurtured a child. Akhenaten had turned out to be the most despicable curse that had ever befallen Egypt. *If I'd brought that creature into the world, perhaps I would be overwhelmed with guilt, too.*

But Tiy hadn't left Egypt entirely without hope. Ay sipped his wine again, savoring its tart flavor, and turned away from the temple to stare northward, along the downstream course of the Iteru, its broad, gray-green expanse shimmering in the morning light. Tiy's steward, Huya, still carried on with some of her work. The man had come to Ay not long after her death, bearing a note sealed with Tiy's ring. The letter had instructed Ay on the best ways to communicate with Smenkhkare, and after some difficult and lengthy work, Ay had finally established communication with his sister's youngest son.

Smenkhkare was amenable to Ay's plan, as Huya had sworn he would be. But now Ay faced a logistical tangle— and a potentially deadly task. Somehow he must contrive to place Smenkhkare favorably in Akhenaten's view, and position the younger man for a co-regency—without sending Akhenaten into a dangerous rage. Clever as Ay was, and ever-alert for the smallest, subtlest opportunity to work his will, he still hadn't found a likely way to slip this new co-regent onto the throne.

One misstep in this delicate task, and I will find myself staked out on the temple floor, exposed to the Aten's judgment. Ay barely suppressed a cold shudder at the thought.

He gazed north, staring unblinking in the direction of Smenkhkare, the savior of the dynasty and hope of the Two Lands. He would have prayed to the gods for inspiration, for guidance, if he'd thought any god might be listening.

He would have even begged the Aten for help, if he'd had any good evidence that the Aten cared one whit for the fate of Egypt.

A man cleared his throat softly from the head of the roof's stairs—one of Ay's household servants. Distracted from his musings, Ay rounded on the man with an irritated frown. But the servant forestalled Ay's anger with a deep bow, palms presented in apology for the interruption, and related his message quickly.

"The King's Great Wife is here to see you."

Ay swallowed his annoyance, fixing a mask of imperturbable calm on his face. What was Meritaten doing in this wing of the palace? The foolish girl had avoided him for years, ever since the japery of Tiy's funeral. And now she sought him out? No doubt she wished to whine and complain, as girls her age always did, eating up his time when Ay had far more important issues to occupy him.

"So early?" Ay said levelly.

The servant's eyes shifted helplessly as he searched for a suitable response. Then he bowed again.

"Very well," Ay said. He gestured for the man to bring Meritaten up to the roof.

She appeared only a few moments later, evidently eager to speak with Ay. His eldest granddaughter had certainly grown into a beautiful young woman. She was even lovelier than Nefertiti, if such a miracle were truly possible. Akhenaten's blood had lent Meritaten an exotic, almost feline refinement that Nefertiti had never possessed.

But even as a girl of seventeen, Nefertiti had claimed far better traits: clear thought and exceptional self-control. These were sadly lacking in the sole remaining Great Wife. Meritaten was far less confident than her mother had been, too—though Ay could see that she tried valiantly to hold herself with poise and presence. He had to admire her effort, inadequate though it was. The past two years surely hadn't been easy for Meritaten, abandoned by Nefertiti to face the public rigors of the throne—and the more private burden of the Pharaoh.

Meritaten stood and gazed at him, face serene, eyes expectant. The only hint of her discomfiture was the edge of her shawl, which she twisted viciously in her fingers. Ay bowed to his granddaughter, as propriety demanded, but he kept his cool, all-seeing gaze on her face, reading easily the strain of desperation and fear that she could not quite conceal.

"Grandfather," the girl said as he straightened from his bow. "I must apologize for having spoken but little to you over these past years."

Ay allowed his brows to rise slowly. He had not expected an apology—nor was one needed. Meritaten had proven herself ineffectual at controlling the king—not with any reliability, at least. Ay had searched for other sources, other hopes, other ways to sink his hooks into Akhenaten's skin. He had found little as yet, save for the rites of the temple. The only time Akhenaten behaved with any predictability was when he felt himself under the direct scrutiny of his strange, distant god. And even though the king's time in the temples occasionally inspired disturbing fits of zeal, close communion with his god seemed to keep Akhenaten placated.

"Think nothing of it," Ay said, waving one hand in dismissal of her words. "We have both been busy, you and I—both preoccupied with important matters. But tell me, what brings you here today? It is so early, Meritaten. Did you not sleep well?"

She sighed, looking down at her toes in their gold-laced sandals. "I'm afraid I did not. My heart has been heavy, Ay—last night, and all the nights before. All the *days* before, too. I have never forgotten your admonishment in Tiy's tomb, when you told me I must control the king. But despite my best efforts, I... well, you know what he is like."

"Indeed I do."

She raised her dark, solemn eyes to his face. She opened her mouth, but no words came forth. He saw her tremble, like a leaf pulled by an insistent breeze. This appearance, here on his rooftop—these words she was about to speak— cost Meritaten dearly. Ay was all the more keen to hear them.

"I need your help, Ay," she finally said. "The king's sanity deteriorates by the day. I'm losing my grip on him—what little grip I ever had. He slips farther from me, faster than I can take up the slack in his leash." She choked out a small, self-deprecatory laugh. "Though in truth, my leash was neither strong nor secure from the start."

Ay sipped his wine. He waited, patient as ever, for the girl to continue.

"We should work together. You are my grandfather, after all. I have come to seek your help. This is not a task I can handle on my own."

Ah. As easily as that, a direct path to the throne opens. Perhaps the old gods still look down on the mortal world after all.

Ay quelled the leap of eagerness in his gut. Now, at last, he would return to his rightful place. Not on the throne, but behind it, guiding the king of Egypt with a firm hand on the back of his neck. And Ay had always worked in precisely this way, too—securing his grip on a woman, who in turn guided the Pharaoh just as Ay directed. First Tiy, wife of Amunhotep the Third... though of course, Tiy had quickly flowered into her own strength and shaken off the better part of Ay's influence. But then Nefertiti had been his instrument, and though she had liked to believe she was beyond Ay's control, he had never truly lost his influence over his daughter's heart.

Now Meritaten. Soft and pliant, frightened and alone, she would afford Ay his most direct control over Egypt's courses, bringing him closer to power than he had ever come before. The girl desperately needed him—hadn't she just admitted as much? She would be no more than a silken glove to cover his hard, confident fist.

But how much sway do I have over you, Granddaughter? He assessed the young woman in thoughtful silence, eyeing her pale, compressed lips, the slight tremor in her frame, the darting of her eyes as she searched for some strength to which she might cling.

Before Ay could be sure of Meritaten's usefulness, he must be sure of her fear. Fear was ever the most direct and reliable way to control any woman—or man. Ay had no need of another Nefertiti, and certainly not another Tiy—a strong-willed woman who would fight his shadow-rule at every turn. But if Meritaten was as weak and yielding as he believed—as susceptible to fear—then she would make an ideal instrument in Ay's hand.

And so, to plumb the depths of her insecurity, he gazed out over the city and smoothly changed the course of their conversation.

"The plague is back—that damnable illness, rising up from the sewer pits on the poor end of the city. Did you know? Have you heard?"

"I hadn't heard, but it is not surprising."

Meritaten did not sound afraid—merely resigned. And why should she not be resigned? The cyclical plague had been a stark fact of life in Akhet-Aten for the past five years. Most of its eruptions were contained quickly, and did not claim so very many lives. But no one had forgotten the worst plague year, when the illness had even overrun the palace, snuffing out the lives of a great many servants and carrying off the majority of the King's Daughters— along with Ay's own wife, Lady Teya.

"Each time the illness rises again," Ay said quietly, soberly, "I am reminded of your dear, young sisters. Those poor little children; they never had a chance."

The reminder of her dead sisters was enough to break Meritaten's mask of courage. She gave a visible shudder and swiped quickly at her eyes, chasing away sudden tears. "What if it strikes Ankhesenpaaten down, as it did my other sisters? Every one of them save her, carried off by the plague. Well... we lost poor Meketaten to *something else*. But still, I would be lying if I said I had no fear of the sickness."

She took a step toward him, hands clasped like a supplicant in the Aten's temple, and Ay thought, *There. I have her.*

"Oh, Grandfather, what if it overruns the palace walls again? Ankhesenpaaten is the last unmarried female of the royal line. If she succumbs to the plague, or if some other evil befalls her..."

She trailed off, pale-faced, lips and chin quivering. The girl's distress was so close to her surface. But what fear truly moved within her? Was it some specific threat that haunted her, more immediate than the plague?

Don't distract yourself with trivialities, Ay told himself brusquely. *The nature of her fear makes no matter.* Meritaten had slid easily into weakness and uncertainty, and had fled at once in his direction, seeking guidance, seeking relief. He savored a brief thrill of triumph. *She will do nicely— perfectly.*

"Tutankhaten carries the royal blood," Ay said, laying a grandfatherly hand on her shoulder. "We need not fear that the bloodline will be lost entirely. But if only I knew where Tiy sent the boy! At least his body wasn't found alongside hers, down there in the Great Aten Temple. That is one small mercy. We can assume the King's Son still lives—we *must* assume he still lives, until we find evidence to the contrary. But of course, Tutankhaten and his royal blood will do us no favors if we don't know where to find him."

"I suppose all knowledge of Tutankhaten's location died with Tiy."

"Perhaps." Ay had pried carefully at Huya, but the steward revealed no information about Tutankhaten. "It grieves me to admit it, but it may be prudent to assume the boy is lost for good."

Meritaten said, "Then Ankhesenpaaten and I *are* effectively the last of our line. We two are the dynasty's only hope." She hesitated, then said in a soft, quavering voice, "I have never conceived..." Her words trailed away. She stared off across the city toward the curve of the cliffs, but her eyes were veiled by a dark shadow, and she seemed to see nothing of the world around her.

Ay could hardly blame her for the grim silence. He assumed that Meritaten's most important duty as King's Great Wife—to go meekly to Akhenaten's bed—no longer interested her as it had when she was young and selfish, when she saw only the material rewards to be gained from her complacency. Neither could Ay fault her lack of enthusiasm. The Pharaoh's very presence was unbearable; his touch must be revolting beyond belief.

Suddenly Meritaten sniffed loudly; her eyes had filled with hopeless tears. Ay's pleasure at seeing her weak—easily manipulated—turned to an unfamiliar twinge. The sensation startled him. Dense and twisting, it was not a feeling he could easily name. Was it unaccustomed pity for his granddaughter's predicament? Whatever it was, Ay pushed the unwelcome emotion away.

"Take heart, Meritaten. You and your sister are not the *sole* hope for Egypt. Even Tutankhaten is not the last drop of our dynasty's blood. One other remains."

Meritaten's eyes widened. She glanced around the

rooftop—empty, save for herself and Ay—as if she feared lurking spies. "Whom do you speak of? What do you mean?"

Ay ignored her breathless questions. "I believe we may have some advantage after all. We must move with great care, and use this resource wisely and well. The king won't like it—no, not at all—but I'm afraid it must fall to you to convince him. Akhenaten almost always spurns my advice, but you are his last remaining wife, the treasure of his heart. You of all people in the world are closest to the Pharaoh—as close as anyone can be."

"Tell me." The girl's voice quavered—with excitement, or fear?

Ay gave her a tight smile, savoring her need, her reliance on him alone. Then, at last, he spilled out Tiy's secret. "Smenkhkare still lives."

"Smenkhkare?" Meritaten shook her head, confused. "Somehow I know that name, but—"

"Tiy's youngest child—her son. He is certainly of the royal line: brother to our king."

The girl clutched her shawl tightly about her slender body. She stepped back, eyes narrowing in a suspicious glare. "But we can't do away with the Pharaoh. You know it would only plunge the world into chaos—destroy the river's floods, bring famine and death across the land."

"We don't need to do away with the Pharaoh. If you can convince Akhenaten to agree to a co-regency with Smenkhkare—"

"I!"

"Yes. It must be you."

"The king has little love for me. He thinks of no one but Baketaten and Sitamun—their spirits, their memories."

Ay shrugged and sipped his wine again. "Of course I

cannot guarantee that the king will listen to you, but you *are* his wife. You have access to him in all his moods, fair and foul. And you are familiar to him. He trusts you, does he not?"

"I suppose." She gazed down at her sandals again, blinking back tears. "I don't think he trusts me very far, but perhaps more than he trusts any other person."

"You see, then: that is why it must be *you* who convinces him to welcome Smenkhkare to the City of the Sun, and offer his brother a partial share of his throne. He is more likely to heed your words than mine."

She shook her head abruptly, rattling the beads in her braided wig. "He'll never accept the idea. He'll be angry with me just for suggesting it." She trembled, and Ay could see how deep her fear ran.

He spoke warmly, lightly, to soothe her fears. He had often spoken just so to flighty horses when he was nothing but a charioteer. "He won't be angry if you present the idea in the correct way—in a way that appeals to Akhenaten. Think—what does he care for?"

"Nothing," Meritaten said with a bitter laugh. "Nothing save for the Aten."

Ay smiled. "Exactly. The Aten. He cares very much about his standing with the god. But now, with Tutankhaten beyond our reach, the king looks a poor symbol of the sun's creative power. He has only one child left—one to whom he is not married, that is. The god has taken away all the rest of his offspring, the living proofs of his generative power—of his godhood."

Meritaten glanced up from her sandals. Her eyes focused on his face, and she frowned prettily in her concentration. Her stare was sharp, but she held her tongue, and the old man could all but see the thoughts tumbling through her heart, fluttering and clamoring like a flock of startled birds as she pieced together what she must do.

This girl may prove quick to learn, after all. Perhaps not as adept a student as Nefertiti, but she suits my purposes well enough.

Finally Meritaten nodded. Ay could see her fear draining away, the tense rise of her shoulders relaxing, her breath slowing. Grim determination crept in, to nest in the places fear had left behind.

"I think I see a way to set the matter before him," Meritaten said, "to make him truly consider the idea. It will be a dangerous conversation, but I think... I think I *can* convince him, if the god is willing."

"Good girl," Ay said. He stroked her smooth cheek with the knuckles of one hand. "Go, then, and speak to the king before you lose your nerve. The sooner we convince him to bring Smenkhkare home, the sooner we can work together, you and I. The sooner we can right Egypt in its course."

Meritaten

Year 17 of Akhenaten
Beautiful Are the Manifestations,
Exalting the Name,
Beloved of the Sun

ERITATEN HESITATED outside the king's chambers, steeling herself, praying for the bravery she would need. She leaned her shoulder against the cool smoothness of a painted pillar and squeezed her eyes tight shut, begging the god to show her favor. *If thou hast ever approved of me, mighty Aten—if all my years of worship in the temple have meant anything to thee at all...* Here in the palace, with cedar beams and a darkened roof soaring high above her head, Meritaten felt far from the warm, glowing presence of the god. She could feel no throb in her chest of the god's response, for its rays were shut out by mudbrick and stone. But still she sent out her desperate prayer. She would need the courage of a desert lion to look Akhenaten in the eye and detail Ay's proposal. *If it be thy will, glorious and singular god, let my voice not shake, and let me stand strong and pure before Akhenaten's scrutiny.*

At last, her prayers exhausted, Meritaten opened her eyes. She gazed up at the huge double doors that barred the way to the Pharaoh's apartments. Though the light inside the palace was dim, still she could make out the image of the Aten with startling clarity. Its great, faceless disc, perfectly round, inlaid with gold and spanning both doors. Dozens of long rays fell from the Aten to bless the figures gathered below—the king with Nefertiti beside him, Meritaten and her five sisters spread around them like flowers blooming in a field.

She stared at the images of her sisters. All of them save for Ankhesenpaaten were gone now—dead. If she angered the Pharaoh too much, Meritaten would join them in the underworld. She swayed, buffeted by fear. She was not strong enough, not clever enough, to do what must be done. The king would be wild with rage when he realized exactly what she was proposing.

She seemed to hear Ay's voice whispering beside her, though the hall outside the king's chamber was empty. *Focus on what the Pharaoh loves best—the god, the temples.* Meritaten breathed deep, pressing her hands to her twisting stomach. She tried to conjure up the sensation of Ay standing beside her, guiding her with his hand on her shoulder—Ay, lending some of his unshakable, unsettling confidence to Meritaten's dangerous cause. But she had never been close with her grandfather. She had resented his cold, calculating ways for most of her life. Even if she could have felt Ay standing with her now, Meritaten wasn't sure the sensation would have conferred the strength she needed.

The scuff and thump of heavy, purposeful footsteps drifted toward her. Meritaten leaned around the pillar and peered down the hall. What she saw nearly crushed the fragile shell of her courage: Mahu strode down the hallway, narrow-eyed and firm of jaw, looking as hard and angry as he ever did.

Meritaten shrank back into the pillar's shadow. Her heart quailed, even as it beat loud and fast in her ears. *You cannot allow Mahu to distract you from this task,* she told herself. She knew she must face down the guard with poise worthy of Nefertiti and Tiy. No matter how he made her bones shake with fear, she couldn't allow Mahu to get the better of her.

Meritaten stepped past the pillar, moving out into the

hall where Mahu could see her clearly. The big man halted, staring at her with his usual impudent, amused expression.

"The king has summoned me," Meritaten told him sternly.

"I doubt that."

"Doubt it all you like. Your opinions make no matter to me."

Mahu shifted, looming subtly over her, forcing Meritaten to tilt her head back to maintain the hold of his dark, glaring eye. The guard was about to make some rejoinder—a thinly veiled threat, no doubt—when Akhenaten's voice cut like a dagger's blade between them, calling out from deep within his apartments.

"Sitamun! Forgive me! My sister, my own dear sister, dead in her tomb!"

A sudden thrill of inspiration raced along Meritaten's limbs, as thick and sweet as honey. The Aten had heard her prayers after all, and blessed her. With a rush of certainty that straightened her spine and calmed her heart, she knew exactly how she must proceed with the king. But first she had to send Mahu away. There was no telling what he might say or do if he learned of Tiy's secret—and no telling whom he might run to with the knowledge.

The one thing Akhenaten cares for is the god. And the one thing Mahu cares for is gold. Oh, yes—Meritaten could bring this man to heel, too.

She softened her expression with an effort. "Mahu, I was hasty to accuse you last night. It was ill-done. And you were right to point out that I had not yet paid you for your... *service.* Even if that service was carried out with rather too much zeal, still we had an agreement, and I must honor it."

Mahu's eyes narrowed with suspicion, but he held his

tongue.

Meritaten slipped a ring from one of her fingers—pretty but insignificant, it was silver set with a small cabochon of turquoise. She extended it toward Mahu. "Take this ring to my apartments and speak to my chief servant, Meha'a. She will recognize this ring as mine. Tell her she is to give you my belt made of golden lotus leaves. You know the one; I've worn it many times at feasts and at court."

Mahu nodded slowly, tapping his square chin with a finger. "I know the one. But I shall go later. Now I—"

"Go now, or I will change my mind. This is your one chance to collect what you feel is still owed. Do not try my patience, Mahu—I *am* the King's Great Wife."

He hesitated only a moment longer. Then he took the ring from Meritaten's fingers with one swift, fierce motion and turned away. Meritaten let out her breath in a long, shaky sigh as Mahu strolled off in the direction of her apartments. The belt of golden leaves was very fine. She would miss it, but a belt was a small price to pay to remove Mahu from her path.

I handled him well enough, by the grace of the god. Surely Akhenaten will play just as easily into my hands.

She pushed open one door to the king's chambers and entered. The receiving room was large, as were all of Akhenaten's chambers, with a soaring ceiling and smooth, brightly tiled floors. A breeze drifted down the windcatchers, sending currents of cool air circulating in lazy ripples. But despite the vastness of the apartments, the grandness of the space, the king kept his personal rooms in startling austerity. That never failed to surprise Meritaten, no matter how many times she came here to tend to the king's needs. Only a single couch stood in the middle of the room, with one long table before it— for taking meals—and beside its curved arm, another, smaller table where an unlit lamp rested. A narrow cedar chest stood in one corner, where the king kept certain documents of state. Otherwise, there was nothing in that grand space—no cushions or stools for entertaining visitors, no instruments to soothe the king's *ka* with gentle music, nothing to beautify the interior or please the eye. The walls were limed, a stark, flat white. Their only ornamentation was one large depiction of the Aten reaching its rays down to caress the royal family, a nearly identical tableau to the one that adorned the Pharaoh's doors. Meritaten shuddered to see them all standing there, the family she had once had. Living and vibrant in their paint, all the sisters she had lost—her mother, too—were vanished from this world. The only trace of them that remained were these murals and carvings, scattered about the palace, etched into the walls and porticoes of Akhet-Aten.

Meritaten stared at the mural; her eyes fixed on her own figure, represented as the child she had been, her father stroking her head while she pointed up at the sun. And little Ankhesenpaaten—she was a small, fragile-looking form, peeking out shyly from between the bodies of Meketaten and Tasherit. *We are all that is left,* Meritaten thought. *Just the two of us. And it is I who must find some way to preserve us—to preserve the whole of the land. Oh, Aten, give me strength!*

Akhenaten swept into the receiving room, trailing a white temple robe that hung half-open in a slovenly fashion, displaying far more of his bare skin than Meritaten cared to see. His chest had grown fleshy with the years; it sagged down toward his soft, round belly, which had just begun to protrude on his formerly lean and strong frame. His dark, staring eyes were red-rimmed from weeping, as they often were of late. He checked at sight of Meritaten and flinched, gathering the edges of his robe, pulling them tight like a shield over his mortality.

"Sitamun? Is that you?" He retreated a few wary steps.

"Are you real, or a spirit?"

She moved quickly to comfort him, smiling, one hand outstretched, hoping she looked beatific. "Father—my king. It's not Sitamun, but I, Meritaten, your loving wife. Come now; you know me."

The king blinked and sighed. "Of course. Of course it's you, Meritaten, my sweet. But you stood below the windcatcher, and the light coming down through it... it made you sparkle and glow. I couldn't be sure."

Meritaten pressed her hand to his cheek in a show of affection, quelling her inner fear. "I may well *be* glowing, for I have just returned from the Great Aten Temple." That was not precisely true, but she could see the temple from Ay's rooftop. She hoped the god would overlook that stretching of the truth. "Father, the Aten blessed me more than it ever has before! The god granted me a vision— such a *glorious* vision! Oh, my king, the god has performed its greatest miracle of all!"

Akhenaten's eyes lost their veil of fearful sorrow. His stare sharpened on Meritaten, and for a moment she felt as if she were pinned against a wall, cornered by some dangerous hunting creature. She made herself stand calm and still, beaming at him with perfect joy.

"What do you mean?" he said. "Tell me of this vision."

"It was given to me to know—why me, I cannot say— that the god has raised your beloved sibling up from death. Life has been restored, where death had once ruled!"

"Sitamun?" There was such pleading in the Pharaoh's eyes, such frantic hope, that Meritaten almost felt sorry to correct him.

"No, not Sitamun, I'm afraid. It is your brother who has been so blessed—Smenkhkare, who died when he was only a small boy."

Akhenaten's brows furrowed. An air of confusion

fell over him; he shook his head slowly, casting about the unadorned chamber as if he hoped to find some explanation carved on the walls or etched into the tiles of the floor. Meritaten resisted the urge to fall on her knees and beg him to believe her, to weep with the crushing tension of her fear. But then wonderment washed over Akhenaten's features. He stared beyond Meritaten at the mural on his wall, the sun-god blessing the royal family. With a hoarse, wordless cry, he rushed to the mural and touched the bright-painted images with his hands, kissed them with his lips, washed them with his grateful tears.

"Smenkhkare!" Akhenaten wailed. "My dear brother, whom I thought so utterly lost for so very long!"

Meritaten permitted herself a dubious frown, so long as the king's back was turned to her. *He hasn't spared one thought for his youngest brother since he helped lay Smenkhkare's coffin in its tomb.* But her cynicism made no matter. Akhenaten was reacting exactly as she had hoped. As the king's oaths of gratitude soared up to the Aten, Meritaten added her own whispered prayer of thanks.

The king whirled suddenly from his doting at the mural. Meritaten hastily re-arranged her face to seem the beaming priestess once more.

"How do you know it, Meritaten? How can you be sure this wonderful news is true?"

She swallowed hard, her heart fluttering in panic.

Remember what he most cares for, Ay's voice whispered in her ear. *The temple, the god—and nothing else.*

Meritaten hesitated. She twisted the edge of her shawl around her fingers, searching for some plausible story.

At once Akhenaten's eyes narrowed; the bliss fled from his face, replaced in a heartbeat by a scowl of dangerous suspicion.

Meritaten spoke without thinking—almost without

hearing her own words, even as they tumbled from her mouth. *Guide me, Aten*, she prayed as she invented a vision for Akhenaten. *My life is in thy hands. Save thy faithful servant from the king's wrath.*

"I was praying at the Sun Altar," she said, her voice trembling—she hoped the king would take it for a tremor of awe. "I had just placed my offering on the table, when I heard a voice calling from the back of the temple. 'Niece! Niece!' it said to me. 'Rejoice, blood of my blood, for the Aten has proven its power by a most miraculous act!'"

Akhenaten stilled. He nodded slowly for Meritaten to continue.

"I looked up from the Sun Altar, and there before me stood a figure I had never seen before. He was a man fully grown, yet somehow I knew that he was also a child. I could not yet see his features as he came toward me, for the Aten's rays were all around him—shining out from his body—and it pained me to look upon him."

"Miraculous," Akhenaten whispered.

"Yes," she quickly agreed. "Then another voice spoke. But it did not come from the glowing figure. I seemed to hear it within my own heart."

Gripped by sudden invention, and trusting her life to that instinct, Meritaten fell to her knees, presenting her palms to the ceiling as if she worshiped in the temple, even now. She swayed like a reed, rocking with a force she hoped the king would take for the bliss of divine revelation.

"Oh, Father!" she cried. "The words I heard could only have been the voice of the god itself!"

She seemed to see herself, to sense her own body, from a great distance. Detached and coolly observant, Meritaten felt tears leak from her eyes and hang like tiny pearls on her lashes. *That is good*, she thought, though she couldn't tell how she had conjured up her weeping.

"What did the voice say?" Akhenaten asked. She could sense the intensity of his voice, his quivering need to know, to feel for himself the power of the vision.

"The voice said, 'Behold! I have the power to conquer death! I have raised up this man from the cold and dark of his tomb for the sake of my most beloved servant, Akhenaten.'"

"For my sake?" Meritaten could not say whether she heard skepticism or wonder in her father's question.

"Yes. That holy being told me the resurrected man's name—Smenkhkare—and said, too, that his purpose was to serve you, even as you serve the Aten. For the god desires more from you, Father—more of your love, more of your worship."

"But I do all I can," the king protested.

"The Aten is an exacting god." Meritaten opened her eyes. The tears, cooled now, slid down her cheeks. "When it tells us we must give more, we cannot make excuses or shirk our duty."

Akhenaten shook his head, mouth agape in an expression of helpless exasperation. "I would give the god all my time, if I could. I would worship in the temple every waking hour, every moment the Aten's light fills the sky. But I have duties here at the palace, too. Surely the god understands that my heart, my *ka*, even my *ba* are always with it, always singing praises to its glory, even when I am occupied with the business of the throne."

Meritaten scowled up at him, as stern as the god itself. "The Aten has already taken away your children, because your efforts in the temple are not enough. And my womb remains empty. The god withholds vessels for your divine seed. Without its approval, you will never breed the gods-on-earth you are destined to sire."

Akhenaten covered his face with his hands. "Bless me,

Aten. I have failed thee! I have fallen short—angered the god! And now it allows these shades of death to torment me—Baketaten, Sitamun. Sometimes my mother, too, and the little girls. I see them reaching for me, accusing me. They want to pull me down into my tomb!"

Meritaten rose gracefully from the floor. She took his hands from his face, brushing away his tears with her own fingers. She kissed him, stroked his shoulder like a hunter soothing an agitated dog. Soon he subsided into miserable shivering.

"Fear not," Meritaten said. "The god always provides a path for the righteous to walk. The Aten has raised Smenkhkare up, and fitted him for service to the throne, so that you, my king, may be relieved of that onerous duty. You will be free to give the god just what it wants: your endless love, unfettered by earthly obligations. Let Smenkhkare handle the dull cares of the throne."

Akhenaten drew a deep breath. He eyed Meritaten with slow, simmering suspicion. "Place another man on the throne? I don't like this idea. The god *cannot* approve of it. No, this vision of yours simply cannot be true. I am the god's chosen vessel, bred for its divine purposes and glorified in its sight! The Aten would never give my throne to another!"

Meritaten's stomach curdled with anxiety. Had she brought him so close to agreement, only to lose him again—and condemn herself? She fought back her fear, painting her face with a gentle, almost motherly smile. "There is nothing to fear. Smenkhkare is not meant to take your throne away from you—only to tend it in your absence, while you see to more important things. He is your younger brother. Let him serve you—you, his overlord and instructor, as befits the roles of elder and younger brothers."

Akhenaten turned away, twitching Meritaten's hand

from his shoulder. For a long moment he stood watching the mural of the Aten, while Meritaten's vision blurred at the edges and sweat prickled beneath her wig. She was certain the Pharaoh had seen through her ruse, certain he would call for Mahu and haul her to the temple, where the ropes and stakes waited beneath the white-fire glare of the sun's ruthless eye.

But Akhenaten's trembling hands covered his face again. He gave a ragged sob, and swayed on his feet, so suddenly that Meritaten reached out to catch him if he fell. "Aten," he cried, "why won't you speak to me? Why is my heart closed to your words, your visions? Ah, Meritaten, if only your mother were still with us. She was a powerful priestess; she could interpret the god's whims with such natural grace, such ease."

"I am her daughter," Meritaten said, thinking quickly. "I have her gift of interpretation. Why should you doubt it? Now that Nefertiti is gone, isn't it fitting that the mantle of her power should pass to me? What could please the Aten more? After all, I was sired by you, my king—I am bred of the same divinity that the Aten wove into your body and *ka*."

"Perhaps," Akhenaten said, sounding unconvinced. "Perhaps you are correct."

Anger surged up in Meritaten. *How difficult must this task be?* Seizing on the king's insecurity, she turned her head and gasped in a frightened voice, "Baketaten! I saw her!"

She had seen nothing, of course, but the king whirled away from his mural, staring about the room as wide-eyed as an animal in a trap. "Where? Where was she? Did she look angry?"

"Very angry indeed," Meritaten said, pressing a hand to her heart. "She had blood on her face, and her eyes were like two coals in a fire. Oh, what a terrible specter!"

The king's tremor of unrestrained fear sent a thrill of

victory through Meritaten's heart.

"She is angry with me," Akhenaten said soberly, as if imparting an important secret. "She wants me to die, too."

Meritaten clutched at his loose robe. "No! No, my king—I have just seen the truth of it! The Aten speaks in my heart, even now. It tells me... it tells me..." She stared, eyes unfocused, as if she saw through the chamber walls and beyond the palace itself, into the heart of the temple. "The god tells me, Baketaten doesn't hunger for *your* death. No, not yours... but Ankhesenpaaten's!"

"My darling daughter! No!"

"And after my sister's death..." Meritaten sharpened her gaze, staring up at her father somberly. "Mine."

"Never! It cannot be! Baketaten, have mercy!"

"The god will take us back, Ankhesenpaaten and I... unless you give yourself more fully to the temple. Unless you toil in the god's rites from sunrise to sunset. Nothing else will appease the Aten, and if the god is not obeyed it will unleash Baketaten's shade to do her worst. She will come for us in our sleep, or while we worship at the Sun Altar. It makes no matter—the god will give her full power, and like a reaper harvesting stalks of wheat, she will cut us down."

Akhenaten moaned in terror.

"Hasn't the god already taken the rest of your children away?" Meritaten went on ruthlessly. "The last of your offspring will soon follow, and then you will have nothing—nothing to prove your generative power, the strength of your holy seed.

"You *must* accept Smenkhkare on the throne, or lose the last of your treasures. Without us, the vessels to bring forth your divine children, you will never become like the god itself. Like any other mortal man, you will die."

The Pharaoh turned in a circle, searching the barrenness

of his chamber—for what, Meritaten could not say.

"Trust me," Meritaten said gently, "your wife, your priestess. Hear my words and believe them. Do as the god wills, my king—and save my life, and the life of my sister."

Akhenaten stared at her, his face pale, the skin around his mouth and eyes taking on a sickly, greenish hue. His mouth worked silently; his eyes stared into a terrible distance, searching for relief they could not find.

At last he took Meritaten's hand and brought it to his lips. "Very well," Akhenaten whispered, and kissed her palm. "I will obey the words of my priestess. It shall be as the god commands."

With a stifled sob, the king drifted into his bed chamber, pulling his robe around his body, staggering as he went. Meritaten watched him go, breathing deep to still the shaking in her bones. With a flare of hot pride, she realized that she had done the impossible. She had convinced the king to share his throne.

She hurried out of his apartments, whisking across the bare floor as quietly as a mouse, for after a brush with the divine, Akhenaten was often seized by intense and frightening lusts. Meritaten slipped through the great, carven doors before he could summon her to his bed. She would not suffer his touch today—not while she still rode high on her wave of victory.

As she made swiftly for her own apartments, Meritaten silently composed the note she would send to Ay.

I have succeeded in my task. Send to the north, and bring the hidden one into the light.

Nefertiti

Year 17 of Akhenaten
Beautiful Are the Manifestations,
Exalting the Name,
Beloved of the Sun

NEFERTITI TOOK THE BOY'S small, soft hand in her own, guiding him as he dipped his reed brush in a pot of ink. Together they dabbed the brush on the pot's rim, then, both of them giggling, she helped him write the characters that spelled his name. Not his true name, of course. It was the name she used here in the seclusion of her small farm, the name that was his mask, his disguise—his safety.

"Ra—mose," she said slowly, as the brush glided smoothly across the papyrus.

Tutankhaten was pleased with his gift of the new writing palette. He made certain everyone on Lady Khenut's farm, from the household servants to the sowers in the fields, knew that he intended to be a scribe when he grew up. At four years of age—nearly five now—he was progressing rapidly in his studies. He was an intelligent child, able to read with very little help, and his interest in writing was keener still.

May the gods grant that a scribe is all you ever become, Nefertiti thought as she watched him attempt to write the name on his own. If fate was kind to both of them, neither she nor Tutankhaten would ever return to the City of the Sun. Every day she prayed that the throne was far behind her, that neither she nor the boy would ever trouble themselves again with Akhet-Aten, its stark, white walls hot with the sun's glare, its temples and palace whispering with schemes and shadows.

She had grown to like life on the farm, as far as she ever enjoyed anything these days, with her *ba* half-severed from her body and her *ka* broken and subdued. Sometimes she could even convince herself that she was only Lady Khenut—that Khenut was the whole of her identity, all she had ever been—and that Ramose was truly who and what she told her servants: the son of her dead sister, an unnamed woman whom Lady Khenut never spoke of.

Those moments were sweet, when Nefertiti could forget the truth and sink into the deep, warm comfort of her fantasy. How she longed for it all to be true. How she wished this idyll could be more than just a temporary disguise. But as Tutankhaten grew, Nefertiti could see Baketaten so clearly in his face—Sitamun, too—and could even make out an eerie trace of the Pharaoh's features, though Tiy had told her Akhenaten was not the boy's father. Day by day he grew, and every one of his traits, from his face to the small, unconscious habits of speech and movement, reminded Nefertiti that the throne still held her heart and her life in an unbreakable grip. It always would hold her, never to let go. That was the fate the gods had made her for, and Nefertiti knew she could not keep her fate at bay for much longer.

Tutankhaten finished his writing. Beaming, he held the sheet of papyrus up for Nefertiti's approval. She stifled a lighthearted laugh. His glyphs scrawled across the page, haphazard, some of them even backward. But for his first attempt, the boy had done well.

"You are practically a scribe already," she said, and smiling through a queer twist of pain, she looked away from him, gazing out from her small, shaded portico over the fields of her farm.

"Aunt Khenut, why do you look so sad?"

"Oh, Ramose," she sighed, "you mustn't mind me. It's only that you're growing so quickly. It startles me, that's all."

Tutankhaten nodded solemnly. "I am nearly a man now."

Nefertiti pressed her lips together to fight back her laughter. She kissed the boy on his cheek. "Put your pallet and ink away. Soon it will be time for supper."

With a cheer, the boy bounded off to do as he was told. The length and leanness of his sun-browned legs startled her. *How quickly he grows!* Duty to the throne, and to Akhenaten's temples, had kept Nefertiti largely ignorant of her six daughters' early lives. She had been obliged to trust them to Mutbenret's care, and to the charge of royal nurses and tutors, but even so, she had spent as much time with the girls as she could manage. She didn't remember any of them sprouting up as quickly as Tutankhaten, who seemed to shed those precious baby years faster every day.

The boy was a wonder to Nefertiti, a little, soft-voiced savior, the only force that had kept her from self-destruction. Guilt over Meketaten's death—over the destruction of all her children—still hung so heavy in her chest that sometimes she thought it might crowd out the breath of life, and leave her empty and bereft, suffocating beneath her sins. But since she had taken Tutankhaten in her arms, at least Nefertiti's flitting visions of her own *ba* had mostly dissipated. The green, flitting bird with her own solemn face rarely appeared anymore, and when it did it seemed a quiet, thoughtful companion, not a threat.

Nefertiti stood up from the reed mat where she had been sitting with Tutankhaten. She stretched with her hands braced in the small of her back, working tight muscles loose and driving out the pains of a body that aged slowly but surely. The fields unfolded before her, green and lush, brushed with the sun's gentle, late-day rays. The simple, quiet peace of this farming life pulsed through her with a poignant ache. She wanted her life in the villa to go on forever—on into eternity. She wanted to raise Tutankhaten to adulthood, watch over him and care for him as she never had done for her poor, beloved daughters. It seemed to her that the gods might provide a way to make amends, to set right all the wrongs she had done, if only she could see that Tutankhaten succeeded and thrived. If only she could be sure the boy was happy.

Paser, one of her hardest-working and most faithful farm hands, appeared around the bend of the farm's long, sycamore-shadowed lane. When he saw Nefertiti in the shade of the portico, he hurried his pace and bowed before her. "Pardon me, Lady Khenut, but there is a man here to see you. He is inquiring about work."

Nefertiti craned her neck as if she might see around the small road's curve from where she stood, but of course it was hopeless. Still, she was always cautious with visitors. She had never lost her fear that she would be found again by someone from the royal family. *If Tiy could root me out, then any of those other schemers might do the same.*

"Who is he?" she asked, trying to keep her tone casual, unconcerned. "What sort of a man?"

Paser shrugged. "He seems a rather ordinary type. Strong, though, and young. We could use more men like him working the property, especially with the harvest approaching. He has two women with him."

"Two women?" The man's wife and sister, perhaps, or female cousins trusted to his care. In any case, the description of the party didn't conjure up thoughts of anyone who might have come from Akhet-Aten, seeking lost Nefertiti. "Very well," she finally told Paser. "Send them to me."

Paser turned to dash back down the lane. Nefertiti called back into her house, into its modest depths, fragrant with supper on the boil. "Teti, we have visitors. Bring bread and beer."

When she turned back to face the lane and saw the strange man approaching, Nefertiti froze. A chill as shocking as the river's depths flooded through her veins, and her shoulders tensed as she drew herself up, bristling, like a cat preparing for a fight. She couldn't say just who the man was. She only knew that she recognized at once his way of walking, its strong, purposeful cadence and the swing of his strong arms. Soldier's arms. She had seen this before—many times—and it could only mean that he had been close to the royal family, a regular fixture of the palace or the temples.

The man clearly recognized her, too. He stopped mid-stride, the color draining from his face, eyes going wide with shock. He had stopped so abruptly that the two women who followed him nearly blundered into his broad, strong back.

Nefertiti grabbed hastily at her frayed composure, drawing its ends back together, forcing a look of calm onto her face. She waved the man on, drawing him closer with the gesture, and prayed fervently to any gods who might be listening that he hadn't come to kill her.

He staggered forward again, staring at her face with a dazed, helpless look that might have been fear. "It's you," he said quietly when he stepped beneath the portico. Then he recalled himself, and bowed low. "King's Great Wife."

"Stop that," Nefertiti hissed, glancing back into her home, hoping her servants were not close enough to hear.

The women who accompanied the strange man gasped, taken aback by the title he had used. Nefertiti assessed the man's two companions quickly. One had the bearing of a noblewoman, poised and cool-eyed, but she didn't recognize the woman's face. Whoever she was, she must not have attended festivals or court often enough to make an impression on the King's Wife.

The other was a northerner, white-skinned with golden-brown hair and a smattering of freckles on her face, shoulders, and arms. When the northerner gaped at Nefertiti, she could see the dark gap of a missing front tooth. The chill in her heart redoubled with terrible force.

Gods preserve me, this is Kiya's servant. It filled Nefertiti with dread, to be confronted with a relic of the long-dead Kiya here in her peaceful sanctuary. The dead have surely come back to accuse me, she thought, bracing herself for whatever terrible wonders the gods might reveal next. *But isn't it their right to haunt me? Isn't that* maat?

Nefertiti made herself breathe slowly, pushed the fear in her gut aside. "Tell me how you found me."

"I didn't," the man stammered. "That is, I wasn't looking for you, Great..." His mouth closed with an audible snap of his teeth. He glanced to the left and right, then finally said, "My lady. What I told your servant was the truth: I *am* looking for work, like any honest man, so that I may provide for my wife and this woman—Nann—who is under our care."

At that moment, Tutankhaten's voice rang out from within the soft shadows of the house. "Aunt Khenut, I have bread and beer for our guests!"

Nefertiti squeezed her eyes shut for the briefest moment. *Careless*, she scolded herself. She should have recalled Tutankhaten. The moment she knew this man for a citizen of Akhet-Aten, she should have told Teti or one of the other household women to hide the boy away. Now it was too late. Tutankhaten stepped out under the portico, carrying a laden tray with ostentatious care.

She turned to him quickly, stepped between him and the newcomers, hoping to shield him from their sight. "Good boy, Ramose. What a help you are! Set it here on this little table, then go inside and help Teti make supper."

She nearly pulled the tray from the boy's hands, eager as she was to get him safely away.

"Can't I stay and listen?"

"No, Ramose," she said, more sharply than she intended. "Run along now. You know better than to question your elders."

With a sulky sigh, Tutankhaten went back inside. Nefertiti glanced warily at the strange man, and her heart fell. His eyes were wide and shining, his face frozen in an expression of strange, unfathomable agony.

"Her son," the man said, hardly louder than a whisper. "He can only be... He has Baketaten's face." Suddenly he covered his face with his hands, drawing a ragged breath. "Thank the gods he is safe. Thank the gods some small part of her was saved."

The man's wife cut him a narrow-eyed stare, but Nefertiti spared the woman's suspicion no more thought. She had more important mysteries to pursue. "How do you know that name—Baketaten? Who are you, and why is your face familiar to me?"

The man pulled himself together, straightening his spine, squaring his shoulders like a guardsman on the alert. "My name is Horemheb. I was a soldier in your... in the Pharaoh's service. Many times I watched over the royal family while they were engaged in worship in the Great Aten Temple. That is how I know Baketaten. And the boy, he is—"

"Ramose," Nefertiti interjected. "He is known as Ramose. No other name is spoken here. Do you understand?"

Horemheb nodded silently.

"I want nothing of Akhet-Aten, nothing of the royal family. My ties to that time and place are severed. I have no desire to mend them. I will not hesitate to have all three of you killed if I must. In fact, I will kill you myself if need be. Believe me, one more sin will not weigh heavy on my heart."

The two women clutched one another's hands. Horemheb's wife tugged warily at his kilt. "Let us go. There is no work for us here. Let us leave this woman in peace."

But Horemheb ignored her. "All my ties to the City of the Sun are severed, too. I want nothing to do with that place, nor with its mad, vile king."

Nefertiti raised her chin slowly, considering the newcomers more carefully now, caution fading slowly. "How did you get out of the city without the king's permission?"

"I'll tell you," Horemheb said, "but it's a lengthy story."

"Very well." Nefertiti gestured to the portico's little table, the fresh bread and jug of beer standing stoutly beside a stack of drinking bowls. "Sit, and eat. I am curious enough to hear your tale."

Horemheb started toward the benches that flanked the table, but his wife laid a hand on his arm. "Horemheb, no!" she said softly but urgently. "We cannot trust this woman. You heard her words! She is hostile, unpredictable. We should leave now in peace—if she will allow us to leave at all. I beg you, don't endanger us by staying!"

He took the young woman's hand gently, smiling at her with obvious affection. "I know her, Mutnodjmet. Or at least, I think I know her. If she is the woman I remember her to be, then she is just and wise. We have nothing to fear from her; we are safe in her presence."

He led the women to the table and poured beer for each of them, and for Nefertiti as well. Then he sat down himself, tearing into the bread, chewing slowly, a slow, heavy bliss sliding his eyes closed.

"You must be very hungry," Nefertiti observed.

"We are," Horemheb said when he had swallowed his mouthful. "We have scraped out a living where we could for the past two years. But the plague has spread outward from the City of the Sun, and we decided it was best to leave our most recent home, and flee south before it can overtake us."

Mention of the plague struck hard and deep into Nefertiti's heart. *Three of my daughters carried off by that terrible disease. And because I left them there to die, I never got to kiss them one last time, nor could I lay them in their tombs.* She reined in her surging emotions with deliberate care, then said, "Anyone who has lived in Akhet-Aten knows how terrible the plague can be. It was wise of you to go south."

"I only want to protect my wife and our friend Nann," Horemheb said. "Their safety was my greatest concern. You see, I want to be a good man now—not a creature of Akhet-Aten. You understand what I mean, don't you?"

Nefertiti said nothing, but held the man's earnest, wide-eyed gaze for a long time. She sipped at her cool, sweet beer, waiting for him to continue.

"If you hear my story, Lady Khenut, I think you will understand. I think then you will know that you can trust me."

"Very well," Nefertiti said. "Then tell me."

Horemheb

Year 17 of Akhenaten
Beautiful Are the Manifestations,
Exalting the Name,
Beloved of the Sun

HOREMHEB RECOUNTS HIS ESCAPE
FROM THE CITY OF THE SUN

THE NIGHT BAKETATEN WAS KILLED, I was ready to run any risk in order to leave Akhet-Aten. I knew Mahu's men lurked in the cliffs, and restricted access to the quays, too, so that no one could leave by the river without Akhenaten's permission. But I no longer cared about the danger. The death of the King's Wife seemed a monstrous cruelty, a symbol of every vile thing that had ever been done by the king and his family. The death of the King's Daughter Meketaten had already soured me to our Pharaoh, but Baketaten's brutal murder was the straw that crippled the donkey, as the *rekhet* say.

That very night, while the palace was in an uproar over the poor King's Wife, I hurried back through the city to my little house at the southern edge of town. Mutnodjmet was terrified at the sight of blood on my chest and my kilt, but she kept her wits about her. While I told her what had happened, she made me change my clothing and wash the blood from my skin. And when all trace of Baketaten's death was gone from me, I told her what I meant to do: leave the City of the Sun, that very night.

Mutnodjmet was, of course, concerned about our prospects—if we even managed to get beyond Akhet-Aten's borders. I'd only ever had a soldier's trade, you see. I had no other experience, no skills to offer, and no means to support my wife without a Pharaoh to employ me. But she could see how very much the violent death of an innocent young woman had affected me. She accepted my decision without complaint. My lady wife has many fine attributes. Good sense and a caring heart are foremost among them.

We didn't have much in our little house, so were able to pack quickly. We put our best things into bags and packs, and left behind everything that had no value or small utility. I woke one of our neighbors and told him I'd received a writ from the Pharaoh to leave the city—to travel to Waset, where I had urgent business with a relative. He sold me a good, strong donkey, and we loaded our belongings onto the animal's back and led it through the streets of Akhet-Aten, slinking quietly from one street to the next, like two thieves scuttling away from the scene of our crime.

Mutnodjmet never made a complaint, though she knew we took a dangerous gamble. That night, in those few hours while we stole away from Akhet-Aten, I came to rely on her and trust to her good sense more than I had in all the prior years of our marriage.

I learned the depth of her kindness, too. As we hurried through one of the slums, she happened to glance into an alley and saw a woman lying there, right in the dirt and cold slime of the lane, curled up and weeping. She thrust the donkey's lead into my hands and rushed to the woman's side. Mutnodjmet bent over the woman, murmuring to her, stroking her hair—even though the plague was always a threat in that district of Akhet-Aten, and she might have caught it, coming so near to a person in obvious distress.

The woman sat up and clung to Mutnodjmet's arms, babbling about the evils of the Pharaoh, about the dangers that lurked in his palace. At first I thought she was simply mad. How many such people had I seen in my years in the city? How many whose thoughts were pathetically scattered by confinement and the growing threat of the king's instability?

But the more I listened to the ailing woman's words, the more certain I became that she, like me, had once been a palace servant—and had obviously served close to the king's family.

"Who are you?" I asked her. "How do you know so much about life in the palace?"

The woman wiped away her tears, leaving smears of filth on her face, and stared at me for a long time. I could see by the clarity of her eyes that she was not mad—only lost in hopeless grief.

"I know you," she finally said, "though I do not know your name. I have seen you standing guard at the Great Aten Temple during ceremonies and daily worship."

Mutnodjmet and I exchanged wary looks. The last thing we wanted was to be recognized that night.

"Tell me your name," I said, "and how you came to be here, in this sorry state."

"My name is Nann," she answered. "I was once the dearest servant of the Lady Tadukhepa—though you Egyptians were pleased to call her Kiya."

"The King's Wife," Mutnodjmet whispered.

"Yes," Nann said. She climbed to her feet and swayed where she stood, but Mutnodjmet was quick to support her. "After my mistress disappeared—was *murdered*—I ran from the palace, for I knew whoever wanted her dead would come after me, too. I knew all her secrets, you see—all her thoughts and dreams. She shared everything with me, as if I were one of her own dear sisters. I fled, because I knew my death was coming—but I wanted to avenge Tadukhepa first."

Her story rang of truth. I could feel it like a vibration deep in my bones—like the rich, inner ringing of *maat*. "Why do you tell me this?" I asked her. "Why not give me a false name, a false history, to protect your identity? You know I am a soldier from the palace. Might I not have been sent to find you, and bring you back to the temple for questioning?"

Nann held me then with those strange, green eyes, her stare very hard and direct. I could not look away.

"Because I don't care anymore," she said. "I have been here in the slums of Akhet-Aten for three years, hoping for some opportunity to escape the city, to get back to Mitanni and bring the vengeance of Ishtar down upon Egypt, for Tadukhepa's sake. Failing that, I have even searched for some way to get back into the palace without being recognized, so I could destroy the Pharaoh and his evil kin with my own hands. But I cannot. Three years of searching, of praying—all in vain. I am trapped here; there is no way out of the city, and no way for one woman to strike at the king. I surrender myself to the goddess's will. I am in Ishtar's hands; let her do with me whatever she wills."

"You poor thing," Mutnodjmet said. "How you have suffered!"

My wife searched through our packs until she found bread and a skin of water, along with a clean cloth. She cleaned Nann's face and hands, then let her eat and drink her fill.

"You must hide, Nann, if you are able," I said. "I'm afraid your mistress Kiya has company tonight in the afterlife. King's Wife Baketaten was murdered, not two hours ago. The Pharaoh's guards will turn the city upside-down.

They'll seize any person whom they might plausibly blame. You, a former servant in the palace, who worked for another King's Wife, the victim of a similar fate—"

"We can't just leave her here!" Mutnodjmet hissed, struggling to keep her voice low. "The guards will hunt through the city for anyone they might implicate. This poor woman will be apprehended and brought before the king—and who can say what he will do with her! She is innocent; I can't leave her to an unjust fate."

And so it was that we took Nann along with us, at Mutnodjmet's insistence. I told Nann the journey would be perilous, and that we might die in the attempt. But she did not care. "If we succeed, and make it past the boundaries of Akhet-Aten, then I might find my way back to Mitanni somehow. Then Tadukhepa's death might be avenged. I will take the risk. Even if I die trying, it is better than remaining here, to face what passes for justice in Egypt."

Nann's strength surprised me. Now that she had found some possible way to leave the city, a certain cool self-possession came over her. All her tears dried away; she stood straight and unshaken. As we resumed our flight through the streets of the city, she moved with the grace and power of a lioness.

Now that a chance had appeared for her to leave the city—however small that chance was—she was convinced that she would find a way to avenge Kiya's death after all. And her gratitude to me was touching—though premature, I thought, since we hadn't won our way free yet.

She said, "When we are clear of Akhet-Aten—" when, not if— "I will pledge myself to your service, and to the service of your lady wife. I'll serve faithfully, as long as you do not prevent me from returning to Mitanni when the time is right—when Ishtar summons me back."

Mutnodjmet readily agreed. The daughter of a noble

family, she grew up with servants in her household, but hadn't had a maid of her own since she was a child. I could tell she was eager for the company of a maid, and wanted one more for female companionship than simply to help her with household duties.

I agreed to Nann's proposal. And why not? I couldn't be certain we would ever leave Akhet-Aten with our *bas* still in our bodies; there seemed no harm in going along with Nann's and Mutnodjmet's fantasy. It kept the women optimistic, to believe freedom was close at hand.

I could not be so cheery about our prospects. Many times, all through my years in Akhenaten's service, I had heard the cliff guards recount what they had done with those who attempted to leave through that high, stony route. But I also knew which trails through the cliffs were most heavily guarded. This allowed me to choose another route—very difficult, and slow going, since the path was no more than an old game trail, once used by goat herds and wild gazelle. In the dim moonlight it was hard to see our route. We often lost the way, and had to retrace our steps until we could make out the faint, narrow line of the game trail once more, winding over slick patches of stone and snaking along the rims of ledges.

Neither of the women complained as we stumbled up the cliffs. Their sandals were no good for this sort of walking; I could tell they were sore and tired long before midnight came. But we kept on doggedly together, climbing as silently as we could.

Whenever we were forced to find the game trail again, I looked back at the City of the Sun. It lay far below us now, but even as we climbed farther up the cliffs, as we put more distance between ourselves and the cage of the city, the palace and its temples seemed to mock me. I was tired, and still in shock from the terrible sight I had seen in Baketaten's chamber. My weary heart got the better of me, and I thought I saw a flood of deep red running through the streets. The sight made me shudder, and seemed to goad me, hard and sharp, urging me to go faster, to get well clear of Akhet-Aten before my blood, too, ran in that dark, treacherous current.

Eventually I realized we were approaching the clifftop boundaries. I hid the women behind a crag; Mutnodjmet fed the donkey tidbits of bread to keep it from braying. I crept forward to scout the way, doing my best to cloak myself in shadow. When I could see the final rise of our game trail, I spotted a pair of guards patrolling along the edge of the cliff, just where we must cross the border to win our way free.

I had no weapon, save for a simple hunting knife, which I kept in my belt. My sword and bow were both in the barracks, though I am a poor shot even in the best of conditions and my bow would have done little good in the moonlight. I knew I would stand little chance if I attacked two well-armed men outright. I would have to deceive them if I hoped to reach our freedom.

Though my heart pounded, I approached them with an easy, casual stride. They seemed to recognize me as one of their own, by my stature and strength, I presume.

"Brothers," I called out, "I've come to relieve you at your post."

"What?" one of them asked, startled. "How so? Our shift only started a few hours ago."

"The city is in an uproar. There has been a murder at the palace. Lieutenant Ranofer wants you back there, to help secure the grounds."

"Cliff patrols are always done in pairs," one of them said, eyeing me suspiciously.

"I know," I replied, "but it's not every day a King's Wife is killed in her own apartments. Special circumstances tonight; Ranofer's orders. Take it up with him, if you've a problem with it. But you'd best get back down to the palace, and be quick. The Pharaoh is in a rage. He wants the killer found within the hour."

The guards exchanged glances, but finally one of them nodded and the other grunted, seeming to accept my story. They set out together toward the main trail—not our game trail, but the more obvious route, the one fugitives usually attempted to use.

I was just about to let out a sigh of relief when one of the men glanced back at me sharply. "Wait a moment," he said, his eyes flashing down the length of my body, taking in my casual kilt, my lack of a sword. "You're off-duty!"

I knew I had to act fast. I snatched my knife from its sheath and leaped at the man. All the tension and fear that had built up inside me seemed to burst out of me at once, propelling me toward him so fast he barely had time to blink, let alone draw his sword. I slashed his throat with one swift motion. He went down with a bubbling scream, and as he fell, I heard his mate draw his sword. I threw myself at the second man with maniacal force, and was able to get close to his body just as his blow fell. I was too near now for his sword to do much damage, but it did slice my arm as it came down. I didn't even feel the cut. I drove my knife hard up beneath his ribs. The blade wasn't long enough to reach his heart, but it did terrible damage. He fell, gasping and wheezing, and I used his own sword to strike deep, straight into his heart.

With both men dead, I helped myself to their swords and daggers—one never knows when weapons might come in handy. I hurried back to where the women waited, and gave one of the swords to Nann. She seemed fierce enough to use it well, even if she wasn't trained in the art.

Mutnodjmet wanted to stanch the blood from my slashed arm and sew up the wound straight away, but I knew our time was short. There was no telling whether any other cliff patrols were close; the two dead men might be found at any moment, and then all hope for us would be lost. She bound a piece of cloth around the cut as we hurried past the boundary stela, rushing out beyond Akhet-Aten's border toward the Red Land. When I could no longer see the cliffs or the river behind us, I sat beneath a thin, scraggly tree—one of the few that sprouted up from the thick red sand there at the desert's edge—and allowed the women to treat my wound properly. We ate and drank a little, but were back on our feet in less than half an hour. We had to keep moving, had to put as much distance between ourselves at the city as we could manage.

We walked south until sunrise, following the desert's fringe. Never will I forget the sight of the sun rising over the desert—the vastness of that place, its stark, frightening barrenness, its violent shade of red. The light of the new day moved toward us with a slow inevitability that seemed conscious, malevolent. It rippled over the distant dunes as it sought us out, coming ever closer, as if mocking our need to hide. We found a thicket just before the light reached us and sheltered there for most of the day, taking turns sleeping and watching the northern horizon for signs of pursuit. But if anyone searched for us, they did not look far beyond the borders of Akhet-Aten. I am sure the city had more pressing concerns that night. Poor Baketaten's death allowed the three of us to live.

Late in the afternoon we pressed on, following the desert's edge when the worst heat of the day had dissipated. By the following morning we found ourselves at a village. It was small—a rather shabby place, if I am honest. So close to the desert, most of the people there were goatkeepers, or raised donkeys and other beasts of burden. But though the place looked unimpressive, we were so grateful to be free of Akhet-Aten that it seemed a glorious, sparkling place. We all found work there for a few days, doing menial tasks—whatever was needed. When we'd labored enough to obtain more suitable shoes, and enough food and water to see us through another long walk, we moved on. None of us liked to linger so close to Akhet-Aten.

My goal was to make it all the way to Waset, but as we worked our way from one village to the next, it seemed less likely that we would be pursued and captured. In time we found ourselves at the town of Nebty, several days' walk from Akhet-Aten, in a welcoming green curve of the river. There I found work at the quays, loading and unloading the freight boats owned by merchants and grocers. Mutnodjmet took up work as a girls' tutor, teaching reading and writing to the daughters of the town's wealthier citizens. Nann here occupied herself on a farm, planting and weeding as the season matured. We all lived together in a two-room house, which we rented with our combined wages. It wasn't a luxurious life, but it was a life free from the king's influence, and free from the strictures of Akhet-Aten, and so we all felt happy and grateful, and glad enough to stay.

In Nebty, we learned that the old gods still thrive outside of Akhet-Aten. Small temples and shrines have been maintained here and there, albeit with careful secrecy. After all, one never knows when a devotee of the Pharaoh's sun-disc will pass through town, and any loyal Atenist might report to the king about illicit activities. So worship is done in secret, inside homes and in temples where the vegetation has been allowed to grow wild, obscuring men's activity. The most visible temples and shrines remain empty and silent now, their gods' statues sadly neglected.

We found joy in worshiping as we used to do, before the Pharaoh cast the old gods away. Mutnodjmet and I were both very young when the Aten came to power, but when we joined in the secret rites at Nebty's shrines we found that the peace and pleasure of the old ways came back readily to our hearts. At night, in our little shared home, Nann even sang songs to her goddess, Ishtar, and those sweet, melodious prayers were the best endings to our long, busy days.

I believe we all would have stayed in Nebty forever, perfectly content with our small lot in life, for our little rented hut felt like a palace of riches after years penned in the City of the Sun. But all too soon, traders from Akhet-Aten came, carrying the plague on their boats and in their cargoes. The illness crept through the town—slowly, taking few lives, but we recalled the signs of the illness with frightening clarity, and we knew soon it would take root and grow in its power.

A ND THAT IS HOW we come to be here, inquiring at your estate," Horemheb said.

The long story had left his throat dry. He quaffed his beer, watching Nefertiti over the rim of his bowl.

She did not seem troubled, but she gazed off into the depths of her estate's lush fields, mulling over Horemheb's story in silence. She was still as beautiful as ever, though the evidence of many worries and woes marked her face with lines around her dark eyes, her lovely mouth. She still held herself with the regal bearing, the arrogant poise Horemheb recalled so clearly from his days in the palace.

"We are in need, my lady," Horemheb ventured when she still remained silent. "Whoever we were before—wherever we came from—we are starting over now, all three of us, just as you are. We want nothing of our past life. We don't want to look back; we only want to go forward. Will you give us your charity, and provide us with work? You will be pleased by how hard we work, I know it. Even Mutnodjmet works hard, though she is nobly born."

Nefertiti rose gracefully from her bench and stepped

to the edge of her portico. She gazed out at her farm, maintaining that inscrutable silence, while Mutnodjmet and Nann shifted nervously on their bench, glancing from Nefertiti to Horemheb and back again.

Tutankhaten burst from the house, squealing with laughter as he ran. A plump maid chased him, scolding, then stopped short when she saw Nefertiti standing there.

"I am sorry, Lady Khenut," the maid said. "Ramose evaded me—such a naughty boy! He insisted he must be with you."

Nefertiti waved her hand. "It makes no matter, Teti. Ramose may stay here and meet our guests."

Tutankhaten turned to Horemheb, gazing up at him with wide, solemn eyes. *Gods spare me—they are Baketaten's eyes. I would recognize them anywhere.* The memory of her was still etched deeply in Horemheb's heart. Time would never wear it away.

Finally Nefertiti turned back to Horemheb, her regal chin lifted high. But she was smiling. It was the smallest, most cautious of smiles, yet still Horemheb could see its warmth.

"As it happens," Nefertiti said, "I am in need of a guardsman. Or should I say, *Ramose* is in need."

Horemheb looked down at the boy again. His heart swelled in his chest with longing and gratitude.

"You know his true identity," Nefertiti said, glancing into her home to be sure Teti was nowhere near. "And so you know why his safety and well-being are vital. There is only so much I can do for him, and as he grows older, he needs to roam and explore. I cannot be everywhere with the boy. But you could be, Horemheb."

A chance to protect Baketaten's child—it was more than Horemheb had dared to hope for. The gods were presenting him with a way to make amends, to apologize to Baketaten's *ka* for his failure to keep her safe.

He nodded humbly. "I would be honored, my lady. So very honored."

A shadow crossed Nefertiti's face. She turned her eyes down to the portico's packed-earth floor. "Wait. Before I agree to take you all in, I must know..."

Her words trailed off, but she returned to the table and sat close beside Nann. She took the woman's pale, freckled hand. "I must know. What happened to Kiya—to Lady Tadukhepa?"

Nann hesitated, holding Nefertiti's stare with a defiant light in her green eyes. But finally she sighed, seeming to crumple in upon herself, and recounted the sad story.

"Mahu came for her. He walked right into her little northern palace, though my mistress's loyal guards tried their best to defy him. But there was no use. No one could ever stop Mahu.

"My mistress had been quiet and restless for days. I could tell there was something weighing on her mind, but she wouldn't speak of it—would hardly speak at all. She said only that she had made a grave mistake, and had told a secret she should have kept. I believe that, in all those strange silences, she heard the gods speaking—telling her she would join them soon. During all those dark days, she seemed at once inconsolable and strangely calm, accepting.

"When Mahu came for her, scattering her maids and guards away, Tadukhepa simply rose from the bench in her garden where she had sat all morning, staring out at nothing. She went to Mahu meekly, saying nothing to anyone who tried to stop her or protect her. But she did pause beside me. She kissed me on my cheek, just here. When she looked into my eyes, I could tell she knew she would never return to her palace—or to me.

"I do not know where Mahu took her, nor what he did with her once he had her alone. I hope he did not make her suffer. Ishtar knows my mistress suffered enough, all the long years of her exile in Egypt.

"After Mahu took her away, I ran from the northern palace and never returned. I knew that whoever wanted my mistress dead would soon come for me, too—just as Horemheb told you—for I had ever been her closest confidante, and all would assume that I was privy to the deadly secret Tadukhepa had revealed. But that was the one thing she never told me. To this day, I don't know what my mistress knew—why she died—to what dark scheme she was sacrificed.

"I ran, but I couldn't get out of the city—not until Horemheb found me. During those years I spent lurking in the alleys and huts of the slums, I always hoped to hear that my mistress was still alive, that she had been brought back safe to Akhet-Aten. But I knew it was a futile hope.

"I suppose Mahu must have thrown her body in the river, for there was no funeral for King's Wife Tadukhepa, no tomb. It seems just the sort of cruelty an Egyptian killer would enact, to deny that gentle woman a tomb. I know you Egyptians believe a person who hasn't any tomb of their own will die twice—once in this life, and forever in the next.

"But that is not the way in Mitanni. Tadukhepa was a good woman—*is* a good woman. I have no doubt that she has found her way to the afterlife—*our* afterlife, the true one—and that she dwells there in comfort and glory. She is far from the pains she suffered here, far from the reach of the Egyptian scum who hated her so. She walks there like a goddess, strong and beautiful. She *was* a strong woman—stronger than any of you believed. She was no cringing mouse; she was a true princess of Mitanni, and a lioness in her own way."

Nann fell silent, picking at her bread with her pale fingers.

Nefertiti hung her head for a moment, her body trembling, her eyes wide and stricken. But she composed herself with a visible effort and drew herself up again. Finally she said in a thin voice, "Thank you, Nann. For telling me."

Nann rounded on Nefertiti with a force that took Horemheb aback. He had never known the woman to be so angry, so fierce. "In Mitanni we are not weak. We are not subject to Egypt's rule, whatever you may believe. We are a force in our own right, and I swear this, by all the gods of brave Mitanni, and by Tadukhepa's memory: I will work any vengeance I can on Mahu, and on every other Egyptian who harmed my mistress in any way. Even the Pharaoh; he is not immune from my wrath. I will strike him down, and Mahu too, with a blade or a club or poison, or my bare hands if need be. Even if I am killed for it, I will go to my death happily, knowing that Tadukhepa is avenged."

Nefertiti paled, staring at the Hurrian in silence. Horemheb, too, felt a knot of anxiety tighten in his gut. It was the worst curse any Egyptian could imagine, to kill the divinely appointed king. To strike against the gods' chosen one was to strike against the Iteru itself, the river whose waters were the lifeblood of the land.

But worse than the chaos Nann's vow promised was the way her desire for vengeance at any cost—even the ultimate cost—echoed in his own heart. Horemheb knew that he, too, would strike the Pharaoh down if given half a chance—even if it meant his own death. Even if it meant damnation.

Nefertiti recovered herself. She lifted Nann's hand and kissed it. "You are brave indeed. All of you. Serve me, if you will; our hearts are aligned. Together, let us bring about all the justice we are due."

Meritaten

Year 17 of Akhenaten
Beautiful Are the Manifestations,
Exalting the Name,
Beloved of the Sun

THE ROYAL QUAY WAS HUNG with garlands of flowers. Sweet, twined ropes of purple lotus and golden lily drooped down to touch the emerald-green surface of the river, reflecting their brilliant glory as clearly as if the Iteru were a mirror. Ranks of children, dressed in bright-colored kilts, lined the wide road that led from quay to palace. The children offered up a hymn to the Aten as the grand ship maneuvered to its mooring. The boat, with its high, pointed prow, its hull as blue as an untroubled sky, was the grandest one Meritaten had ever seen. Its deck was crowded with men in the striped kilts of the king's soldiers—a royal escort for this most anticipated arrival.

Beside her on the royal platform, Akhenaten twitched impatiently upon his throne. Their vantage was shaded by a canopy of soft white plumes, held aloft on golden poles by ranks of servants. But despite the pleasant coolness of the shade, Akhenaten seemed irritable, his inscrutable thoughts turned inward where Meritaten could all but hear them simmering.

The Pharaoh's feelings about Smenkhkare had vacillated wildly in the ten days since Ay had summoned the younger man to claim his place as co-regent. For every moment the kin spent staring about him in wonder at the miracle of Smenkhkare's resurrection, he spent an hour raging, shouting at stewards and servants, knocking away his meals with disgust, glaring at Meritaten as if he knew full well what she and Ay were attempting. But Meritaten kept her composure in the face of the king's anger, wielding an aplomb that would have put Nefertiti to shame. By invoking Nefertiti, by claiming her mother's gifts as High Priestess of the Sun and the authority of divine vision, she was able to soothe away every one of Akhenaten's rages and bring him around once more to blissful anticipation of Smenkhkare's arrival. Whenever she called upon her mother's strength as High Priestess, the king would cease his fretting and cup Meritaten beneath her chin, examining her face with his red-rimmed eyes. He would kiss her tenderly, and whisper in her ear how much she resembled her mother, how pleased he was that Nefertiti lived on, and continued to serve the god through Meritaten's presence.

She did not mind Akhenaten's kisses, nor did his touch trouble her heart, but the king's attentions did not precisely please Meritaten, either. He was a tedious chore, a necessary task easily seen to, and quickly forgotten once finished. And if her affections kept the king under control—a weighty obligation she had struggled with for two long years—Meritaten was prepared to tolerate the work.

She settled him now as he fidgeted on his throne, reaching out to stroke his forearm, an unconscious gesture, as one might soothe a bristling cat or a fussing baby.

"Isn't it wonderful, my lord, that the Aten has wrought such a miracle—and all for you? The god is greater than we ever imagined, to bring your brother back from the realm of the dead." She had spoken these words so many times they were like breath to her, flying from her throat without the least bit of thought.

Not quite mollified, Akhenaten gripped the arms of his

throne, muttering, "But can I trust this man? This is my kingdom, after all, and—"

"Dear father—mightiest Pharaoh! Of course you can trust him!" She laughed lightly. "The Aten would never entrap you. It loves you far too well. Are you not the god's most beloved son, the most favored being it has ever made? You overbrim with the god's own power! What can you possibly fear from a servant such as Smenkhkare?"

That pacified Akhenaten, as it always did—the reminder that he was practically a god, on the very brink of ascending to his full, divine power.

This sagging vehicle of flesh, a god! Meritaten thought wryly. But she turned a gentle smile on her father, betraying nothing of her true thoughts.

Akhenaten nodded, his eyes fixed on the mooring ship, but his stare distant, looking beyond the boat and the river itself to some unknown distance. "That is right—that is good. The longer I remain in the temple, the more the Aten will feel my devotion. Then at last, then—"

"Precisely." She broke into his ramble with brisk energy. "The god provides a way for us to glorify it, no matter our circumstances, if we only look for the opportunity. A co-king who may stand as junior to you—supporting your acts, so that you might rise even higher in the god's esteem—is a gracious gift from the Aten. Now, let us welcome this Smenkhkare as befits a servant of the god. We owe him good courtesy, since he will give you the respite the god requires."

As the last of the ship's heavy lines were tied securely to the quay's pillars, the children ended their song. Each child held a woven bag over one shoulder, and they tossed out handfuls of bright flower petals, covering the road with a sweet and fragrant carpet. The nobles assembled on the quay began to talk excitedly; the hum of their gossip rose in pitch as the boat's ramp touched the land and the junior king's entourage of stewards and servants debarked.

Ay had selected most of Smenkhkare's staff. Meritaten had no doubt that they were loyal to the old man, and would report to him all that Smenkhkare did and said. But they were also well suited to their work, adept and clever, and would help guide the new king as he settled into his important role. They were dressed richly, too, as befitted the close personal attendants of a Pharaoh. Their long white kilts, pleated intricately and embroidered with bright threads at their hems, brushed the flower petals as they strode toward the palace.

A group of court musicians, arrayed near the boat's landing site, played a tumbling fanfare. Then they struck a triumphant tune that buoyed the mood of the crowd even further, until the nobles cheered and clapped and laughed with the joy of this novelty. The music even seemed to lift the king's uncertain mood. He leaned to the edge of his throne, watching the boat avidly for his first glimpse of his god-sent companion.

Smenkhkare pulled aside the red curtain that shrouded his private cabin, protecting him from the hot sun as well as from the gaze of onlookers. He stood still for a moment beneath that gently waving canopy, gazing out at the city of Akhet-Aten. Though he was some distance away, Meritaten could see that he was young and strong, his body ready and capable. He moved with a careful grace that spoke of inborn nobility and a finely honed confidence that filled her with a tingle of hope.

There stands a man who is worthy of the title Pharaoh, she thought, unable to tear her eyes away.

Attended by the few members of his staff who had remained onboard, Smenkhkare made his way down the ramp to the shore. He seemed entirely unperturbed by the shouts of approval, the music, the petals he crushed underfoot. He moved through this new world as the birds flew through the skies, as the fish darted in the river—as if the palace, the throngs of subjects, the splendor of Akhet-Aten had always been his by right.

Meritaten flushed as the crowd cheered louder. *They do not even know this man, yet they show more enthusiasm for him than they do for their true king.* She should have been outraged on her husband's behalf—but she could only sympathize with the court. Akhenaten was not an easy man to love, but this new king, this Smenkhkare, exuded charm and aptitude with his every step.

Smenkhkare approached the two thrones beneath their canopy of white plumes. He bowed to the Pharaoh and the Great Wife. When he straightened, he held Meritaten's gaze for a moment that seemed to stretch into eternity, and her breath caught in her chest. He was a singularly handsome man, with features that resembled Akhenaten's but were more masculine, less eerily refined. She saw that he was older than she had first assumed. At close range, noting the faint lines on his face and the depth of wisdom in his eyes, she guessed his age at about thirty years. Yet he still possessed a youthful air, a certain inclination toward amusement that gave him a charming sense of energy and vitality. He painted a stark picture of contrast beside the sagging, twitching Akhenaten. No wonder the people had cheered him.

Smenkhkare turned to Akhenaten. "Brother," he said warmly. "It has been many years since I saw you last."

Akhenaten's knuckles whitened as his grip flexed on the arms of his throne. But then he pushed himself up from his gilded seat and gestured for Smenkhkare to climb the few steps to the top of the royal platform. "The god has given us a most miraculous gift," Akhenaten said, loudly enough for the nearest nobles to hear. "Let us have two kings now—brothers, both blessed by the Aten and doing its holy work."

He wrapped his arms around Smenkhkare, an embrace that went on for what seemed to Meritaten an uncomfortably long while. Smenkhkare looked at her over Akhenaten's shoulder; his eyes sparked for a moment with humor, as well as a probing, searching light that made her heart beat loudly in her ears.

When Akhenaten released him, Smenkhkare bent over Meritaten's hand. His lips brushed her skin with a gentle kiss. "Niece and King's Great Wife."

Again Smenkhkare held Meritaten's eye. She sensed a promise in his gaze, an intimacy that made her stomach leap and her breath quicken. But before she could do more than wonder at the intensity of his look, Akhenaten tore Smenkhkare's attention away again.

"Now that I see you, strong as a bull and so very alert—and glowing as you are with the god's blessing—Meritaten, my priestess, does he not glow?"

"Ah, indeed," Meritaten managed.

"Now that I see you, Brother, I know the Aten has blessed me a hundredfold. You are prepared to bear the burden of the throne, and act as my loyal servant, aren't you? Aren't you?"

Akhenaten's fervency did not seem to disquiet Smenkhkare in the least. No doubt Ay had prepared him well, instructing him in the king's strange habits, his flights of zeal. Smenkhkare showed nothing in his cool expression but quiet curiosity. He offered the senior king a deferential bow. "I am always ready to serve the throne and the god, Brother. I will ever be your most faithful servant."

"Then let us feast! We have prepared grand entertainments to welcome you. The City of the Sun is the finest place in all Egypt. Let us show you our gratitude. Come now!"

Akhenaten led them from the dais. The crowd of nobles

and stewards parted to make way; he found the petal-strewn path and strode along it, heading toward the palace with such speed that Meritaten and Smenkhkare nearly had to run to catch up to him.

Meritaten caught her husband by the elbow, threading her arm through his, slowing him to a more seemly pace. Smenkhkare walked on her other side, and she could feel his nearness as a warm flush along her skin.

"This is good. This is *maat*," Akhenaten said, wrapping one arm around Meritaten's shoulders, pulling her tight against his side.

Just moments ago, before Smenkhkare had kissed her hand and looked at her with that strange, searching gaze, the Pharaoh's touch had not disturbed Meritaten. But now, still feeling a throb on her hand in the exact spot where Smenkhkare had kissed it, she fought back an urge to twist violently away from Akhenaten, to thrust herself out of his reach.

"How was your voyage?" she asked Smenkhkare, to distract herself from the growing revulsion in her gut.

"Very pleasant," he said. His voice was low and smooth. She seemed to feel it vibrating gently inside her own chest. "But I am glad to be here at last, in your company."

"I hope you will find Akhet-Aten agreeable."

From the corner of her eye, she saw him turn toward her, caught the faint trace of his smile. "I already find it quite lovely, my lady. It surpasses all my expectations."

Akhenaten's arm tightened around her body, like a hawk seizing its prey. Meritaten walked on calmly in the Pharaoh's grip, praying that her new disgust at his touch would never show on her face.

THE FEAST WAS SUMPTUOUS, the great hall ringing

with laughter and music, rich with the odors of roasted goose, sweet wine, and the perfumed cones of wax that adorned the ornately braided wigs of Akhet-Aten's noblewomen. Meritaten, seated between the two Pharaohs, felt herself pulled in one direction, then the other—allowing her heart to fill with the joy and splendor of the lavish celebration, then wilting inside as her frustration with Akhenaten grew. His presence seemed to cast a shadow over the feast, one that fell on Meritaten alone. Among so much warmth and happiness, she shivered as if in the grip of winter.

But the sun was still up, painting the western sky with a ruddy glow as it sank slowly toward the night. Akhenaten watched it anxiously through the feast hall's huge double doors—opened wide, to welcome cool river breezes. The Pharaoh fidgeted and muttered as sunset approached. At last he stood abruptly, cutting off his distracted conversation with Smenkhkare.

"I should be at the temple," Akhenaten said. "Now that you are here, fulfilling the god's will, I must serve the Aten, too."

Smenkhkare exchanged a glance with Meritaten. She raised her brows, silently urging him to go along with the Pharaoh's sudden change of plans.

"As you wish," Smenkhkare said. "If the god wishes you to commit yourself more fully to the temple, then you may as well begin now."

Meritaten forced herself to take the Pharaoh's hand, giving him an encouraging squeeze. The feel of his skin, dry and rough like crumbling brick, turned her stomach. "I am sure the god is eager to hear your praises, before it departs from the sky. Let us remain here and entertain all these guests in your name. Isn't that what your brother Smenkhkare is for?"

"That is good—yes, very good," Akhenaten said. Without

another word, he descended the dais and strode from the hall, ignoring the praises of his subjects as he passed.

Meritaten breathed a long sigh as he left, sinking gratefully back in her chair as relief washed over her. The music of horns and harps seemed brighter, more vibrant, with Akhenaten gone from the hall, and when she popped a honeyed date into her mouth the sweetness seemed to burst through all her senses. She turned to Smenkhkare with an unfeigned smile.

"Tell me, King, now that we are alone—what do you truly think of Akhet-Aten?"

Smenkhkare's brow raised and he gave a short, uncertain laugh. He licked sweet onion sauce from his finger before he answered. "It is... a most impressive place," he said carefully.

"Impressive? How do you mean?" She leaned toward him on her throne, so their closeness became almost conspiratorial. "Indulge my curiosity."

"It's large," he said. "There are a great many more people than I expected to find here."

There would be fewer people living here, if they had any say in the matter. But she kept the smile on her face. She found it easy to do, so close beside him. "Go on."

"The buildings are all quite lovely, especially this palace, yet I find the art so... *original.*"

Alienating, he means to say. Off-putting. It was true that Akhenaten had turned traditional forms on their ears. Meritaten had not been outside the City of the Sun since she was a baby. But she had heard many older courtiers speak of the art and architecture of Akhet-Aten, comparing this city's appearance to the Egypt they had known before—the Egypt that had flourished under the old gods. *Eerie,* many of them had said of Akhet-Aten's buildings and murals. *Strange, otherworldly. Isolating.* And all of it made after Akhenaten's unique vision. Her whole life, she had believed her father when he'd said that his city was the grandest, the most striking and lovely in all the world. She had felt lucky to live there, privileged to be a part of its singular beauty. But now she wondered what Smenkhkare preferred—what he considered beautiful. She longed to see the cities and districts beyond Akhet-Aten, to the north and the south, with a sudden, burning desire so strong, it unsettled her stomach.

"I think you are being polite," she told him playfully. "I think you find Akhet-Aten strange."

He shrugged in mild agreement. "You must understand, my lady: I lived most of my life in a small, traditional village, surrounded by common folk and their plain, homey ways. I may be royal-born, but I have not set foot inside a palace since I was ten years old—and even then, it was the House of Rejoicing on the West Bank, a more old-fashioned place than where I find myself now. Your city *is* beautiful, but even so, I fear it will take some getting used to."

"It's so odd—absurd, even, that a man of the royal blood should live so far from the capital city."

"Perhaps, but it was necessary. My mother Tiy was wise and far-thinking. And it's a good thing she thought to send me away. Imagine where we might be now otherwise. I thank the gods—" he caught himself, smiling wryly at the mistake, so easily made— "I thank the *god* that I am able to serve Egypt at this moment, when the need is so great."

Meritaten couldn't keep the smile from sliding off her face. The pleasantries of the feast seemed to recede from her, the music and light rushing away down a long, dark tunnel that left her in cold blackness. At least she no longer had to bear the weight of her responsibility alone.

"The Pharaoh wasn't always like this," she said quietly, so only Smenkhkare could hear. "I remember when he was stronger—confident, capable—and full of a magnificent belief in his own power. I believed in his power, too. I was only a young girl then, a naïve fool—I understand that now, just how foolish I was. But I did believe he was a great man—the very greatest, the most glorious person the god ever made."

"How could you have thought differently? Akhenaten was the window through which you viewed the world. He controlled what you saw, what information you received, and so he controlled the very thoughts of your heart. I would have thought him glorious, too, had he restricted my view of the world the way he did yours."

She sipped her wine, silent among a host of complicated musings. "Yes," she said at last. "That is true. But I see him differently now. He's not as strong as he once was—if he ever *was* the monument of power I believed him to be. When Sitamun died—and later, Baketaten—something broke inside him. His heart has fractured like a dry bone. I don't believe it can ever be repaired. He is mad as a doddering old grandfather now, and I'm certain our Pharaoh will never be sane and whole again."

"What was it, do you think?"

She looked up at him, questioning—and the brightness of his eyes, their intelligent focus, stole the breath from her chest.

"I mean," Smenkhkare clarified, "what was it about the deaths of those two ladies that affected him so badly?"

Meritaten sighed heavily. "I wish I knew. The Aten knows, I have prayed for the answer to that question more times than I could ever count. I am left with speculations. They seem rather useless to me."

"Let us hear them, all the same." Smenkhkare eased back against his throne's backrest, drinking idly from a bowl of beer, its rim dotted with bright faience colors.

"I think..." Meritaten said slowly, carefully, "I think the king believed that nothing that was *of him* could ever die. I think he truly felt himself immortal, invincible, because the Aten loved him so, and blessed him above all other men. I think he believed that because he was set apart, the god would preserve all that was his—his sister-wife, his daughter-wife—and his children, too. My sisters."

She fell silent, picking disconsolately at the leg of a roasted goose. Her appetite had fled, but the rich, greasy meat was a distraction from her dark thoughts.

"Akhenaten must have loved them all very much—Sitamun, Baketaten, and all your poor sisters."

Meritaten dropped the goose leg into her silver supper bowl. Its bone clattered against the rim. "Loved?" She laughed bitterly. "Akhenaten does not, has *never*, loved anyone in all his life. Except for himself—and he loves his own person, his own power, with far more passion than most people adore their children, their parents, or their lovers!"

Smenkhkare set his beer carefully on the table before them and gazed at her, waiting with patient sympathy for her to speak on.

Meritaten was distantly aware that she had said too much—that to say more might condemn her. But she couldn't seem to hold back her hurt, her fury. The words tumbled out like water from a courtyard fountain.

"Don't you see? It wasn't the loss of Baketaten or my sisters that pained him. It wasn't *they* he mourned. They had no value to him as people—no one does! He values a person only for what he can wring from them, not because each life is sacred in its own right. Oh, I know the priests of Aten tell us that the god loves life and rejoices in its goodness, but to Akhenaten, *his* is the only life that matters. He expected his strength to multiply through Sitamun and Baketaten—and through my sisters, may the god keep them safe. He expected that they would elevate him further, by bringing forth gods from their wombs. He thought no harm could come to them, because he saw them as sacred vessels for his own seed, tools to use in his own designs.

"Their deaths shocked him—not because he loved them, but because in dying, they took away the illusion of powers he believed were his alone, and his forever. It's not grief that has broken him and reduced him to the creature he is now. It's disillusionment. It's faltering faith. It's fear of what powers the god might drain from him next. Power— divinity—his place at the pinnacle of all creation: that's what Akhenaten cares for. That, and *nothing* else."

Smenkhkare took her hand, a gentle display of support that made Meritaten's chest tighten with the sobs of relief she held back. "Several times now, I've heard you call yourself a fool. But you are no silly young girl, Meritaten. You have as sharp a heart as Tiy ever did. You are very fit indeed for the throne of the Great Wife."

She blushed, turning her face away. But she left her hand in his warm, soft grip. "Ay would disagree with you. Most strenuously."

"Then it's Ay who is the fool."

Now Meritaten stared at Smenkhkare, wide-eyed with fearful surprise. "It's dangerous to think so. Ay is ten times cleverer than he lets on. If there is anyone in this palace whom you should fear, it's Ay—not Akhenaten."

Smenkhkare gave a confident, good-natured laugh, loosing her hand from his grip. But his confidence did nothing to comfort Meritaten.

"I'm not afraid of Ay, but I give you my word that I will treat him with caution. Though there is a vast difference between caution and fear."

I see little difference, she thought. *Little that truly matters.*

But she did not wish to argue with Smenkhkare—not when she could still feel the heat of the blush on her cheeks and feel the memory of his hand holding her own. She said only, "Good. I will trust you to handle Ay wisely and well."

A troupe of dancers entered the hall, their bodies adorned with nothing but long, trailing ribbons that floated behind them as they moved, drifting on the fragrant air like wisps of vapor. Meritaten settled in to watch, glad to release her fears and enjoy the simple pleasures of music and dance. Smenkhkare might be new to the City of the Sun, and unaware as yet of its subtle political currents, but she liked his smooth voice and easy, confident manner. She was happy to place her trust in him. Their hours together, watching the delights of the feast unfold, talking shoulder to shoulder with their hands so near to touching, made for the best time Meritaten could ever recall having. Despite her mistrust of Ay and Akhenaten, the stresses of the past two years lifted from her like a cloak discarded, and she seemed to float above the feast hall on a cloud of bliss.

When the dancing troupe had finished several numbers, the musicians altered their tune to a low, insistent throb. The feast had turned toward its natural conclusion; the eldest and most dignified of the guests departed, while those who were young and adventuresome strolled about in pairs, seeking out secluded alcoves in which to make entertainments of their own.

"It's time for us both to depart," Meritaten said reluctantly. *If only we could go off in one another's company.* Her wish to engage in the typical feast-ending debaucheries was compelling and fierce. But she knew it would be a scandal—or worse. It would not be fitting, for the new Pharaoh and the Great Wife to partake of such delights— particularly when Meritaten was not *his* Great Wife.

She frowned as she stared out through the hall's great doors, to the violet dusk and the western horizon where the sun had sunk into darkness. *If only you had saved me, Aten, for this man—for a true king, capable and feeling and strong! How happy I would be then.* But the Aten did not require happiness from the people it had made. It only required loyal worship.

The sight of gathering night filled Meritaten with dread, as it never had before. With the sun set and Akhenaten returned from the temple, he might very well call her to his bed chamber. For the first time in her life, the thought of lying with him was unbearable—so repulsive that a wave of nausea swept through her, and cold sweat collected on her brow. She pictured the Pharaoh's aging body, his red-rimmed, staring eyes. Beside Smenkhkare, who was so beautiful and courtly, even if he had been raised in a *rekhet* village—and who had told Meritaten that she was not a foolish girl, but worthy of her throne— Akhenaten seemed revolting as a leprous rat.

She stood from her throne so quickly that dizziness seized her head. She reached out instinctively and grabbed the closest thing to hand: Smenkhkare's shoulder.

"Are you all right, my lady?" He gazed up at her with concern.

"I'm quite fine. But will... will you walk with me tomorrow in the garden?" She flushed at her own boldness. "I have enjoyed speaking with you tonight."

He smiled. "As have I. Let us make it a habit. I shall see you tomorrow, Meritaten."

The sound of her name on his lips shivered all through her body. It took a force of will greater than the strength of the river's current to let go of Smenkhkare's shoulder and walk away.

O NLY THREE WEEKS had passed since Smenkhkare arrived at Akhet-Aten, but already Meritaten felt as if their evening strolls in the garden were a long-standing habit, the routine of many years. These were the gentle hours when the cares of the court—and the pressure of being Akhenaten's wife—drifted away from her like boats down the river. Side by side, so close she could feel the warmth of his body brushing her bare arm, she and Smenkhkare wended aimlessly among the flower beds and ponds, where lotus blooms dotted the water like bright stars fallen to earth.

"The senior king seems most content with his temple service," Smenkhkare noted, plucking a stalk from a waist-high clump of ornamental grasses. He twirled the stem in his fingers idly, and tapped it now and then against Meritaten's thigh, like a herdsman driving a goat.

"Thank the god for that. The temple is where he belongs, surely—out of the throne room."

If not for the way the garden relaxed her, she might have shuddered to think what could become of Egypt now, as Akhenaten descended further into his madness. She and Smenkhkare were required to attend the morning services at the Great Aten Temple, and there she could see the stark changes wrought in the Pharaoh. His skin had darkened to the deepest brown from hours spent standing in the sun. He sang hymns to the Aten with more fervor than he had ever shown before. He was more demonstrative than before, too. Whenever Meritaten approached him at the Sun Altar, he would kiss her on the mouth, long and deep, and tell her how happy he was with this change, how thankful for her sacred visions, which had brought about this new elevation of his glory.

The kisses and caresses infuriated her—especially with Smenkhkare looking on. And in her moments of introspection, she could admit that she was frightened by the rapidity of Akhenaten's decline, his steep slide into unchecked zeal. But Meritaten was willing to accept the king as he was now, if it meant *she* could be happier with her lot in life, as well.

And she was happy. Overjoyed, in fact—so full of hope and blessed warmth that sometimes she thought her chest would burst open and the bright fire inside would escape, blotting out the god in the sky with the strength of her happiness. Smenkhkare learned the duties of a Pharaoh quickly, as one would expect from a man born of the royal line. He was adept at ruling; he took to the throne and all the responsibilities it conferred with the same natural readiness of a duck bobbing in water. Meritaten was impressed with Smenkhkare's fair judgments and level thinking. He often made pronouncements she found wise, even inspiring. Before he had come into her life, Meritaten had viewed her daily duty on the throne as another chore to be discharged, as dull and uninteresting as seeing to the king's appetites. But with Smenkhkare at her side, she found she enjoyed ruling as the Great Wife. Like him, she was born to rule. She had lacked only a competent partner, but now that he was here, she found joy in her task.

"I heard him crying out last night," Smenkhkare said, breaking into her pleasant musings. "He was weeping over Baketaten."

Meritaten's spirit crumpled a little; the colors in the garden seemed to wilt and drain, and the approach of evening raised a chill along her arms. She hadn't thought of Baketaten or her death in some time—not since she had spoken so passionately to Smenkhkare at the welcoming feast. But in a heartbeat, all her guilt and regrets came flooding back, settling in her belly with a sickly weight.

"He does that often," she said. "I'm surprised this is the first time you've heard it."

She found she couldn't look at Smenkhkare. Her hastiness and immaturity in the matter of Baketaten seemed to stopper her throat; she could say no more.

Smenkhkare told me I was no fool, but he doesn't know the half of it. If he found out how I overstepped myself—how I alone sent poor Baketaten to her grave, and for nothing! —he would despise me. He would cast me away from his side. And he would be right to do it. Shame buffeted her *ka*, so strong it made her tremble. *Oh, Smenkhkare, I am not the good woman you believe me to be.* But with him at her side, she wanted to be good. She wanted to be worthy of his friendship—and if the god was kind to her, she might yet be

For a moment, inspiration flashed in her heart like lightning, quick and hot and terrible. She must confess the part she had played in Baketaten's death—yes! That would alleviate her feelings of guilt and shame. Before she could talk herself out of it, she took Smenkhkare's hand—the gesture surprised even her—and opened her mouth to speak. But before she could draw a breath, she closed it again. The confession simply would not come. She couldn't share her guilt with anyone. Her shame over the incident went too deep—so deep it cut off her words.

Smenkhkare looked at her quizzically, amused, then tapped his stalk of grass on her nose. He kept hold of her hand, and she made no move to release him, either, but smiled shyly down at her feet as she and Smenkhkare strolled along the garden path.

"In the evening light, you are so beautiful," he said. "But then, you are beautiful in every kind of light. In starlight, too, I imagine."

She smiled tremulously. "Thank you."

He turned to her with sudden fervency, his eyes burning, his mouth tight and turned down. "You're too beautiful for Akhenaten. That twisted madman..."

"But I *am* for Akhenaten," she said, her stomach churning with remorse. Perhaps this was her punishment, Baketaten's revenge from the mists beyond her tomb: she would be Akhenaten's forever, even as her longing for

Smenkhkare grew, day by day.

He sighed and cast his grass stem off into the flower beds, tossing it like a spear. "It's easy to forget that. We are together so often, and work together so well. But we see *him* so little—"

"Thank the god for that. Without Akhenaten in the throne room, I am beginning to believe we might actually set Egypt to rights again—repair matters with the northern client-kings, drive back the enemies that harass them, and—who knows?—perhaps even expand the empire once more." She tried to laugh lightly, but it sounded pinched and forced, even to her own ears. "It is amazing what we can accomplish, with the senior Pharaoh distracted by his precious temple."

Smenkhkare's laugh did not sound false. It was rumbling and rough, but had a note of gladness in it that raised her spirits even from their present dejected state. "We might do anything at all, we two."

He still kept hold of her hand. Meritaten would have gone on holding it forever if she could. They walked that way in contented silence for some time, fingers interlaced, bare flesh against bare flesh. Her heart fluttered madly in her chest and her face heated for no good reason—merely because she was happy and full of a soaring, singing warmth. She could scarcely believe that only a few weeks ago she had felt old and used up, at the end of her wits. Smenkhkare had made her feel alive once more, vibrant and young.

"Great Wife!" A woman's voice drifted across the garden from the direction of Meritaten's apartments. "Great Wife! We are ready for you."

"My bath is ready," she said to Smenkhkare. Already she ached inside with the pang of their parting. "I shall see you in the morning, at the temple."

"I am looking forward to it, as always," Smenkhkare said.

Then, with another of his alluring laughs, he plucked a flower from a nearby bed. He extended it toward Meritaten, holding it before her nose so she could breathe in its perfume. The scent was as sweet as the music that seemed to swell and throb inside her heart.

Ay

Year 1 of Smenkhkare,
Holy of the Manifestations

Year 17 of Akhenaten,
Beloved of the Sun

THE GREAT WIFE'S ATTENDANTS whispered behind their hands, squinting at Ay with suspicion even as they admitted him to Meritaten's chambers. The hissing of common snakes meant nothing to him. Women of the servant breed had no understanding of necessity, of power—of the forces that moved Egypt, and therefore moved all the world. Men of their class had no understanding, either. It was theirs to fetch and carry, to go where they were sent and do as they were commanded. They were not the masters of their own fates, and so their dislike for him bounced away from his *ka* like drops of water from oiled linen.

"The Great Wife is still in her bath," the eldest of the servants said. "She will not see you yet. You must wait here in the—"

"Admit him," Meritaten called, her voice floating out languidly from the tile-lined bathing room.

Ay stepped over the threshold, into the thick, perfumed humidity of Meritaten's bath just as she rose from the water. Her maids bustled past him, all but flapping their arms with agitation. The women rushed to wrap her in thick linen, to shield her nakedness from his eyes. But Meritaten scattered them with a wave of her hand and dried herself, running the long, white towel unhurriedly over her slender arms, her shoulders, her breasts.

She was a beautiful young woman. Ay was willing to admit that much to himself. But her unconcern at standing naked before him was unsettling.

"So ready to display your body to a blood relative?"

Meritaten smirked at him, but did not answer.

"Have you grown so fond of the incestuous web your father has tangled you in?"

Her bold smile turned to a sickly frown, and she wrapped the towel quickly about her body.

"Perhaps so." Ay pressed on relentlessly. "I think a current of true depravity runs not far below your surface. And why not? It makes sense; you are the offspring of Akhenaten."

"How dare you speak that way to me? Don't forget yourself, old man: I am the King's Great Wife." Meritaten came toward him, her feet slapping lightly on the tiles. Despite her frown and the alacrity with which she abandoned her wanton display, her pace was direct and steady, her head high, her stare unflinching.

She stopped before him, just close enough that he felt encroached upon. Then she let the towel fall to the floor with a whispering slide, a soft thump. "Does my nakedness disturb you, Grandfather?" Her dark eyes held his defiantly.

"No," Ay said honestly. He was not disturbed, merely mystified by her shamelessness. To prove his point, he allowed his gaze to travel down her body, the soft brown curves of her flesh. "Nor do your tendencies surprise me—not truly. It seems Akhenaten has trained you well."

Her face darkened at the sound of the king's name. She breezed past him, out of the tiled bath with its cloying smells of rose oil and myrrh, into her bedchamber where her women waited to dress her. "Do not speak to me of *him*." She cast the words back over her shoulder. "Not here. My chambers are my sanctuary, where I may forget all about the king."

"You forget one king, but not the other."

The indignant flash in her eyes told Ay all he sought to know. His suspicions were correct. He had watched the girl over the past few weeks since Smenkhkare's arrival. Meritaten was a fool after all—and a good deal more foolish than most girls her age.

"I am sure," Ay said casually, "your uncle Smenkhkare will be pleased to hear that you are adept in the ways of incest."

Though she was only half clothed, Meritaten clapped her hands sharply to dismiss her women. They went in a bluster of scoffs and rustling skirts, casting spite-filled glances at Ay.

Meritaten pulled her robe around her shoulders, belted it closed with a vigorous jerk of its violet sash, and gave Ay her bitterest stare. "You don't know anything of it—of my life, my heart. You don't know what it's like, old man, to deal with the Pharaoh—with the first Pharaoh, I mean—Akhenaten."

"I am one of his most trusted advisors. I know what he is like."

"It's not the *same!*" She shouted the word, and Ay could feel the tension of her distress like a cord of pleasure stretched tight inside him. Every beat of the pulse leaping in her neck plucked that cord and raised from it a sweet, familiar music. *How easily you are pushed to your limits, little King's Wife. How easily I move you.*

Meritaten mustered her serenity with obvious effort. After a moment she went on, more calmly this time: "Smenkhkare is in full control of his own wits. I can have a conversation with him, without fear of interruption by Baketaten's ghost, without it devolving into praises to the god. That is where my delight in Smenkhkare's company begins and ends. It is a relief to discuss the throne and Egypt's business with a man who can comprehend such things—whose decrees make sense, whose judgment can be trusted. If you believe I have some other designs on the new co-Pharaoh, you are wrong."

Ay smiled. "Am I wrong? I saw you together in the garden. I saw the way he held your hand."

Meritaten's cheeks flamed red. "You were spying on me? On us?"

He shrugged. To deny it would be foolish. He had nothing to hide, and if he hadn't wanted the girl to know he was keeping an eye on her, he wouldn't have told her so.

"You are making much out of nothing," Meritaten said, lifting her chin and turning regally away, a cold dismissal—how like Nefertiti she was! "An uncle may hold his niece's hand without any *spies* calling incest. Tend to your own business, Ay, and do not trouble me with this nonsense."

She brushed past him, toward her bed on its gilded lion's paws, its curved ivory head rest and coverlets of imported silk and soft linen. Beside the bed was a great, free-standing wardrobe chest, made of expensive cedar, oiled to a night-dark luster. She pulled open its doors and pawed absently through her collection of night dresses.

Ay followed her, and would have grabbed her by the wrist to turn her attention back to him, but she flinched away before he could touch her.

"This *is* my business," he said. "Egypt is my business. Whatever your personal feelings for me, I am your most capable advisor—yours and Smenkhkare's—the man who can best guide you in your roles as King's Wife and Pharaoh. You would be wise to listen to me, even if you despise me. Need I remind you after all that you wouldn't have Smenkhkare's companionship without my help? It was my suggestion to bring him to the throne, my idea to seat him beside you."

Meritaten left her night dresses alone and turned to him with a look that said, *Make your point quickly and be done with it.*

I would have taught Nefertiti her place for stares less insolent than that, Ay thought, his palm itching with the desire to slap the haughty look from his granddaughter's face.

But he kept control of his perfect calm. It was ever the best leverage over an opponent, especially a flighty, arrogant girl. "You claim you have no designs on Smenkhkare, no attraction to him—well and good. You may *claim* anything you like. I only wished to warn you, after I saw you in the garden this evening: do not be so young, Meritaten. Do not be such a fool. Akhenaten is your husband, not Smenkhkare—and Akhenaten is a singularly jealous man. You know he is capable of drastic measures if he is crossed."

"I have no intention of crossing the Pharaoh."

"Every time you make calf-eyes at Smenkhkare, or stroll with him in the garden, you are crossing the king. Are you so eager to ruin everything—all the plans we've made, Smenkhkare's claim to the throne—for the sake of alleviating your loneliness? If you give Akhenaten any reason to mistrust Smenkhkare, it will all be over. He'll send Smenkhkare away, or worse, have him killed."

She tossed her head, a terse dismissal of his warning. "Akhenaten believes the Aten itself resurrected Smenkhkare. He believes Smenkhkare is singularly blessed by the god."

"He believes that now. How much longer will be trust to the story?"

"Akhenaten is a sun-blinded fool. He sees only what he wants to see."

"I doubt that very much," Ay said. "He's mad, but he's

not dim. And those who are both insane and keen-hearted are the most dangerous people of all."

Meritaten narrowed her eyes at him and pressed her pretty mouth into a thin, pale line. *Like you, Grandfather?* Ay could all but hear her thoughts.

"I know Akhenaten better than anyone," Meritaten said at length. "You told me so yourself, in those days past when you insisted that I control him."

"You are placed the closest to him—to his body and his thoughts—but he is still a force well beyond your control." *And well beyond mine, if I am honest.* "We must all work together to keep him in line. We must act as one—Smenkhkare, you, and I—to keep the king focused on his temples."

Meritaten pulled a gauzy night dress from her wardrobe and tossed it across the foot of her bed. Then she brushed past Ay to a table that stood near the room's windcatcher, where the evening breezes, funneled into the chamber, cooled a jug of wine. She poured herself a cup, but did not offer any to Ay.

"He *is* focused on the temples," she said. "He practically never leaves them. There is no danger he'll see my harmless strolls with Smenkhkare and grow envious. Unlike you, he doesn't lurk about in gardens." She sipped the wine, and her eyes held a hint of a mocking smile as they watched him over the rim of her silver cup.

Ay thought, *There was a time when Akhenaten did nothing but that—peered at women in the gardens.* Those West Bank days. Tiy had thought Akhenaten—Young Amunhotep in those days—an unbearable burden simply for his disagreeable habit of spying on the ladies of the harem. What Ay wouldn't give now to reverse time, to return to a world where degenerate creeping through flower beds was the worst of Akhenaten's offenses.

There was no reason why the Pharaoh might not return

to his old habits, and catch his wife in the midst of her dangerous, foolhardy game. But Ay did not bring up the possibility. He kept his peace, waiting to see what Meritaten would say next—how she would reveal yet more of her weakness.

"My time with Smenkhkare does no one any harm," she said, then gulped at her wine again.

Still Ay waited.

Finally Meritaten burst out, "And I won't give him up! I won't! I won't have Akhenaten for my sole companion. His touch is *repulsive* to me. You cannot comprehend it, how his kisses, his lecherous looks—how the mere *thought* of him turns my stomach!"

Ay grunted in satisfaction. "So you are not as far gone into incest as I'd initially thought."

She rounded on him, snarling. "Don't you dare cast aspersions on me, old man. I am what the god has made me. More to the point, I am what the royal family has made me—my father, my mother, and *you*, Ay. You're no stranger to these vile manipulations. Don't think I'm unaware of your part in this long line of outrages—how you made Nefertiti into what she was, an object for you to use, so you might work your private designs against the throne. You think I'm a fool, but I'm not. I am a servant of Egypt, and I have only gone where the god has sent me and done what the god commanded. Despise me for it if you like, but *someone* had to be Akhenaten's Great Wife!"

"And someone must stay his Great Wife. If you persist in mooning after Smenkhkare, you will end staked out in the Great Aten Temple, tinder to be burnt by the very god you revere."

The girl blanched, but she did not back down. Her hand tightened on the wine cup, the knuckles of her fine, slender fingers going yellowish-pale. For a moment, Ay thought she might hurl the cup at his face. But she had learned more self-control than that.

"Smenkhkare is worth that risk," Meritaten said quietly, firmly. "You've seen how he has taken to the throne. He is a more capable king than Akhenaten ever was. Soon the god will see it, too, and will remove my father from the throne."

Ay chuckled, hooking his thumbs in the belt of his kilt sash. "As long as it's not *your* hand that removes him."

"Why not yours, you scheming old toad?"

Amused, Ay shrugged. The girl was surely a fool, but at least she was a courageous one.

"The god will remove Akhenaten," Meritaten went on, "because in the City of the Sun we glorify the Aten; we are its dedicated people. It will grant our prayers, if our belief is strong enough. And when Akhenaten is no more, Smenkhkare will be our sole king—our true king. I look forward to the day. I pray for it. If you are wise, you'll pray for that day, too."

"And with Smenkhkare on the Pharaoh's throne, will you still sit beside him?"

Meritaten drew herself up, fixing Ay with an arrogant half-smile. He nearly gasped; she was the very image of Nefertiti, but twice as defiant as that lost beauty ever was.

"I am the King's Great Wife," Meritaten said levelly. "Someone had to do the job, and the god chose me for it. Don't question the will of the Aten, Grandfather. And don't try to undo its holy works. I will reign on my throne for as long as the god wills—no matter which man rules beside me."

Ay had delivered his warning. Let the girl heed it, if she was wise enough to see the sense in what he said. There was nothing more here for him to do. He bowed low, showing her his palms with an ironic flourish. "Great Wife, with your leave, I will—"

"Go," Meritaten snapped.

He obliged her, turning away, surprised at the sensation that burned between his shoulder blades. He wasn't embarrassed, was he? *Surely not.*

"And Ay," she called after him as he made for the door.

He paused and looked back at her. Twilight was gathering in the garden outside; a soft veil of blue shadow hung about her, making her look far more strong and confident—even mysterious—than she truly was. He waited.

"Stay out of my garden," Meritaten said, and turned away.

Meritaten

Year 1 of Smenkhkare,
Holy of the Manifestations

Year 17 of Akhenaten,
Beloved of the Sun

IT WAS ALL MERITATEN COULD DO to keep herself from fidgeting on the throne of the King's Great Wife, like a child eager to slip away from lessons and scamper off to play. The stewards of the audience hall gathered up their scrolls and wax tablets of notes and figures, preparing to close the chamber to all petitioners and business of state. In another moment Smenkhkare would dismiss the court. Meritaten wanted nothing more than to leave the throne room behind and stroll with him through the flower beds, blushed pink with the approach of evening. Perhaps she would hold his hand again, as they had done the evening before.

Ay's unexpected visit to her apartments the previous night had unsettled Meritaten, though she would rather have died than allowed her grandfather to see her disconcertment. Nevertheless, though his warning still hung about her heart, haunting her private thoughts as the shades of dead women tormented the Pharaoh, Meritaten still felt confident in her strength as King's Great Wife. Akhenaten's madness was safely contained within the temple walls. It would not spill out to infect the rest of Egypt—it *could* not. The god was distant and often inscrutable, but the priests of the Great Aten Temple taught that the god was the very embodiment of justice.

Nothing could be more righteous, more perfectly *maat*, than for Akhenaten to while all his time away in worship, leaving Smenkhkare and Meritaten to the business of ruling the Two Lands.

As Smenkhkare bent on his throne to exchange a few quiet words with one of his stewards, Meritaten watched him from the corner of her eye. He was so handsome, so strong—the very embodiment of goodness and light. He sat the Pharaoh's throne with an air of natural ownership; Smenkhkare looked born to rule, as indeed he had been. Surely this was the king the Aten had always intended for Egypt's throne.

It was only a matter of time before some act of the god took Akhenaten from the world of the living, carrying him off into merciful oblivion. Perhaps one of his great statues would topple onto him while he worshiped at the Great Aten Temple. Perhaps the god would send a cobra into Akhenaten's path, or would simply stop the breath in his throat while he slept. Then all of Egypt would be free to rejoice in Smenkhkare as its true, good, perfectly made king—and Meritaten would be the gladdest of them all.

Concluding their business, Smenkhkare nodded to the head steward. The man raised his staff of office to rap out the dismissal on the limestone steps of the dais. But before the staff could strike, the chamber doors opened at the far end of the hall. Two of Mahu's guards came in, dragging a frightened man between them. A cloud of murmurs rose up from the attendants of the Pharaoh's hall. The man the guards dragged was weakened by fear, feebly pawing at the floor with his feet but unable to stand, to walk under his own power. The guards brought him to the foot of the throne and cast him down roughly at Smenkhkare's feet. The man caught himself against the floor with a loud, stinging slap of his palms. He lay there, panting and trembling, not daring to raise his eyes from the ground.

"What is this?" Smenkhkare said, startled.

"Apprehended," one of the guards said gruffly. "Blasphemy."

"Seized by Pharaoh Akhenaten's orders," the other added.

Meritaten glanced between the guards and Smenkhkare, her ears full of the sound of the prisoner's shaking breath.

"Explain," Smenkhkare said.

"According to King Akhenaten," one of the guards began, but Smenkhkare silenced him with a wave of his hand.

"Not you." The co-regent rose from his throne and descended the dais. He bent and touched the prisoner on the shoulder, gently.

The man looked up. When he saw Smenkhkare, wrapped in the finery of state, leaning down to peer at him, he whimpered and all but wept. His distress was so extreme that Meritaten felt tears of sympathy sting her own eyes.

"Please, my lord," the man stammered. "I am a good and devoted servant of the Aten. I do not know what I might have done that angered the Pharaoh. I have done my best to live my life righteously. I have never blasphemed against the one true god, nor has any member of my household, so far as I know. Please; I know I am unworthy, but have mercy on me. I beg you!"

Smenkhkare said nothing, but straightened and looked up at Meritaten on her throne. His brows raised slowly, a cautious, searching, unspoken question.

Meritaten cleared her throat. "Guardsmen, perhaps you can tell us: how did the king know about this man's blasphemy?"

The guards exchanged wary glances. Finally one of them shrugged. "It seems, my lady, that the king had a vision while worshiping in the temple this morning."

"A vision?"

"Yes, Great Wife. We do not know all the details,

of course; we are only soldiers, and not privy to the Pharaoh's confidences. We were merely told that the god had revealed to the king that this man—"

Meritaten silenced him with a wave of her hand. "Enough. Thank you." She leaned toward Smenkhkare as he climbed back up to his throne. Her whisper barely more than a breath, she said, "I thought Akhenaten seemed more... *zealous* than usual at this morning's ceremonies."

Smenkhkare nodded grimly. "But what's to be done?"

"It's only Akhenaten's madness that caused him to lash out against a loyal man. Surely there can be no real offense here. The guards would have heard something more substantial, some rumor or tale, if any blasphemy had been done. You won't judge this poor man harshly, will you?"

"Of course not. I doubt very much he has done anything wrong. But how to appease your husband, and make him forgive his subject?"

Meritaten leaned closer still, shielding her mouth with her hand. She whispered in Smenkhkare's ear, "Akhenaten's wits are scattered. By now he doesn't even recall the charges he brought against this man; I'm sure of that. Simply let him go free."

"Are you certain? If the Pharaoh does recall, and still believes the man guilty—"

"You'll see what I mean. Akhenaten has already forgotten all mention of a vision, and any hint of blasphemy. He is cutting up meat for the altar even now, I'll wager, and singing hymns up to the sun. This was nothing but a flicker of his madness. It's passed from him now. No harm will come; I'm sure of it."

Smenkhkare gestured for his head steward to approach the prisoner. The steward lifted the man from the floor by his hand. "Brace up," Smenkhkare said to him kindly. "I believe you, sir, that you are a loyal subject of the throne, and that you worship the Aten most honestly. Go free, and do not fear for your safety. You and your household have the protection of the king now—of *this* king. I will see to it that no harm befalls you."

The man bowed so low his face nearly touched the floor, and he was obliged to hold his wig on his head with a shaking hand. "Thank you, my lord! You are merciful!"

Smenkhkare called to a pair of his personal servants. "Habu, Iufni, you will escort this man back to his home. There is no need to trouble Mahu's men any further. They may return to their barracks, with my thanks for their hard work in the king's service. And we shall have to tell Mahu that he must check such orders from the king with me before he issues any arrests. We can't have the citizens of Akhet-Aten suffering, or living in fear because of a fleeting fancy of Akhenaten's."

There was another rumble of mutters as Smenkhkare's men led the still shaking man from the throne room.

But Smenkhkare paid no more heed to the audience hall. He extended his hand to Meritaten. "Great Wife, will you join me in the garden? The throne room has grown stuffy. I would rather discuss the northern borders with you in the open air than here in this room."

Meritaten walked from the throne room with her hand demurely on Smenkhkare's arm, but once they were free of stewards and servants, out among the flower beds and thin, swaying trees, she slid her palm down his warm, smooth skin until she found his hand, and laced her fingers with his. His grip on her tightened, as if he were reluctant to ever let go. But he remained quiet and thoughtful for some time, his eyes staring distantly, beyond the high garden wall toward a vista only he could see.

Finally Meritaten asked, "What is troubling you, my lord?"

"This incident in the throne room—that poor man. Are you sure Akhenaten will forget all about it?"

"I'm quite sure. I admit I've never seen him lash out at a citizen this way—not without some true grounds for suspicion. He has apprehended and tried people before, and even executed some. But always for guilty acts—for violating the laws of the city."

"Such as trying to leave without the king's permission," Smenkhkare said, a force of bitterness in his voice that Meritaten had never heard before. "Or worshiping gods other than the Aten. Are those the laws you mean?"

"But there is no god other than the Aten. And why would anyone want to leave this city? It's beautiful here, and good. All of our citizens have everything they could ever want or need. The god asks nothing from them in return, save for their loyalty and praises."

Smenkhkare shook his head harshly. The braids of his short wig tossed about his square chin. "You have only ever known this lone god, and have only known this one city. But Egypt is so much vaster, Meritaten! And I have seen the power of other gods at work in the world. I know that they live yet, and love Egypt, even if our Pharaoh— *one* of our Pharaohs—suppresses them."

Meritaten's heart thumped painfully in her chest. "You cannot speak that way. You, of all people!"

She had always believed as her father had taught her— that anyone who cleaved to the old gods was a dangerous person, a heretic and a madman. But Smenkhkare was kind and gentle, clear-hearted and good. She could never believe him bad or corrupted in any way... yet here he was, denying the supremacy of the Aten. She stopped on the garden path and shuddered, wrapping her arms around her body, half-expecting the god to strike them both down.

"You must trust me, Meritaten." She turned her face

away from him, but Smenkhkare lifted her chin with a gentle touch. "You and Ay brought me here to help heal Egypt. Part of that healing is to order the Two Lands as they once were—to restore the world that was."

"As it was? You mean in the days before my father came to power—before my family, my bloodline, ruled."

"I mean no offense. After all, I am of your same bloodline. But I have seen more of the world than you have. I have lived among the old ways. They are nothing to be feared; we should embrace them. Even you. And I believe we *can* restore Egypt. We can tear down the walls of Akhet-Aten, so the power of the Pharaoh reaches all up and down the length of the Iteru once more. We can stop the edges of our empire from crumbling, and rebuild what we once had, so the Two Lands are once again the greatest power in the world. *We* can do it, Meritaten—you and I."

She stared up into his eyes. His smile was soft, encouraging, and he looked so earnest and eager. Despite his blasphemous speech, warmth built inside her, and she longed to feel his arms around her. In her seventeen years, she never had felt such desire for any man.

"You must trust me," Smenkhkare said. "Trust that I can do the job well—that I can be a righteous king. I will never steer Egypt, or you, wrong."

Meritaten's voice had fled, abandoning her to this trembling, this melting desire, when she most needed the strength of her words. She could only nod in acceptance. Her breath shook in her throat, like a wind in a grove of sycamores.

Then Smenkhkare bent and kissed her, his mouth soft but insistent against hers. And fire like the sun's midday rays coursed through her body.

THERE WAS PRECIOUS LITTLE to mark the passing of the seasons in Akhet-Aten. Here in the dry curve of the Iteru, where the current slipped quickly past, the river's annual flood barely made a difference in the water level, and the cliffs around the city prevented one from observing the fields, the long, wet line of the Iteru valley that stretched to the north and south. Only the merchants who traveled abroad, seeking rich goods to bring back to the City of the Sun, could say if the fields sparkled with still water or if the rich, dark soil of the sowing season blanketed the fertile lands in black.

In the Great Aten Temple, the priests kept intricate calendars to track the cycles of the stars, but the only indication Meritaten had that winter had nearly come was the almost imperceptible shortening of the days, and the blossoms fading in the garden.

Had it truly been ten months since Smenkhkare had come into her life? That seemed an impossibility. Never had she known such joy, such bliss—or such chilling fear. All through the seasons of growing and harvest, Akhenaten's baseless accusations against his own citizens had grown more frequent, until they were almost commonplace. Now at least one accused person was brought before the throne each week. Sometimes several were hauled to judgment in a single day, weeping and trembling at the foot of the royal dais. It was clear to Meritaten that her father's wits were eroding faster all the time, like a ditch carrying too much water. Was this growing madness his fate? Or was it brought about by too much time spent under the glare of the sun? Meritaten couldn't say.

Akhenaten continued to level accusations of blasphemy and treason against his own people, yet Meritaten and Smenkhkare agreed it was best to keep Akhenaten distracted by his god, sequestered in the temple. Together they had already worked many positive changes in

Egypt's policy, reopening lines of communication with embittered client kings far to the north. Now, as winter closed in, they were making slow but steady progress toward decentralizing power, extending the king's reach beyond the borders of Akhet-Aten, into the heart of the Two Lands where it belonged. To bring Akhenaten back to the throne room now would only thrust the country back into the darkness, after such painstaking work to claw their way up into the light.

Akhenaten's virtual disappearance from the palace pleased Meritaten for other reasons, too. The kiss she had shared with Smenkhkare had progressed along its natural course. Her heart was his completely, and she felt no shame at that. She spent each day wondering when she might be alone with him again. Sitting beside him on their thrones through the long hours of court, unable to touch him or feel his body pressed against her own, was a lovely, blissful torment. With Akhenaten gone all day in his temples, Meritaten could pretend he didn't exist at all. She could tell herself that Smenkhkare was her true husband, always had been—that neither she nor Egypt had ever suffered under Akhenaten's control, and everything was well.

Despite Smenkhkare's secret belief in the old gods—something Meritaten now tolerated with lighthearted fondness, the way one humors a child's belief in an imaginary playmate—Meritaten was still a devotee of the Aten. And why should she not be? The Aten was a god she could see as it moved across the sky. She knew the Aten lived—there it was in the heavens!—and heard her prayers, too. She knew it was only a matter of time before it granted her daily petition, before it gave in to the passion of her heart and removed Akhentaten from this life. Then she would be free to love Smenkhkare openly. Then there would be no more need to hide her affection for the junior king, or to hide all that they did together.

Today there would be no strolling with Smenkhkare in the garden. He and Ay were closeted to discuss Akhenaten's latest round of accusations against his innocent subjects. The Pharaoh had ordered a larger number of men and women arrested than he ever had before, and both Smenkhkare and Ay feared he would soon move on to more drastic actions.

These arrests were a tedious subject for Meritaten now; in the ten months since Akhenaten had taken up the habit of flinging out accusations like a farmer flings out feed to his geese, Akhenaten had not countermanded a single one of Smenkhkare's dismissals of the baseless charges. She was more certain than ever before that Akhenaten forgot all about the visions and accusations the moment he'd uttered the commands for the arrests. Nothing would come of them; there was no need for Ay and Smenkhkare to take this all so seriously.

But they did take it all so seriously. That was how she found herself walking alone in the garden, scowling at the fading blooms, contemplating the approach of winter. She plucked a withered flower from its stem and brushed it against her lips, remembering her first walk with Smenkhkare in this very garden. She could still recall the sweetness of the flower he'd held to her nose, and the look of warm promise in his eyes. How she wished he were with her now! To be separated from him—even by a few walls, even for a short time—seemed an intolerable cruelty.

She rounded a bend in the path and there, sitting on the ground in front of a bench, was Ankhesenpaaten. Aunt Mutbenret perched on the stone bench behind the girl, combing out her hair. Mutbenret and Ankhesenpaaten were often together, close as cats curled up in a basket. They were a natural pair, for they were both retiring and quiet, and seemed to enjoy their mutual silences far more than they ever enjoyed music or gossip or even more sedate conversation. Meritaten often wondered whether they had worked out some secret way of communicating, some code of gestures and blinks that she knew nothing about.

She wandered over and sat beside Mutbenret on the bench, watching the ivory comb slide smoothly through Ankhesenpaaten's long, tightly curled hair. Mutbenret smiled at Meritaten, but said nothing, as was her custom. She separated the girl's hair into even locks and began to work an intricate braid, which Ankhesenpaaten could coil tightly around her head and wear beneath a more fashionable and courtly wig.

Meritaten twirled the wilted flower in her fingers. "Winter is almost here. We'll have another festival soon—and a feast to go with it. Is that what the braid is for? Are you ordering a fine new wig for the occasion?"

Ankhesenpaaten did not look around; Mutbenret still worked deftly at her hair, so she held still, staring out into the garden. "I suppose you'll sit beside Smenkhkare at the feast," she said.

Ankhesenpaaten's tone would have sounded neutral to anyone who was not her sister. Meritaten caught its subtle note of scolding.

"Of course I will. And what exactly is that supposed to mean?"

"You should be more careful, you know." Still Ankhesenpaaten did not look at her.

Meritaten glanced uneasily at Mutbenret, but their aunt only shrugged as her fingers worked to the end of the braid. She had been with the girls for all their lives, and was more of a mother to them than Nefertiti had been. If there was one person in all the world Meritaten knew she could trust, it was Aunt Mutbenret.

"You don't know what you're talking about," Meritaten

said to her sister. "I *am* careful. The only one who sees anything amiss is you, and that's only because you're such a creeping little thing, always watching everyone and everything around you, like some mouse in the shadows."

"Father sometimes sees as much as I do." The braid finished and tied off, Ankhesenpaaten turned and gazed up at Meritaten, her large, black eyes sober with warning.

"When he leaves his temples," Meritaten conceded. "But how often does that happen? He doesn't know what's going on within his own palace; he's only ever here at night, to sleep in his bed. And then he rushes back to the temples again before the sun rises, so he can be ready to greet the god. He's so tired out from his worship that he hasn't wanted anything to do with me in ten glorious months. He has forgotten all about me, and that suits me fine. I haven't lain with him once since Smenkhkare has been here. The very idea of it is repulsive to me now; I can't believe I could stomach his repugnancy before. And for so long, too! Don't I deserve a little happiness, after my long and arduous toil?"

"If you ever wonder why I speak so little," Ankhesenpaaten said quietly, grinning to herself like a cat by the fire, "it's because you talk enough for the both of us."

Meritaten nudged her with her sandal.

"What will you do if Akhenaten does remember you?" Mutbenret asked quietly. "What will you do when he calls you back to his bed?"

"I won't go," Meritaten said petulantly. She threw the wilted flower over her shoulder, into the browning winter shadows.

"If only it were so easy to deny the command of a Pharaoh."

"Watch me do it," Meritaten said. "I am Smenkhkare's now—his and no other's."

119

"Those are dangerous words," Ankhesenpaaten said.

"What do you know of it—a girl of thirteen?"

Ankhesenpaaten stood, brushing dried leaves and pale dust from her dress. "I'm a woman now."

"Good; then when Akhenaten wants someone in his bed, I'll send you in my place."

Mutbenret leveled a hard stare at Meritaten; the poisonous fury in her eyes took Meritaten aback. She had never seen her gentle, soft-spoken aunt look so full of hate before.

"If you did try to send me," Ankhesenpaaten said calmly, "I would take my own life."

"And I would help her," Mutbenret added, tucking the ivory comb into the basket at her feet.

"You would not. I wouldn't allow it."

"I would," Ankhesenpaaten insisted. "Remember what happened to Meketaten."

"Well, cheer up," Meritaten said gloomily. "You may be barren like me. In all my years with Father, and in these blessed months with Smenkhkare, I have never fallen pregnant."

It had never bothered Meritaten before that she remained as barren as a pit of sand. But now it gnawed at her heart with a sudden, fiery pain. How she would love to give Smenkhkare a son, or even a daughter! She felt certain he would be a good and devoted father—and would never make his children suffer as Akhenaten had done to his daughters.

They don't understand, either of them, what it's like to love a man so very much. I cannot lose Smenkhkare, not now that I know the joy of love!

She clutched Ankhesenpaaten's hand, and leaned her head on Mutbenret's shoulder. "Oh, don't tell anyone!

Please! Especially not Ay. I have him complacent—fooled. He believes all my dealings with Smenkhkare are chaste."

Ankhesenpaaten, ever preferring silence to speech, gave Meritaten a dry, doubting look. Those raised brows and pursed lips said clearly that she doubted *very much* that Ay was either fooled or complacent.

"Well, our father *is* complacent," Meritaten said defensively. "I've kept him nicely in line by telling him I have visions—just like the High Priestess of the Sun. I won't be surprised if he makes me the High Priestess in truth someday soon. That's how much he believes in me. And it's the simplest way you can imagine to control him. He'll believe anything that comes from the Aten."

Ankhesenpaaten gave her another infuriating stare, this time with her head tipped to one side, her mouth curling wryly. *False visions from the god are a dangerous policy*, her sister's look said.

Meritaten flared at her. "I do what I must! And you shall see how well I keep Father complacent. If ever he suspects anything of Smenkhkare and me, I'll simply tell him that I've had a vision, and that the god told me to do what I do. He will believe it. He will—you'll see!"

"I hope you're right," Ankhesenpaaten said after a lengthy pause. "You may feel the king is becoming easier to control, but I believe he is only growing more unpredictable— more dangerous."

"What do you know of it? You aren't around him as often as I am. You don't see what I see."

Mutbenret stroked Ankhesenpaaten's head, favoring her like a beloved pet. "This girl sees more than you would believe, Meritaten. You would be wise to listen to her advice."

Stiff with offense—and frightened by the depth of Ankhesenpaaten's observations—Meritaten rose from the bench. "*Thirteen*," she said with fierce emphasis. "I'd be a fool to listen to her advice. And now if you will excuse me, I have duties waiting."

She strode down the garden path, slapping at the pale, drooping blooms as she passed. She did not look back once as she left her sister and her aunt behind.

Meritaten

Year 2 of Smenkhkare,
Holy of the Manifestations

Year 18 of Akhenaten,
Beloved of the Sun

T HE AFTERNOON LIGHT had taken an alarming
slant. The hour was growing late—too late for
Meritaten's purposes. She scowled at the bright beams
spilling through her garden window, at the patch of
golden glow that crept across the floor with the speed
of a snail. Smenkhkare was late for their arranged tryst,
and her pleasant anticipation had long since turned to
annoyance. The festivities of the New Year were finally
over. Throughout the celebrations, she and Smenkhkare
had been too busy to while away time in one another's arms,
but at last the pressures of court had eased, and Meritaten
was more eager than ever before to lounge about on her
bed with her beloved. Miu-Miu jumped up onto the bed
where she sat staring disconsolately at the garden door,
which remained undarkened by Smenkhkare's frame.

"What is keeping him?" she asked the cat as she stroked
his fur. "Surely he hasn't forgotten." When she'd whispered
her intention to entertain Smenkhkare this afternoon, he
had seemed every bit as eager as she was.

Her mouth was dry, since she had no one but Miu-Miu
to kiss. "A drink would be welcome," she muttered. Miu-
Miu purred inquisitively and butted his head against her
shoulder, but he could offer nothing else. Sweet beer or
watered wine—either would be just the thing to raise her

mood. But she had sent all her servants away, claiming she had a fierce headache and needed absolute silence to recover.

"He's not coming," she told the cat. She slid from the bed, turning her back on the garden and the afternoon light, and stalked to the door of her apartments. She would summon any passing servant and have them fetch her some wine. But not watered—the strongest they could find. If Smenkhkare was going to forget all about her, then Meritaten would get riotously drunk and make merry on her own. "Who needs a man to have a good time?" she called out to Miu-Miu.

But when she opened the door, she paused, staring out into the pillared hall. A ceaseless noise bubbled far down the corridor, tense and urgent. It was the sound of many voices talking at once—shouting, now and then—in clear agitation.

Meritaten shut her door carefully and hoisted the hem of her dress. She hurried down the corridor, the quick scuff of her sandals against the floor quickly lost to the buzz of voices as she drew nearer. The hall was alive with stewards and men she recognized from the court—nobles, advisors, treasurers. Even scribes flew along the corridor, carrying their folded wooden writing palettes under their arms. Most of these palace denizens seemed intent on particular destinations. Those who weren't rushing in the direction of the throne room crowded into meeting offices where nobles shouted and called for order. They collided and cursed as they dodged this way and that on their errands.

Meritaten found a knot of her own serving women, speaking with their heads together, darting looks around the corridor and clinging to one another's hands in obvious distress.

Meritaten grabbed the nearest woman by the elbow—

Sadhe, one of her bath maids. Sadhe jumped with a strangled shriek, fluttering away from Meritaten with her hands up as if to ward away an attack. But when she and the rest of the women realized it was only the Great Wife, they bowed to her hastily with murmured apologies.

"What is going on?" Meritaten demanded. "Why do you all look as if you'd seen a demon?"

Tentkheta, the lady who painted Meritaten's face each morning, looked up from her deep bow. Her face was streaked by tears. She said, "At least twenty men and women have been apprehended by the Pharaoh, my lady."

Meritaten sighed. "So many this time! But it's no reason to lose your wits. They'll be brought before the throne tomorrow, and Smenkhkare will dismiss all the charges against them, just as he has done with the rest of the king's prisoners."

"Not this time!" Tentkheta's voice rose to a whine. "Akhenaten has taken them directly to the Great Aten Temple. He means to try them all in the god's light!"

Meritaten couldn't suppress a shiver. She knew what it meant, to be tried in the Aten's light: staked out to suffer piteously, exposed to the heat. Even in late winter, the Egyptian sun was hot enough to kill—especially inside the temple, where the slant and slickness of the walls reflected the heat like an oven. Such was a fitting end for a proven criminal, perhaps, but not for the innocents Akhenaten had taken to persecuting.

"One of them is my brother," Tentkheta wailed. "My lady, please, you must intervene! My brother is a good man, and devoted to the one true god! He never did any blasphemy—such sins are not in his heart!"

"All right, all right." Meritaten patted Tentkheta's shoulder awkwardly. "I will go to Smenkhkare straight away. Don't be afraid; I'll do everything I can for your brother, and for the rest of the prisoners, too."

"These twenty today," Sadhe whispered, her eyes wide and frightened. "But who will be next? How many will be taken?"

Hotepti, who was older than the rest and should have had firmer control of her wits, cried out in a sudden panic. "It's only a matter of time before he comes for us all! We have to find some way to get out of this city!"

"Silence!" Meritaten hissed. "Don't say such things—any of you! You know what will happen to you if Mahu or his guards hear those treasonous words. Be silent, all of you, and go wait in my chambers. I'll come to you when this matter is resolved. Where is Smenkhkare? I must speak with him directly."

Sadhe pointed down the corridor. "In the throne room with Ay, my lady."

Meritaten hurried toward the throne room, shouldering her way through the agitated crowd of stewards, who were so intent on their tasks that they did not see it was the Great Wife who walked among them. As she passed a garden portico, Ankhesenpaaten emerged from its blue shadows with Mutbenret close beside her. Both of them stared at the tumult in the corridor, startled and confused.

Meritaten grabbed Ankhesenpaaten by the hand, unsure exactly why she did it. Perhaps she only wanted someone with her now, so she would feel less helpless and alone in the face of the king's madness. All her control over Akhenaten was crumbling, it seemed—or perhaps Ay was right, and she had never had any control to begin with.

I've thought to hide my sins from the king, but he sees through me— sees through what Smenkhkare and I have done, circumventing his commands, freeing those he tried to kill. Does he see everything Smenkhkare and I do? Will I soon join these poor innocents in the scorching sand of the temple?

Fear sickened her—and she was all the more terrified for knowing that unlike the prisoners, she was guilty.

"Let me go," Ankhesenpaaten snapped. She jerked her hand, but Meritaten only hardened her grip.

"It's father," Meritaten said. "Come on; we're going to the throne room."

"Why me? Leave me out of it."

Meritaten had no good answer. She could not say, *Because I'm afraid, and I want my sister with me.* She was the King's Great Wife—for now, at any rate—and she must maintain her dignity. "You might be useful," she said instead, and hauled Ankhesenpaaten along behind her as she plunged back into the crowd, working her way ever closer to the throne room.

The guards on the doors opened them straight away when Meritaten gave the command. The long room with its soaring ceiling and bright pillars was largely empty now, most of the clamoring nobles and stewards shut out so Smenkhkare and Ay could speak together freely. Their voices echoed high among the pillars' lotus-carved crowns.

Ay stood halfway up the dais, holding sheaves of papyrus in one hand and glancing at them now and then as Smenkhkare spoke.

Meritaten let go of her sister and rushed toward the throne. "I'm here," she called. "If I can be of any help. I've only just heard—"

Smenkhkare smiled down at her, though she could tell his body was tense with worry. "I'm glad you're here," he said.

But Ay scowled as he crunched the stacks of papyrus in his fist. "You were meant to keep the king under control. But look now! He's more addle-witted than ever! Look at all these charges against innocent citizens—" he shook the papers at her; they rustled like the scales of a coiling cobra— "but no chance for Smenkhkare to save them.

They've all been taken straight to the temple!"

To drive home his point, Ay read off a few notations from his list. The information had been hastily scrawled by some harried scribe—facts about the people apprehended, details of what exactly they were charged with. The list was grim indeed, and all the more frightening because the charges made little sense.

"Djefari of the House of Two Bows, arrested for spitting over his right shoulder when the sun was rising—spitting in the direction of the god! Lady Idut, apprehended for trying to work a spell to prevent the sun from rising. Have you ever heard of such a thing? Khaneffere, a soldier in the king's guard, taken because the king had a dream that Khaneffere laughed at one of the sacred hymns. A *dream*! Iterti, arrested on suspicion that he likes his pet cat more than he likes the Aten. Wadj, apprehended for—"

"Enough!" Meritaten drew herself up bravely. "You're wasting time by reading the charges. This won't bring Akhenaten to heel."

"Nothing will," Ay said venomously, stepping down the dais toward her. "You've proven that admirably, Meritaten."

"I *can* control him. You'll see—if you'll just let me go and speak to him..." Meritaten wasn't at all sure she could control the Pharaoh. She had thought him easy enough to enthrall before, but that illusion was shattered now. *Still, I must try. Who can do it, if not me?* "I shall go to the temple now, and—"

"No," Smenkhkare said at once. "You must be kept safe. You must stay far from Akhenaten until we can be sure his fury is contained."

He fears we'll be found out, too, Meritaten realized, gazing up at Smenkhkare with tearful eyes. *He knows how close we now stand to discovery—to destruction.*

From somewhere behind her in the wide, empty throne

room, Ankhesenpaaten's voice came softly. "The king's fury will never be contained."

Meritaten rounded on her, the tears spilling over her cheeks. "You never speak when your words are wanted, yet you speak *now*, when you can only spout this useless drivel? Be silent!"

The girl drifted forward, Mutbenret trailing cautiously behind her. Ankhesenpaaten came to the foot of the dais and stood gazing coolly up at Smenkhkare on his throne. "You all know what must be done. There is only one way to end the Pharaoh's madness."

Ay and Smenkhkare exchanged slow, laden stares. Then they both turned to Ankhesenpaaten, silent and expectant.

"Akhenaten must be killed," the girl finally said.

The breath left Smenkhkare's chest in a loud rush. Even Ay's face paled.

Meritaten gaped at her sister. "Don't you know what it means to kill a king? Chaos! Darkness! The river's flood destroyed forever—every kind of evil unleashed upon the land!"

"Would that be worse than what we have now?"

Meritaten shook her head in disgust and turned away from her sister. "You're as mad as Father."

But even as she rejected Ankhesenpaaten's dangerous words, the thought thrilled her with blasphemous excitement. Kill Akhenaten, and be done with it. Such a simple thing, on the surface—but it was the worst evil a mortal could perpetrate. No one would willingly take the life of a Pharaoh, and damn his or her eternal soul. Not even a king as terrible as Akhenaten could make that price seem reasonable.

"The girl may be right," Ay said quietly.

Smenkhkare stared at him in frank shock. "How can you

say such a thing? Meritaten is right: the risks to Egypt are far too great, to say nothing of the risks to one's own eternity."

"I didn't say *we* should do it," Ay said smoothly. "But Akhenaten's death may be the only thing that will save Egypt now. You came to Akhet-Aten to assist him, Smenkhkare, and for a time he was content to let you do your work. But now he takes back his old power, and takes innocent lives into his hands. He is reckless, mad—"

"But he is still a king! Divinely appointed by the gods!"

"The *god*," Ay said with emphasis.

Smenkhkare's face darkened—with embarrassment or fury, Meritaten couldn't tell.

Ay continued, "Don't let Akhenaten or any of his lickspittles hear you speak of a plurality of gods. He is already trampling over your position, Smenkhkare. He will be on the lookout for a way to rid himself of you, too—any plausible excuse." He lifted the papers again, smacked them against his other hand for grim emphasis. "Clearly, he needs very little inspiration to move against his perceived enemies. He may already be planning accusations against you, for all I know."

"No!" Meritaten cried. "He can't harm Smenkhkare—he can't!"

Ay rounded on her, disgust dripping from his every word. "Keep silent, you worthless fool! If you had done your job and kept the Pharaoh on a short leash, none of this would be happening. Instead you've gone chasing after Smenkhkare like a bitch in heat."

Smenkhkare all but leaped from his throne, roaring down at Ay. "Don't speak to her that way! You are my subject, Ay, and under my command. Do *not* forget that."

"Stop *fighting*!" Meritaten shouted. "We must be united. We must—"

A new, rapid tumult rose outside the room's huge double doors, excitement flooding the corridors and flowing down the palace halls. Everyone in the throne room fell silent at the sound, turning to stare at the doors in wary surprise. Clear notes of disbelief and wonder rang in the voices of so many servants and stewards. And then, as the crowd drew closer to the throne room doors, Meritaten could make out words: "My lady!" and "King's Great Wife!"

She glanced at Ankhesenpaaten. The girl looked as startled as she. "What are they talking about?" Meritaten asked. "I am the Great Wife."

But as she stared at her sister, the look on Ankhesenpaaten's face turned from confusion to disbelief, then to wondrous awe. Eyes sparkling and face flushed with a sudden, fierce longing, the girl stumbled a few steps toward the throne room's doors.

The doors groaned as guards on their far side pushed them open. The crowd of stewards and nobles in their fluttering kilts parted; a woman walked through their midst, moving with regal poise, with a grace Meritaten knew she should recognize—but a fog of confusion and fear seemed to shroud her vision, obscuring her memory. She stared at the woman, who paused on the throne room's threshold. The newcomer was dressed as finely as a legend, in draped linen of the purest white, her neck and arms gleaming with gold. The long, curled locks of her wig were beaded in lapis lazuli, and a simple golden circlet rested on her brow.

Recognizing the woman at last, Meritaten gasped and covered her gaping mouth with one hand. But she could not speak. No one could.

Silence filled the throne room and the corridor outside. It was Ay who finally broke it, releasing the spell of disbelief that held them all in place. "Nefertiti."

Nefertiti

Year 1 of Nefer-Neferu-Aten,
Effective for Her Husband

Year 18 of Akhenaten,
Beloved of the Sun

W HEN THE GILDED DOORS of the throne room swung ponderously open, Nefertiti's gaze fastened on her daughters. She had thirsted for the sight of them like a man in the desert thirsts for cool, clear water, and now that they stood before her, she found it nearly impossible to tear her eyes away.

Meritaten and Ankhesenpaaten had grown. They were women now, both of them, slender and graceful, clear-eyed and strong. Even in their surprise at seeing her again, they seemed as confident, as self-possessed as any mother could have hoped. She longed to run to them; her arms trembled and ached with the need to embrace them. Her throat was tight with cries of love, with pleas for their forgiveness—for leaving them alone, and for all the other wrongs she had heaped upon them. But this was not the time for sentimentality. And it was certainly not the time to beg her daughters' pardon. She had come to save Egypt, and to do that she must remain strong.

As she strode into the throne room, Nefertiti raised one hand, gesturing over her shoulder. Nann hurried to her side, holding young Tutankhaten in her arms, and Horemheb took his place on the boy's other side, bristling and fierce like a lion of the hills, one hand on his sword, ready to defend Nefertiti and her young ward if need be.

Tutankhaten looked around him at the long, pillared hall of the throne room. The boy was brave, unconcerned with the ruckus his appearance—and Nefertiti's—had raised within the palace. Nefertiti led her people straight to the dais and halted there, raising one brow at the man who sat on the throne. Closeted in the isolated comfort of her farm, she had heard of Smenkhkare's miraculous *resurrection*, his ascension as Akhenaten's co-regent. *So Kiya's secret got out after all*, she had thought at the time.

She had known she would find Smenkhkare here when she came to claim the throne, but in her imagination he had been a mirror image of his brother, just another Akhenaten, easily contained by harnessing his zeal. But she could tell at once, by the focus of his eyes and the serious set of his mouth, that Smenkhkare was no Akhenaten. *Good*, she told herself. *Egypt needs a stronger Pharaoh*. It was a shame Smenkhkare was not the one the gods had chosen for the role.

Ay's frown was as deep and cold as Nefertiti had remembered. "So this is what Tiy had in mind for Tutankhaten's rearing," he said. "I wondered where she sent the boy. But you have brought him back to us now."

Nefertiti sniffed at her father, then looked casually away. "I have not brought him for *you*."

"But your timing is god-sent." Ay gestured toward the doors, closed now—but the milling of the palace and the city beyond could still be heard clearly through that carved and gilded barrier. "Do you have any idea what is happening out there?"

"Better than you do, it seems. Akhenaten's wits have slipped entirely away, but these things never happen all at once, like a landslide among the cliffs. They come about little by little, one piece of a mad heart breaking away, falling down the precipice. But you have all left him to his devices, and allowed him to crumble bit by bit, until the ruin of Egypt is all but assured. He will destroy even his own city, and you have done nothing to stop him. You should all be ashamed of such weakness."

Smenkhkare rose slowly from his throne. He came down the dais one step at a time, his eyes never leaving Tutankhaten. He seemed not to have heard Nefertiti's chastisement at all. She did not stop him as he approached. When she'd heard that Smenkhkare had been called to the co-regency, she had puzzled out the identity of Tutankhaten's real father.

Tiy, that sly old she-cat. She has husbanded this bloodline like a grower of grapes or a breeder of horses, refining it, crossing it, bringing about by her own schemes the very crown of the dynasty— and the salvation of the Two Lands. But it was Nefertiti whom Tiy had entrusted with this precious gem, Tutankhaten, the purpose-made lord of Egypt. Tiy in her wisdom had appointed Nefertiti with this most crucial task. She would not give the boy up now, not even to his father. She had a duty to Egypt—to Tiy—to the gods themselves.

Smenkhkare touched Tutankhaten's face gently. The boy stared back at him with solemn eyes, silent and observant.

"So the little one survived," Smenkhkare said. "I have often wondered... By all the stars in the sky, he looks just like Baketaten. I remember her so well."

"As far as I know," Nefertiti said with significant emphasis, "this is the only son of Akhenaten, your senior king."

Ay edged closer to Tutankhaten. Nefertiti and Horemheb both stepped between them, so that Ay could come no closer.

"This makes everything even more secure, more certain," Ay said. Blocked from the boy, he stood at the co-regent's side instead. But he was near, so near she could smell the ink-and-papyrus odor of his body, the faint trace of watered wine and an old man's sweat.

She felt no fear at her father's proximity—not anymore. She was pleased to note it.

"We have a co-regent in Smenkhkare," Ay went on, "and now we have an heir as added security. Better—you, Nefertiti, have always been adept at controlling Akhenaten. With your help we can tame him, and then the way will be cleared for the god to work its will, and remove Akhenaten from the throne."

Smenkhkare finally tore himself from his study of Tutankhaten. He turned to Ay with a pinched, irritated expression. "And how will *the god* do it? There is still that small detail—*how*? No one is willing to risk his own—"

"You mistake me," Nefertiti broke in smoothly. "You mistake the reason for my coming, and most of all, you mistake my role in your machinations. I did not bring Tutankhaten back to the City of the Sun for you to squabble over him, nor for you to work him into your doomed, foolish schemes." She held Ay's stare for a moment, then shrugged and turned away. "You will find that I have plans of my own, and that I am far better placed to succeed."

"Speak plainly," Ay said, his voice thin with mistrust.

"Tutankhaten is my ward, and he will remain in my care." She took the boy from Nann's arms. Tutankhaten clung to Nefertiti's neck, familiar with her embrace, content in her arms. She climbed the dais and sat easily upon the throne—not the throne of the Great Wife, but that of the Pharaoh. She held Tutankhaten on her knee as she looked down at them—watching them from her rightful place, high above them all.

Everyone gathered below her—Smenkhkare, Ay, the girls and Mutbenret—seemed to hold one shared breath, stunned by the sight of Nefertiti sitting in the place of the king. Even Nann and Horemheb goggled up at her in obvious surprise. They, her most trusted companions, had known nothing of this plan. She had told no one what she meant to do, save for the flitting specter of her *ba*.

"I am not here to tame a king, Ay." Nefertiti spoke smoothly into the silence. "I am here to claim my throne. I am your Pharaoh now, by right of my strength and experience, and I will rule as the king of Egypt until Tutankhaten comes of age."

Ay burst out laughing. The sound of it rattled among the pillars, clattering up into the shadowed ceiling. "You are as mad as your husband! No woman will rule as king."

Nefertiti raised her brows, a wry dismissal of his protest. "Women have held the Horus Throne before. Sobekneferu did it. And then Hatshepsut, who ruled Egypt better than any man could have done, for twenty-two long years. I have already done the work, already acted as king, even if it was from the shadows. While the rest of you plotted and schemed, or shivered in your chambers for fear of the plague, I steered Egypt in its course from behind my husband's throne. I have more experience than any of you. Better, I have demonstrated aptitude. Don't let your pride turn you into fools. Yield the throne to the one person who knows how to handle it."

Smenkhkare began, "But I—"

"You've made a valiant effort, Smenkhkare, but apparently you are too soft to keep Akhenaten in line. You cannot even keep one city from falling prey to that madman's fits of insanity. How can you hope to save all of Egypt?"

"We have been making progress," Smenkhkare said. His face darkened with embarrassment as he spoke. Surely he knew how defensive, how weak he sounded.

Nefertiti shrugged. "Not enough progress, and not fast enough. Outside the boundaries of Akhet-Aten, we can see how Egypt declines in power year after year. What the Two Lands need now is a strong, experienced hand to guide them."

"A female hand!" Ay's scoff was so loud, so forceful, it was nearly a hoot.

"Better than a madman's hand, or the soft touch of a neophyte king. Don't fear, Father. I don't intend to rule forever. Once my ward Tutankhaten reaches his majority, I will hand the throne to him without any qualms. But when I bequeath this boy his kingdom, it will be ordered, whole, and freed from Akhenaten's influence. Make no mistake about that."

"I will rule for Tutankhaten," Smenkhkare said fiercely. "He is my—"

"He is the King's Son," Nefertiti broke in sharply. "If you want to maintain the slightest leverage over Akhenaten, you will not forget that this boy is the King's Son. Save any other suspicions you have until that glorious day when Egypt is freed from the fetter of Akhenaten."

Smenkhkare subsided, but he glared up at Nefertiti, his black eyes hard and promising.

Ay threw up his hands in exasperation. "This is the height of foolishness. At a time when we cannot afford to play-act, you sit there, preaching to us about your qualifications to usurp the throne! We have more immediate concerns just now. Get out of that seat, girl, and behave as befits a woman of the royal court."

"This is my throne now, Ay. You would be wise to accept that fact. All the people of this palace—the ones who work for the throne, who make this administration function— what do you think they saw when I walked down those corridors? They saw a miracle. They saw their beloved beauty, Nefertiti, risen from the dead. If there is danger at the Temple just now, what could be more reassuring, what could be a better talisman? Those men and women out there, on whom you depend—they would be sorry to see me pulled down and cast aside. And in any case, you are in no position to marshal forces against me. All of Akhet-

Aten is roiling with fear, threatened by the Pharaoh in his Temple."

"That may be true today, Nefertiti, but it will not be true for much longer. Don't be rash; think ahead."

"I am thinking ahead already, Ay—to the work I must do to repair Egypt. I am thinking ahead to all the many ways a king might die. If you want Akhenaten gone from the throne, you would be wise to support me *on* it."

Ay stilled. The scowl faded from his face, replaced by the studious calm that indicated he was thinking—churning his plots and schemes in his heart, sifting and sorting them until he found just the right game to play. His eyes sharpened on her face, and Nefertiti could read his thoughts as easily as an opened scroll. *Is she truly willing to kill the Pharaoh? Can she afford to be so reckless with her own soul? If she is willing to try it, then perhaps it is worth leaving her on the throne.*

How well I know you, Father. But you do not know me at all. Nefertiti kept her gaze fixed on Ay, but even without looking at the girls she could feel the presence of her daughters—her two remaining daughters, all she had left in the world—and her sister Mutbenret, burning in her *ka*, filling her with the choking smoke of guilt and shame. *My soul is already damned, Ay, and damned beyond any hope of salvation. What is one more sin, weighed against all the others?*

"If you are so frightened," Nefertiti pronounced from her throne, "then let Smenkhkare and me *both* reign. For now. Once Akhenaten is dealt with, then whichever king the gods love best will continue on. The other will be discarded in due time." She tilted her head, smiling down at Smenkhkare lightly, happily. "Do you agree?"

The younger man sighed and gave a tiny shrug. "I have no objections—for now. Truly, I see little other option at the moment. Ay is correct: we do have more pressing concerns just now; we must act quickly, and together, if we hope to stop Akhenaten from destroying his own city and people. I will welcome your help, Nefertiti. The more who join me in this fight, the better."

Nefertiti nodded. "A wise move."

"As long," Smenkhkare added, "as you do not restrict my access to... the *King's Son*. We will have peace between us, Nefertiti, on that one condition, and until Akhenaten is dealt with. Once we have solved that problem, then let the gods choose whichever Pharaoh they prefer."

"Very well," Nefertiti said. "I will agree to your truce, until our most pressing and immediate concerns are alleviated."

"You're as mad as your husband, Nefertiti," Ay said.

But I am the only one who has nothing to lose—the only one who can save you from your own king. And you know it, Ay. You know it.

She stared down at her father from the height of her throne. "My name is not Nefertiti. Not any longer; not to you. I am King Nefer-Neferu-Aten, and you would be wise to remember that, Ay."

Meritaten

Year 2 of Smenkhkare,
Holy of the Manifestations

Year 18 of Akhenaten,
Beloved of the Sun

M OTHER..." THE WORD was pulled from Meritaten's throat by an unseen hand. She couldn't have said whether she spoke it with longing or rebuke, but under the power of that simple word—that irresistible spell—she stumbled toward the throne.

Nefertiti looked down at her. All the stern haughtiness fell from her face; her eyes softened, and Meritaten saw her throat tense as she swallowed hard.

But before either of them could speak, Ay brushed past Meritaten, climbing halfway up the dais. "Your cozy arrangement with Smenkhkare is all well and good," he said, "but we have pressing business. What do we do for the innocents whom Akhenanten has taken to the temple?"

"Yes," Smenkhkare added. "You've had long experience with the Pharaoh. Advise us, please."

"Akhenaten will never cease to persecute them," Nefertiti said, "even if you can free them from his grasp."

Meritaten's anger flared, burning away any warmth she might have felt. "How do you know? You have been absent these many years, while we have proven already that Akhenaten *will* forget, that he can be distracted—"

"Not for long," Nefertiti said. Her tone was not harsh,

yet it held a sharp edge that seemed to say, *Leave this matter to your betters, girl. Don't meddle with things beyond your strength.* "Absent or not, I have known Akhenaten very well, and for longer than any of you. You might distract him for a time, but he always finds his focus again, always comes back to his selfish desires. The only hope for those he has targeted—for punishment or for any other purpose—is to remove them entirely from his reach. Tiy knew that; it's why she sent Smenkhkare away. These prisoners must be taken out of the city. Otherwise they will all die, sooner or later. Akhenaten may be diverted, but he does not forget."

"Remove them from the city?" Ay said. "As soon take the stars from the sky as get citizens out of Akhet-Aten. Especially when the king has decided he doesn't like them. He'll only send soldiers after them to pluck them from the southern road, or send men by boat to catch them if they try to leave via the river. There is no safe way out of the City of the Sun."

"There *is* a way out," Nefertiti said. "I found it myself. The hard part will be to snatch them from Akhenaten's immediate grasp. How many soldiers are loyal to you alone, Ay? And to you, Smenkhkare?"

The men conferred quickly. "Fifty," Smenkhkare said. "Perhaps sixty at the most."

Nefertiti's lips thinned. "Not many, but it may be just enough. Akhenaten is already in the temple with his captives; we will need to approach him carefully."

Ay turned to regard Meritaten. She could feel his narrow eyes probing her worth, assessing her utility. "I've had my complaints about you, Meritaten, but in the past you *have* reined the king in smartly with your High Priestess act. Now is the time for you to show your worth, King's Wife."

Meritaten's heart pounded in her ears. The floor seemed to spin dizzily beneath her. "I cannot face him in the temple." There, at the seat of his strength, where his strange, frightening power wreathed him...

Smenkhkare came to stand beside her, pulled her close in an embrace. "You leashed him once as a priestess. You told me how you did it, how you convinced him to accept me as his co-regent. You can do it again. You are strong enough, brave enough."

She could not speak. She shook her head in denial.

"Meritaten must go to him at the temple," Nefertiti said, letting Tutankhaten slide to his feet as she rose from her throne. "She must convince him to bring all the prisoners up to the top of the cliffs."

"What," Ay said, "to throw them off?"

"Of course not. I know a ruse—one that will appeal to Akhenaten's sense of drama and grandeur. Meritaten, you need only work your influence over the king and convince him to bring the prisoners up the eastern path to the top of the cliffs, to the place where the tallest boundary stone stands. I will tell you everything while we go to the temple, but we must go now. We haven't much time."

Nefertiti came quickly down the steps of the dais. Meritaten lunged for her, seizing her hand. "You speak to him," she begged. "You were once his most cherished High Priestess of the Sun. He'll listen to you!"

"Not anymore, he won't." Nefertiti pulled her hand from Meritaten's grip, but she took her by both shoulders, holding her firmly, looking deep into her eyes. "Don't be afraid," she said softly. "You are my daughter, and stronger than you know."

It was small praise from a mother who had been absent too long, and who had left Meritaten to face too many tragedies alone. She knew this—yet somehow Nefertiti's words bolstered Meritaten's courage all the same. She uprooted her feet from the floor and followed numbly behind as Nefertiti made for the double doors.

"Nann, Horemheb, take Tutankhaten somewhere safe. Do not let him out of your sight."

"When have we ever?" Horemheb retorted.

"I'll send for you when this business is done." Nefertiti gestured impatiently for Ay and Smenkhkare to keep up. "I've a chariot waiting outside. It will be a tight fit for us all to ride together, but it will get us there faster than walking. Come! Time is fleeting."

AY AND SMENKHKARE had no time to muster their full force. By the time Meritaten climbed into the chariot beside Nefertiti, no more than two dozen of Smenkhkare's loyal soldiers had joined them, milling about the courtyard, eager to turn their attention on the temple. Ay took the chariot's reins, and Smenkhkare sprang up beside Meritaten, one protective arm wrapped tight around her shoulders.

The chariot rolled out of the palace gate and into the wide, straight road that led to the Great Aten Temple. The loyal guards ran beside it, to the left and right, protecting those within from the angry, surging crowds that jostled and clamored in the streets of Akhet-Aten. Nefertiti leaned close to Meritaten's ear so that she could be heard above the crowd. She laid out the plan in detail, but it seemed a desperate gamble to Meritaten, more likely to fail than succeed. But what choice did any of them have? She couldn't allow so many good and loyal people to perish for the sake of Akhenaten's madness.

All too soon, Ay reined the horses to halt. They stamped and snorted at the base of the temple's towering gate.

"Are you sure," Meritaten said, resisting the urge to cling to Nefertiti, "are you *sure* you can't speak to him yourself?"

"He doesn't love me like he once did. I'm afraid I would only enrage him. But you—he trusts you."

Does he still? she wondered, glancing at Smenkhkare with a guilty flash of her eyes. *Or does he know about my iniquities?*

"All you need do is get the prisoners up to the cliff-tops," Nefertiti said. "They will do the rest for themselves."

"You make it sound so simple." Before her lone thread of courage could snap, she jumped down from the chariot and strode resolutely toward the temple gate. Smenkhkare was close beside her—at least she had that comfort. But she would rather have had him elsewhere—beyond the reach of Akhenaten's anger. For only the god knew whether Akhenaten still believed Meritaten and Smenkhkare his pure, devoted servants—or whether he had finally seen what others saw, Ay and Mutbenret and Ankhesenpaaten. *Who else? Who else has seen my faithlessness, and told the Pharaoh I have sinned against him?*

All she could do was trust her safety to the Aten. She and Smenkhkare pushed their way through crowds of shrieking women and men who called out for justice, their voices hoarse from too much shouting, their demands still unanswered.

"Let us pass," Meritaten said sharply to the wall of guards who blocked the temple mouth. "The Pharaoh has summoned us. Move aside, and let us in!"

Two guards edged apart, creating a gap between their bull-strong shoulders, just wide enough for Meritaten and Smenkhkare to wriggle through. The moment they were past the line of the guards, that gap closed again, trapping them inside with Akhenaten's delusions.

Meritaten turned to Smenkhkare, wishing she could take his hand, wishing they could both turn into birds and fly far away from this place, the shouts and screams, the madness, the terror coiling in her gut.

"You are brave," Smenkhkare said softly. She could hardly hear him over the noise of the crowd.

Meritaten bit her lip, bracing herself, and made for the temple's hot sanctuary. As she passed the gate, her feet sank into deep, hot sand and waves of reflected heat buffeted her from the temple's inner walls. Her legs shook; her stomach clenched with nausea. But when she caught sight of Akhenaten—slouching on his sun throne at the end of the temple's great length, positioned between two huge statues of his own mighty self—calmness fell over her, as quickly and wholly as if she'd been plunged into water.

Perhaps Nefertiti's sudden reappearance is *a talisman after all, a sign from the god meant just for me.* Now was the time— Meritaten could sense it, with growing awe—now was the time to take up Nefertiti's mantle of power, to wrap the majesty of the sun priesthood around herself, and speak to the king in the only language he could understand.

She approached the king across the sand, passing by the people who fought the guards, struggling to evade the bonds and stakes that would pin them to the ground. Some were already down, their arms and legs stretched against the burning sand, crying piteously, weeping for forgiveness of sins they never committed. Meritaten passed them by, sparing them neither glances nor tears. She walked calmly to her father's throne and smiled, even as he cast a hateful glower down upon her.

"Mighty king," she said.

"Where were you?" Akhenaten grated. "You should have been here, at my side!"

She bowed. "I did not receive your summons until now. But I came most gladly, ready to see the will of the god done."

When she straightened, Akhenaten's expression had changed. A new fire burned behind his eyes—a heat she hadn't suffered in many blessed months, but she recognized his lust in an instant.

Not here—not with Smenkhkare looking on, she thought

frantically.

But she recalled Nefertiti's perfect composure, and pushed her fear and disgust far from her heart. *I will do what I must. I am the Great Wife, clever and strong. For Egypt, for my people, I will do what I must.*

Akhenaten seized her by the arm, pulling her against his body so roughly that she stumbled in the deep sand. Her knee cracked against the seat of his throne; she swallowed a cry of pain. He kissed her, his mouth greedy and forceful. Her heart pounded, her pulse throbbing in her head amid the stifling heat, and anger flared in her at the thought of Smenkhkare forced to watch this farce of passion.

But Meritaten did what needed doing. She returned the Pharaoh's kiss, playing at hunger until his breath quickened against her cheek and his fingers dug painfully into her arm.

I can still move him, she thought. *I can still influence him, in this way if in no other.* She saw, too, that she was the last of the people who could exert their will over the Pharaoh— and that soon her influence would fade. *Let this be my final act as priestess—the one great and heroic act of my life.* She would not fail, nor balk in her duty. She would play her advantage wisely and well, and if the god was willing, the king would relent.

"Meritaten," he whispered, desire roughening his voice.

"My great and mighty lord." She stared deep into his eyes, stifling her instinct to flinch away. "I rejoice in your strength and righteousness. The god has brought me here to witness justice done."

His hand moved from her arm to her breast, and his teeth clenched with rage and power. "When my enemies are dead, then the god will be pleased. When I have done the Aten's will, it will lift the curse on your womb, and together we will bring forth—"

Now, Meritaten told herself. *While this mood is still upon him, while I am in his favor.*

She cried out as if in ecstasy and staggered backward, into the narrow shadow of one of the statues. She let her knees buckle, and dropped into the sand, then pitched forward, prone at the king's feet. There she writhed, twisting like a thing possessed, gasping and crying out, clutching at her own body. Over the sound of her display, she heard Akhenaten panting in excitement—in arousal.

"I know!" Meritaten shouted. "I know what the god wants! I have seen his desires! He imposes his desire upon me—ah! I feel the Aten's longing in my own flesh!"

Suddenly Akhenaten's hands were on her, gripping her arms, pulling her bodily from the sand. He sank back on his throne, holding her on his lap while she squirmed and arched her back, throwing up her hands as if fighting off some assailant—or embracing the power of her vision.

"Yes," he hissed in her ear. "This is good. Tell me what the god wants!"

"He wants," Meritaten panted, eyes tight shut, "a greater act than can be carried out here, between these temple walls. The god's fire is hotter than any heat the temple can hold, for this place was built by the hands of men. Blasphemers must burn so hot that not even ash remains! For that, they must be cast into the Red Land itself!"

Akhenaten's grip loosened. He shoved her slightly, pushing her away from his body, suddenly wary. "What do you mean?"

"Take them up to the cliffs!" Meritaten moaned, still mimicking ecstasy. "Let them walk out alone into the temple the god made for himself. Ah, the heat of the sun! It fills me!"

"Send them out to perish in the desert," Akhenaten said. "Out into the east, the place of the god's origin. Yes, that is fitting—yes."

The king stood, spilling Meritaten from his lap; she rolled in the hot sand and clambered to her feet to stand at the king's side.

Please, she prayed, turning her face up to the pounding sun. *Please, let it work. Let him do as I said.*

"Pull up these wretches' stakes," Akhenaten shouted, "and form up to surround them. We are going up to the cliff-tops with these traitors and vermin. The god has commanded it! I have heard it from the mouth of my own priestess!"

M ERITATEN LED THE WAY up into the cliffs, the prisoners trailing her in a sad procession. Akhenaten's guards surrounded the train of condemned, offering no escape to any who might have been foolish or brave enough to run.

Smenkhkare trudged along beside her as they toiled up the trail. He maintained perfect silence, and Meritaten could feel his confusion, his sorrow—his disgust at the scene he had witnessed in the temple. She wanted to tell him that all would be well, that she and Nefertiti had devised a brilliant plan as they'd whispered together in the throne room... and most of all, she longed to reassure him that she was still his, forever his—that her performance for Akhenaten had been play-acting, and had revolted her as much as it did him. But she kept her silence. The danger was not past—not yet. And until the captives were safely away, she must maintain her guise as the devoted priestess in Akhenaten's service.

When they reached the top of the cliffs, Meritaten rushed forward to press her forehead against the narrow, pointed boundary stone of Akhet-Aten. *We have arrived,* she told herself, relieved. *Now let the prisoners be wise* enough to do what must be done.

The prisoners straggled up to the bare, flat ground that surrounded the boundary stela. Akhenaten had not yet appeared over the edge of the cliff, but his guards spread out and ringed the condemned, hemming them in. Meritaten scanned the prisoners quickly. One of them in particular seemed a likely accomplice, a man well past his middle years with wise, observant eyes.

She darted toward him. She must confide the plan before Akhenaten appeared. The god alone knew what might happen then—the Pharaoh might decide to pitch these innocents from the cliffs after all.

He flinched back from Meritaten as she approached, but she comforted him with a shake of her head, a softening of her gaze—and after a moment that felt much too long for Meritaten's liking, the man ducked his head and allowed her to approach again.

"What is your name?" Meritaten whispered close to his ear, so quietly she could barely hear the words herself.

"Panefer, my lady."

"Listen closely, Panefer. I won't have time to repeat myself. There is a way to safety, but you must follow my directions precisely. Keep all the prisoners together, and walk directly out into the desert for one hour. By then, the king and all his men will be gone from the cliffs—I will see to that. After an hour's time, turn south and walk for half an hour, then turn toward the river again. You will be beyond Akhet-Aten's boundary stones. Go south along the desert's edge. Keep to the places where there is still some vegetation, but do not venture farther west than that, or patrols from Akhet-Aten may find you. By nightfall, you will find water in an old shepherd's well that stands beside a tree with a forked trunk. There are thickets there, enough to shelter you from tomorrow's sun. One more day's walk to the south will free you from

Akhet-Aten forever."

Panefer squinted at her, searching her eyes, her face, weighing her sincerity.

"It's not a trap," she said. "We are going to bring down Akhenaten, one way or another. But first I would see you all safe from harm."

The old man took Meritaten's hand. Regardless of her status as King's Great Wife, he raised her fingers to his lips and kissed them gently.

"I was a priest on the West Bank, in the days before Akhet-Aten. I was a priest of the old gods, the true gods. I bless you, my lady, and all your works and designs. In the name of Mother Mut, and of Maat, and of Iset, who knows all names, I bless you. Iset knows the name of your heart, and she will keep you close to her bosom forever."

The whispered blessing took Meritaten aback. She had never known any god, save for the Aten. But Panefer's kiss and his earnest words filled her with a queer, floating warmth. But before she could make any reply, Akhenaten gained the cliff-tops, and Meritaten stepped quickly away from Panefer's side.

"You traitors against the Aten," Akhenaten bellowed, "for your crimes and sins I sentence you to perish in the god's own forge. The Red Land awaits you—the Red Land, your only tomb! Go; do not think to beg for mercy, for there is no place for you in the City of the Sun, nor in the Aten's graces!"

The condemned moaned and cried out—even Panefer, who betrayed nothing of Meritaten's aid—for every Egyptian knew that the Red Land was the source of all chaos, the place where no river flowed, where no green thing grew, where no redemption came. But the guards advanced on the prisoners, goading them with their spears, and Panefer was the first to turn his back on the king and the cliffs, and walk out into the desert to face the violent blows of the sun's rays. Meritaten could not breathe until the rest of the twenty followed him, and then her breaths came in ragged sobs, which she did her best to stifle.

Akhenaten stood at the desert's edge, shielding his eyes with a hand, watching as the group of condemned men and women dwindled in size, then finally vanished against the wavering glare on the horizon. When he could see them no more, he gestured for his guards and started back down the trail. Meritaten and Smenkhkare hung back, pressed into the shadow of the boundary stone, watching Akhenaten and his men disappear among the boulders and the shadows of rocky crags. The Pharaoh was wrapped up in his bliss, unconscious of Meritaten's absence from his side. He sang a hymn to the Aten as he walked away. Its cheerful refrain echoed from the cliff walls.

All the poise and strength ran out of Meritaten, like a slashed water-skin draining. She gave a strangled, wordless cry and sagged into Smenkhkare's arms. She shook violently, all the pent-up fear releasing from her body at once, and she gagged and heaved with the force of her nausea.

"There, there," Smenkhkare said gently. His touch was all she could feel, his soft caress along her arm, bruised where Akhenaten had clutched her. "You did well. I didn't know exactly what you and Nefertiti intended, nor did I know quite what I was looking at, down there in the Temple. But now I see it. You are a strong Great Wife, my love—stronger than you know."

But Meritaten didn't feel strong. She was weak as a day-old kitten, and weighted as she was by her sins, she felt undeserving of the mercy the god had showed by allowing the ruse to come off so easily. She clung to Smenkhkare, weeping against his chest. *Iset knows the name of my heart*, she thought, recalling Panefer's strange blessing. *And what if that goddess does exist, after all? What else does she know? Will she condemn me, too, for loving you, Smenkhkare?*

Horemheb

Year 1 of Nefer-Neferu-Aten,
Effective for Her Husband

Year 18 of Akhenaten,
Beloved of the Sun

TUTANKHATEN LAUGHED as he splashed in the warm shallows of the palace lake. Now and then he broke out into simple, rhyming tunes—children's songs, the sort Horemheb half-remembered from his own boyhood—stomping among the floating lotus leaves in time to his chants. Nann moved protectively beside the boy, her skirt tied up around her waist, following the heir to the Horus Throne like a pale, long-legged wading bird, her eyes sharp and watchful. The Hurrian woman provided a nurse's care to Tutankhaten, and Nefertiti offered a mother's guidance and discipline. But it fell to Horemheb to protect the boy from bodily harm, a task he had taken to with earnest focus and grim determination.

In the week since Nefertiti had re-appeared in Akhet-Aten, Horemheb, Mutnodjmet, and Nann had settled into their wing of the palace with varying degrees of comfort. Nefertiti occupied the palace wing watchfully, haughtily, like a lioness occupies a plain—but the transition had been less natural for her servants and friends.

Horemheb was left with a persistent feeling of vague discomfort, like an itch between his shoulder blades. After Baketaten's death, he had sworn he would never return to Akhet-Aten again. He still hated the city, hated the pain of its memories, and loathed the dark stain of

Akhenaten, which he saw everywhere he looked: in the images of Aten-worship that adorned every wall, in the strange, distorted art Akhenaten favored. But he had sworn to protect Tutankhaten. He would go wherever the boy went, guarding him as he had failed to guard Baketaten. Tutankhaten was Horemheb's chance at redemption, his opportunity to make things right with the spirit of his lost love.

Nann, too, seemed conflicted about her return to Akhet-Aten. Horemheb could read the hatred of this place clearly on his friend's face. Nann's scowls and hard-eyed stares never left her now. She seemed haunted by the need for vengeance; a tense, dangerous energy seemed to propel her through her daily tasks, even the simple and gentle ones. Often Horemheb feared the stress of confronting Akhet-Aten again would prove too much for Nann to bear. But at least under the protection of Nefertiti, the self-proclaimed king of Egypt, Nann could move about the palace safely, searching for the opportunities she craved to wake her slumbering vengeance.

Nann seemed to have no particular fondness for Tutankhaten, as far as Horemheb could tell—nor did she seem disposed toward any child she encountered. To her, Tutankhaten was a means to an end, the magical talisman that guaranteed her safety as she sought a way to begin her grim task of avenging Lady Tadukhepa's death. But because she valued Tutankhaten for the protection he conferred, and the access he allowed to the royal family, Nann looked after the boy with assiduous care. That was enough for Horemheb. He could trust Nann with Tutankhaten's life, for her own life depended on the boy's safety.

Mutnodjmet, for her part, seemed entirely untroubled by life in the palace. Born into nobility, the palace suited her much better than their old shack had, on the southern edge of town where they had lived in the earliest days of their marriage. Mutnodjmet had proven herself brave, loyal, and hardworking during their trials outside of Akhet-Aten—Horemheb could fault his wife for nothing. But now, with his new appointment as guardian of the heir, Horemheb felt more keenly than ever before the differences between them. She was made for this world of courts and power—bred for it. But he was still the common-born soldier, simple and unrefined. Often when he returned to the small but beautiful apartment they shared, close to Nefertiti in her private wing, Horemheb felt more distanced from Mutnodjmet than ever before. Even when she pulled him close and purred into his ear how happy she was here, how pleased she was to live in the royal palace as the wife of an important official, Horemheb felt the gulf between them stretch wider. And he didn't know what he could do to change it.

A life with Baketaten, had such a life been possible, would have left him feeling far more disconnected and unworthy—Horemheb was sure of that. Baketaten had been even farther above his station than Mutnodjmet was, as high above him as the stars in the sky. Yet she had loved him—he had never forgotten the moment when she had told him so. And with a sharp stab of loss, he sensed that somehow he would have found a way to overcome his unworthiness if the gods had just given him the *right* wife—if they had found some way to marry him to Baketaten instead of Mutnodjmet.

There was a stir and murmur from the portico that served as an entrance to Nefertiti's private garden. Tutankhaten trailed off in his song and looked around; Horemheb followed his gaze, and across the bright, sunlit grounds he saw Nefertiti's guards snap to attention.

"My lord," one of the guards called to Nefertiti, "Smenkhkare seeks an audience."

Nefertiti had been relaxing on a blanket spread in the shade of a tall hedge, its branches swelling with new flower buds. She uncoiled herself and rose, gesturing for the guards to admit the other king.

Smenkhkare came across the garden with a stride that spoke of ownership. He spared a hard look for Nefertiti but turned aside, going instead to the lake's edge. He sat on its stone wall, watching Tutankhaten with an intense, painful hunger. Nefertiti planted herself resolutely near Smenkhkare. Horemheb did, too, his hand never straying from the hilt of his blade.

"Good day, Tutankhaten," the other king said.

Tutankhaten hopped and sloshed among the lotus leaves, sending up a great splash that nearly reached Smenkhkare. "Good day, sir."

"You speak with such admirable formality," Smenkhkare said. He tried to make the words sound casual, but Horemheb could hear the twinge of desperate longing in his voice. "But you know, King's Son, you may call me Smenkhkare. It would please me if you would."

It would please him if the boy called him Father. Horemheb kept his silence, but did not ease away from where Smenkhkare sat.

"Once I was called Ramose," Tutankhaten said, pulling up a lotus vine and idly slapping his own back with the wet tendril. "And my aunt Nefertiti had a different name, too. Do you have many names?"

Smenkhkare chuckled. "No, I'm afraid I have only the one name now. Though I used a different name once."

"It's good fun to have lots of names," Tutankhaten said.

"It is."

He reached into the carrying pouch that hung beside his kilt's sash. Horemheb tensed, but Smenkhkare shot him a withering glance, and he subsided. Smenkhkare produced a small wooden crocodile from the pouch, a cleverly-made toy painted bright green with large blue eyes.

"See what I've brought you," he said.

Tutankhaten same splashing over to the lake's edge. He examined the toy solemnly, turning it over and over in his small hands.

"See how the jaws snap," Smenkhkare said, demonstrating.

The boy looked up with a sudden grin. "It's terribly fierce!" He made the crocodile bite one of Smenkhkare's fingers, and for a few moments the two lost themselves in play, Tutankhaten roaring and thrashing in the water, Smenkhkare crying out for mercy.

When the boy pulled himself out of the water and scampered away over the grass—Nann in pursuit—to play with his crocodile among the flower beds, Smenkhkare stood in his soaked kilt, doling out a bitter laugh to Horemheb and Nefertiti. "You don't truly believe I would harm my own son, do you?"

Nefertiti lifted one brow and peered at the guards on the portico, but they were far enough away. There was no danger they'd heard Smenkhkare's words. "I wouldn't put it past any person of your particular lineage to harm his own child, if he saw some benefit in the act."

For the briefest moment, a flicker of pain passed across her face. But it was gone again in an instant, and she was the same regal, unmoved Nefertiti, ruling over her garden and her palace with astonishing self-control. But gone from her face or not, Horemheb knew the pain still lingered. Over the year they'd spent raising Tutankhaten on her secluded estate, Nefertiti had often spoken frankly, telling him in heart-wrenching detail of her regrets, of the sins that shadowed her. He knew she had never forgiven herself for allowing her daughters to suffer.

"I am not like the rest of my family," Smenkhkare insisted. "You know that, Nefertiti. I spent most of my life out of the palace, away from court. The corruption that has steered this dynasty into madness never touched me."

"Yet here you are," she rejoined, "back in the thick of it, vying for my throne just as one would expect the son of Tiy to do."

"I am only doing my sacred work. I cannot alter the circumstances of my birth. I cannot deny that I am of the royal blood, that I have a duty to the Horus Throne."

"Exactly. You cannot deny who and what you are."

Nefertiti eased herself down on the lake's edge and gestured for Smenkhkare to sit beside her. After a moment of pained hesitation, glancing after Tutankhaten scampering in the flower beds, he sat.

"I cannot deny who I am, either, Smenkhkare." All the hardness had fled from Nefertiti's face, lifted from her shoulders. She spoke to the other king now as an equal, reasonable and concerned. "As Akhenaten descended into madness, it was I who held Egypt together. It was I who ruled as Pharaoh. His body sat upon the throne, but it was my heart that thought for him, my voice that dictated his writs, my hand that enacted his works. These things have already been done; they cannot be undone. We cannot unmake reality. Now, when Egypt is so very weak and fragile, why would you strive to take power away from hands more capable than your own?"

Smenkhkare shook his head, sighing. "I don't mean to discount your sacrifices, your work, but after all—it was I who was appointed by this administration, not you."

"Do you call my father and my vain, selfish, addle-hearted daughter an 'administration'?" Smenkhkare's face darkened and his mouth turned down; Nefertiti held up a hand to stay his protest. "Smenkhkare, I do love Meritaten—make no mistake about that—but I also know what kind of person she is. The girl is not suited to ruling. I had hoped she might be, once, but even then, I never intended her to become the Great Wife. She never should have been in a position to appoint you at all. I am here now to correct that mistake."

"You don't know your daughter at all," Smenkhkare said, his voice low and tight with barely controlled anger. "Meritaten is stronger and more capable than you give her credit for."

She smiled at the passion in his voice, and Horemheb saw that it was a genuine smile, warm with real happiness and gratitude. "I am glad you love her. She deserves love. She *is* all the things I said of her—vain, and a poor ruler— but she has many fine qualities, too. And every mother wants her children to be happy."

"How can you presume to judge Meritaten as a ruler— or even as a daughter—when you abandoned her years ago? You've been hiding out somewhere—"

"As you were once hidden," she interjected, "for many more years than I."

"You haven't had time to know Meritaten as a ruler, as a King's Wife. Not *every* drop of this bloodline is fouled, Nefertiti. There are still some in this family who are pure of heart, whose *kas* are good. I am one such, and your daughter is another. And Baketaten—I remember her well, when she came to me to get a royal heir. There was no stain in her *ka*. She was as good and pure a person as the gods ever made."

Horemheb bristled. Unconsciously, he stepped forward to block Smenkhkare's view of Tutankhaten. All the old, painful memories flooded into his body, searing in his chest, shivering his limbs. With brutal vividness, he recalled the loamy smell of Smenkhkare's olive grove, the stars glimmering through the branches overhead while he lay there on his bedroll, knowing that Baketaten was even at that moment tangled up in Smenkhkare's arms instead of his own.

Smenkhkare looked up at Horemheb and paused, examining his hard-set jaw and fierce, wounded eyes with a thoughtful air. Finally he said, "I remember your face, soldier. You were there, too. You knew Baketaten." He turned to Nefertiti. "This man will tell you: Baketaten was as pure as the sacred heron. There was no evil in her, and you know there is no evil in her son—in *our* son. Why, then, do you not trust me? Why do you oppose me, and make an already difficult reign more complicated?"

"Because Egypt is not your land to rule. I have already proven myself adept, and I have sacrificed too much, Smenkhkare—more than you can comprehend—to see to Egypt's safety. I will not turn my back on my sacrifices. I will not allow all that pain, all that suffering, to come to naught. It is my country; I have already handled its reins with more skill than you. I will not stand aside until Tutankhaten sits on the throne, a grown man who has been raised on good counsel. You must make your peace with that fact, for I will not change my mind."

"He is my son," Smenkhkare repeated. "He should be raised as *I* see fit, under *my* good counsel."

"But he will not be. I will see him safely to his kingship, and I will see that he is untouched by Akhenaten's influence, or by Meritaten's blundering, or by your naïve good intentions. He will be a strong ruler, a servant of *maat*, but only if I guide him."

Smenkhkare stood abruptly, towering over Nefertiti, who remained seated on the lake's edge, her hands folded in her lap. "I can take him from you. I know how to find Mahu; I can—"

"Do not threaten me," Nefertiti said coolly. "Only a fool believes that Egypt has a plague of Pharaohs. Horemheb here knows which king is the rightful one, the true one. He will not hesitate to slay a pretender."

Horemheb slid his dagger from its sheath, rejoicing in the whisper of the steel. He would gladly take this Smenkhkare's life out of pure spite, just for the sake of the love he never got to share with Baketaten. Even if the gods thought Smenkhkare a true Pharaoh, and would damn his soul for the crime, Horemheb would do it—and relish every moment.

Smenkhkare stepped back, raising his hands in placation. "Sheathe your knife, man. Nefertiti is in no danger from me."

But Horemheb kept his dagger bared until Nefertiti herself gestured for him to subside.

"You won't have Tutankhaten," Nefertiti said again. "Understand, I don't do this to pain you. I am simply thinking of Egypt—of the future of the whole Two Lands. And as for Mahu, well... You can try to kill me over this, Smenkhkare, but trickery and violence are the first things I'll be expecting from you."

"I told you already, I do not work that way. I do not think that way."

"But as you said for yourself, you are who and what the gods have made you. You are the son of Amunhotep and Tiy; you are the brother of Akhenaten. No matter how good your intentions, you cannot escape your own blood."

"I don't want violence," Smenkhkare insisted. "But neither will I cease to fight for my son. I am sure we can find a peaceful resolution, Nefertiti, if only you will meet me halfway. I am sure there are peaceful ways to solve *all* of this family's problems, and all the problems Egypt faces, too."

Nann, stooping over Tutankhaten in the flower bed, straightened abruptly and caught Horemheb's eye. The cynicism was plain on her pale face, and he knew it reflected his own like a well-polished mirror.

Nefertiti rose gracefully. "You have said all you mean to say, I think. I have said all I mean to say, too. I will see you in the throne room, Smenkhkare."

He held her gaze for one long moment, then turned roughly away. He went to Tutankhaten, bent and kissed the boy on the forehead, then strode from the garden without looking back.

When he had gone, Horemheb sighed with relief. Smenkhkare's anger and insistence had made him tense; he shrugged and rolled his shoulders, stretching out the knots that threatened to form.

Nefertiti's sigh had nothing of relief in it—it was pure exasperation, pure strain, and loud as a winter wind. She paced along the lake's retaining wall, pinching the bridge of her nose with her long, delicate fingers. "It's Ay who has put these thoughts into Smenkhkare's head. For six years Smenkhkare never spared a single thought for Baketaten's child—I am certain of that. But now that Ay knows Tutankhaten lives—now that Ay knows just where to find the boy—he is whispering in Smenkhkare's ear, pushing him to steal the boy away from me, so I will have nothing to secure my place on the throne."

"Smenkhkare only had eyes for the boy from the moment you brought him into the throne room."

"But Ay is pushing Smenkhkare know. Using his interest in the boy to control him. I know Ay; I understand how he works." She stopped her pacing and shook her head. The ornaments in her long wig chimed. "There is a part of me that wants to trust Smenkhkare. There is a part of me that desires nothing more than to give up my place on this accursed throne and let him be the king. But I *cannot*. The gods put Tutankhaten into *my* hands, not his—and Tutankhaten kept me alive when I should have been dead. That means something, doesn't it?"

"Of course, my lady. It must." Horemheb was not at all sure of his words. But he felt it was what she wanted, what she needed—an affirmation to secure her in this rare moment of fear.

"It doesn't matter that Smenkhkare is the boy's father," Nefertiti went on. "He doesn't know Tutankhaten as I do, and the gods didn't give Smenkhkare this heir to raise. This is my purpose. I am only doing what the gods direct me, Horemheb, even though it... it *frightens* me to be back in the palace again."

Her admission of fear took him aback. Nefertiti, the unfailingly composed, the stunningly regal—frightened? He stared at her, bereft of words, and her eyes darted suddenly, her head turning as if a bird had flitted past her face—but there was nothing in the air around her, nothing Horemheb could see.

"It is dangerous to be here again—dangerous for me. But we do what we must, don't we? To make amends for past sins, to set things right."

"Of course, my lady," He said soothingly. But he felt in need of comfort himself. Her unusual slip of confidence utterly confounded him.

"The one grace that saves me—so far, at least—is that Akhcnaten has remained cloistered in his temple and hasn't yet grasped how vigorously this pot is boiling, right under his own nose. I don't think he has comprehended what it means at all—that I have returned. He hasn't come to see me, thank the gods. He hasn't asked after Tutankhaten, as far as I know. But how much longer do you suppose that will last?"

"Not long," Nann said grimly from amid the budding flowers.

Horemheb suppressed a shudder. He had reconnected with his old friend Djedi since returning to Akhet-Aten, sharing strong beer in a drinking shop to reminisce and reacquaint themselves. Djedi had been on duty in the Great Aten Temple that strange, dark day when Meritaten had rescued the innocent citizens from Akhenaten's madness. Horemheb had stayed behind to protect Nefertiti, but his friend had told him everything. Meritaten's performance had been marvelous, to hear Djedi's report of what he saw—but how long would it be until Akhenaten realized the truth? How long until he learned that his Great Wife had tricked him into sparing the so-called traitors and blasphemers, and setting them all free? Sooner or later, the Pharaoh would realize that his co-regent and his Great Wife had played him for a fool. When he did, his rage would be implacable. He might do anything at all— *anything* to express his anger and assert his dominance. Young Tutankhaten might be safe from the mad Pharaoh, if he still thought the boy his own son. But Horemheb was certain Nefertiti would not be spared.

"We can't count on Akhenaten staying occupied by his god forever," Nefertiti said darkly. "It is only a matter of time until he lifts his head and looks beyond the temple walls."

"I'll protect you," Horemheb offered. Never in his life had he felt so weak, so useless—so helpless against the gods and the cruel fates they wove.

"You will," she agreed gently, "if anyone can. May the gods send us deliverance from this viper in Egypt's bed."

Nefertiti

Year 1 of Nefer-Neferu-Aten,
Effective for Her Husband

Year 18 of Akhenaten,
Beloved of the Sun

A S EVENING FELL, Nefertiti sat in her garden alone, watching the stars turn slowly in the plush, cool dark of the sky. Those distant, silver lights were her only comfort here, their presence the only beautiful thing in a palace of riches. And they were only beautiful because they were far from Akhet-Aten—as far away as she wished to be.

Even out in the garden, with the endless expanse of sky above, she felt the walls of the palace constrict around her. She was enclosed, caged—trapped in this place where all her sins still lingered, where every terrible act she had ever committed in the name of power and vengeance seemed pressed and painted on the mudbrick of the walls. The gentle approach of night did little to drive the self-loathing from her *ka*, but at least the stars afforded a glimpse of another place—another world, far beyond this dark and base realm of the living.

She watched twilight unfold in dull detachment. Even here, alone, beneath the open sky, she was set apart from the world, attached by nothing more than the small, thin, fragile tether of Tutankhaten. How strange, that a child who was not even her own should become her purpose in life. But he was her reason—the last duty she must discharge before flying up to the stars, if they would have her. And perhaps they would, after all. Perhaps an afterlife was not entirely barred to her. If she could but guide Tutankhaten safely to the throne, some of her wrongs might be righted. Perhaps she would even find forgiveness—some—for the things she had done to her daughters. That forgiveness would only come from the gods, though, not her daughters themselves. They could never love her again, never accept the things she had done, the way she had bound them like sacrificial beasts on a temple altar. Nefertiti knew she had no real hope of redemption, no right to expect the Field of Reeds when she died. The peace and ease of that reward would surely be denied. But she could perhaps hope that the gods would dispose of her quickly; that Ammit, the Eater of Hearts, would consume her in one sharp-toothed bite, and not gnaw at her for eternity, drawing out her suffering. And perhaps when Ammit had eaten his fill, whatever remained of her would fly up to the sky, and settle somewhere in the cold, distant dark between the stars.

If I find myself there, will I be able to look down on the world? Will I see Akhet-Aten from that distance? The West Bank, where I was a girl, where I still had hope of love and light and a life that was worth the living? Or was the night sky simply too far away, raised too high by the arch of Goddess Nut's cool, dark body?

Large, pale moths flitted around a bower of vines as the fragrant white flowers opened to the night. The green *ba* darted among them, flicking its emerald wings, its black eyes watching, burning in the starlight. *Death is near to me, here in the City of the Sun.* The thought did not frighten her; it was merely a fact to be acknowledged. *It will come for me soon, if it can. My* ba *is eager to fly free—up to the vacant black between the stars. I must hold off death as long as possible, for Tutankhaten's sake—for Egypt's sake.*

The boy was in his chamber now, being readied for bed.

Horemheb was with him as usual, so it was another guard who called softly across the garden to announce a visitor.

"The Lady Mutbenret, my lord Nefer-Neferu-Aten."

Nefertiti's heart leaped into her throat. Her chest swelled with unexpected pain. She stood—the moths scattered at the sudden movement—and gestured for the guard to admit her sister to the garden.

Mutbenret came to her across the blue twilight. She moved in a direct line, a slender, delicate form cleaving the night in her simple, white-linen smock. She stood before Nefertiti and looked at her with eyes as distant as the stars, but she did not bow, did not so much as incline her head in the presence of the king. Nefertiti had had no time to speak to Mutbenret—no courage, in truth—since her return to Akhet-Aten—and she suspected a reunion would not be entirely welcome, at any rate. *I had a little sister once, a shy, biddable girl.* But this was a woman who stood before her, firm and unbent. The luminous stars revealed a tracery of fine lines around Mutbenret's eyes, the marks of age and wisdom just beginning to form. Nefertiti had remembered Mutbenret as a quiet, broken creature—*my doing*, she thought sadly—but now her sister held herself with a poise she had never possessed before.

"'My lord'?" Mutbenret asked when she stood in front of Nefertiti. But there was no wryness, no amusement in her voice. She spoke the words with a hint of scorn.

"I am king now. It's a fitting form of address."

"You have certainly achieved all your ambitions now— you have climbed to the very highest peak of power."

And trampled on you along the way. And on my own dear daughters, may the gods forgive me. Nefertiti did not know what to say. She could think of no words that might answer the bitterness in Mutbenret's voice, and so she kept her silence.

"I will not waste your time with idle talk," Mutbenret said. "Since the king's permission is required, I have come to ask your leave to depart the City of the Sun. I hope you will grant me that one kindness, since you denied me all others."

Don't go. Please, not yet. Allow me to make amends, or to try, at least. "I only just saw you again, for the first time in years—and now you wish to leave?"

"Yes," Mutbenret said flatly. "I feel I must put as much distance as I can between myself and you, Nefertiti. Akhenaten cast me aside; he no longer troubles me. And at any rate, he is mad, and perhaps unaware of the evils he did to me. But you put me in his bed with all your wits about you, knowing full well what I would face."

Nefertiti swallowed hard. Tears stung her eyes, but she made no move to conceal them from her sister. "I was trying to—"

Mutbenret shook her head abruptly. "It doesn't matter now. In any case, I will not listen to your excuses. The past is the past; we cannot change it. But I have no desire to suffer your company in the present."

The truth in what she said—the simple, undeniable *maat*—struck Nefertiti like a blow from a soldier's club. She hung her head, fighting to breathe, to hold the breath of life in her unworthy body. After a long moment, she nodded. "I understand." It was no more than what she deserved. It was a good deal less than what she deserved.

"I would ask one favor more," Mutbenret added, folding her arms across her body, drawing herself up, bracing for a fight. "Let me take Ankhesenpaaten with me."

Nefertiti looked up sharply. "No."

"Why not? I looked after all your children when you were so occupied with your precious Aten temples. I was their true guardian. It was I, not you, who mourned in their tombs as they died one by one. And I am the one who cares for Ankhesenpaaten now. If you ever loved her—if you ever pretended to love her—you will let her go."

"I cannot," Nefertiti said. Her voice was thick in her own ears, her throat tight with self-loathing. "I need her close."

"Close? For what purpose? So you may use her as a pawn, as you did me—as you did Meritaten, and Meketaten?"

That last name stung Nefertiti like a slap to the face. "You will never know how I fought to win Meketaten back from her father's clutches—how I suffered to protect her."

"But you didn't win her back, and you didn't protect her. Not in the end. You failed her, Nefertiti."

Tears broke from their dam and spilled down her cheeks, running hot and fast. "I don't want *that* for Ankhesenpaaten—believe me. I have a kinder fate planned for her. I intend to marry her to Tutankhaten when he comes of age—and when he reaches manhood, Egypt will be a better, more stable place. She will be King's Great Wife and live with ease—as you should have lived, Mutbenret. As all my daughters should have lived."

"There is no such thing as a life of ease in the royal court. This is a place of unending evil. Surely by now you know that is true."

It will not be true for much longer. If the gods will just sustain me... The *ba* flitted past her eye again, and Nefertiti flinched.

"Ankhesenpaaten is a sensitive girl," Mutbenret went on. "She should be spared the horrors of royal life. Let me take her somewhere—someplace distant and secluded. I will see to it that she lives in peace, with the quiet and solitude she craves. Let her go, Nefertiti. Give yourself that one small gift, the knowledge that *one* of your daughters slipped away, and had a chance at happiness."

More than anything, Nefertiti wanted to say yes. A yearning for Ankhesenpaaten's happiness, for her to live an untroubled life, for her to simply *live*, crowded into her heart with such force that she gasped aloud. But she couldn't relent. She lived in service to Tutankhaten now—all her efforts must be for him, if she was to make amends to her dead daughters, if their deaths were not to be in vain. If their short, precious lives were not to be wasted. She must restore the Egypt that was, give it a strong, capable king... or her daughters' *kas* would hate her forever.

"Ankhesenpaaten is..." How could she explain it, in a way that would make Mutbenret see sense? "She is too valuable. Politically. I *cannot* let her go. She is fifteen now; if she leaves Akhet-Aten, meets some common man and marries him, I can never use her to fulfill—"

"Listen to yourself," Mutbenret whispered. "*Use* her. Your own daughter. You are as sick as Akhenaten—sick to your very core."

Nefertiti bore the insult with the best grace she could muster. When she could marshal her voice again, she told Mutbenret gently, "Go now. Before you anger me."

Mutbenret held her eye for a long moment, saying nothing. But volumes of anger, screeds of despair, hung in the air between them. Finally she turned away.

Nefertiti reached out for her as she went, grasping at the place where she had stood. "Wait! Please, sister..."

When Mutbenret paused and turned back, isolated on the garden path, Nefertiti went to her with arms extended, begging silently for an embrace, for forgiveness. But Mutbenret stepped back, denying her touch.

Nefertiti's arms fell like the stone weights of a fisherman's net. "Very well. If this is the way it must be—very well.

You must be gone from Akhet-Aten before the sun comes up. Otherwise—"

"I shall be," Mutbenret said coldly, and left the garden.

NEFERTITI STUMBLED into her bedchamber an hour later, exhausted from her weeping, craving the succor of sleep. But when she saw what awaited her there, she knew the gods had not yet finished punishing her for her sins.

Meritaten was perched on the edge of Nefertiti's bed, trembling and pale-faced, decked in provocative finery that accentuated the fullness of her breasts, the curve of her hip, the smooth, brown expanses of her bare skin.

Nefertiti pawed hastily at her cheeks and eyes, wiping away the last of her tears. She said brusquely, "What is it?"

"I've come to ask for your aid." Meritaten jumped up and paced in agitation. The bangles on her wrists and ankles chimed with every step. "Just as you aided me in the matter of the temple's prisoners. You remember!"

Nefertiti waited, eyeing the girl cautiously.

Finally Meritaten drew a long breath and said, "Akhenaten has sent for me. After so long... he has ordered me to return to his bed."

Nefertiti's heart stilled in her chest. "You are the King's Great Wife. It is your duty."

"Yes, but I love Smenkhkare!" Meritaten's face crumpled; she wept openly, sending the black kohl coursing down her face.

You fool of a girl. But the thought was laden with pity.

"How can I do it, Mother—how can I suffer his touch when I have known true love in Smenkhkare's arms?"

"You have...?" Nefertiti shook her head. "That was

foolish, Meritaten. And terribly dangerous, for both you and the co-regent."

"I know. But I have been so very much *alone* since you left! I didn't intend to love Smenkhkare—it just *happened*. And I cannot undo it now; I cannot change the way I feel about him. And he loves me, too! It will wound him, if I go back to Akhenaten as his amusement, as his whore!"

"Smenkhkare should have been wiser than to allow this. If he takes a wound to his heart, then he is to blame. Not you."

"There must be some way to change Akhenaten's mind." Meritaten reached out for Nefertiti, clung to her hands. "He was always fond of you. Won't you go to him in my place?"

She laughed bitterly. "Look at me, Meritaten. My face may still be attractive, but I am nearly forty years old, and I have borne six children. I will not suffice in his bed. And besides, I am not the King's Wife—not anymore. I am Pharaoh in my own right. It is not my place to entertain Akhenaten."

"You *are* still the King's Wife," Meritaten insisted. "It's even in your throne name—Effective for Her Husband. You can do it... you *must* do it!"

"Do not take that tone with me."

"Why not?" Meritaten dropped her hands and stepped back, eyeing Nefertiti with cold venom. "Isn't it the least of what you owe me?"

"I don't owe you anything," Nefertiti snapped. But she knew full well that she did—that the debt she owed Meritaten and her sisters could never be repaid, no matter how long or hard she labored in that service.

"Oh, don't you! You manipulated me into my father's bed when I was just a girl, too young to understand all it would mean, all I would give up."

"It's no worse than what I suffered. My father did the same to me—used me as his implement to gain more power."

"And you think that excuses you?"

Meritaten's words were too much like Mutbenret's. The pain was too close to Nefertiti's heart, constricting and fierce. She could take no more of this punishment from the gods. Throwing up her hands, anger filling her heart, Nefertiti shouted for her guards. When the men filed in, she pointed coldly at her trembling daughter. "Escort the Great Wife to Pharaoh Akhenaten's chambers. See that she goes in. Meritaten, clean up your kohl. It won't do to be seen like this."

Meritaten gaped at her a moment, then her face reddened with rage. She clenched her fists. "*You* are to blame for my misery. *You* pushed me into this—made me into what I am, a mad king's plaything. I will never forgive you for abandoning me, for selling me to this fate! *Never!*"

"Neither will the gods," Nefertiti assured her. "Now go; your duty waits."

Meritaten pulled herself together, shedding the role of hysterical girl and donning the guise of a royal woman in control of herself, body and *ka*. Even as Nefertiti hardened her expression, driving her out the door, she felt a wave of pride in her daughter, in her natural poise and strength. *Perhaps Smenkhkare was right—perhaps she is more a King's Wife than I ever suspected.*

Closing off her misery in the cage deep within her heart, Meritaten breezed from Nefertiti's apartments, never once looking back at her mother. She went to her odious duty as self-possessed as a goddess.

Meritaten

Year 2 of Smenkhkare,
Holy of the Manifestations

Year 18 of Akhenaten,
Beloved of the Sun

AS MERITATEN STRODE down the brazier-lit hall between her mother's two guards, the fury burned so hot inside that her footsteps might have scorched the tile floor.

"I don't need your escort," she told the guards shortly. "I know the way to the king's chamber."

One of the men ducked his head, bobbing in embarrassment. "Apologies, Great Wife, but Pharaoh Nefer-Neferu-Aten herself commanded—"

"My mother is *not* the Pharaoh!"

Exasperation and awe overwhelmed her, drowning her in equal measure. The loyalty Nefertiti could still command was stunning—loyalty from these men, and from others scattered throughout the palace and the City of the Sun. They believed in her strength, her right to the throne, even after a three-year absence from the court. Against such blind devotion, what could anyone do?

Meritaten quelled her surge of desperation. In the incident of the Temple's prisoners, she had felt a strength come over her she had never known she'd possessed. In that moment she had been a true King's Wife, capable and strong. She had even felt herself worthy of the title of Great Wife. Of course, much of the dealings with the prisoners had been Nefertiti's idea. But it was Meritaten who had carried out the plan. Surely she still had access to that strength, that perfect aplomb.

After the success of the Temple incident, Meritaten had allowed herself to hope that she and Nefertiti might work together, partners united in secret against Akhenaten. But their encounter tonight had proven how false that hope had been. Nefertiti was still the callous manipulator she always had been, still eager to make use of anyone who crossed her path, daughter or not.

With or without Nefertiti, I am still the woman who stood up to Akhenaten and diverted his anger, and changed his mind before he knew what trickery I worked. I will do it again, if I must.

Nefertiti would not win. Nor would Akhenaten. Meritaten had given her heart to Smenkhkare; the god meant them to be together—otherwise, the Aten never would have allowed their love to grow. Nothing would change Meritaten's heart now, nor her resolve to avoid Akhenaten's attentions.

Why, Aten? Why does the king want me now, after ignoring me for so many months? What has recalled me to his thoughts?

She would have given anything to slip away from the guards and avoid Akhenaten's chamber altogether. His desires were always fleeting; with another hour of delay, he would forget he had ever called for her. But the guards were resolute, and cruelly exact in their duty. The high double doors to Akhenaten's apartments loomed at the end of the hall, and Meritaten knew she couldn't turn away now.

Mahu, leering at his post outside Akhenaten's chamber, admitted Meritaten with a quiet snicker. She stormed past him with her chin held high, refusing to give that beast of a man the satisfaction of seeing her cringe.

But the moment the doors were shut behind her— when she was alone in the receiving room of Akhenaten's apartments—the wild, strained light in the Pharaoh's eyes did make her flinch. He was panting with desire already, his teeth bared in a grimace of anticipation. He rushed at her, hands outstretched, and Meritaten's fragile confidence broke.

"Ah," Akhenaten breathed, rubbing her too roughly down the length of one arm.

She couldn't help jerking away. Once his attentions had been noting to her, a dull duty best seen to quickly and forgotten. But now his touch was like the slime in the bottom of an old cistern. She could not bear it, and though she trembled and tears filled her eyes, she would not suffer it, either.

Anger flashed in the Pharaoh's eyes—the same deadly fury he had worn when Meritaten had arrived to rescue the prisoners at the Great Aten Temple. "Hold still," he commanded.

She did, willing herself to remain unmoved, unfeeling, as she had in the old days. He stroked her back, the locks of her wig, and bent close to sniff the myrrh of her perfume.

"I had a wondrous vision," he purred beside her ear. "Those who blasphemed against the god and conspired against me—"

"Do you mean the sacrifice I took from the Temple?" Her voice shook, though she tried to make it as firm as blocks of sandstone. "The ones we cast out into the Red Land?"

"The very ones. I saw them withered and desiccated beneath the rays of judgment!"

Meritaten swallowed the lump in her throat. She hoped it was just his madness, and not a true vision. She thought of Panefer, the old, traditional blessing he had given her, and hoped the innocents had found their way to safety, as Nefertiti had promised they could.

"And I had a better vision still," Akhenaten went on. "I saw two sons—twins—born of your body."

Her eyes widened. She had never been with child; she assumed her womb was as barren as the Red Land itself.

"These children were gods, with golden skin and hair of lapis lazuli. They remained young forever and served at my right hand and my left, while I sat on a throne made of sunlight. Beautiful boys, young and fresh as new-sprouted papyrus fronds."

Meritaten clenched her teeth as her stomach roiled. *If I ever had a child, you would never come within a thousand spans, whether it was a daughter or a son.* But she made herself say placidly, "How wonderful."

"Yes—a glorious vision! A true vision! The god has blessed you with ever more insight, Meritaten. Your powers and holiness grow. You were well-named: Beloved of the Aten. Surely the god loves you well, and now that you are flowering into the station of a High Priestess, the Aten will allow my seed to take root within this field."

He laid a hand on her belly. His touch was surprisingly gentle at first, almost tender. Then his fingers clenched, digging into her flesh. Meritaten cried out and spun away from him, rubbing at her bruised skin.

"Do not deny me!" Akhenaten shouted.

"You were hurting me!"

"The Aten will not allow you to feel pain, if your faith is pure and true. I feel no pain anymore when I stand beneath its rays. I feel only warmth, only light."

Meritaten blinked back her tears, taking in his darkened skin, thick and deep-lined as worn leather. He had been far too long in the sun; the light and heat had addled what little remained of his sanity.

Akhenaten advanced, reaching out to touch her again, and Meritaten cringed away from him. She tried to marshal her power, the strength of a Great Wife. She tried to recall how brave she had felt when she had crossed the sands of the Temple to face him on his throne. But this was different. Alone with him, knowing what he wanted—what he would use her body for—she had never felt less powerful in all her eighteen years.

He seized her by one arm, shook her so hard her teeth rattled. "We must fulfill the vision! The twin boys—my golden servants! They are waiting in the god's light, waiting to come to me. Go into the bed chamber and undress."

"No!" The word ripped from Meritaten's throat with such passion she knew she never could have held it back, even if she had tried. The denial surprised her at least as much as it shocked Akhenaten. He stared at her blankly for one heartbeat; Meritaten trembled. But she made herself speak. "No. I cannot do this. I will not!"

"Why?" He loomed close, his eyes flicking over her face, her body, narrowed and suspicious. Then, quick as a cobra, his hand flashed down and pulled up her skirt. Meritaten screamed in fear and outrage, hitting his hand away, letting the linen fall again. But he had already seen. "This is not your bleeding time. So why do you deny me? Why do you deny the will of the god itself?"

"It is *not* the will of the god," she said, her voice thick and harsh with conviction. "If you trust the truth of my visions, if you believe in my power as a priestess, then you must believe me when I say that I have seen nothing of—"

"You are not High Priestess yet."

Meritaten grasped desperately for some defense. "But Nefertiti *is* still High Priestess of the Sun." She held still and silent for a few ragged heartbeats, waiting for the king to deny it—but he did not.

Nor did he mention Nefertiti's madness, her unseemly presumption of kingship. *Perhaps he doesn't know*, Meritaten thought, stricken with wonder and possibility. *Perhaps he doesn't yet realize that she has set herself up as king. Perhaps he hasn't yet heard—or if he has, his visions and greedy desires have already made him forget.*

She ventured, "And as your High Priestess, Nefertiti has finally returned to Akhet-Aten. Surely *she* is the one to bear your golden twins, not I."

"But you are of my own blood, my own seed! Through you, their bloodline will be pure."

Her confidence grew—by only the breadth of a cat's whisker, but it was just enough. "It is true that I am your own daughter. Yet I have never been blessed with a child. Nefertiti, though... she has borne you many healthy children. It's her womb the god favors, not mine."

"Many children," Akhenaten mused darkly. "I have seen her now and then, going about the palace in the evenings, after the sun has set. Who is that boy she keeps at her side?"

"He... he is your own son," Meritaten said, confused. "Didn't you know? He is your child, the one you got from Baketaten."

The Pharaoh jumped at the sound of Baketaten's name, turning in a quick circle, darting looks into the shadows of his chamber. "Don't," he hissed. "Don't say it. She will hear you."

"No. She will not hear me. She is dead in her tomb; she can't hurt you. And the boy with Nefertiti is your own child—your heir! She raises him as if he were her own. What more proof do you need that Nefertiti is the one who must bear your sacred twins?"

His fear discarded for the moment, Akhenaten stroked her shoulder. "But Nefertiti is not as beautiful as you. Not anymore."

He leaned closer, his mouth diving for her own. Meritaten shoved away from his kiss. "I won't!"

The king's hand flashed up from below, grabbing her so hard by the jaw that she thought the bones would break. He stared deep into her eyes, searching, and Meritaten had the nauseating sensation that he could see into her very *ka*. "What are you hiding? Why this sudden aversion to my touch?"

"Sudden?" Clamped in his grip, she spoke with difficulty. "You have ignored me for nearly a year! You do not want me anymore! Let us part ways as bedmates, knowing it is best for us both."

He released her jaw; she gasped and kneaded her tender flesh with one hand, trying to soothe away the ache. But in another moment he grabbed for her again. It was her breast this time—and he seized it so hard that she cried out in pain as well as revulsion.

"But I *do* want you," Akhenaten hissed. "And the god wants it. You must obey the god, and you must obey me."

Meritaten kicked him hard, the sole of her sandal catching him just below his knee. He bellowed in pain, but he released her, and she twisted out of his reach.

"I must *not* obey you. There are more kings than just you now. Smenkhkare is my king—and even Nefertiti is a better Pharaoh than you! You will never touch me again! I'll *die* before I'll allow it!"

Akhenaten advanced, his furious breath grating in his throat, his eyes as hot as coals in a burning brazier. With a flutter of her heart, Meritaten remembered the stories she had heard about Sitamun, his own sister and wife. She had died alone in Akhenaten's chamber, a victim of his rage. Would he kill her now, too?

But before he could seize her, Akhenaten stopped short, staring at her quizzically. "What did you say? About Nefertiti?"

The sudden flux of his mood, from rage to idle curiosity,

lit the wick of Meritaten's anger. She exploded at him, flailing her fists in the air, screaming. "You're such a *fool*! A mad, blind fool! Nefertiti has come back to the city, and set herself up as king! She rules here now like Hatshepsut! She has taken the Pharaoh's throne! She wields the boy like a dagger against her enemies! Through that boy, she keeps Smenkhkare's power at bay—Smenkhkare, your own co-regent! Soon enough she will move on you, too, and by then she'll have all the palace, all the city in the palm of her hand! You'll not be able to stop her. She is more powerful than—"

Akhenaten's roar of rage silenced her. Meritaten braced for his strike, certain her life had reached its wild, bloody end. But he turned and sped from Meritaten, bulling through his chamber doors and out into the hall, shoving past Mahu, storming through a group of startled stewards and maids.

Meritaten and Mahu both stood stunned for a moment, holding each other's wide, startled eyes. Then they rushed after the king together, Meritaten hoisting the hem of her thin, revealing dress high enough to run in Akhenaten's wake. Guards at other posts along the way joined them as they passed, leaving their duties to trail after the screaming, raging king. But no one dared touch Akhenaten, or stop him. As he ran, he shouted for Nefertiti, demanding she come out and face him—face the judgment of her husband. His howls rattled and rang high among the pillars, like birds trapped within the palace walls.

When Akhenaten reached Nefertiti's wing of the palace, she was already waiting for him, standing coolly at her apartment door, observing the Pharaoh's rage with detached unconcern. The guard Horemheb stood close beside her, and Nann held Tutankhaten protectively in the doorway, just behind Nefertiti.

Akhenaten stumbled to a halt, face to face with Nefertiti. He panted harshly, his shoulders heaving with his effort and with the heat of his fury. "So you think to steal my throne, you vile bitch!"

"It is not your throne," Nefertiti said calmly. "The gods have given it to me, by right of my strength and competence."

"The *gods*! There is but one god, and I am its vessel in the mortal world!"

"Oh, are you?" One kohl-dark eyebrow raised. "Divine? But I think not, Akhenaten. I am certain you would bleed, if one were to cut deep enough."

Akhenaten clawed at the air between them, struck mute for one moment by the audacity of Nefertiti's words. But he found his voice again, strangled though it was by hate. "You dare to threaten the Aten's chosen one?"

She took one easy step toward him. "I am not afraid of you." And as Meritaten watched the scene with unfold with growing horror, she realized with envy that her mother's words were true.

"You are a false king, a pretender," Akhenaten grated. "And a blasphemer! Meritaten knows what I do with blasphemers! She can tell you; she knows!"

Nefertiti cast a faintly amused glance at Meritaten, then sniffed a wordless dismissal of the king.

Akhenaten's molten gaze skated past her, to Tutankhaten, who clung to Nann's neck but did not cry, did not fuss in her arms. "Meritaten tells me you use this boy like a dagger, to threaten and secure your way. He is an instrument of your blasphemies!"

"How dare you," Nefertiti snapped. "He is your own son, and heir to your throne."

"I have no use for sons. I need only females to propagate my divine seed. Watch how easily I defang you, Nefertiti— the bitch who would be king! Mahu, take the boy. And kill him."

Meritaten screamed. She grappled with Mahu, clinging to his arm, trying to drag him back with her slight weight, with the force of her sudden regret and fear. But Mahu flicked his arm as if she were no more than a fly, and Meritaten stumbled backward, her shoulder and back colliding painfully with a pillar.

Mahu slunk toward Nann and the child, smooth and deadly as a stalking leopard. Nann shrank back against Nefertiti's door; her hiss was like a cobra defending her nest, but the woman was no more substantial than Meritaten. Mahu would put her out of the way just as easily.

Horemheb stepped in Mahu's path. Nefertiti moved with him, shielding Tutankhaten with her poised, confident body.

She looked Mahu in the eye as he reached for the child. "Are you so corrupted, Mahu, that you will commit the most terrible crime of all? If you want this boy, you will have to strike down the king of Egypt. Do it now, if you dare. Do it, and throw your eternal *ka* in Ammit's mouth." She spread her arms wide, offering him her undefended chest, her belly. "Do it, if you dare."

Horemheb

Year 1 of Nefer-Neferu-Aten,
Effective for Her Husband

Year 18 of Akhenaten,
Beloved of the Sun

HOREMHEB SAW the hard, cold light in Mahu's eyes dim as he hesitated, face to face with Nefertiti. Her words hung like a thick river fog in Horemheb's heart. *Strike down the king of Egypt. Do it, if you dare.*

Time slowed and contracted. Mahu's dagger slid from its sheath with terrible, unstoppable slowness, its blade singing on a long, hissing note.

Do it, if you dare.

This was Horemheb's chance—the only chance he would have. This was his one opportunity to reach Akhenaten when he was vulnerable, standing apart, devoid of his ever-present guard's protection. It was the moment Horemheb had waited for since he had cradled Baketaten's shattered body in his arms.

Don't think, he told himself even as he side-stepped, as he lunged past Mahu with the furious drive of a falcon striking its prey. *Don't think about the consequences. Consequences be damned...* As his own *ka* would be damned. For Horemheb knew this was the ultimate evil, the invitation of chaos that could unmake the world. And yet he knew it must be done. Who in this blighted family, this shadowed palace, would avenge the woman he loved, if not him?

His dagger sprang eagerly from its sheath, leaping to his hand. He was on Akhenaten in two purposeful strides. The blade flashed golden in the light of brazier flames as he brought it up with a smooth, powerful stroke. Akhenaten had no more than a heartbeat to react—to see that death had come for him. The Pharaoh emitted a high, strangled scream, a squeal like a beast in a trap. He tried to scurry backward, away from the dagger that thrust toward him with the inevitable force of *maat*.

But there was no escape. Horemheb drove hard at his hateful target, ramming the dagger up beneath Akhenaten's breastbone, through the robe and loose flesh, past bone that shivered along the blade into the sinews of Horemheb's own body. When dagger met heart, he felt Akhenaten's shudder ring through him like the blow of a temple's gong. And though he knew in that moment that he was damned, still he rejoiced when the king's hot blood spilled out over his hand.

Akhenaten's eyes were wide with shock, glazed with the death he could not evade. He stared into Horemheb's face with an expression of piteous fear.

Meritaten screamed again, a loud, harsh shriek of pure panic that must have torn her throat raw. The few female servants who had huddled in the colonnade to watch the confrontation joined her, and soon the palace hall filled with a clamor of sound—the screams of the women, shouts of disbelief from guardsmen and stewards, the frightened cries of Tutankhaten—who had never seen such violence, never seen blood like this, pouring like a fountain, running thick and red along the tiles.

The screams distracted Mahu from his task. He spun, his blade up to defend the king—but too late. Far too late. He watched in horror as Horemheb jerked his blade free, as Akhenaten toppled, face-down in his own pooling blood, twitching at his guard's feet.

Horemheb dropped the dagger beside Akhenaten. It was useless to him now. As Mahu overcame his shock and lunged, Horemheb grappled with his sword's hilt, but his hand was too slick with blood; he could not get a sure grip. He darted back and to the side; Mahu followed, slipping, unsteady on the spill of blood that grew with each slowing pulse of the king's dying heart.

That's it, Horemheb thought grimly, still struggling to wield his sword well enough to fight. *Forget Tutankhaten. Come at me, and fight a real man—a man brave enough and foolish enough to kill a king.*

The crowd of terrified onlookers grew rapidly as servants and ambassadors rushed down the hall toward the shouts and screams. Scribes and soldiers raised the alarm. Mahu lunged at Horemheb and he fell back; the crowd shrieked as the two combatants plunged into their midst. Bodies pressed and jostled, hands tearing at clothes; in the panic, decorum was forgotten and prayers for mercy and deliverance were shouted up to outlawed gods.

"Not here!" Horemheb shouted as Mahu's blade hissed toward his belly. He parried it with a clumsy slap of his uncertain sword. "Let these people go—let them clear a way!"

"Save your breath," Mahu panted, "for when the god makes you plead for mercy!"

A shout cracked down the hall, ringing with authority. "Stop!"

But Mahu did not cease; Horemheb's sword hilt slid in his fist, threatening to fall.

As he parried desperately, Horemheb saw a hand flash out from the crowd, a hand glinting with rings of gold and precious stone. It landed on Mahu's bull shoulder, pulling him back, restraining him.

"Your king commands you to stop! Mahu! Drop your blade!"

Mahu subsided, lowering his dagger slowly, his glaring

eyes locked with Horemheb's. Horemheb could feel the fire of his hatred, flaring and hot. But Smenkhkare pulled Mahu back, back, away from Horemheb—while a cadre of guards moved quickly to take Horemheb into custody.

Smenkhkare, pale-faced, looked down at Akhenaten's flat, still body, a gruesome island in a sea of blood. "What is this? What have you done?"

Every voice in the hall fell silent, save for Meritaten's frantic weeping, her shivering, hysterical wails. Smenkhkare found her huddled against a pillar, pressing her face against the stone as if to shut out the terrible sight of the Pharaoh slain. He pulled the King's Wife into his arms, murmuring in her ear until her cries ceased and her sobs faded. But as she looked up from Smenkhkare's embrace, her kohl-smeared eyes found Horemheb, staring at him as if he were a crocodile loosed among them.

Horemheb turned to Nefertiti for—what? Support? Approval? —but even she looked stunned, blinking at him in dull shock as if he had just batted the sun from the sky.

It was Nefertiti's face that drove home to Horemheb the full weight of his act, its staggering enormity. His mistress—always so sharp and clever, always thinking, watching, knowing—stared at him with the vacancy of a sun-struck goat. He had terrified the wits out of her— even her, Nefertiti, the strong and implacable.

By Horus, Horemheb told himself. And then more darkly, *By Set. What have I done to my* ka? *What have I done to Egypt?*

He let his sword fall with a jarring clang and raised his hands in surrender. He would accept whatever blow the gods saw fit to deal him. There was no denying the truth, no escaping his fate. He was a king-killer, and damned forever.

Y OU DID *WHAT?*" Mutnodjmet's face blanched in horror. Her hands flew up to cover her mouth.

Horemheb, escorted by far more guards than necessary, had been dragged roughly to his chamber and shut inside, the guards barring the door and patrolling outside the room's one small window. He would not be allowed to leave—nor would Mutnodjmet—until his punishment could be determined. Certainly he could not expect to live—what hope did a king-killer have of mercy?—but he hoped Smenkhkare would show mercy toward his wife. Mutnodjmet had played no part in the terrible act. She hadn't even come out into the hall when she heard the shouts and screams; a sensible woman, she had stayed inside, even hiding herself in the wardrobe until the clamor had settled. For her to die along with Horemheb would be a terrible injustice. He offered up a hasty prayer to Horus, to Mother Mut, that they would inspire leniency in the Pharaoh's heart.

But he couldn't speak the words again—couldn't admit the crime. Not to Mutnodjmet. "I... Akhenaten..."

She turned away from him, gaping, speechless with disbelief. She walked to their bed slowly, like a woman in the grip of a magician's spell, and sat on the edge of the mattress, staring at the chamber's wall.

"I'm sorry," Horemheb offered. A dim, distant part of him wanted to laugh at the apology. If ever a thing could be called inadequate...!

Mutnodjmet said softly, "I should think you are."

"We must... we must stay here for now. Until Smenkhkare decides..." He trailed off. There was no need to finish the thought. "I don't know exactly who is guarding our door, but I wouldn't be surprised to learn it's Mahu. He wanted me dispatched at once, but Smenkhkare wouldn't allow it. The king wants to consult before..."

"Consult? With whom?" Mutnodjmet did not seem truly interested. They were just words to say, a distraction from the terrible weight of fate that was bearing down on them both.

Horemheb shrugged awkwardly. "Priests? Nobles?"

Mutnodjmet turned her face toward him, but not her eyes. She seemed incapable of looking at him, of acknowledging that he was in fact her husband and had truly done this terrible thing. *If only I could comfort her,* Horemheb thought miserably. *If I could spend one last tender moment with her, before I am brought to justice.* She was a good woman, admirable—brave and loyal—and he loved her, even if he didn't have for her the same fatal passion he had for Baketaten, the brutal, demanding love that had made him cast his own *ka* into the flames. But the guards were just outside his door, and anyway, Mutnodjmet couldn't even look into his face. How could she suffer the touch of a damned man?

Horemheb sank onto a stool beside their little round dining table and waited. There were no thoughts in his heart save resignation; no hope he would be spared. There was a blunt, uncomfortable throb inside him, a hard stone of anger pressing against his heart. Anger at Baketaten—how could she have placed such a spell on him? How could she have made this demand, from beyond her cold, dark tomb, to destroy himself for her sake? And anger at himself, too, for he could have chosen another path. Instead, he had foolishly leaped into Ammit's mouth for the sake of a dead woman's memory.

An hour of silence passed—perhaps more. There was a rustle and stamp outside their chamber door, the sound of guards snapping to attention. Horemheb rose from the stool, his joints aching from the long spell of inactivity. Death had come for him, and he found it was almost a relief. At least now he would suffer no longer with the waiting.

He expected some lieutenant, perhaps even a general. But when the door opened, Smenkhkare himself stood in the threshold, his brows lowered, his mouth pressed in a hard line.

Horemheb bowed low, and heard Mutnodjmet hasten to do the same. "My lord."

"May I come in?" Smenkhkare said. There was a hint of a sigh in his words.

"This is your palace," Horemheb said, confused. Was he not to be dragged away, then, to a prison or to the temple? "You may go where you please."

Smenkhkare entered, pushing the door shut behind him. "My palace in full now. I'm the co-regent no longer." He didn't sound thankful—only resigned.

"Mutnodjmet, bring the king some wine."

Confused and startled, she hurried to do as Horemheb asked. She blushed when the Pharaoh took the cup from her hands.

"Meritaten is weeping," Smenkhkare said. He drank a long draft from the cup, then abandoned it on the table. "I don't know whether she cries from grief or happiness. She bore no love for her father and husband. None of us did."

Horemheb shifted his weight uncomfortably, staring down at his feet. "What will be done with me, my lord? I would rather know straight away, and not drag out this torment any longer."

Smenkhkare nodded thoughtfully. "I have decided to disband Akhet-Aten. I will move the court back to Waset, the original seat of power—where the king dwelt even before the days of the West Bank. It is not good, for the Pharaoh to think he is better than any common man. I will take Tutankhaten with me. I don't want you to worry on the boy's account. I will treat him gently. He is my own son, after all."

An unexpected pain wrenched his heart at the news. Whatever his feelings now for Baketaten, Horemheb still felt a great sense of duty toward her little son. He didn't like to be parted from him, didn't like to surrender him to Smenkhkare. Father or not, the king didn't know Tutankhaten as well as Horemheb and Nefertiti did.

Smenkhkare paused, examining Horemheb in silence. His gaze was not unkind, not unsympathetic, and it seemed to reach so deep into Horemheb's *ka* that it squeezed around his heart. "Baketaten," Smenkhkare finally said, "my son's mother... she was a great and pious woman. She loved the gods—the *true* gods—and Egypt, more than anything else. She put her duty before the desires of her heart. There are few people in the world who can claim such devotion. For her sake, and in her memory, I will keep Tutankhaten safe. Do not fear for him."

Horemheb closed his eyes, fighting the sudden welling of tears. "You can't possibly keep a child safe in this vile, blood-stained court. There is no safety here."

"Not even for kings, it seems." Smenkhkare sounded almost amused. "But I have made up my mind, brave and reckless Horemheb. Tutankhaten will remain with me."

"What about Nefertiti? She is a king now, too."

Smenkhkare laughed abruptly. "The gods won't suffer a woman pharaoh—not anymore. These aren't the days of the conquerors; times have changed. Nefertiti and her ambitions are problems that will solve themselves. I have faith in the gods; let them see to it."

Horemheb lifted his gaze from the floor. He studied the king's face in silence. It was clear from the small, dry smile, the arch of his brows, that Smenkhkare thought Nefertiti's reckless ambition would lead her straight to her death—or that she would simply give up once he took Tutankhaten away. But Horemheb had come to know

Nefertiti well during the years he had spent in her service. If Smenkhkare disregarded her power or her ability, he did so at his own peril.

The Pharaoh turned toward the door. Mutnodjmet made a small sound of fear in her throat, reaching out toward the king. Horemheb said quickly, "My lord, please. What is to become of me?"

Smenkhkare paused with his hand on the latch. "You have done a great service to Egypt, Horemheb. You put the needs of the many ahead of your own interests." He shrugged. "Or perhaps I mistake you, and credit you too much. Perhaps you acted out of base hatred, and thought only of vengeance. But in either case, *maat* has been served. I fear it's at the expense of your own eternal *ka*, but still— *maat* has been served. You are free to go wherever you will, with one exception. You must not come to Waset, to meddle with my court and my son. I have a plan, you see: a vision to undo all the damage my family has done. I will revive true kingship in the Two Lands, and rule Egypt the way it longs to be ruled. I fear your new status as a king-killer—and whatever motives direct you to hover over Tutankhaten—will only get in my way."

"We can go?" Mutnodjmet's cry was breathless with disbelief. "Horemheb is not to be killed?"

"That is so, my lady. Go with my blessing, but heed my warning, too. Your husband must stay well clear of Waset. This is the only warning I will give you."

Moving as one, as if the same *ka* dwelt in their bodies, Horemheb and Mutnodjmet fell on their knees and kissed the hem of his kilt.

"Rise," Smenkhkare said abruptly, stepping back from their gratitude. "Make your peace with the gods, Horemheb. You will need whatever mercy they may grant you."

Ankhesenamun

Year 1 of Horemheb
Holy Are the Manifestations,
Chosen of Re

I T WAS MY MOTHER who told me Akhenaten was dead. She came to me in my bed chamber, where I was practicing the harp when I should have been preparing for sleep. I will never forget the way she looked when she stood in my doorway, how the light of my two small lamps illuminated her face, accentuating the high cheekbones, the thin nose, the dark, piercing eyes. She was still beautiful, but the years of her life had been hard, and she looked aged and tired in the deep-golden underlight of the lamps. Yet through her obvious weariness, a light of triumph shone. I set down my harp on the cushion beside me and waited, watching her as she stood, watching me. I expected some momentous news, though I couldn't imagine what it might be.

Finally Nefertiti left my door and came to me. She sank onto another of the cushions strewn across my floor, close by my side. "Your father is dead," she said, her voice weak with relief. "Ankhesenpaaten—thank the gods, you are safe."

I heard the rest of her words, the unspoken ones: *One of my daughters is safe—one of six, the gods damn me. In this trap of power which the gods made for me, I let the rest of my children suffer and die. But at least not all were lost.*

I did not know how to answer her. I only looked at her,

waiting to see what she would do next. She sat straight for a long moment, holding my gaze. Then all the strength left her—mask of regal poise wilting like a spent flower, body drooping. She fell slowly to the side, like a tree felled when the *rekhet* clear a field for planting. Her cheek came to rest on my leg. She lay in absolute stillness, and did not make a sound. But after a time I felt dampness soaking the linen of my night-dress, and I knew that she was weeping.

I was a young woman, but I had reached fifteen years. How I managed to escape my father's notice for so long, I will never know.

Smenkhkare wasted no time mobilizing the court. He and Meritaten moved the seat of government back to its traditional home of Waset—not to the West Bank, where the generations before us dwelt apart from their subjects, but into the city itself, in the thick of Egyptian life. The old palace—home of the conquering kings named Thutmose, and home, too, to Hatshepsut, the woman who reigned as king—still stood in Waset, not far from the temples which had once teemed with devotees to the old gods.

While Smenkhkare waited for word that the historic palace was finally ready to receive him, I spent my last few days with Meritaten, watching her spin and frolic in the garden, hearing her songs of pure, matchless joy. She was finally free to love Smenkhkare, and to be loved in return without fear of punishment. It was all she had ever wanted.

I was happy for my sister, even if I thought she was a fool who couldn't see beyond the tip of her own nose. But my happiness could only reach so far. I knew that Egypt's needs must come before the whims of any woman's heart, no matter how long or how terribly that woman had suffered. There was a quiet fear in me, a creeping caution on Meritaten's behalf. She was a King's Daughter and a King's Wife. The gods had never made her for happiness— as they never made me for happiness. We were made to tend Egypt. That purpose was the debt we paid in exchange for our privileged lives. I feared that her happiness would soon be tempered, that reality and duty would strike her, with a blow like a soldier's club. But there was no use in telling her. She wouldn't hear of it. Her *ka* been imprisoned too long. Free to fly now, it stretched its brilliant wings and soared, far beyond the reach of sensibility.

Meritaten hardly spoke to our mother while the Waset palace was being readied. I think Nefertiti would have tried to build a road into her eldest daughter's heart, but Meritaten was thoroughly embittered. She would not hear of making amends. Whenever Nefertiti tried to approach us in the garden, or while we gossiped together in our chambers, Meritaten would simply get up and walk away, right in the midst of speaking. Such rebuffs always left my mother with a pained expression, but she seemed all the more grateful that I, at least, was willing to offer my forgiveness.

At last the day came when Smenkhkare would move his court to Waset. He left with Tutankhaten—Nefertiti let the boy go with only a little regret, understanding the wisdom in parting with him, now that Akhenaten was no threat to anyone. Smenkhkare, we all understood, was a gentler soul than our bloodline had ever before produced. He would ensure the heir to the throne was kept safe and treated well.

With Tutankhaten gone, Nefertiti turned her attention to me. I was a resource nearly as valuable as Tutankhaten himself: the last marriageable daughter of the royal blood, and the best possible choice for Tutankhaten's Great Wife. Nefertiti tended me like the treasure I was, nurturing me with all her time and attention.

I do not think I flatter myself too much when I say that I am not now—and never was—a fool. Even as a girl of fifteen, I understood that I was first and foremost a tool to Nefertiti, just as Tutankhaten had been—as most people were. But despite my obvious value and utility, she treated me with great affection. What was more to me, I could read all her regrets plainly on her face, every time we spoke— and could see, too, that she would never recover from the loss of my sisters, never forgive herself for leaving us. That regret seemed a peace offering between us, a promise of amends to be made. And my *ka* longed for my mother's love, despite her aloofness and her preoccupation with politics. So I accepted my usefulness, my fate as a pawn in the games she played. My acceptance of our hard reality allowed me to cherish the time we spent together.

With the borders of Akhet-Aten open at last, it didn't take long for most of its citizens to leave. Life ran out of the City of the Sun like water from a shattered pot. Only a few people remained—here and there a handful of nobles who supported Nefer-Neferu-Aten in her unorthodox claim to the throne; and of course, many priests of the Aten Temples remained. I supposed then, as I do still, that the Aten priests stayed to worship their cold, distant god not because they felt any great affiliation with that religion, but because they could not countenance the things they had done in the Aten's name. If they abandoned their faith and went back to the old gods, they would be forced to confront many dire atrocities. But if they maintained the cult of the Aten, they could rationalize what they had done. I cannot blame them for it. They were put into as hard a position as ever my sisters and I were. We all do what we must, for the sake of our hearts and *kas*.

Ay was among the first citizens to leave. He supported Smenkhkare as Pharaoh, and now that Smenkhkare had possession of the heir, Ay cleaved to the most obvious power. Such was ever his way. But I think something else spurred his departure. He was eager to be away from Nefertiti. Those who were loyal to our new female king were *fiercely* loyal, and Ay was growing older. The moment her lifelong hatred of Ay was known to her followers,

Akhet-Aten would have offered him no refuge.

Mahu, too, followed Smenkhkare to Waset—though by the king's orders, not by his own choice. Smenkhkare suspected the brutal guard of many crimes, including Baketaten's death, but he had no evidence to prove his guilt in any wrongdoing. He wanted Akhenaten's hound kept close, on a tight and restrictive leash, where he could be carefully watched—and hopefully controlled.

Horemheb and his wife stayed at Nefertiti's side. They could not go to Waset, of course—or at least, Horemheb could not. But all the rest of the Two Lands remained open to him, and he might have chosen any favorable clime he pleased, put any distance imaginable between himself and the palace where he had witnessed so many terrible deeds—and committed one of his own. But now his life seemed inextricably bound to Nefertiti's. It had hurt him badly to let Tutankhaten go, but the debt he felt he still owed to Nefertiti, who had taken him in and given him new purpose when he thought he had none, could not be easily discharged. He suspected—as we all did—that the gods had yet more planned for the woman who was king. Though her devotees were loyal, they were relatively few, and Horemheb knew Nefertiti needed a protector.

Horemheb's decision to remain with Nefertiti did not truly surprise me. But Nann's did. She did not feel Tadukhepa was properly avenged—after all, Mahu still walked free, the one whom she could be certain had made her mistress suffer. She might also have given up her dark mission and returned home to Mitanni, if she wished. But she was not eager to leave Nefertiti's side, any more than Horemheb was. I often tried to discern her reasons, to make sense of her dark, brooding ways. But Nann was a scroll that refused to be read.

She was an endless source of fascination to me in those days. Now that the Aten's power was rapidly declining, she was quite unabashed about worshiping her frightening

196

goddess Ishtar, whose fearsome clawed feet and eagle's wings both drew me in and repulsed me. Once—one of the many times I questioned Nann about her decision to remain in the City of the Sun—she told me that she stayed because she liked to watch the place die, liked to see it empty a little more each day, and liked most of all to watch its memories crumbing and blowing away in the dust and debris of the empty, untended gardens. Besides, she added, showing the gap of her missing tooth in a mysterious smile, Ishtar had revealed to her that she would take revenge on Mahu—but not yet. Nann was patient and faithful enough to bide her time, until the goddess told her to strike.

Why some of the others remained in Akhet-Aten, I shall never know. A few merchants, a few builders and artisans, bakers and brewers. The City of the Sun stood on a terrible scrap of land, infertile and sere. Surely by remaining, these common people were reminded each day of the very worst of times. Perhaps, like the nobles, they saw in Nefertiti the makings of a true king, and understood how desperately Egypt needed her strength and wisdom.

Whatever their reasons, they provided Pharaoh Nefer-Neferu-Aten with a tiny kingdom all her own. The power itself meant nothing to Nefertiti. But it was useful to her—useful to me. She used that small, self-contained kingdom as my school, taking advantage of the palace, the miniature court, the modest trade that still flowed in and out of Akhet-Aten, to teach me how to rule. We stayed at Akhet-Aten for nearly a year, and little by little I took the reins of power while my mother carefully shaped and guided me, grooming me for the role I must someday play as Great Wife to Tutankhaten. And as I further honed my already keen skills of observation, I came to see that Nefertiti was waiting for something I could not yet understand—some sign from divinity, some alignment of the stars. She was as patient and keen a watcher as Nann, who waited for

Ishtar's sign.

Once, as I roamed the dying, withered gardens of the palace, I found my mother weeping beneath a bower of crackling brown vines, calling out for Meritaten. The image rent my heart. I, too, missed my sister, though I had always thought her vain and reckless. But later that very night Nefertiti summoned me to her chamber, and I listened as she and Horemheb discussed how they might seize Tutankhaten on his throne, and how they might contrive to put Meritaten out of the way. I think by that time my mother knew her eldest daughter was a threat to Egypt's stability. Meritaten was not brave enough, not strong enough to rule. Suddenly my mother's tears in the garden made a grim, terrible sense. She had been contemplating how to seize and dispose of her own child—one of only two who remained to her. It's a terrible thing for a mother to face. Even a mother as hardened as mine.

That night I resolved to make myself a lioness—strong, with unflagging courage, and with wisdom to match Nefertiti's own. For I understood that if I ever proved disappointing or too weak to rule, Nefertiti would put me out of the way, too, and find some other woman to take my place at Tutankhaten's side. She loved me, as she loved Meritaten. But she loved Egypt more—as was fitting, for a king.

My resolve had nothing to do with my own desire for power. I did not want it—but I accepted it as my lot in life, the task the gods had bred me to perform. I never could have cared less for ruling Egypt—but I wanted my mother's approval, more than anything else in the world.

There in the dry, hot wreckage of the City of the Sun, we all awaited the signs that would call us back to battle, back to power—Nefertiti, Nann, and I. Then, just before the third year of Smenkhkare's reign dawned, dire news reached Akhet-Aten in a letter bearing Ay's seal—and my mother knew our time had come.

Meritaten

Year 2 of Smenkhkare
Holy of the Manifestations,
Living Appearance of the Sun

THE SILENCE IN Smenkhkare's bed chamber was absolute, save for the soft sighs of the king's breath. Meritaten held his hand, counting the rise and fall of his chest. Each inhalation was weaker than the last, the exhaled breaths fading. A gentle afternoon light fell in through the windcatchers and through the garden door, opened to admit a healing breeze. The golden softness of the sun's lowering rays fell on his body like a mantle, like a comforting blanket.

It had been four days since Smenkhkare had fallen. He'd been descending the dais of his throne at the end of a court session when, without the least warning, his left leg had given out beneath him. He fell hard to the slick malachite floor, which seemed in that moment the dark, murky depths of a crocodile pool, from which any fierce, thrashing danger might emerge to haul him below the surface. Meritaten had run to him, of course, and tried to help him to his feet. But his leg as well as his arm defied him, weak and nearly paralyzed, gripped by some power beyond his control. As Meritaten bent over him, Smenkhkare had tried to smile at her in reassurance. But the left side of his mouth would not curve, and when he spoke his words were scattered and senseless.

The court had reacted at once, calling in physicians and magic-workers to cast out whatever demons possessed the Pharaoh. He did not seem to be in pain, which was a blessing. But his inability to speak with any clarity terrified Meritaten, as did the way his face drooped on the left side, like beeswax half-melted in the sun.

For four long days, Meritaten had stayed at his bedside, listening in misery as the physicians discussed the strange ailment. They had seen the same ill spirit take men and women before, but never had they seen a man so young afflicted in this way—though one of the physicians had read of a similar case, a girl of no more than ten years who lived far to the north, in the Delta. That anomaly aside, this was an ailment reserved for the old. The king was a man in the prime of his years, not a doddering old grandfather with bent back and bald head.

The physicians had at least reassured Meritaten that these patients sometimes recovered—even the spectacularly old ones, bouncing back with nearly all their faculties restored when the right spells and chants were applied. That had given her hope as she kept her vigil at Smenkhkare's side. But as the days passed, he seemed to grow weaker, his heart farther away than ever before, his body weak, his wits feeble and scattered.

Now he would not wake at all—had not opened his eyes since early that morning, when he had watched the darkness fade through his garden door, watched the night graying into day with an expression that was solemn and sad. She clutched his hand and wept, praying for the god's mercy, wishing she could return to happier times and relive the months since their arrival in Waset. Everything had seemed restored, *maat* finally come to stay in her life. They celebrated their great joy in one another before the whole world, unashamed and rejoicing. She had even hoped she might bear him a child—but it seemed the Aten in its inscrutable wisdom still saw fit to leave her womb as barren as a sandy field. Instead of giving the king a son from her own body, Meritaten had thrown herself into caring for Tutankhaten, taking the part of the boy's mother. Not because she bore any special love for Tutankhaten—she did it because it made Smenkhkare happy.

At least the boy had made her work as substitute mother easy. He was bright and kind-hearted, eager to please, as easy a child as any woman could hope to raise. But though she did her best to care for him, Meritaten couldn't help feeling a faint resentment whenever he was near. He was Baketaten's boy—Baketaten, who had given Smenkhkare the one thing Meritaten could not.

Spirits often hung close when a death was near, and with a sharp stab of terrible acceptance, Meritaten knew Smenkhkare would die soon. *I must not think ill of Baketaten now.* If Meritaten thought of the woman—if Baketaten was watching—then Baketaten's spirit might draw too near and be trapped here... and her *ba* would haunt Meritaten, just as it had haunted her father. And so when Tutankhaten's nurse ushered the boy in to see his father one last time, Meritaten made herself smile, even though the sight of him was a bitter rebuke from the god.

She moved aside on her bench, allowing Tutankhaten to climb up beside her. He sat, hands folded politely in his lap, and looked solemnly at Smenkhkare.

"You must be brave," she told him, knowing she could never be brave herself. "Your father the king will die soon."

Tutankhaten's eyes filled with tears, but he did not sob, nor even sniffle. "Must he truly?"

"It is the god's will. We would keep him with us, if we could. But the Aten's purposes are too great and complex for mortals like us to understand."

The boy nodded in reluctant acceptance.

"Do you know what this means for you?" she asked quietly, watching the faint rise and fall of Smenkhkare's chest.

Tutankhaten nodded again. "I must be the Pharaoh now."

"Yes. That is so."

"But I am so small."

The boy was hardly seven years old—perhaps not even that old; Meritaten could no longer recall his exact date of birth. He was young indeed to rule as king, but it seemed the god had decreed his fate.

"I will be with you," she said, "to guide you and help you."

The very thought made her feel dry and hollow with exhaustion. There was nothing she wanted less than to take the throne as Tutankhaten's regent. She had had enough of thrones, enough of power. Without Smenkhkare beside her, every moment on the throne would feel like a thousand thorns in her skin. But over these four dark days, as she watched Smenkhkare weaken, she had been forced to confront the possibility. *If I must rule, then please, mighty Aten, make me a better ruler than anyone in my family.* She intended to pattern herself after Smenkhkare, to be just and open-hearted and fair—to leave the scheming, plotting ways of her bloodline behind.

Yet even as she set her heart to the hard reality, Meritaten knew, down unshakably deep, that she could never be the ruler Smenkhkare was. No matter how she tried to suppress the person she had been, the place she had come from, the damage of her strange upbringing still reared its head more often than she liked to admit. As she held and stroked Smenkhkare's thin, motionless hand, she could feel her woeful unsuitability in the trembling chill of her own fingers. She couldn't be anyone other than who she was: a woman prone to fits of temper, who often felt control over her own heart and *ka* ripped away by the forces and events around her. Guilt over the role she had played in Baketaten's death still gnawed at her often, clouding her thoughts—and the guilt she felt over stirring Akhenaten into the rage that had spelled his doom crept up on her, too—even though his death had set her free, and brought her more joy than she had ever thought possible.

My thoughts are all a mess. If I'm honest, I cannot call myself stable enough to rule. Was it only her grief over Smenkhkare that made her feel this way, like a dropped pot just hitting the floor, its pieces ready to fly apart in a thousand different directions? Or was it something worse—something that had been fated since her birth? *Perhaps I am mad. Just like Akhenaten.* Even before Smenkhkare's illness, Meritaten had often lashed out when she didn't mean to, and more times than she cared to count, she had stared down blankly from her throne, paralyzed by indecision, before the eyes of the whole court. It had always been better, easier, safer to keep silent and leave Smenkhkare to think, to decide—to rule.

I am no fit regent. Aten, take this task from me. I cannot do thy work.

Blinking the tears from her eyes, she watched Tutankhaten kiss Smenkhkare's hand. *What will become of us now?* she wondered, stroking the boy's braided side-lock. *If only there were someone else to bear this burden, instead of me.*

The chamber door whispered open. Meritaten glanced up, expecting to see another physician or a magic-worker come to try another useless spell. But it was Ay who stood in the doorway, looking unaccustomedly hesitant, questioning. She had never seen him look so uncertain before. She watched him in silence, wondering what he meant by this strange reluctance.

Then, with a lurch of her heart, she realized he was asking silently whether the king still lived.

"It won't be long now," she said, wondering how she spoke the words without choking on their bitterness.

Ay drifted closer. He stood at the foot of Smenkhkare's

bed, gazing down on the king's diminished frame, his haunting stillness, with a look of confusion and defeat.

But as Meritaten watched Ay's deep-lined face—Ay, who had known so much more power and potency than she ever had—inspiration dawned.

"I cannot do this, Ay," she said quietly.

"We all must bear our burdens."

"And I was Great Wife to two kings. Haven't I earned the right to set my burden down?"

Ay narrowed his eyes at her; she sensed an angry lecture coming. She forestalled him. "Haven't I earned the right to pass my burden on to another?"

Slowly, comprehension overtaking him, Ay lifted his chin. His eyes swept over her, the familiar, swift assessment, his knack of seeing, of knowing. At last he said, "Yes, my lady. I believe you have earned that right."

Meritaten clung to Smenkhkare's hand. She lifted it, pressed it against her cheek, feeling the boniness of his knuckles, his essence wasting away. "But you must swear," she said with a sudden, fierce fire. "Swear to step down as regent when Tutankhaten comes of age. The boy is his heir. It's what my love would have wanted—to see his son on the throne."

Ay did not hesitate. He never had hesitated, when power was so near—when it was so easy to reach out and pluck. "I swear," he said, and with a swift, sure step, he came forward and took Tutankhaten's hand in his own.

Meritaten

Year 1 of Tutankhaten
Lord of the Forms of the Sun,
Strong Bull, Perfect
Who Satisfies the Gods

MERITATEN WAS STILL HOLDING Smenkhkare's hand when, an hour after Ay's departure with Tutankhaten in tow, the king breathed his last. She did not leave him until dawn the next day, lying in the bed beside him, holding his cold, unfeeling body in her arms. She was inconsolable in her grief. The night felt like a hundred years, and every moment the realization would dawn on her once more that she would never speak to Smenkhkare again, never kiss him, never stroll with him in the garden, with her hand on his arm and the sun bright and hopeful in their eyes. Even when her maids came in to tend her, and threw themselves on the ground to wail with the voice of her grief—even then the crushing weight of sorrow would not lift from her body.

Throughout that long night, lingering in the distant reaches of her heart, a fearful reservation about Ay's oath plagued Meritaten. It did not lift as the rites of embalming began, as Smenkhkare's body was committed to the dry, crumbling natron in the House of the Dead, prepared for his resurrection into the Duat. She could not shake from her memory the image of Ay stepping forward, taking Tutankhaten's hand with a quick, grasping greed.

She could only pray she had done the right thing in relinquishing her place on the throne to her grandfather.

Even if she hadn't been locked in the grip of loss, Meritaten was sure she lacked the strength and intelligence necessary to resist Ay. She had once had courage and influence. She still remembered walking through the sands of the Great Aten Temple on the day she had freed Akhenaten's condemned. But that small measure of power had drained out with her tears as she wept for Smenkhkare. Ay held the key to Egypt's future now. Meritaten had placed it in his hand, because she knew she was not strong enough to hold it. She could not regret that decision. She could only trust that everything was as the god willed it, and hope that if she had erred in the Aten's sight, she would be forgiven.

But as the seventy days of Smenkhkare's embalming proceeded, Meritaten felt farther away from the god than she ever had before. Now and then, as if her ka worked a secret rebellion, she could still feel the place on her hand where the old priest Panefer had kissed her. Sometimes the words of his blessing sprang unbidden into her heart. *In the name of Mother Mut, and of Maat, and of Iset, who knows all names, I bless you. Iset knows the name of your heart, and she will keep you close to her bosom forever.* But though the names of the old goddesses still raised a burning wonder in her chest, they seemed even more distant and unconcerned than the Aten. The old goddesses had done nothing to save Smenkhkare—nor had any gods, Aten or otherwise. They had all left Meritaten, broken and alone, to face a grief that could never be borne.

One morning as the seventy days neared their end, Meritaten let herself into the throne room early, well in advance of her courtiers. She climbed the dais one slow step at a time, then sank onto her gilded seat, staring out across the silent hall. The emptiness of Smenkhkare's throne seemed to vibrate and echo beside her. He was so frankly, so completely *gone*. She would be in his presence only one more time, when he was carried to his tomb, when little Tutankhaten was led through the ceremony of the Opening of the Mouth—and then Smenkhkare would go below the ground, into the maze of his eternal rest, and his son would be Pharaoh, and Meritaten would fade like morning clouds burned away by the sun. And Ay—he would take over in Tutankhaten's name. He would sit upon Smenkhkare's throne, for better or worse, and let any god who cared damn Waset to ashes. Just a few more days, and Meritaten could retreat to privacy and grief. She could forget she was ever a King's Great Wife. The promise of that respite was her only comfort now.

One of the double doors at the hall's distant end creaked slowly open. A head, covered in the blunt wig of a court steward, popped into the hall, vanished again—then appeared once more. Even at a distance, Meritaten could see the surprise on the man's face. She waited as the man hurried down the length of the hall.

"My lady! We have all been looking for you." He bowed at her feet, but the gesture had something of a cringe in it, and Meritaten frowned at him warily. "Your mother has come to Waset, and wishes to speak with you."

Meritaten shook her head, mute and stunned. *Nefertiti—here? What could Nefertiti possibly want in Waset?* She didn't know what to do. If Smenkhkare had been here, he would have reacted smoothly, confidently, telling the steward—

The man cleared his throat. "As you are here already, Great Wife, shall I admit her to the throne room?"

"Yes," Meritaten finally managed. "Yes, by all means."

A brief, foolish hope flared in her breast, that Nefertiti had come to comfort and aid Meritaten in her time of grief. That hope was extinguished by the look on her mother's face the moment Nefertiti entered the hall. She crossed the malachite floor, moving with that infuriating air of natural command which Meritaten knew she could never replicate. The guard Horemheb followed in her wake.

"Why have you come?" Meritaten said before Nefertiti could speak. She feared that if her mother had the first word, she would cast some mysterious spell over Meritaten, and take away what little strength she had here. "And that man, Horemheb—you know Smenkhkare banned him from Waset!"

Nefertiti halted before the dais, but she did not bow. *Is she still playing at Pharaoh, then?* The thought exhausted Meritaten far more than it angered her.

"I have heard of Smenkhkare's untimely death," Nefertiti said in a clear, untroubled voice. "By my calculations, the Opening of the Mouth will be performed quite soon. I have come to resume my place as Tutankhaten's guardian."

"No," Meritaten said.

"He was Smenkhkare's heir, but now that our good king is dead, we find ourselves with a boy who is too young to rule. Tutankhaten knows and trusts me. I am the wisest choice to guide him on the throne."

"The choice has already been made." Ay's voice rang clearly down the hall. Meritaten and Nefertiti looked up together, watching as Ay strode into the room.

"You?" Nefertiti said scornfully.

"Why not?"

She narrowed her eyes. "You are old, for one thing. Shall we risk Tutankhaten losing another guardian to the tomb?"

In spite of her sex, Nefertiti truly looked like a king, confident and wise, ready with a bold, intelligent energy. Even Meritaten could see how suited she was to rule. Power shone from her, and Meritaten knew that much of Waset's court—to say nothing of its *rekhet*, who still remembered Hatshepsut fondly—would sway to her favor with very little effort. Ay was withered and old. He seemed an unstable regent by comparison, despite his reputation for shrewdness.

Meritaten stood. "I will not allow this."

Nefertiti shot her a piercing look, but just before she spoke her eyes softened with something that might have been regret. "Whether you allow it or not, it must happen. We must think of Egypt's needs now, not our own preferences—or our pains."

Meritaten felt the goaded by that fleeting look of sympathy—stabbed by it. Pain? What did this woman who called herself 'mother' know of Meritaten's pain? Where was Nefertiti when she had suffered alone with only Akhenaten for company? Where was she when Smenkhkare's life had ebbed away? She had left Meritaten alone to struggle, without any of the guidance she offered now to Tutankhaten. Should the boy now have everything Meritaten had lacked?

Impulsively, she descended to stand before her mother. She was gripped by the need to look her in the eye, to stare boldly into her perfect, haughty face as she spoke. "Some may have accepted you as Pharaoh in Akhet-Aten, but this is Waset. Smenkhkare and I made this place anew. It is *my* city, not yours—and Egypt is my country, by right of my status as consort to two kings. You must do as I say. And I say you shall not rule as Tutankhaten's regent."

Nefertiti was unfazed by Meritaten's anger. "You were the consort of two kings. But I *am* a king. Stand aside, girl, and give the reins of power to those who know how to handle them."

"The work we have done here," Meritaten protested, "Smenkhkare and I—working to restore the old gods, the old ways..."

"Very good," Nefertiti said. "I, too, have found peace with the old gods. Don't be afraid; I will work for the same causes as our departed Pharaoh. Smenkhkare's work will continue beyond his death. I will pass it on to Tutankhaten, too. Your late husband's legacy will be safe in my hands."

Ay's laugh was as harsh as the cry of the *geb-geb* bird. "But you *cannot* rule as king, Nefertiti!" The triumph in his words reverberated through the room. "Why? Because you cannot make the holy trinity. If you believe in the old gods as you claim, then you know that a king must have a Great Wife, and also a child. Otherwise he is not like the gods he claims to represent. You, a woman! Where is your Great Wife?"

Nefertiti cast a sharp glance at her guard. Her flashing eyes, the jerk of her chin, were eloquent with a language Meritaten did not understand. But Horemheb did understand. He moved with the speed of a striking cobra, lunging toward Meritaten. He seized her by the arm before she could cry out. She jerked in his grip, and the few stewards in the room gasped and murmured in tense surprise.

Ay snapped his fingers toward the stewards. "Call the Great Wife's soldiers!"

"Don't be foolish," Nefertiti said just as loudly. "She is my own daughter. Why would I harm her?"

The stewards milled, unsettled, but clearly torn between Nefertiti—splendid, commanding, like Hatshepsut come again—and Ay, grizzled and old.

"Ay!" Meritaten shouted. "Call my men in! Do it yourself!"

But Ay wasn't looking at Meritaten, the King's Wife. He watched Nefertiti with narrowed eyes, and folded his arms across his chest in a posture of cautious waiting. "It hardly matters, Meritaten. You don't want the throne, anyway."

She heard the words he didn't speak aloud. *You are of no use to me now. I have Tutankhaten; what do I need with a useless, ineffective King's Wife?*

Meritaten kicked out at Horemheb, but he dodged and danced, keeping beyond the reach of her feet.

"Here is my Great Wife," Nefertiti said, turning to Ay with a mocking smile.

Meritaten gasped in horror. "You can't be serious. Ay! You cannot let her do this!"

But Ay said only, "Wait for the right time, girl. It will come. Sooner or later the winds will change on Nefertiti's luck. Even if the court comes to favor her, she will fall again, and quite soon. The gods will not be mocked. Soon enough order will be restored."

Tears blurred Meritaten's vision. "And until then, you would subject me to this madness? This perversion of tradition?"

"Oh, calm down, girl," Ay said in disgust. "Can't you keep your wits about you? Look at it as an opportunity. I would, in your position. You never know what new fortunes might arise from this arrangement."

"Damn you," Meritaten cried. "I'm not *like* you, Ay!"

The moment the words were out of her mouth, Meritaten felt their harsh, brutal truth. She wasn't like Ay—nor was she like Nefertiti, nor like any who had come before her. She was a pitiful, broken thing, the failed cast-off of a mad dynasty. She sagged in Horemheb's grip, surrendering with a sob. Nefertiti jerked her head in command, and Horemheb pulled her back down the hall, away from her throne forever.

Nefertiti

Year 2 of Nefer-Neferu-Aten,
Beloved of the Beautiful Appearance

Year 1 of Tutankhaten,
Lord of the Forms of the Sun

NANN HAD ALREADY COMMANDEERED a choice wing of the palace for Nefertiti, with spacious apartments built and decorated in the old, traditional style. Horemheb led the way, Meritaten held firmly in his grip. The girl didn't even look up from the floor as they strode past pillars and dry, stone-walled courtyards, yellow in the sun. She seemed as limp and lifeless as an overused rag.

But when they reached Nefertiti's new quarters and Nann shut the door behind them, life leapt back into Meritaten's *ka*. She rounded on Nefertiti, eyes sharp with fury, her words snapping like sails in a storm wind. "Your Great Wife? What kind of twisted relationship are we to have now?"

This anger was good—better than the alternative. Nefertiti would rather see hatred in her daughter's eyes than that dull, uncaring vacancy, the torpor that had hung over Meritaten even before Nefertiti had made her shocking announcement.

"That is not my intent," Nefertiti said. "I am not debauched like your father was."

"What difference does that make? You certainly are as corrupt as he was—and every bit as ravenous for power."

212

Nefertiti knew she would be a fool to argue with Meritaten. The girl wasn't entirely wrong. What she did now, she did for Tutankhaten's sake—and, by extension, for Egypt's sake. But however she excused it, this *was* a seizing of power. As for corruption—her heart had long since been soiled by the creeping filth of royalty. *No one in this family can escape corruption, Daughter—not even you.*

"Listen to me, Meritaten. With your help, this can be a clean, straightforward coup."

"At least you admit this is a coup."

"I won't dance around the issue. Of course it's a coup. Is there any other way to remove Ay from his proximity to the throne? You condemn me for immorality, but 'Corruption' is Ay's *ren*, the name written on his heart! Half the iniquity of this bloodline began with Ay—with his insatiable greed for power."

Meritaten folded her arms over her breasts, her fine jaw tensing. "Whatever you may think of him, Ay is also wise and experienced."

"So am I."

"And humble," Meritaten added drily.

Nefertiti drifted to an ebony table, its edges inlaid with ivory stars. Nann and Ankhesenpaaten had already seen to everything: a tall jug of wine stood waiting on a tray, several cups made from polished horn standing nearby. Ankhesenpaaten poured two cups of wine, and Nefertiti took one, sniffing the robust, sweet vintage. The younger girl held the other cup out to Meritaten, but she turned her face away without so much as a word of thanks to her sister—a condescending refusal.

"Humility," Nefertiti said, "is a useless virtue, and therefore it is no virtue at all. Should I pretend I don't know how to rule the Two Lands? Should I pretend I never did it before, that I can't do it better than Ay? And why should I act out such a farce? Because I am a woman?"

Meritaten sat on a long couch strewn with leopard skins. She sank down gingerly, as if she feared the skins might revert to live leopards at any moment and savage her. "Why do you think you can rule better than Ay?" she asked quietly.

"Because unlike him—and whatever you may believe of me—I don't want power for my own sake." She nodded to Ankhesenpaaten, and the girl set the cup of wine Meritaten had refused on the table. "I want it for Tutankhaten's sake. I want to protect his claim to the throne. He is the one the gods have chosen for succession, by right of his birth and his male sex."

"So you admit a female Pharaoh has no place on the throne." Meritaten's voice was growing rough. She needed a drink.

"Stop being so stubborn and have some wine. Your own sister poured it, and you've seen me drink it; you know it isn't poisoned. Besides, you're no good to me dead. I need a King's Great Wife."

Meritaten stared at the cup, her lashes lowered over her eyes like the dark plumes of an ostrich-feather sunshade. They were matted with kohl and tears. But finally she lifted the cup and drank—long and deep, as if her throat were as dry as the Red Land.

"The river will hardly dry up if I rule on Tutankhaten's behalf," Nefertiti went on. "Egypt never suffered under Hatshepsut."

"If you truly mean to rule on Tutankhaten's behalf, then act as his regent. Don't claim you are a king."

Nefertiti added more wine to each of their cups. "A regent only has so much power... but a king is unfettered by any convention."

"Clearly," Meritaten said. "Apparently a king might even

take her own daughter as a wife!"

"Spare me your sulks," Nefertiti said. "You've faced far worse before."

She gestured, and Nann carried a chair across the room, positioning it on the other side of the table. Nefertiti sat easily, as if she had spent her whole life in this foreign, old-fashioned chamber. Ankhesenpaaten sank onto a small, three-legged stool close beside her. The wine jug and its remaining horn cups stood like a fortress wall between Nefertiti and her eldest daughter. Meritaten sipped her wine again, glaring over the vessel's rim, looking with increasing suspicion between Nefertiti and her sister, who stuck like a servant to Nefertiti's side.

Nefertiti continued, "Would you like to know how this arrangement will differ from your marriage to your father? I'll tell you: I will never call you to my bed. You may count on that. You will be my Great Wife in name only—but it is a vitally important role.

"Ay was right to point out that without a Great Wife, the nobles of Waset will never accept me as their king. And that's to say nothing of their priests. Waset is such a traditional place; I find it tiresome. But here we are in its palace, working to restore its old gods. We must play by Waset's rules, whether we like them or not.

"You will perform the necessary ceremonies at the Temple of Amun, hold the necessary office—and stand beside me, the third part of the trinity that guarantees Tutankhaten's divine status. That is all I will require of you. The duties are light, as I'm sure you can see."

Meritaten slumped against the back of the couch. She sighed deeply, a lonely, rattling sound. "Marry someone else, Mother. I am done being a King's Wife. Marry Ay, if you are so keen to make a holy trinity with your own blood."

Nefertiti could feel a flush spread hot across her cheeks.

Was it alarm or anger that quickened her heart? "Ay will never come near the throne—not while I have a say in the matter. That's why I've come: to save you from your own foolish maneuver. To save Egypt from your blunder."

"There is nothing wrong with Ay."

Meritaten didn't even sit up in response to Nefertiti's needling. *Perhaps the girl truly has reached her limit.*

"There is *everything* wrong with Ay," Nefertiti said. "He is cold—unfeeling. And his thirst for ever more power simply can't be quenched. Believe me, I know. I suppose he swore to hand the throne over to Tutankhaten as soon as the boy grows up, didn't he?"

Now Meritaten did sit up, rising slowly from her stupor until she sat stiff-backed on the edge of the couch.

Nefertiti could have ground her teeth to dust. "Of course he swore it. And you believed him. Meritaten, you trusting fool."

"He swore it on the Aten *and* the old gods!" The wine cup trembled in her hands.

"Oh, I have no doubt about that. Ay will make any oath, no matter how terrible, if it suits his purposes—if it will bring him the power he craves."

"But an oath to the one true god is binding! His *ka*—"

"Binding?" Nefertiti grunted in flat dismissal. "No oath binds Ay. He doesn't fear *any* god, and so he doesn't fear to swear with one breath and blow the same oath away with the next. By giving him the regency, Meritaten, you have barred the rightful heir from his throne forever."

Meritaten sniffed. Tears gathered in her eyes.

"But if you will only cooperate with me," Nefertiti went on, gentle and cajoling, "we can undo the damage now. We shall be heroines for Egypt's sake—together! I have a plan to bring the Two Lands back to stability, to tear down Akhet-Aten and everything it stood for—to revert our land to its old ways. And by the time Tutankhaten is a man, he will rule as the gods intended Pharaohs to rule, wisely and well, with the good of the people foremost in his heart. Don't you want that, Meritaten? Isn't it worth working for?"

Meritaten's tense mouth softened. Her eyes lowered, then her chin, and for a moment Nefertiti's heart leaped with triumph—and gratitude for the girl's good sense. She was on the verge of accepting, of committing to the plan, and Nefertiti saw the way clear for her, for Tutankhaten. With her heart's eye she saw a long, black, lightless tunnel, and at its end the Horus Throne, golden and gleaming. A shadow drifted away—a shadow that had Ay's face, her last enemy, her final and most terrible foe. As his shadow passed, the tunnel became a path, well-lit, smooth, and straight, a welcoming road to the throne.

We will do it, by the gods. United, Ay can't hope to stand against us.

But just as a smile began to form on her lips, Meritaten looked up suddenly. Her eyes were wide with horror, her face pale. She lurched to her feet, knocking her cup of wine to the floor, where its dregs spilled across the tile like blood. "You planned this from the start!"

"Planned what?" Nefertiti couldn't stop herself from pressing a hand to her chest, the girl's outburst was so sudden and vehement.

"Smenkhkare's death!" Meritaten cried. Her hands were clenched tight at her sides, fists to beat back her pain. "I remember your words back in Akhet-Aten, when you slunk back out of hiding. Perhaps you don't remember, Mother, but I do. *I do!*"

Nefertiti waited, eyeing the girl cautiously. *This sudden fury—has she gone mad?*

"You said, 'Whichever king the gods love best will

217

continue on. The other will be discarded.' But it wasn't the gods who chose, was it? Was it! It was you!"

"I don't know what you're talking about."

Meritaten rushed around the table, closing with Nefertiti—but Horemheb was there, stepping smoothly into her path, holding out an arm to bar her way. Nefertiti watched her daughter calmly as she threw her slight weight against Horemheb's restraint, weeping and ranting.

"You poisoned Smenkhkare! Or if you didn't poison him, then you killed him through some sorcery—some foul magic you worked from Akhet-Aten! You wanted him dead, because he was in your way. And you saw to it!"

"I never touched Smenkhkare." Nefertiti hadn't needed to. She too recalled the words she had spoken when she came back to Akhet-Aten with Tutankhaten in her possession. There had never been any cause to hurt Smenkhkare. Nefertiti had known the gods would choose their proper king.

"I *won't* help you," Meritaten spat, clawing at Horemheb's arm. "I *never* will! You wanted Smenkhkare dead—out of your way—so you could get your claws around Tutankhaten again. But you didn't think what it would cost you, to act so selfishly! You killed the only person in all the world whom I loved—the only one who loved me. I will never forgive you—*never*! And I swear by the Aten's holy rays that I shall work against your foul cause, every moment of every day! Every breath in me shall be turned against your work!"

Nefertiti rose smoothly from her chair. She leaned toward her daughter, eye to eye, so close she could have kissed her. "You *will* help me," Nefertiti said, "if you want to survive."

Meritaten gasped. She stared at Nefertiti in horror, her hands loosening on Horemheb's arm, falling back limply to her sides. Nefertiti had never seen such fear in the girl's eyes before, nor such helplessness. Guilt and hatred swelled inside her, filling her gut until she was certain she would burst. But she made herself stand before her daughter, erect and unmoved.

Nefertiti said softly, "Tutankhaten's claim to the throne is all I live for now. That boy—his right to rule—is my only remaining purpose in this world."

Meritaten drew a few shaky breaths, gathering herself in. Finally she said, "You could have lived for your daughters. But you cast us aside."

Nefertiti heard Ankhesenpaaten shift restlessly on her stool. She thought perhaps the younger girl would object, but she held her tongue, as usual.

"You are both King's Daughters," Nefertiti said. "You have more pressing concerns than a relationship with your mother. The gods made you with a greater purpose. You are not *rekhet* girls; you are half divine! You must act like it, Meritaten."

"Act? I have acted on Egypt's behalf for long enough. I am *done*—do you hear me? Finished! Make Ankhesenpaaten your King's Wife, for all I care."

Nefertiti did not answer. Ankhesenpaaten's path was already set, its bricks level and laid. The gods knew, Nefertiti had worked hard to set each of those bricks firmly before the girl's feet. She would not change Ankhesenpaaten's fate now.

"You *will* work with me," Nefertiti insisted. "If I must, I will set guards on you day and night to ensure that you help our mutual cause. I would prefer you worked with me of your own accord, but I will do what I must, Meritaten— never doubt that. You will see the sense in working side by side, and working for Tutankhaten's sake. Together we *will* restore Egypt—for we have no other choice. With time you will come to like the work. You were bred for it, after all—it is your divine purpose."

"Working for Tutankhaten's sake? To restore the old gods?" Meritaten tossed her head in bitter amusement. "Well, Mother, Ay still has Tutankhaten. He was sworn to the regency before the old gods—and their priests. Whatever dim view you hold of Ay's loyalty to the gods, that oath cannot be undone."

Nefertiti smiled. "Ay won't be in my way for long. Leave the old man to me. Now go back to you chambers and get yourself used to the idea of serving as my Great Wife. Our work begins tomorrow. I need you at my side for the morning's ritual at Temple of Amun, and you must be alert, ready to work for Egypt's cause."

Meritaten turned away from Horemheb and stormed out of Nefertiti's apartments. Ankhesenpaaten watched her go. Then she turned a reserved, dark gaze up to her mother. That look was full of caution—and worse, fear.

"Don't worry," Nefertiti told her. "Everything will work out as the gods will it. Meritaten will come around. She has to."

Ankhesenpaaten still said nothing, but Nefertiti could feel the girl's doubt in her silence, hanging heavy in the room, as stifling as the heat of summer.

Horemheb

Year 2 of Nefer-Neferu-Aten,
Beloved of the Beautiful Appearance

Year 1 of Tutankhaten,
Lord of the Forms of the Sun

S HE ISN'T LIKELY to come around, my lady."
Horemheb shook his head sadly. "What are the chances she'll really cooperate with you?"

Nefertiti stared at the apartment door, brow furrowed. The door's slam still seemed to shiver along the chamber walls. "She thinks I killed Smenkhkare." Horemheb wasn't sure if it was hurt he heard in Nefertiti's voice—or calculation. Perhaps it was both. "I swear I never did, Horemheb. I would swear to it on any god you please."

"I believe you, no oath required. It's your daughter you must convince."

Nefertiti lapsed into thoughtful silence. She returned to her chair and picked up her wine cup, rolling it absently between her palms. After a long moment she said, "No. I should not convince her—if such a thing could even be done. It's of more use to me if she believes I did kill Smenkhkare. Meritaten has never been an especially courageous girl—"

"She was brave that day in the Great Aten Temple, when she rescued the prisoners."

"Yes." There was real pride in Nefertiti's voice, in the brief smile that lit her eyes—for only a moment. But then she subsided again, losing herself in darker musings. "She has shown courage a time or two. But by and large, she has no spirit for these games we all must play. She will never be like Tiy—or like Baketaten."

"Nor will she ever match you."

She waved a hand, brushing away Horemheb's praise. "The gods alone know whether I will succeed. I've been wrapped up in the throne's foul dealings for my whole life, yet it still remains to be seen whether I am a shrewd player... or as naïve as a child. I could be on the verge of failure—of death—this very moment. I simply cannot say. So we must keep Meritaten complacent and obedient, ready to go wherever I send her, for I need all the help I can get. If I must allow her to believe I killed the man she loves—and that I may kill her, too—then I will let her believe it. I must keep Meritaten beside me as Great Wife, no matter the cost. As king, I can overpower Ay. As just another potential regent, the gods alone know what schemes he might be able to work against me."

"How long?" Ankhesenpaaten had cleaned up the spilled wine, and now settled on the couch among the spotted skins. "How long do you think it will take to put Ay out of the way and make the throne safe for Tutankhaten again?"

Nefertiti made a helpless gesture, palms up toward the ceiling, as if offering the weight of her troubles up to the gods. "I wish I knew. Somehow I must hold my place in the palace—and more importantly, increase my support among the priests and nobles—until I can consolidate enough power to face Ay down. Then I'm sure the gods will guide me—will show me the way to undo Ay's appointment as regent, and get Tutankhaten back under my own care."

She dropped suddenly into her couch with a sound that was very close to a sob. She pressed her lined, harried face with her hands, then bent until she was hunched over herself, hidden—weeping, for all Horemheb knew—

behind the screen of her fingers. Ankhesenpaaten stroked her back like a nurse tending a fussy child.

At length, Nefertiti looked up at him. Her eyes were dry, her kohl unsmeared. "I hate myself for this, Horemheb—for doing this to my daughter. To both my remaining children." She reached out blindly; Ankhesenpaaten put her hand into Nefertiti's, squeezed. But Nefertiti did not look at the girl. "I have no choice. The gods maneuvered me here—by my birth, and later by sending Tutankhaten to me. I am bound by their power. I can't just walk away from my duty, with so much still undone."

Horemheb thought of Tutankhaten, his fragile innocence, his good-natured, cheerful ways. *The duty we all have now, the task the gods have given me, too...* But *should* Tutankhaten be under Horemheb's care, even indirectly? He was tainted now—a king-killer. Might his influence permanently stain the boy, and ruin what was good and useful in his *ka*?

"It's... all such a delicate balance," Horemheb offered weakly.

"Delicate," Nefertiti agreed, "and more deadly than ever it was at Akhet-Aten, or even in the House of Rejoicing. I loathe myself all the more for playing this game, for who knows better than I how terrible it is? But once the gods have set our paths, we cannot change them."

She paused, looking up at Horemheb with desperate hope. "Can we?"

Once Horemheb had believed that mere mortals could change the course of their fates. And more than anything, he wanted to reassure her, to tell her that she could be the mistress of her own heart, the ruler of her own life. But he had the blood of a Pharaoh on his hands. Who put him in that terrible place—who set the course of his life, made him lose his heart to Baketaten, made him burn with desire for vengeance—if not the gods? Who used him as the instrument to rid the world of Akhenaten, at the cost of his immortal *ka*? No... mortals could not change their fates. Horemheb had seen too much, lived through too much, to believe it now.

When it became clear that Horemheb could offer her no comfort, Nefertiti sagged back on the couch, eyes closed. The silence, dark and significant, stretched on and on. Finally Ankhesenpaaten let go of her mother's hand. She gathered the discarded wine cups and picked up the tray. "I'll go to the kitchen," she murmured, "and bring back food. Beer, too. We could all use some strength now. Full stomachs will put everything into perspective."

Nefertiti watched the girl walk away with a look of pained longing. When she vanished, closing the chamber door far more quietly than her sister had, Nefertiti covered her mouth with one hand—holding back cries of regret or wails of sadness.

"My lady?" Horemheb knelt before her, gazing earnestly into her face. All pretenses of kingly composure had fled. Her eyes were deep, tragic pools, ready to spill over with tears. "You must hold yourself together," he reminded her gently.

Nefertiti reached for him suddenly, clinging to both his hands. The touch surprised Horemheb. In all the years he had known her, Nefertiti had never been demonstrative. Though her grip was strong and untrembling, still he could feel the desperate need, the fear running through her veins.

"Promise me," she said, "that you will always serve me."

Horemheb nearly laughed, the demand was so unnecessary. "You know I will."

"Not only to protect me, but to watch over me." She glanced again at the door—the place where both her daughters had disappeared. "Promise me you'll keep me from going too far. You must be for me what Huya was for Tiy."

Horemheb shrugged uncomfortably. "I'm not nearly as intelligent as Huya."

"You have something far better than intelligence—rarer and more useful." She squeezed his hands, and smiled. And despite her obvious pain, Horemheb could tell that the smile was unforced. "You are good, Horemheb. All the way down to your *ba* and *ka*, you are good and kind, in a world where so few are."

Gently, he pulled his hands from her grip. "You are mistaken, my lady. My *ba* and *ka* are damned. I killed a king—a god."

"Akhenaten was no god. But Tutankhaten may be divine enough to bring Egypt back to its old ways, to restore the gods-that-were to their full glory. If we can only pry him out of Ay's grip, the boy may grow up as pure and good-hearted as you."

Tutankhaten. Baketaten's loss was distant now, a dull ache rather than a sharp, lancing pain. But Horemheb still felt the same duty toward her son. That responsibility had never left him. *For Tutankhaten, I will do anything—even if I am so stained by my act that I must flee from his presence.*

Horemheb stood, and offered his hand to pull Nefertiti to her feet. "My lady, I swear to be your man, whatever may come. For Tutankhaten's sake."

"Good," she said. And now she smiled again, lightly, shaking off the sorrow her daughters had raised in her long-bruised heart. "With your oath, Horemheb, I can almost feel hope for the future."

Nefertiti

Year 2 of Nefer-Neferu-Aten,
Beloved of the Beautiful Appearance

Year 1 of Tutankhaten,
Lord of the Forms of the Sun

You are restless tonight, my lady." Nann was like a pale ghost drifting at Nefertiti's shoulder, her feet almost perfectly silent on the garden's gravel path.

They walked through a grove of ancient sycamores, which were surrounded by high, dense banks of vine and shrub. It was night. The rising moon was full and bright, scattering a pale, powdery light along the path, the high reaches of the broad-leafed trees, the tops of the overgrown hedges. The small garden was an appealingly secluded place, little more than a pocket hidden among the folds of palace corridors and alcoved chambers. Though it was still mostly untamed—a holdover from the days before Smenkhkare had revived the Waset palace—the remnants of protective hedges and maze-like paths indicated its original purpose: a place for secret conversation, for private, protected thought. It suited Nefertiti well tonight. She paced its winding paths in silence, then turned and wandered back along their lengths, musing in the sheltered dark.

"My lady?" Nann tried again, her voice pitched cautiously low.

"Thinking," Nefertiti said. "Only thinking."

"About Meritaten?"

Nefertiti looked sharply at Nann, a rebuke ready on her tongue. But when she saw Nann's face in the moonlight, pale skin eerily luminous, eyes darkened by shadows, she held back those harsh words. She considered Nann more closely. The Hurrian servant was a danger to Nefertiti. It was foolish to keep her so close, a serpent cradled to her breast, for the moment Nann learned of Nefertiti's role in Kiya's disappearance, the woman would not hesitate to destroy her. But despite the threat she posed, Nefertiti liked Nann. Or at least, she admired the woman's intense focus, her dedication to righting this mad world's wrongs... and her implacable, awe-inspiring patience. Rather than rebuke her, perhaps Nefertiti could learn from her. Conspire with her.

"Yes," she said at last. "You saw how she reacted today. She hates me—not that I blame her. It's only a natural reaction. But—"

"But she is problematic."

Nefertiti cast a sideways smile at Nann, wryly appreciative. *Made by the gods as a Hurrian servant, yet your eyes are sharp, your heart discerning... and your calculation as coldly accurate as Tiy's ever was. Your* ka *went to the wrong body, Nann. You should have been born into Egypt's royal family.*

At length, Nefertiti agreed. "Problematic. Though in truth, my trouble isn't with Meritaten—not truly. If she won't cooperate and come to me willingly, to serve me in the place of a Great Wife, then Ay is more a danger to my cause than ever."

Nann nodded solemnly. "I see it. He will gather forces against you, cite your female sex, your unfitness for the role of king."

"Yes. And he'll do it soon—as soon as he hears that Meritaten has refused to work by my side. He may be working even now to unite his followers in opposition, and to find still more. But here I am, strolling in the moonlight." She laughed bitterly. "What else can I do? Without Meritaten, my hands are tied... at least until I find another to take her place."

"That could take a very long time, my lady."

"I know. And I fear we don't have any time left."

They walked on, rounding the familiar curve of the path, treading it all over again. The gravel was churned and darkened by the passage of their own sandals, crossing this ground so many times. In the sycamores above, some small night bird called repetitively, a small, croaking noise, rhythmic and dull, as if to emphasize the futility of this aimless pacing.

All at once, unsure what moved her to speak at all, Nefertiti said, "There is one way I might proceed. One thing I might do." But she fell silent again, quickening her pace, the gravel crunching louder underfoot. It was dangerous and reckless. But it stirred her to excitement, filling her chest with a great, bounding flutter of eagerness.

"Kill Ay?" Nann guessed, utterly unscandalized by the thought.

"How did you know I was thinking of just that?"

Nann shrugged. "It's the only sensible thing to do. If Ay is removed from the picture, then Meritaten—"

"Meritaten will have no one else on her side. She will have only me to support her. I will be the only refuge for her trust."

It was a cruel manipulation, a hard blow to bring Meritaten into line. *Poor girl. She has suffered so much. If I had any other choice... if I could afford to set her free, to live her life free of these dreadful games...* But Nefertiti had no other option. The gods had moved them all into their places, casting each of their *kas* in these roles. *We are players on a divine stage. We are powerless to change the plot, to rewrite our lines. What the gods require of us, we must do.*

"Without Ay," Nann added, "Meritaten will have no one else to scheme with."

Nefertiti blew out harshly through her nose, a graceless snort of irony. "Meritaten never schemed with anyone. It's Ay who plotted with her, who used her as a pawn on his *senet* board. That has always been his way. He used my sister and me in the same manner, until I could finally break away and take Mutbenret with me."

And then I used her in just the same way, may the gods damn me. The gods and their damnable plans, the traps they've set for my ka. She pressed her hands against her forehead, her cheeks, cooling the heat of anger and fear, brushing away the damp sweat of disgust at her own scheming heart.

"I would free Meritaten if I could," Nefertiti said softly. "If only the gods would allow it, I would just... let her go. But I cannot. And she hates me for it. She doesn't despise me half as much as I do myself."

Nann stopped on the garden path. She reached out and took Nefertiti's hand. The gesture surprised Nefertiti, and for the briefest moment offense reared up within her. Nann was a servant. It was gross presumption, for someone of her status to touch a woman of the royal blood, unless duty demanded it. And to be so forward with the rightful Pharaoh...! But in the next heartbeat she pushed those feelings aside. Nann's grip was firm, strong—a show of support and simple camaraderie. Nefertiti hadn't felt the sympathy of a friend in... how long? How many years of her life had she spent alone, isolated by duty, by power?

"You should do it," Nann said. "Ay, I mean. The time is right. Don't you feel the goddess speaking in your heart?"

She didn't know how to respond. Where Ay was concerned, Nefertiti felt the same things she always had, even in her earliest years. Anger, helplessness, mistrust. The fear was gone, but only because she knew what to expect of him. But the hunger for her long-delayed vengeance was as hard and cold as ever, gnawing at her gut with the same familiar pain. Certainly she felt no whispers from Nann's strange northern goddess. But would she know Ishtar's voice, even if she heard it? She stared hard at Nann; as moonlight rippled through the sycamore leaves, the shifting subtlety of light and shadow seemed to wreath Nann's body with a feathered cape— with an eagle's wings. The pale woman drew herself up, and her hand squeezed Nefertiti's.

Perhaps the goddess has spoken to me after all.

Nefertiti glanced around the garden, searching for the emerald wings and darting speed of her *ba*. But it was nowhere to be seen. *Does that mean my death is not close at hand? Or does it mean my* ba *has already flown, already given me up for lost?*

It didn't matter. The time had come to act. Let the gods do with her whatever they pleased in their unfeeling caprice.

She nodded.

Nann's grin was slow and satisfied, a leopardess gloating over prey. "Shall I send for Horemheb? He can do the deed."

"No." The suggestion struck Nefertiti with instant dissatisfaction. Her whole body tensed and quivered, rejecting the very notion that anyone else *should* do this deed, that any hand but hers should deal out Ay's justice. *This is my task, and no one else's.* "Horemheb has done enough killing in Egypt's service. I shall go alone."

"Let me come with you, then. To protect you."

The offer touched Nefertiti—and also fanned her guilt into a blaze. *I don't deserve your care. It was I who wanted Kiya dead.* But she said only, "No. I'll have to get close to Ay, and he's a cunning old man. He'll suspect something if I bring anyone with me."

"Certainly he would suspect a guard, a soldier," Nann said. "But a maid?"

"A clever woman who is devoted to me, who can watch the door and give the alert if any witnesses come? No, Nann—Ay is too cautious and too far-thinking. He won't be alone with me and anyone who might aid me. Not anymore; not now that I've made myself king. But he will consent to see me if I am alone. He believes I still fear him. He thinks he can still control me, if I've no one around to support me."

Nann sucked in her lower lip, mulling over Nefertiti's words. Finally, though, she brushed her hands together as if the deed were already done. "How will you do it, then, my lady?"

Nefertiti hadn't thought that far ahead. She tapped her chin, examining her options quickly, as one riffles through stacks of papyrus with a deft finger. "It must be a blade," she said at last. "I don't have any poison handy, and in any case, I can't be sure Ay will eat or drink at this hour. And he's old, but still rather wiry; I doubt I could overpower him without a weapon."

Nann smiled. She smacked her fist into the palm of her hand. The sound cracked in the still night air, and in the moon's blue-white glow, Nefertiti could have sworn the woman's fingers had turned to an eagle's sharp talons. "I know just the blade to bring," Nann said. "Come back to my room, my lady. I will help you prepare."

NEFERTITI FOUND IT DIFFICULT to walk serenely through the brazier-lit corridors of the Waset palace. She felt predatory, dangerous, full of ruthless power. Slinking would have been more suited to her mood—prowling from shadow to shadow, watching from the dark as the meek servants scurried about their small, menial tasks. She was sleek, sharp-eyed; she ran her tongue along her teeth and though she knew it was only her imagination, still she could have sworn she had the fangs of a lioness, pointed and hungry for blood. Waset was a place of old traditions, old gods. The *kas* of long-dormant goddesses seemed to resurrect and fall toward her from the star-swept sky, drawn to her fury like flakes of iron to a lodestone.

I am Pakhet, She Who Scratches. I am Sekhmet, who thirsts for blood.

But though all the rage of a great, fierce she-cat coursed through her veins, Nefertiti made herself walk sedately past pillars and alcoves, moving openly through wavering rings of lamp light and silver drifts of moon.

As she made her way toward Ay's chambers, she felt the sword's weight at her hip, bumping along her thigh with each unhurried step. It was the blade Nann had taken from the cliff-top guard at Akhet-Aten, one of the two Horemheb had killed on the night of their escape.

When Nann pulled the short, curved sword from beneath her sleeping pallet and explained where it came from, Nefertiti had shaken her head in wonder. "You kept it all this time?"

"Of course," Nann had replied. "Ishtar knew it still had a purpose—that in my hands it had work yet to do. And now I give it to you. Let its duty be done by you, Nefertiti, as the goddess wills."

The folds of a long, flowing shawl covered the sword completely, giving no hint that Nefertiti was armed. Nann had seen to that, draping the shawl just so, tying it carefully, standing back with her head at a critical tilt while Nefertiti walked and walked across her small chamber, more times than she could count, until finally the Hurrian was satisfied that the sword was well concealed. And then came better practice—Nefertiti reaching below the shawl, drawing out the blade, practicing the motion until it was as natural to her as breathing. And each time she whisked the sword from its scabbard, each time she saw its blood-bronze shimmer in the lamplight, her heart leaped with righteous glee.

She was ready. Egypt's oldest and fiercest goddesses walked with her—as did Ishtar, that foreign queen of the stars whose strength seemed to burn in Nefertiti's limbs.

She reached Ay's door. No soldier guarded it; Nefertiti smiled, amused. Ay thought he needed no protection— was that the way of it? Soon he would learn how wrong he was.

She knocked on the door frame, a brisk, commanding rap. One of Ay's servants answered, a man in his middle years who raked Nefertiti head to feet with a suspicious scowl.

Nefertiti had expected a guard on the door—one who could easily be shut outside while she did the goddesses' work. But she hadn't counted on servants inside Ay's chamber. Not at this late hour. She had lived in the all-but-abandoned City of the Sun for too many months, with a dramatically reduced staff. She had forgotten Ay would have a whole assortment of men and women about him, tending to his needs. Nefertiti flushed under the man's assessing gaze. She felt like a fool; for a moment she hesitated, unsure how to proceed—or if she ought to continue. But beyond the servant's shoulder she saw Ay's lamplight flicker, leaping up the wall of his chamber to illuminate a painting—perhaps a hundred years old—of Sekhmet, the lion-headed goddess of war. It was a good sign, encouraging. *I shall find a way to send the servants away—all of them. I'll only need a moment alone with Ay, to do what must be done. That moment will come, and I will know when it arrives.*

"I've come to speak with my father," she told the man. "It's an urgent matter; it can't wait until the morning."

"The Lord Regent cannot see you now. He is preparing for bed. He—"

"Is that Nefertiti?" Ay's voice rose up from the chamber, heavy with self-congratulation, already certain he had won whatever argument was yet to unfold between them. "Let her in, man. By all means, let her in."

Lounging on a low couch of indigo silk, the remains of his supper spread on the table before him, Ay squinted up at her peevishly. "What do you want? Be quick, and then be gone."

The sword felt like a live thing against Nefertiti's hip, vibrating with eager energy. "I've come to discuss the regency—and Tutankhaten."

"I won't give him up, Nefertiti. The regency is a done thing, sworn before the High Priest of Amun *and* the god himself." His bony old fingers made a brushing motion in the air, a dismissive flick, as if he were driving away biting flies. "You are dealing with the king's own representative now, so listen when I tell you that your rebellious behavior will not be tolerated. Nor will this foolishness of taking Meritaten as a wife."

"Foolishness?" she said coolly. "Surely you can see the sense in it. You're not so old and doddering yet that subtleties escape you."

"There is no sense in having a Great Wife unless you are the Pharaoh. You are *not* a king. One does not simply proclaim oneself the ruler of the Two Lands. It is a divine birthright, an appointment of the gods. If one could simply take the throne by strength or wit alone, I would have worn the Double Crown long ago."

Nefertiti sighed, but she gave her father a tolerant, almost playful smile. She leaned casually against the great lotus pillar that stood beside his chamber door. "I have a feeling I can make you see the sense in what I do—and make you consent to my plan, too. But it will take some doing; I can see that. My throat is already dry. Is there anything left in that wine jar?"

Ay pressed his lips together, watching her suspiciously. Finally he said, "No. It's empty."

"Send your man here for more, then. We'll have a nice, pleasant talk, you and I."

"I doubt that very much," Ay said. "There are no pleasant talks with you anymore. And anyway, I won't waste my time or my breath on a mad woman. Declaring yourself king—it defies belief. You should have stayed with Akhenaten, girl. You suited one another perfectly."

She tossed her head, as if in amusement. "No wine for me, then?"

"None." Ay licked his lips, his eyes darting about the room before they landed on her face again and lingered there, cautious and glittering. "Go to the kitchens and get it yourself, if you're so thirsty."

He suspects me, Nefertiti realized. *He won't be alone with me, no matter how I try to convince him. I shall have to attack anyway, witnesses or no.*

She opened her mouth, ready to make some ribbing comment. But the high, piping sound of a child's laugh rang out suddenly, and a moment later she heard a few lines of one of the songs Tutankhaten loved to sing. Nefertiti looked toward the sound. Beside the mural of Sekhmet, a side door hung barely open. The crack along its edge flickered with cheerful light.

"Tutankhaten is here, in your apartments?"

"Why not?" Ay said with a dismissive shrug. "As I am his regent, I thought it fitting to keep him close, where I can teach him." He added with emphasis, "*Protect* him. His personal staff are readying him for bed. It is already far too late for a boy of his age to be up, but he was excited by the move."

I won't like to kill Ay where the boy can see it. He's a sensitive child, and he won't understand why I do it. Perhaps I can convince Ay to come outside, to walk with me in the garden... But no. Ay had many faults, but no one could accuse him of gullibility— least of all his own daughter. And there he sat on his couch, watching her with those searching, penetrating eyes. He was on the alert, waiting for Nefertiti to betray the purpose, to reveal the need that had brought her here.

"Why don't you sit down?" Ay asked smoothly.

Nefertiti shook her head. "I am quite comfortable standing." If she sat, the shawl might part and reveal her weapon—or she might not be able to draw it quickly enough when her moment came. She and Nann hadn't practiced any seated maneuvers. She couldn't take the chance.

"Well," Ay said, "I don't see what purpose you serve here—standing there like a lady's maid, when you claim to be a Pharaoh. That pillar doesn't need you to hold it up."

"I've come to talk about Tutankhaten," she said again.

"There is no point in talking about the boy. You won't have him back from me. Make your peace with that fact, Nefertiti. You've proven yourself a most egregious mother, especially in this mess with Meritaten. The boy doesn't need your maternal influence. He is better off without it, I think."

"Look at you, throwing stones when your house doesn't even have walls. You were not a good father, Ay. Tell me, have you found a whipping boy for Tutankhaten? Do you make that poor boy watch while another child takes his punishments?"

Just for a moment—so brief it might have been a trick of the dancing lamp light—real pain flitted across Ay's face. It took Nefertiti aback. Suddenly she could feel the coldness of the stone pillar reaching through her shawl and smell the char of the roasted bones scattered on Ay's tray. The jolt of surprise seemed to heighten all her senses, sending a panic deep into her chest, as if she had just stepped outside to find the river in the sky and the stars spread across the earth. Nefertiti had never known her father to have regrets—not of any kind. But in that moment she had seen the self-accusation plain on his face.

"I erred," Ay said. "I was very hard on you and your sister. Harder than I needed to be."

It was not an apology, but it was very close. The sheer rarity of it took Nefertiti's breath away, stunning her to stillness. She stood gaping at him, unable to speak anymore.

Ay rose from his couch, straightening his old joints gingerly. He came to stand in front of her, so that she was caught between him—his hard, all-seeing eyes—and the pillar. "I will not give up the regency," he said, "but you and I could work together to raise Tutankhaten. It isn't... *necessary*, that we should be forever at odds."

Slowly, Ay's hand raised. It took all of Nefertiti's composure to resist flinching, to hold herself still instead of ducking and spinning away. Her father's touch had always been like iron, cold and unforgiving. But now he laid a hand on her shoulder, and it was gentle—almost friendly.

Nefertiti frowned at him in confusion, in wonder.

"What are you—?"

She didn't have time to finish the question. Fast as a soldier's arrow, Ay pulled aside the drape of her shawl. His eyes fastened at once on the sword in its scabbard, then darted back up to pin her against the pillar, dark and shining with every drop of his accustomed fury.

"You viper," he spat. Then he shouted over his shoulder, "Mahu!"

The door that hid Tutankhaten from her view flew open. Mahu filled the frame like a flash flood, crashing, inexorable. The guard's jaw clenched when he saw Nefertiti, her sword exposed. Her stomach twisted violently as she recalled Mahu's cold calculation, the ease with which he had disposed of poor, lost Kiya.

Nefertiti shoved her father hard; he was braced for her reaction, but still he stumbled back just enough that she could dodge out of his grasp. As she rushed for the relative safety of the outer corridor, she heard Mahu's stride behind her, his heavy footfalls like an army's drums, driving soldiers on toward their deaths.

Nefertiti scrambled out into the hall, but Mahu caught the edge of her shawl. She turned to face him, panic draining away, the confidence of her goddesses returning in a warm, buoyant flood. Death would not find her while she ran like a frightened hare. She faced Mahu squarely, meeting his hard stare with all its dire promise with look just as ready, just as fierce. With a smooth, singing hiss, the sword emerged from beneath her shawl, steady in her hand.

Nefertiti levelled the blade at Mahu's heart. The big man blinked down at it, then burst into laughter, as if were the best joke in all the world, to feel the point of a sword at his chest. But Nefertiti was not shaken, nor did lower her blade. She stepped firmly toward him, digging the point against his breastbone. His flesh split; a red stream ran down his hard, flat belly to stain the white of his kilt. Mahu yielded before her advance, but the condescending grin never left his face.

He lifted his own blade, a long, wicked dagger that was nevertheless not long enough to reach Nefertiti's body. Mahu clashed its blade against her sword. "You don't know the first thing about fighting, Lady Pharaoh. Put down your blade and surrender. I'll be merciful if you do."

"I know you better than that, Mahu."

She pressed again, and he sucked a thin gasp through his clenched teeth, retreating another step. She could see the tension in his body, how ready he was to spring and slash at her face, her neck, the moment Nefertiti gave him an opening. What Mahu had said was true; she didn't know the first thing about fighting with blades. But she could sense by some instinct—by the wisdom of the war-goddesses that still possessed her—that she had blundered into a treacherous place. As long as she kept her arm straight, her sword hard against his chest, Mahu could not reach her. But the moment she tried to hack at him, or to parry his own testing blows, she would lose her fragile advantage.

I must make a decisive move soon. But how? Desperate, she pressed forward again, backing Mahu toward a pillar. If she could only find the right angle, the leverage she needed to deliver one strong thrust. It might be enough to strike through to his heart—to end the threat of Mahu forever.

His back connected with the pillar. Nefertiti's breath burned in her throat; her legs shook with the violent energy that seemed to burst out from her chest.

Mahu's laugh was like stones falling in the cliffs of Akhet-Aten, loud and cracking and hard. He paid no heed to the blood that coursed down his body. He slapped at her sword again with the dagger's long blade. "What will you do now, Lady Pharaoh? What, take my heart?"

Nefertiti glared up at him—and froze. A thin, pale arm emerged from the shadow of the pillar. It twined around Mahu's neck—a fluid gesture, tender, like a lover's embrace. Nefertiti's sword hand quivered; her blade drooped, even as Mahu's eyes widened in shock. Another hand appeared. Nefertiti could see the freckles scattered on its skin, across knuckles tensed on the grip of a short, sharp knife. The knife flashed as it cut through the air. It slid smoothly over Mahu's throat, and the sound he made was terrible—a rasp, a gurgle, the cut-off breath of a groan. The red fountain gushed forth; Nefertiti shouted in disgust and staggered back, dancing away from the spreading pool that shone grotesquely in the lamp light.

Mahu fell face down into his own blood. Nann stood in his place, her white face calm, still with grim satisfaction.

"Aunt!"

Nefertiti turned, dazed, toward the cry. Tutankhaten ran from Ay's chamber; he checked and stared at the blood, at Mahu stretched along the floor.

Now! Take him! At once! The goddesses cried out sharply in Nefertiti's heart. She swept him up in her arms and held him tightly. The boy was heavy, and the strength was quickly leaving her body, replaced by wracking shivers. She still held the sword in her fist. She would not let it go.

"I have you now," she said to Tutankhaten, unsure whether those words were triumph or relief. "Nann, quickly—where is Ay?"

Nann darted around the blood, peering into the chamber. Ay's servants came bowling past her, scattering, crying out at the sight of Mahu and dragging each other away, down the long corridors into the dark. Nann caught one of them by the arm. "Where is Ay?"

"Gone," the man panted. "The garden door!"

With a growl, Nann shoved him away. His feet slipped in the blood; he nearly went down, but with a cry he righted himself and hurried after his fellows.

"Horemheb," Nefertiti ordered. "Quickly. Horemheb must find Ay—apprehend him—he mustn't escape the palace! Go now!"

"But you—"

"No one will harm me while I have the heir in my

arms. Go!"

Nann gave her a steady look, brows lowered with determination, lips pressed white in her moon-pale face. Then she spun and sprinted away, shouting for Horemheb.

Nefertiti's fist tightened on the sword's hilt, even as she settled Tutankhaten on her hip as gently as she could manage. Ay was out there somewhere—alive, furious, knowing full well that Nefertiti had planned his death. He would act without any hesitation. He must he found straight away, before he could leave the palace and go to ground in some obscure shelter to plot and plan. For Nefertiti was certain that Ay would not give her a second chance to strike. Green wings beat close beside her ear. Her death was close—but there was no knife at her throat yet. She might yet survive, with the gods' mercy.

She turned away from Mahu's corpse and strode toward her chambers.

Horemheb

Year 2 of Nefer-Neferu-Aten, Beloved of the Beautiful Appearance

Year 1 of Tutankhaten, Lord of the Forms of the Sun

He saw Mutnodjmet sitting alone on the pale limestone wall of the lake. She gazed down patiently into her lap, running her bare toes through the short grass. In the light of moon and stars he could just make out the shade of her dress: pale pinkish-red, simple in cut but suited to a well-respected servant placed highly in the hierarchy of the palace. Horemheb would have preferred to see her in something much finer. It wasn't that he didn't find Mutnodjmet beautiful in this garment. With her shoulders and delicate collarbone bared, limned in the white light of the full moon, Horemheb couldn't have thought her lovelier even if she were draped in all the jeweled finery of a King's Great Wife. But he knew Mutnodjmet would have preferred more—a better, more fashionable dress, more status than that of a servant, a private home, a finer life.

I will give it to you one day. I will make all your fondest dreams come true. Before he went down into the Duat to face judgment for his grievous sin, he would build a life for Mutnodjmet that made her happy—the life she truly deserved. *I will do one good thing before I die.* It wouldn't be enough to save his ka, but it would make him proud and satisfied, to make his wife more than what she was now.

She looked up at the sound of his footsteps on the garden path and smiled. The lake behind her reflected the dazzling moon; she was haloed in ethereal light, as pretty and benevolent as a goddess in a shrine. Horemheb sat close beside her and kissed her gently on the neck.

"It's like old times, isn't it?" she said. "Meeting in the dark of night, sneaking away from our duties to kiss under the stars."

"We were foolish and reckless then," Horemheb agreed.

"Not so foolish, I think." Her soft hand stole into his. "Here we are, living in the palace, close to the king. We turned out all right in the end."

"I think your parents would still like to flay me alive for stealing the heart of their youngest daughter."

"Mother always scolded me. 'He's just a common-born soldier! He'll never take you anywhere in life!' But look what my soldier has done for me. I am body servant to the Pharaoh! My mother would have killed for a position of such honor."

Mutnodjmet giggled, rocking on the lake's edge. She gave every appearance of satisfaction with her lot in life. But Horemheb couldn't shake his guilt. She deserved more. Brave as she was—all the years of their struggle while they freed themselves from Akhet-Aten's insidious influence—she deserved a status that was higher still. She deserved to be set amid the stars that glowed against her skin.

Wrapped in these thoughts, Horemheb blinked in surprise. Had he ever loved Baketaten so much? He must have. Did he not commit the ultimate sin in Baketaten's name? But he had never lived with Baketaten, never grown with her. Mutnodjmet had cast a spell on him, by her simple proximity, her persistence in his life. And now he couldn't imagine that he had ever thought her a burden. The gods had blessed his foolish heart a hundred times over—more than he deserved, certainly. He doubted there was another man alive who could claim his wife was not only unfailingly loyal but brave and resilient as a war horse—and as beautiful as the full moon shining.

He wrapped his arm around her, rejoicing in the shape

of her body, her fragrant warmth. "It certainly is like old days in one respect. Our duties have kept us both so busy that I haven't been able to see nearly enough of you. I've been hungry for you."

"I won't do anything here," she warned. "Even if there's no person prowling through the garden, there are owls and bats in the trees, and frogs in the water. I won't have *them* watching us. Can you imagine?" She shivered.

Horemheb laughed. "That's not what I meant. I've hardly *seen* you for days. Just to sit beside you, to talk to you, is like the breath of life to me."

She smiled at him shyly. "I've missed you, too. It's so strange, to see you so often while we're in Nefertiti's company, but to be unable to..." She trailed off, squeezing his hand.

"How have you liked your duties?"

"Very well," she said, but there was a hint of sadness in her voice. "Nefertiti is a kind and gracious woman. But if I must work in the palace, I do wish I could care for the little king again."

Horemheb nodded in sympathy. He too longed to watch over Tutankhaten as he once had. He worried about the boy's safety, and feared Ay would prove a wicked influence on his tender young heart. The loss must be greater for Mutnodjmet. Without any children of her own, she had grown especially close to Tutankhaten. She must miss him almost as much as a mother would.

"Let's not stray toward sadness," he said. "We finally have a night together, and—"

The sound of panic erupted on the other side of the garden, the thud of many feet running, incoherent shouts as a dozen voices clamored together. It seemed the people were fleeing along the length of a portico. As they passed the opening and plunged on into the heart of the palace, their voices were muffled by the palace walls, but Horemheb could still make the faint cries of alarm.

"What's happening?" Mutnodjmet sprang to her feet.

Horemheb rose more slowly, a wary tingle creeping up his spine. He had heard shouts like this before— the running feet clattering along a palace corridor, the chorus of panicked cries. The night of Baketaten's death returned forcefully to his memory. Akhenaten's death, too. "Someone has been killed," he said.

Mutnodjmet clutched at his arm. "How can you be sure?"

"Where is Nefertiti?"

Before Mutnodjmet could answer, a pale figure came sprinting into the garden, skirt flying, arms pumping at a dogged pace.

"It's Nann!" Mutnodjmet cried.

Horemheb called to her; the Hurrian veered toward them and stood panting, her breath spent. But despite her exertion, a strange fire of confidence burned in her *ka*. Her green eyes were wild, but not with fear. "Nefertiti wants you. Come at once!"

Horemheb pressed a hand to his fluttering stomach. "Thank the gods she's all right."

"Not for long, if you don't hurry. Come now!"

Horemheb took Mutnodjmet by her shoulders, gazing down earnestly into her face. "Back to your room. Quick as you can. Bar yourself in and don't open the door, unless it's for me, Nann, or Nefertiti herself."

Mutnodjmet nodded, trembling. "All right."

Horemheb turned to follow Nann, but his wife cried, "Wait!" He glanced back at her—and grunted in surprise as she threw herself into his arms. Her kiss was fierce and passionate, but she parted from him quickly. Mutnodjmet was no fool; she too could sense the terrible urgency that suddenly colored the night. "Be careful," she said. Then she darted away through the garden.

HOREMHEB AND NANN found Nefertiti in her own apartments, close beside the garden gate, thank the gods. She sat on her feather-stuffed couch, surrounded by burning lamps, calmly holding Tutankhaten on her lap. Ankhesenpaaten was there with her, too. The girl moved unhurriedly around the room, lighting ever more lamps until the air smelled hot and singed.

"More light," Nefertiti said as Horemheb slid through the door and barred it shut behind him. Her voice was perfectly controlled, fearless. But as she watched Ankhesenpaaten move about the room, her eyes were wide and strained with fear or some other unaccustomed emotion—shock? Disbelief?

"My lady," Horemheb began.

Nefertiti cut him off, snapping a hard glare at Nann. "I told you to send Horemheb after Ay!"

"You need protection," Nann replied. "Ay has many loyal followers, from servants to soldiers to fat, balding noblemen. Anyone at all may strike against you, knowing what you planned to do."

"Nonsense!" Nefertiti clicked her tongue in disgust. "Now Ay has slipped free."

"He has nowhere to go but into the palace."

"Oh, he won't remain here. He has allies in the city— he seeds them everywhere. The gods alone know where he is now. Nann, you blasted fool!"

Nann shrugged. Then, to Horemheb's amazement, she cast a rather withering look at Nefertiti. "Then I'll go out into the city myself and track him down. Do you think I can't? You saw what I can do."

Horemheb stepped into the space between them. Both women's eyes snapped to him. "What did you do?" he asked Nann, half afraid of the answer.

She answered casually. "Killed Mahu. Slit his throat. It was easy, like slaughtering a goat."

"The gods never made a goat as strong or fierce as Mahu," Horemheb muttered.

He jumped as the door thudded against its bar. Tutankhaten squirmed and whined on Nefertiti's lap; Nann produced from somewhere—her belt, perhaps—a small, sharp knife with a blade like a lion's claw. She slunk close to the door, her body like a bow bent and ready to fire. Horemheb drew his own dagger and joined her on the door's other side.

"Let me in!" It was Meritaten's voice, shrill with anger. "What have you done, Mother? Open this door!"

Nefertiti nodded to Horemheb; he flipped the bar from the door and pulled it open quickly while Nann dragged Meritaten inside. The door slammed shut again as Meritaten jerked herself out of Nann's grip.

She rounded on Nefertiti. "Answer me! What have you done?"

"Not half of what needed doing," Nefertiti said wryly.

"How like you," Meritaten seethed, "to lash out for your own ends. How like you, to turn the palace upside-down for your own gratification. I shall be surprised at nothing, after this!"

"Sister," Ankhesenpaaten said, reaching out toward Meritaten.

But the furious young woman batted her hand away and strode toward Nefertiti, ringed by her dozens of lamps. Meritaten stretched out an imperious hand. "Let Tutankhaten go. He belongs with me, not you."

Nefertiti's eyes narrowed, withering, unamused. "You aren't his regent. You sold that position to Ay, for all the power he could ever desire."

"You aren't his regent, either, whatever you may believe."

Tutankhaten twisted in Nefertiti's arms. "Put me down!" he whined. "I'm not a baby; let me walk."

"Hush, child." Nefertiti jerked her head at Nann, summoning her to take the boy. But Nann stared back belligerently, holding her tiny knife up in a fist crusted with dried blood. She edged closer to Meritaten, ready to strike if need be.

It was Ankhesenpaaten who took the boy. "Come now, Tut," she said softly. "Let's leave these grown-ups to their dull talk and play a game. You'll stay with me, won't you?"

The boy nodded and took Ankhesenpaaten's hand. She hurried him away—out of reach of Meritaten—into a corner of the brightly lit room.

"Nann was right to bring me here, to you," Horemheb said to Nefertiti. "You need protection, my lord. And Tutankhaten—we should send him away, somewhere safe. If I know how your bloodline works—" he cut a suspicious glance at Meritaten— "this palace is about to burst into a storm of violence. It's not safe here for any child, but especially not for one as important as he."

Nefertiti raised a hand, abrupt, silencing. "No. Tutankhaten must stay here. He needs to learn—needs to see what he will face when he is grown."

"It's *you* we should send away!" Meritaten scuffed the toe of her sandal hard against the floor, kicking imagined dust at her despised mother. "Just *leave*, let us go on in peace, before you pull the whole palace down around our ears! You aren't welcome here, and you tempt the Aten's patience. The god will not long abide your blasphemy, this sick twisting of the kingship."

Hatred burned hot in Meritaten's eyes and smoldered in her words. Unlike Ankhesenpaaten, this daughter had never forgiven Nefertiti, never cultivated any fondness for her mother. Her anger at Nefertiti would only rise, growing up like a sapling from rich soil—until finally it stretched out its dark limbs and bore fruit. She would do something drastic, foolish—dangerous. She would try to put her mother out of her life forever. By instinct he moved closer, towering over his mistress protectively.

Meritaten scowled at Horemheb. "Don't look at me as if I'll harm your precious jape of a king. I am not vicious and corrupt. But my mother is. It's she you should look to for outrages, not me!"

"Not vicious and corrupt?" Nann said breezily. "Do you truly think so?"

Meritaten gaped at her. "You dare to insult me with

such talk! You, a *rekhet*—and not even an Egyptian!"

Nann grinned. The gap in her tooth made her look positively cheeky; Meritaten's already flushed face heated like fanned flames.

"I'm going to find Ay," Meritaten said, turning her nose up at Nann. "I've no time for your games, Mother. If you're wise, you'll be gone from this palace by the time I locate him. I've reached the end of my patience with you. An exile to Punt would do nicely."

"She won't be exiled." Ankhesenpaaten spoke up, calling from the corner of the room where she sheltered Tutankhaten behind her skirt. "She is not soft and broken, like Kiya's daughter. You'd be wise to cooperate with her, Meritaten."

"You always stay so silent, until your words aren't wanted," Meritaten raged. "And then you're quick enough to speak! Leave now, Nefertiti; you won't appreciate the farewell I give you once Ay is beside me again."

She stormed to the door, knocked the bar aside with a furious blow, and vanished from the chamber. The room was silent in her wake, save for the crackle and hiss of the lamp wicks.

Horemheb broke the silence. "It's Meritaten who should be exiled. Her hatred is intense. She's dangerous to you, my lord."

"I won't hear of it," Nefertiti said softly. "As much as it pains me to admit it, Ay was correct: I must have a Great Wife, or the traditionalists will never accept me. And if I'm to overpower Ay, I must hold the king's throne—at least until Ay is finally dealt with. I almost managed tonight—*almost*. But though I failed, by the grace of the gods I have survived to try again. I *will* succeed. I must. And when I do, I will gladly give the kingdom to Tutankhaten. But until Ay is gone, the throne is safe with no one but me."

"Can't Ankhesenpaaten stand as your Great Wife?" Horemheb could hear the pleading in his own voice, but he couldn't temper it away. The night's panic—and

Meritaten's boiling rage—had been too much. Nefertiti was in danger; he was sure of it. If he could only make her see it, acknowledge it. Then she might consent to a safer course, a wiser, more stable path.

"No," she said. "The moment I'm able—the moment this chaos in the palace settles—I'll marry my daughter to Tutankhaten. That way, if anything should happen to me—" she gave Horemheb a tolerant smile, a look that said such an event was unthinkable, impossible— "he can take over his own kingship smoothly, immediately—with no obstacles to his succession."

Horemheb bent his head and said softly, so neither Tutankhaten nor Ankhesenpaaten could hear, "Then kill Meritaten. You *must*, my lord; she is dangerous. I've seen that fire in a person before, but only when they're willing to kill." *And I've felt that fire in my own heart, just before I plunged my blade into Akhenaten's chest.*

Nefertiti returned a hard glare. "I've wasted enough of my children's lives. If I can keep Tutankhaten's throne safe for him without killing another daughter, then I will do it, Horemheb. And that is my final word on the subject."

Horemheb straightened, sighing. He could still feel the violence of the night, shuddering deep in the bones of the old palace. It tingled along his nerves; the clatter as Meritaten knocked the door's bar aside still seemed to echo in his ears. He stared at that door, at the place where Meritaten had vanished. Spots of color danced before his eyes, the ghosts of the lamps Nefertiti had lit to drive back the cold reach of night.

Ay

A Y PAUSED IN THE DARK of the alley's mouth, concealing himself behind a stack of old, clay beer jars while a handful of men, dressed in the short kilts and red sashes of palace stewards, hurried along the street. He breathed in the stink of Waset's air—rotting refuse, piss and worse from the slimy puddles at his feet—counting his breaths until the stewards were past him. Then he slipped out of the shadows and fell in behind them, moving with the same brisk, efficient air toward the palace, a slab of indigo darkness against the predawn sky.

He took a great risk in returning to the palace, for the gods alone knew how well Nefertiti had done in his absence. Had she grown her feeble power, bringing more supporters to her cause? With Tutankhaten in her possession—as the boy surely was now, three days after she had attacked Ay—she might be capable of nearly any miracle of state. He might return to find the palace and even the priests in the temple district beyond swayed to Nefertiti's favor. But Ay knew he had little choice. The situation with Nefertiti had reached its tipping point. One of their lives would be forfeit—she had decided that when she'd brought the sword into his chamber. Nefertiti may be his daughter, but Ay was determined that *he* would not be the one to die. What good was a daughter now, anyway? Unmarriageable as her age advanced, so full of dangerous hubris that she would grasp and take for her own benefit, she was of no further use to Ay. She could safely be discarded—more to the point, she must be disposed of now, before she struck again.

He had hidden in the city, taking a room at an inn under a false name, and there watched and waited for his opportunity to re-enter the palace under some plausible disguise. He knew he had found that chance when Nefertiti called for a host of additional stewards to plan and coordinate the wedding of Tutankhaten to Ankhesenpaaten. The work was to begin shortly after sunrise.

It had taken very little effort to procure the garments of a palace steward. He knew a certain rich man whose wealth was nonetheless insufficient to feed his gambling debts. The man's wife was made to work in the palace laundry, and for a promise of a few trinkets from the palace treasury—which he would throw down on the betting boards the moment he had the chance—Ay had a steward's garb delivered, freshly washed and pleats pressed, to his room at the inn. A simple cloak with a hood—not so fine that it would look suspicious on a man of modest means—completed his camouflage.

Blending among the bustling stewards—the men already discussed their grand visions for the wedding to come, its spectacles and rich, bounteous feast—Ay was all but invisible. They passed through the great, towering pylons of the palace gate without comment or suspicion from the soldiers who guarded it—double the usual number, for Nefertiti was keen to find Ay. If she did apprehend him, Ay had no illusions that he would find a daughter's mercy. The end would come swiftly—immediately. But he was calm as he passed through the gauntlet of soldiers. Without the long, formal kilt of a well-placed nobleman, without a rich man's fashionable wig, no one had reason to look twice at Ay's face. Stewards, like soldiers, were both numerous and interchangeable, no more individual than birds in a flock. The men who guarded Nefertiti's gate were like most people in the world, never looking deeper than the surface of the water, never caring what creatures swam below. They saw short kilts and red sashes, not faces, not features—not a threat to their would-be king.

Beyond the largest courtyard, with the gate guards far behind him, Ay slowed his steps, hanging back as the group of murmuring stewards pressed on toward the throne room. Once free of the group, it was a simple matter to slip through little-used corridors toward the grand central garden, the hub of the palace. There he paused, gazing up at the sky. The stars were rapidly fading, the moon small and weak, sinking below the edge of the palace wall. Dawn would come soon—in an hour, perhaps a little more. *I haven't much time. I must act now.*

Ay cut across the middle of the garden, skirting the long, artificial lake. Water lapped smoke-gray against the retaining walls as night lost its darkness. He passed through a grove of sycamores and saw the wing of the palace where Meritaten kept her rooms. A single light, small and golden, burned in one of her windows. *A good sign. The gods are with me, for whatever that's worth.*

Ay went directly to her bed chamber door. As he hurried through the grass, a figure passed across the window—not Meritaten; this woman was both tall and plump. One of her ladies, then. She noted Ay's approach and cried out in alarm, but a heartbeat later Meritaten appeared at the window, peering out, all the soft planes of her lovely face blued by the last remnants of night. Quickly, Ay pulled back the hood of his cloak and stood waiting. She blinked at him, then recognition dawned on her face, brows lifting, mouth open in silent surprise.

When Meritaten pulled open her chamber door and beckoned for him to hurry inside, Ay saw that her chambers were empty. She had sent all her maids away—a caution he appreciated. She was still dressed in her night clothes, but Ay could see a bit of blue linen spread across her bed—she had just risen, it seemed, to prepare for the great meeting of the stewards, the state-sanctioned fuss over Tutankhaten's wedding.

"I've looked for you," she whispered, "all over the palace! I even sent men into the city, but they never found you. Where have you been hiding?"

"It's better for you if you don't know. Nefertiti might go to any lengths to find out. She is more viper than mother."

Meritaten's eyelids slid down heavily. "You don't know how right you are. But what can we do now? She has Tutankhaten, and the palace guards are all in a tangle; they won't do anything useful for anybody—not until they're clear about who is in charge."

"I am in charge," Ay said, biting back his annoyance. "I am the regent, sworn before the gods, by your command when you were still King's Great Wife."

"You needn't tell me that. But it hardly matters; without you here, they were all ready to take orders from Nefertiti— the guards, the priests—everybody." She hesitated, then said, "And it seems a good many of them feel she is king by rights, now that she has claimed me as her Great Wife."

Ay cursed inwardly. How many had already defected, trickling over to Nefertiti's cause? He was more certain than ever that he must get rid of his meddling daughter— and keep his own hands clean in the matter, if he had any hope of winning back the support he'd already lost.

"She hasn't married you yet," Ay said. "Or at least, she hasn't dragged you to the temple for a *farce* of marriage."

"No, not yet," she agreed. But her voice was flat with defeat. "I have no doubt she will, though. Last night she told me to dress beautifully this morning, and to be ready early. For certain, she plans to announce our wedding to the whole court, as soon as the stewards have worked out all the details for Tutankhaten's own ceremony. Isn't that sweet?" Her voice dripped bitter irony. "A double wedding, the young heir and the ruling Pharaoh, taking sisters as their brides. It's like something from a story."

"You can't let her force you into the marriage ceremony," Ay said, pushing the blue dress aside, sitting on her bed. "I fear for you, Meritaten. She will drag you down and use you up. And then she will dispose of you. She does it with ease, without any thought—removing people from her path."

The girl was silent for a moment, staring out her window into the gray garden. "I know."

"You don't know the half of it." Ay's pause was dramatic, and he sighed, a gust of regret that sounded authentic, even to himself. "I must tell you, girl—I feel it is my duty. But you must be brave."

She turned away from the window, one hand at her throat as if clutching the stone of tension she suddenly found there. "What must you tell me? Speak!"

Ay lowered his gaze. "Nefertiti killed Smenkhkare."

Meritaten's stricken gasp seemed to fill the whole chamber. Ay peered up quickly from the floor to find her staring at nothing, face pale, eyes wide and tragic—and slowly, slowly, her hand curled into a fist. *Perfect.*

"I always suspected," Meritaten finally said, her trembling voice no louder than a breath. "But I had no proof. How do you know?"

"She told me herself." Ay shrugged helplessly. "She was quite proud of it. She hired a poisoner, a very skilled man from Akhet-Aten, and positioned him in our kitchen, here at Waset. Little by little—so slowly its effects would not be noted until it was far too late—she sickened Smenkhkare from afar."

With one great cry of pain, Meritaten overcame her shock. Rage filled the place where it had sat in her heart—rage and cold, well-cultivated hatred. "I knew it—I *knew!*" She threw herself toward the window, pounded her fists against its frame until finally she fell back, wincing at her skinned hands, unable to break free of her prison. She whirled and ran to her bed, then fell prone along it, weeping into her bunched-up coverlet. "Oh, Smenkhkare! My love!"

Ay laid a gentle hand on her back. "Your love, your feelings, meant nothing to Nefertiti—*mean* nothing. She does not feel. She is as cold and hard as bronze, as impersonal. Smenkhkare was in her way—he, the righteous king who kept Nefertiti from the throne she imagined could be hers. And so she destroyed his life callously, to satisfy her revenge. His life, and your heart with it."

"I hate her," Meritaten wailed. The bedding muffled her cries, but her body shook with the force of her sobs. "I wish the god would strike her down! Why has the Aten never taken her? Why, when so many others of greater worth have been taken?"

Ay took Meritaten by the shoulders, lifting her gently, guiding her up so that she sat with her head drooping against his shoulder.

"Perhaps the Aten was waiting for the right instrument to do the job."

Ay's voice was so laden with meaning that Meritaten calmed her weeping. She looked at Ay soberly, blinking back her tears.

"What do you mean?"

"No one has more cause to strike against Nefertiti than you—no one's actions could be more righteous. She took Smenkhkare from you, and now she tries to trap you in a mockery of marriage so that she may use you for her own ends."

Bewildered, Meritaten shook her head. "Are you... suggesting...?"

Ay reached beneath his short cloak and found the dagger he had concealed in the thick wrapping of the red sash. He slid it from its hiding place, held it up between them. In the flickering lamp light, the dagger's point glinted like the last stars in the sky. Then, deliberately, he placed the hilt in Meritaten's hand.

"*Maat* is on your side," he said quietly. "You know the Aten hates murder, but a killing is not murder if it restores righteousness to the world. Nor is it murder if the one who does it is undeniably just."

Meritaten stared down at the blade in her hand, thoughtful and silent. Finally she asked in a tremulous tone, "I... how can I do such a thing?"

"You are strong enough. *Maat* gives you power." Ay laid his hand on her shoulder and squeezed. "Do you not wish to avenge Smenkhkare's death?"

The girl's dark, tear-reddened eyes flashed, locking with his. And Ay could read their hardness, their pain: *I am ready.*

Meritaten

Year 2 of Nefer-Neferu-Aten,
Beloved of the Beautiful Appearance

Year 1 of Tutankhaten,
Lord of the Forms of the Sun

Meritaten dropped her night dress on the tile floor of her bath. A chill crept up her legs, settling in the small of her back as she knotted the steward's kilt around her hips. She didn't know whether the shiver in her spine had more to do with the waning night's cold, or with the dread that hung around her like a thick perfume, choking her breath. She pushed that fear away, refusing to examine it, to feel it. Righteousness would soon be done. She would bring justice to Smenkhkare, to her own heart—to all of the Two Lands.

She left her night dress where it fell and hurried back to her bed chamber. She felt naked, vulnerable, though she was only bare below the knees and from her waist up. She would look just like a palace steward, if not for her breasts.

Ay, wrapped in one of Smenkhkare's embroidered robes—which Meritaten had kept folded in her wardrobe ever since his death—nodded in approval. He held out the red steward's sash and guided her as she tied it. Then he swept the short, hooded cloak he had worn around her shoulders.

"There," he finally said, stepping back to examine her. "That ought to do for a disguise, as long as no one looks too closely."

Her stomach tightened. "As long as—?"

"Don't fret. It's quite simple to go about unseen. You

257

just need to know the trick of it. Walk confidently, and in the open—don't slink about in shadows. Act as if you belong exactly where you are. Then no one will look twice at you, and with the cloak no one can tell whether you are a woman or a man. Besides," he added, "you won't need your disguise for long. Just long enough to get inside her chamber."

Meritaten felt far distant from herself, as if she floated high against the ceiling, like a *ka* reluctant to return to its body after a long night of dreaming. "I am ready," she said, sliding the dagger into her sash. But she wasn't at all certain that she *was* ready.

Ay squinted at her, weighing her courage. "You will not falter?"

"Never. For Smenkhkare, I will do anything." That, at least, she knew was true. Now that her long suspicion of Nefertiti's guilt had finally been confirmed, she was eager to avenge the only man who had ever delighted her heart. *When I join you someday in the Field of Reeds, Smenkhkare, you will greet me as a heroine. And together we will spend eternity satisfied, knowing justice was done.*

Ay opened the garden door and held it while Meritaten slipped through. "I won't be here when you return," he told her. "But I will know when the deed is done. By and by, I'll return."

"When you do, I shall give you a great reward. You have served me well, Ay, in telling me the truth."

He smiled at her, and in the warmth of his gaze, in his unflagging support, Meritaten felt *maat* rise within her. She was a vessel for righteousness, an instrument of good.

"Go now," Ay said softly, "and do the Aten's work."

She went swiftly through the garden—walking, as Ay had advised her, with a confidence as smooth and direct as the river's flow. The sky overhead had lightened. It was starless now, the black of night having given way to a pale, feather-soft gray. The faintest suggestion of a rosy blush spread low along the eastern horizon. The god would rise soon, spilling its righteousness down to drive away all darkness, all shadows, all vile, corrupted deeds. But the palace servants would be awake then, too, and would stop her if they found her. Meritaten had very little time.

The door that led from the garden into Nefertiti's bed chamber was painted a garish red; Meritaten found it easily, even in the pre-dawn dimness. She hesitated beside a cluster of rose bushes, watching the palace wing carefully: the grounds that surrounded the old mudbrick building, the rooftop where soldiers might be stationed, alert for threats to their pretender king. But if anyone patrolled the rooftop, they were not in sight at that moment, and the red door was completely unguarded.

It's barred from within, then, Meritaten decided. Nefertiti's haste to bring about these royal marriages could only mean that she lived in constant fear of Ay's retaliation. She would not sleep unprotected.

She considered knocking, allowing Nefertiti's maids to think for a moment that she was a male steward, come on some business pertaining to the wedding—and then pulling her knife, slashing her way inside. But Nefertiti would be on the defensive by then, wakened by the screams of her women—if not by Meritaten's knocking.

As she chewed her lip, raking the building's façade with impatient eyes, she saw the dark, narrow mouth of a window, open beside a trellis of climbing vines. The window was certainly too narrow for any man to fit through—and for most women, too. But small and slender as Meritaten was, with the god's help she might just squeeze through it.

She hurried closer to inspect the window. Hardly wider than her two hands, it was little more than a ventilation slit, angled to catch the prevailing breezes from the river. It would be a very tight fit indeed—and she must work her way in silently, which made the task all the more difficult. But the god had provided a way. Meritaten knew she had to try, no matter how daunting the window seemed.

She took off her cloak and laid it gently in the soil below the window. Then she tightened her sash and tucked the dagger in more securely, afraid it would loosen and clatter against wall or window sill. Then, with one deep breath to brace herself for the struggle, she reached hands and feet into the vine-covered trellis and began to climb, slowly, cautiously, placing her body with painstaking care so she would not rattle the leaves. It felt as if an agonizing hour dragged by while she pulled herself up the trellis, one hand's breadth at a time. Finally she was high enough that she could stretch out one leg and brush the rough, cool edge of the sill with her bare toes. She stretched farther, the muscles in her leg and groin straining, and managed to set her foot flat upon the sill.

As she pushed and pulled herself inch after aching inch closer, Meritaten bit the inside of her cheek to keep herself from crying out in pain. Muscles stretched to the verge of tearing, and then, when she finally worked her left leg and shoulder into the chamber, she was obliged to pull her bent right leg so tight across her chest that she couldn't breathe. But at last she scooted, turned, wriggled as much as she dared, and found herself sitting on the inner edge of the window slit, looking down on Nefertiti's bed chamber.

Nefertiti tossed and murmured on her grand, gilt-legged bed. She had kicked her sheets aside; her body was bared to the dawn air, the tones of her skin warming by the moment as the first rays of sunlight crept in past Meritaten's body. Two maids lay on pallets spread across the floor. The door that led from the bed chamber to the receiving room beyond was closed, but not barred. Meritaten held her breath, listening, and heard the faintest scuff of sandals on tile, a whisper over the sleeping breath of the three women in the room.

The pains of her struggle ebbed from her body as she sat there in the window frame, hesitating. Nefertiti turned heavily onto her side, and Meritaten's heart froze.

She felt sure her mother would wake and find her there—and then what? *Find the knife in my belt. She'll know why I've come. She'll know Ay sent me. It will be all over then.* But in another moment Nefertiti shifted again, flat on her back, and Meritaten saw that she still slept, albeit poorly.

Fitting, that her sleep should be disturbed. Do her sins haunt her in her sleep? I wonder.

Still Meritaten could not make herself move, could not force herself to leap lightly down from the window sill and carry death to her mother's bedside. The longer she looked at Nefertiti's face, beautiful even when furrowed by a haunting dream, the faster a terrible ache spread through Meritaten's *ka*. Nefertiti had done great evil to her—and to Smenkhkare; him most of all. But she was still Meritaten's mother. *Why couldn't you have loved me?* she cried silently to the sleeping woman. *Why couldn't you have been glad for me to simply to be your daughter?* But Meritaten—the simple fact of her, the mere existence—had never been adequate. She was nothing to Nefertiti unless she was useful. Neither her heart nor her *ka* existed in her mother's reckoning. There was never any love for Meritaten—only pushing and pulling, only the tangled expectations of royalty, wrapping her like a hunter's net around a doomed, flapping, desperately crying bird.

Meritaten jumped down from the window sill, landing lightly on the balls of her feet and the spread fingers of her hands. Like a cat she held the pose, arched, bristling, waiting for any stir from the women. But the two maids slept on, and Nefertiti lay still on her bed, the dream subsiding, leaving her to relax in a more peaceful sleep.

Meritaten rose from her crouch and walked silently past the maids on their low, narrow pallets. She came to Nefertiti's bedside and stood gazing down. Through the dull force of her commitment, tenderness for her mother welled up again, quite against her will. *Is it possible to truly hate one's mother, even if she is as heartless as mine?* Perhaps if she woke Nefertiti now—perhaps she could climb into bed beside her, feel her mother's arms around her, the embrace of that purest love, which she had longed for all her life but had never felt. Perhaps before the sun rose, before the demands of court rose up to fill her day, Nefertiti would in fact love her—would behave as instinct told Meritaten a normal mother should behave—caring and gentle, forgiving and kind.

But in a flash, Meritaten recalled looking down in just this way on another bed, where another sleeper lay, still and distant, lost to his unknowable dreams. *Smenkhkare.*

That had been love—the best, the purest, unstained. And Nefertiti had snatched it away from Meritaten. Taken it, and never apologized, never repented.

All shadows of tenderness fled from Meritaten's heart, just as the shadows of night scatter before the Aten's golden truth. She would not hesitate, would not fail Smenkhkare now.

She drew the knife from her sash.

The whisper of the blade woke Nefertiti. Her eyes flew open, wide with fright—but she did not cry out for her maids. She blinked rapidly, dazed by the sleep that still clung to her—and finally, when she recognized Meritaten, when she saw the fury that bent her, that set her jaw, that surely flashed in her eyes like the god's own light, Nefertiti sighed and sank back against her cushions.

She held Meritaten's gaze for a long moment. Her face went still with understanding—acceptance.

Meritaten acted before she could think, before she could talk herself out of the deed. Her hand jerked up; the blade drew easily through Nefertiti's throat. Hot blood rushed out, covering Meritaten's hands. Nefertiti's face paled; her eyes bulged with pain, with the force of the instinctive scream she held back. But through that mask of suffering, Meritaten saw a gentler force move. Nefertiti watched her daughter as she died, and in that look Meritaten saw forgiveness—clear as a lotus pool—and a woeful surrender that told Meritaten plainly that even if she could have, even if there had been time, Nefertiti would not have cried out, would never have fought her. Death had come for Nefertiti—she knew it was her time— and she found no regret in dying at her own daughter's hand. She too knew it was *maat*.

Meritaten swallowed hard. The blood burned on her hands, hot as a boiling kettle; she stepped back from the bed, her stomach surging with a sudden roil of nauseous fear. As the last of her blood drained, Nefertiti's legs kicked hard; the bed shook on its golden lion's paws. The sound of it woke the maids. They sat up blearily, both in almost the same moment, and gazed around the chamber, filling slowly with morning light. But when their blinking eyes found the blood, the river of it pouring down from the bed to land noisily on the floor, both women leaped up, tossing their blankets aside, screeching like snared rabbits.

In that moment, with the force of Nefertiti's sympathy— her *love*—beating hard inside her chest, Meritaten knew with bitter clarity that Ay had played her for a fool. The maids' panicked screams were so loud, so frantic that Meritaten could all but feel them slapping against her face, stinging every bit of her bare, vulnerable skin. She would not be allowed to escape. She would never get back to her apartments, where Ay waited, smug in his victory. She would not come out of his terrible, cruel trap with her life.

The chamber door flew open. Horemheb, Nefertiti's favorite soldier, bulled inside the room with his dagger drawn. He stopped dead when he saw the blood still dripping down from the bed, falling like a cursed rain. He stared in horror at Nefertiti's limp, lifeless form, the gash marring what had once been her lovely, long, proudly-held neck. And Meritaten, standing over her with the knife still clutched in her fist.

She commanded her fingers to open. Through the shock and sadness they did; the hilt adhered to her palm for half a heartbeat, sticky with blood. Then it dropped, ringing on the floor tiles, tolling like a gong in Meritaten's ears, even over the screaming of the maids.

Horemheb approached slowly. At first he made no move to seize her. He merely stood beside her, looking down at the ruin of Nefertiti's sleep, his face pinched and stricken, struggling to hold back the tears that glinted in his eyes. Finally he looked at her, and Meritaten could read the question plainly on his face. *Why?* She did not resist when he took hold of her, his huge, strong hand encircling her upper arm.

"Go," Horemheb said briskly to the maids. "Send Nefer-Neferu-Aten's guards to protect Tutankhaten. He must not fall into Ay's hands. There is no time for grief! Stop screaming and go!"

When they had gone—still uttering cries of terror— Horemheb's shock turned all at once to helpless rage. He gave Meritaten a strong shake. "Why? In the name of the gods, *why?* She was your own mother!"

"A foul and corrupt mother," Meritaten said. But she wept as she spoke. What she said was true—Nefertiti had been a failure as a mother. But the pain of Horemheb's words still cut down to her *ka.*

She was your mother!

"You know they will kill you now," Horemheb said. "The Priests of Amun, and Nefertiti's soldiers. Her dedicated men—she had many, more than you know. I will not protect you from justice, merely because you were Nefertiti's daughter."

"I know," Meritaten said. She felt entirely calm now, resigned to her fate. "It doesn't matter. I've been played for a fool... but it doesn't matter. My whole life was fouled and corrupted, and taken from me, made... not my own. But hers was, too, wasn't it?"

She gazed up at Horemheb, hoping for some confirmation from the soldier—some acknowledgment that Meritaten and Nefertiti had had this secret kinship, this likeness that bound them together, even if Meritaten never knew it until now. But Horemheb only shook his head, dazed and sickened.

"We are all touched by darkness," Meritaten said. "My family, this blood. I am evil, too, am I not? The only good and pure thing in me was my love for Smenkhkare. But now he is gone, and I have nothing left to live for. Let the Aten do whatever he pleases with me. I don't care anymore."

Horemheb grunted in disgust. "It's not the Aten I'd worry about. They don't kill here in Waset the way your father did at Akhet-Aten. You won't be left for the sun to claim, but still they will make you suffer."

"No more than I have suffered already. And no more than I will suffer beyond. I am ready to face my judgment... for this—" She nodded forlornly toward the terrible, red mess she had made of Nefertiti— "and for everything else. I know what will become of my eternal *ka*. I'll be thrown to the Eater of Hearts. I'll be endlessly devoured. What other fate can I expect, for doing Ay's bidding like the fool I am? For killing my own mother?"

Horemheb dropped his head, shutting his eyes as if to block the sight of Meritaten's foulness as well as pale, still Nefertiti. He let out a ragged breath. But he didn't release his grip on Meritaten's arm.

"Even that will come as a relief, I think," she said quietly. "Ammit's teeth in my heart. The pain will be nothing beside losing Smenkhkare—and this is an even worse pain, this knowing that my love for him—the only good thing in my *ka*—was my weakness."

"Your weakness?" Horemheb's voice was gruff, disgusted.

"It was my love that let me be manipulated." She felt very far away, light, flitting—was her *ba* already departing, even while her body still lived? "Love turned me into the instrument of my own mother's death."

Horemheb was silent for a long moment. Meritaten heard, far down the palace's distant corridor, the sound of running feet, the shouts of hard, male voices.

Finally Horemheb said softly, "You poor girl."

She looked up at him in surprise. She was back suddenly—in herself, not drifting away. She felt everything, the blood cooling on her hands, the ache in her fingers where she had gripped the knife so tightly. The pounding of her heart, the quiver in her legs. And Horemheb's grip, locked tight in the flesh of her arm.

"All of you," he said. "Your sisters, all of them dead—and the one still living, too. I pity you, even now. Even seeing what you have done. I remember the night Meketaten died. Ankhesenpaaten came to me, asked me to protect her. But I didn't. I turned away."

Meritaten kept silent, watching his face. Pity was there, for certain, turning down the corners of his eyes. And regret, too, tightening his broad, square face.

"You were not the cause of Nefertiti's death," Horemheb said. "You were only the instrument. It was Ay who truly did it. I know it—but how can I prove it, when his friends speak in his defense? And they will speak. They will put him back on the throne. Easily now, with Nefertiti... dead."

A sudden sob, strong and unstoppable as a clap of thunder, ripped through Meritaten's chest. "There is no resisting Ay! He is too clever." Tears washed her cheeks, but all the tears in the world could never rinse the blood from her hands. "Nefertiti was too clever too—my mother. My mother! One of them had to die, Horemheb, don't you see? There was no way to make peace between them. Oh, but why—*why* did the gods let this burden fall on me?"

"Don't blame yourself," Horemheb said. "You wielded the knife, but it was Ay who truly struck the blow. I know it's true. Somehow I'll make them all see. Or if I can't, then I'll avenge Nefertiti. Somehow. I give you my word on that."

"And me," she said, choking on her tears. "Avenge me, too."

He stared down at her soberly, pressing his lips into a

hard, silent line.

"Don't let them take me to the temple, Horemheb! They'll punish me—they'll execute me! They'll make me suffer; you said so yourself! I don't want to hurt anymore. Ammit already gnaws at my heart. I cannot bear more pain!"

"I... I can't just kill you, my lady. It is not *maat*."

Meritaten laughed through her tears, the feel of it sour in her throat. "The man who struck down a Pharaoh— you fear *maat*? If you don't kill me, I will run from the palace to the river, and throw myself to the crocodiles. And then there will be no afterlife for me at all, no hope for redemption, if there *is* any redemption to be had. There will be only the Eater of Hearts—his teeth in my *ka* forever, rending and tearing. Would you do that to me?"

"No," he whispered.

The pounding of guards' feet drew closer. The shouts were loud in the hall outside.

Her own words echoed in Meritaten's heart, rising above the clatter of the soldiers. *Why did the gods let this burden fall on me?* She swallowed hard, remembering the old man's face in the red reflected light of the desert. Panefer the priest, taking her hand, kissing it, blessing her. *The gods?*

Horemheb drew his knife. The sharp glint of its blade, reflecting the bright morning sun, was like a forgiving touch to Meritaten. But his hand trembled, and he hesitated.

"You must," Meritaten pleaded. "Quickly. I am ready now—do it!"

"Bless you," Horemheb said, "in the name of Mother Mut, and Maat, and Iset, who knows your *ren*."

Meritaten gasped. The place on her hand where Panefer had kissed her burned with a sudden, welcome fire. With a thrill, she could feel those goddesses reaching for her, calling to her. She had never known them before, but still their arms opened wide to welcome her, to forgive her—

to wrap her in a mother's pure embrace.

Horemheb bent quickly. His rough lips rested for a moment on her brow. "You will see Smenkhkare in the afterlife. I know it."

She smiled up at him then, tears of hope blurring her vision.

Then his blade flashed, quick and clean. She felt no pain when it sliced her; only cold. And then heat—a wondrous, potent heat, more intense, more magical than the fire of the Great Aten Temple. The blood ran fast and thick down her chest. Horemheb guided her gently as her legs buckled, as the strength went out of her in a long, hot rush. He lay her across her mother's body, face to face, heart to heart.

Ankhesenpaaten

Year 1 of Tutankhaten
Lord of the Forms of the Sun,
Strong Bull, Perfect
Who Satisfies the Gods

ANKHESENPAATEN!
The voice called into the depths of her dream, cutting through the vision, the memory of Akhet-Aten's garden in full bloom. Bright sunlight, pure-golden like the king's own throne, danced among the open blooms of roses and jasmine. Leaves swayed, fragrant in the shade, and from somewhere in the garden the childish laughter of her sisters rose, splendid and sweet.

Ankhesenpaaten!

It was Meritaten's voice. No, she realized, sitting up in the shade of the rose bush, looking around the garden, confused and half frightened. It was her mother's—her mother.

A strange ache filled her... then a chill, despite the warmth of the sun.

"Ankhesenpaaten!"

She lurched up in bed, sucking in her breath with a long, croaking gasp. She had blocked her window with a shutter that night—why? She couldn't remember now. The room was dark, though a thin strand of gold shone in the crack of her shutter. The morning sun, just risen.

A broad, dark figure bent over her bed; the panic returned to her and she gave a squeak of fear, thrashing backward and away.

"Peace!" the man said urgently. "Ankhesenpaaten, it's me!"

She recognized the voice. "Horemheb?"

"Yes." He reached out tentatively, like a charioteer calming a skittish horse. "You must get up. Now—quickly!"

Ankhesenpaaten frowned in the darkness. She felt the voices of her sister and her mother fading rapidly, flying away from her heart. She knew, without knowing *how* she knew it, that Nefertiti and Meritaten were both dead.

She stood quickly, bare feet slapping the cold tiles of her floor. She wrapped her arms around her body, holding back the shivers of early-morning chill. Or was it fear that trembled her?

"I am the last, then," she said quietly.

Horemheb was leaning away from her, his head cocked alertly, listening to the sound of many feet pounding along the corridor. He turned back to her, distracted. "What did you say?"

"I said, 'Where are we going?'"

"To the Temple of Amun. But we must move quickly. Here—" He pulled her cloak from its peg by the door and tossed it to her. "Sandals, too; be fast. We must go on foot, I'm afraid. No time for a chariot."

Dressed only in her cloak and the wisp of her night-dress, with neither wig nor jewels, Ankhesenpaaten looked like any servant girl scurrying along in the sudden clamor of emergency. No one wasted a glance on her as she and Horemheb rushed through the corridors. Stewards, maids, distracted noblemen shouted and cried out as they came from their chambers, spilling into the halls, blundering against one another as the grim news reached them each in turn.

"The Pharaoh is dead," someone yelled, and another man shouted back, "Which one?"

She knew which one. The knowledge goaded her on, pushing her along the route Horemheb indicated, out through the palace's main courtyard to the Royal Road. The broad, ancient track ran north to the city of temples, the dwelling-places of the old gods. They walked briskly down the road, the noise of awakening Waset—and of the palace in uproar—dwindling behind them.

Ankhesenpaaten said nothing. That was ever her way. But she did watch, as was her custom, seeing with perfect clarity the determination that hardened Horemheb's face, the terrible purpose of his stride. *To the Temple of Amun.* And her mother the Pharaoh was dead. Pain welled in her, a surge of loss that threatened to stop the breath in her lungs. Resolute, she pushed it away. There would be time to mourn later. For now, she must focus on her duty—this thing the gods had made her for. Nefertiti was gone, but it seemed Tutankhaten still lived. Why else would she be wanted at the temple? *He will need me. He won't understand what is going on, why this has happened.* Ankhesenpaaten hardly understood, herself.

When they had walked in silence for nearly a quarter of an hour, a strange, dark shape appeared on the road far ahead, moving rapidly out of the morning haze that clung around the base of the distant temple complex. Horemheb stopped Ankhesenpaaten with a hand on her arm. They watched as the unidentifiable shape resolved into a small cart, the kind *rekhet* farmers used to bring their crops to market, pulled by a single horse.

"Come," Horemheb said. He pulled Ankhesenpaaten off the road, pressing her back into a thick tangle of weeds that stood along its verge. He waited nearby, tense and bristling like a dog bred for fighting, until the cart drew almost level with their position. The driver reined the horse in sharply; it grunted in protest, throwing up its head, white

271

spittle flying from its mouth.

Ankhesenpaaten recognized the driver at once. Her skin was white as alabaster in the morning sun, her hair gleaming like polished bronze. She scrambled out of the weeds. "Nann!"

"Thank the gods you're here," Horemheb told her.

The Hurrian reached down to pull Ankhesenpaaten up into the cart. "Mutnodjmet and the boy are already at the temple," she said to Horemheb. "I drove them there myself. Traded away a much too valuable bracelet for this farmer's cart, but it was the first one I saw as we stole though the gate, out into the city. I figured it would be faster than walking."

"Speed is worth any price now." Horemheb hoisted his bulk into the cart, and Nann slapped the reins on the horse's rump, wheeling it around in the middle of the road.

"They're with the High Priest," she called over the clatter of the horse's hooves as they sped toward the Temple of Amun. "Tutankhaten is well. Your lady wife has him in hand; the moment she heard Nefertiti's maids screaming she ran to the boy's chamber and snatched him up in the chaos. It was fortunate that Ay and his men didn't get there first."

"Fortunate indeed."

"All is ready at the temple. I came back to find you."

"You have found us," Horemheb said. "Now drive!"

Nann hissed the horse to greater speed. The cart jounced hard along the road; Ankhesenpaaten pressed herself down into its wooden bed, bracing arms and back against the cart's high sides. Her teeth rattled as they sped over the old, hard-packed road. She looked up, past the horse's twitching, swiveling ears and its dark, flying mane, and watched in awe as the huge pylon gates—the first of several—flashed past. The cart flew by *seshep* crouching on great stone plinths, their lion bodies reclining, their human faces watching the road like sentinels from an eerie vision. Then they passed more pylons—older, carved with the names and images of ancient kings—then the outer shrines, the small houses of lesser gods that clustered close to the vast, blue-shadowed wall that surrounded the great temple precinct of Ipet-Isut. She saw more: fleeting images of priests like drifting ghosts, pale as incense smoke in their white robes; a few early supplicants moving dream-slow between the shrines with offerings of meat and milk in their outstretched hands. Then at last the grandest temple of all reared up before them, its wide, slanted façade spread like the hood of a cobra.

Nann's cart shuddered to a stop just at the foot of the temple steps. Ankhesenpaaten did not wait for Horemheb to help her to the ground. Her duty was waiting—and the sooner she did what needed doing, the sooner she saw to Egypt's great and terrible need, the sooner she could be alone again, silent with her thoughts, mourning the death of the mother she had only begun to know. She sprang over the cart's wooden side, then ran up the steps without waiting for Horemheb or Nann.

As Ankhesenpaaten rushed up the long, broad stairway toward the temple's black maw, Mutnodjmet appeared on its threshold, materializing out of the darkness, holding little Tutankhaten by his hand. The boy stood as tall as he could, trying to look unafraid. But when Ankhesenpaaten reached him she saw that his eyes were wide, his lips pale and trembling.

She bent, smiling, and took his hand. "Are you ready, my lord?"

"For what?" His eyes darted, and he glanced back over his shoulder into the temple's intimidating shadows.

"We must marry now. I am to be your wife."

For a moment he sucked his lower lip. "So soon? But the Pharaoh—"

"Smenkhkare is dead, my lord, and now Nefertiti has joined him." The ache swelled in her chest again, but she kept her face calm, her voice confident and steady... for the boy's sake. "You are the Pharaoh now, Tutankhaten, and I am your Great Wife."

He looked down at the laces of his sandals—not fearfully, but with a meditative air. "It will be hard," he said. "To be the king."

How wise he is already—and yet he doesn't know the half of it. Hard and dangerous and trying, but we have no choice. The gods made us for this purpose, and set our fates on the midwife's bricks at the moment of our birth. What the gods have done cannot be undone. We are powerless before them.

Ankhesenpaaten made herself smile. "But we will rule together. We will always be together, you and I, and the gods will not abandon us. This is what we were meant for, Tutankhaten. This is why we *are*."

Another long moment contemplating the well-worn stones beneath his feet. Another thoughtful pause. But the boy looked up, squaring his small shoulders. "Very well, then," he said. "Let us do what we must."

Mutnodjmet turned, calling into the black for the High Priest of Amun. The man came forth, carrying a clay lamp in his upturned palms, ready to light the way. Tutankhaten looked wide-eyed at the leopard skin that draped the man's shoulders, the fanged and snarling leopard mask that hung from a cord around the priest's neck. But he smiled down kindly at Tutankhaten, and nodded at the fierce certainty in Ankhesenpaaten's eyes.

The priest led them deep into the heart of the temple. They went alone—just the two of them, hand in hand, following the dancing, golden circle of the High Priest's light. Not for a moment did she let go of Tutankhaten's hand. When they reached the sanctuary where the god waited in perfect, cloaking darkness, the very air felt black, the shadows close and cold. And when the priest's lamp flared, its light whisking up the golden body of the god to illuminate Amun's face, she felt as small and vulnerable as the little husband who stood beside her. Amun was a strange god to her—to Tutankhaten, too. They had never learned to love him, never come to know him.

Will you be kind to us, Amun? Although we do not know you yet, will you grant us a father's guidance? For we have no father, no mother. We have only each other, this brave little Pharaoh and I.

As the priest began a hasty ceremony of marriage, Ankhesenpaaten gazed up at the god's face, dimly defined in the weak light of the single lamp. Amun's smile was soft and benevolent, his eyes wise and knowing. The fact that he had a face at all sent a warm ripple through her *ka*—eyes to see her, a mouth to speak into her heart. Amun would be a gentler god than the Aten, which had nothing to offer a human heart but the brutal power of its rays.

Amun, you see me. You know me. Ankhesenpaaten was sure of that. With this god to guide and protect her, all would be well. And she had Tutankhaten there beside her, his small hand firm and unshaking in her grip.

Horemheb

Year 1 of Tutankhaten
Lord of the Forms of the Sun,
Strong Bull, Perfect
Who Satisfies the Gods

NANN SHOUTED from the driver's seat as the horse trotted into the palace's courtyard. "Make way! Move!"

Agitated crowds of stewards and officials, nobles and soldiers milled and muttered, watching the cart with suspicion, even shock. A *rekhet* farmer's shabby vehicle had no place here, in the sunlit courtyard with the splendid walls of Waset's palace rising all around.

But the small wagon's cargo raised a greater sensation. Horemheb cringed inwardly, watching eyes widen and hands fly up to shield whispering mouths. There was not a single person in the courtyard who didn't recognize Tutankhaten, peeking out over the cart's side, his side lock bouncing against his face as the horse clattered to a stop. They knew Ankhesenpaaten, too, even in her simple night dress and cape—now that the morning's initial furor had died back somewhat and men once more found themselves capable of rational thought, of careful observation. Far more startling was the man draped in leopard skin: Merymentu, the High Priest of Amun. A man as exalted as he certainly had no place in a wagon that still stank of half-rotted vegetables.

Nothing for it now. Horemheb jumped down from the seat beside Nann and lifted Tutankhaten from the cart.

One of the stewards pointed, shouting, "Tell Ay the heir is found!"

"Stay close," Horemheb told the boy as Ankhesenpaaten clambered down to stand beside them.

"What must we do now?" the girl asked. She was calm, despite her mother's death—solemn and focused, a well-trained and ready King's Great Wife. "Where do we go?"

"To the throne room."

Horemheb led the way, brushing past the clustered stewards, Tutankhaten's small hand swallowed by his own. Merymentu walked only a step behind, the leopard robe and mask of his sacred office plain for all to see. Horemheb was glad of the man's support. No one would have dared assault the High Priest; his presence, so close to Tutankhaten, added an extra layer of protection. The crowds of nobles and their attendant scribes, scribbling furiously on small palettes strapped to their forearms, fell back as Horemheb's small but powerful entourage cleaved through their numbers.

When they reached the two great doors to the throne room, Horemheb shoved them open without hesitation and led Tutankhaten down the long, cavernous hall. Vast pillars soared high above them; the air was sweet with myrrh, an old scent, the clinging memory of generations of Egyptian kings. Below their sandals, the well-worn malachite floor—trodden by courtiers for uncountable years—shone like the water of the river. Tutankhaten walked across it gingerly, for it was slick and its reflective surface had a disorienting effect. But the boy did not complain. He kept moving, doing his best to match Horemheb's stride.

Horemheb and his supporters stopped at the foot of the dais. He stared up with a dry frown at the two thrones at the top of the painted stair—one seat empty, the other occupied.

"Ay," Horemheb growled, "step down. The throne is not yours."

Ay's sigh of relief and small smile seemed genuine enough—glad to know Tutankhaten was safe, Horemheb assumed, for the boy was the old man's only link to power. But Ay's mask of impassivity quickly returned. "Step down? I think not, soldier. Though I do thank you for bringing the heir back safely. Your work is done now; you may go."

Horemheb had expected this—Ay's slithering and dodging, Ay's careful manipulations. He gathered himself to speak, to shout his accusations of scheming, of treason planned and waiting to be done. But Ankhesenpaaten stepped forward before Horemheb could open his mouth.

Though she stood in only her night dress and sandals, she held herself with poise worthy of all Nefertiti's meticulous training. She said in a ringing voice—a voice that carried all along the hall's great length, "He is not the heir any longer. He is the king."

"Not," Ay said, smiling drily, "until he performs the Opening of the Mouth for Smenkhkare." Then he added in a low voice, almost a mutter, "No need to do the same for Nefertiti; she was never a king."

"He has married me before the eyes of Amun," Ankhesenpaaten said. "He has a King's Wife, as tradition demands. As soon as Smenkhkare is laid in his tomb, the mantle of power will pass to Tutankhaten. Your time as ruler has ended, Ay. Step aside now, so no more blood will be shed."

Ay grunted in amusement. "So many words from Ankhesenpaaten, our silent one."

"I have words, too," Horemheb said. "Would you like to hear them?" He raised his voice to a deafening shout; it boomed among the pillars like the drums of war. "Come, all you loyal to the throne! Come and see your Pharaoh!"

A thin trickle of nobles and their attendants had followed Horemheb into the hall, but as his shouts went on the trickle became a flowing stream, and then a flood as strong as the river's inundation. Ambassadors from far-off lands, servants in their simple garb, noblemen and their wives crowded into the throne room, lining its long walls, jostling and craning their necks to watch this new drama unfold. Horemheb could read wonder in the nearest faces, as the people looked from the two children, so gentle and pure, and the priest in his sacred robes who stood behind them, Horemheb with his bull-strong body and watchman's glare who stood at their side.

Someone called out, "King Tutankhaten! The rightful ruler of Egypt!" Murmurs rippled far down the hall, and then shouts answered back, "Tutankhaten!" "Pharaoh!" "Blessed by Amun!"

Ay listened to the acclaim, his sharp-angled face still and thoughtful. Then his gaze narrowed on Horemheb. "I have no desire to usurp the boy's throne," he said loudly. The shouts died down so the people could listen. "But he is young yet, and I am his regent."

Horemheb set one foot on the lowest step. Ay's chin raised, a brief concession to the anxiety he surely must have felt. But he did not cower or cringe. Nor did he vacate the throne. "If you are truly his regent and nothing more, then get off that throne. Let Tutankhaten sit in his rightful place. Let some order come back to Egypt, to drive back the chaos that is churning all around us, eroding our borders and depleting our strength!"

A few men in the great hall cheered at Horemheb's words.

Ay smiled lightly. He held Horemheb's stare, his eyes small and unblinking, his body at ease on the golden seat, unintimidated by anyone's measure. Then, abruptly, he stood and descended the dais, one step at a time. His eyes never left Horemheb's; they were locked together like two gazelle bucks, grappling with their horns.

"Do not think I will yield my position to you, *rekhet*," Ay said quietly when he reached the step where Horemheb stood. "You had Nefertiti's favor, but she is no more. And you are nothing here in Waset without her. Nothing."

"I don't want your position," Horemheb said.

"Then why do you defend the boy from his own regent?"

Ankhesenpaaten pointed at Ay, her accusatory finger flying like an arrow toward his heart. "You are no rightful regent. You took the position by deceit!"

"Child," Ay said coolly, his thin lips curling in scorn, "you don't know what you're saying."

"I know more than you think. I see more than you know."

Ay gestured toward Merymentu, an exasperated flip of his hand. "Look, Horemheb was kind enough to bring the High Priest of Amun. This man will attest to you, Ankhesenpaaten—to all of you gathered here—that I swore before the god to act appropriately, to shepherd Tutankhaten to his throne and to set him fully upon it in due time."

"That is so," Merymentu said, plainly reluctant.

"There you have it," Ay said. "It was a holy oath. How then can you doubt me?"

Horemheb snorted in disgust. "A holy oath! What have oaths ever meant to you? What has honor meant to you? You, who manipulated Meritaten into killing her own mother!"

"Such accusations," Ay said placidly. "I wonder, do you have any proof of the calumnies you sling?"

Flushing with fury—for of course he had no proof, and he had told Meritaten as much—Horemheb held his tongue.

"Meritaten was always unstable," Ay went on, "a fool who should never have been in charge of Egypt. I had my doubts about her sanity, too. A valid concern, given her father Akhenaten's... affliction." He cast a significant gaze at Ankhesenpaaten, and a stir of whispers spread through the crowd.

"Ankhesenpaaten is strong and good—wise for her age," Horemheb said. "I would swear to it before any god. Egypt can trust her, and Tutankhaten, too, for he has grown up without Akhenaten's influence. But no one can trust you, Ay. You have been the architect of—"

"Indeed," Ay broke in with a bitter laugh, "no one does trust me, even though I alone, of all my family, have never steered Egypt wrong."

Ankhesenpaaten tossed her head in dismissal. "That is only because your desires have thus far happened to coincide with Egypt's needs. The moment they diverge, you will put your interests ahead of *maat*."

"Is that what you suppose?"

Horemheb said, "Anyone who has had close dealings with you knows the Great Wife's words are true."

Merymentu raised a hand, an apologetic gesture, stepping between Horemheb and his adversary. "Ay was sworn to obedience and loyalty before Amun himself. And the god granted him the office of regent. That cannot be undone— not without a directive from the oracle. To deny Ay his position as Tutankhaten's regent is to countermand the express will of Amun."

Horemheb's teeth clenched hard, but he made his shoulders relax, made himself yield a hand's breadth of ground. *I've angered the gods enough. I cannot push them further.* "Very well," he finally said. "But if you will not leave your position, then I will not leave mine—the post

281

Nefertiti gave me. I am the young Pharaoh's protector, Ay. I will be beside him always... watching. Remember that, and be wary."

Ay nodded graciously, but his eyes as he brushed past Horemheb were sharp with triumph. Before the eyes of the whole court—the whole palace, even down to the meanest servants—Ay took Tutankhaten's hand.

Ankhesenamun

Year 1 of Horemheb
Holy Are the Manifestations,
Chosen of Re

I CAN OFFER LITTLE PRAISE to my grandfather Ay, save for this: no person the gods made ever surpassed him in cunning, stealth, or patience. He could wait as long as circumstances demanded to bring his plans to fruition. This, too, I can say in Ay's favor: he and Horemheb worked side by side throughout the early years of Tutankhaten's reign, as effectively as anyone could have hoped—and far more amicably than I expected.

I have no doubt that if Horemheb had ever left the Pharaoh's service, even for a day, Ay would have maneuvered my young husband into a trap in the very hour of Horemheb's departure. My sweet little husband was a clever, clear-thinking child, but he was only six years old when he became our Pharaoh. No boy of such an age can be called sophisticated, even if he is bright and eager to do good works. Horemheb was the only bulwark that protected Tutankhaten from his own youth and inexperience. And though Ay gave every appearance of supporting and guiding the king, we both knew, Horemheb and I, that the old man was alert for his smallest opportunity.

Had any chance arisen to put Tutankhaten out of his way, Ay would have taken Egypt's crown for himself. The danger was plain to all of us—Horemheb and I, Mutnodjmet and Nann, Merymentu High Priest of Amun—all of us who surrounded the tender young king, offering him our guidance, our protection... and our love.

For all his inexperience, and despite his trusting nature, I believe some secret, instinctive part of Tutankhaten's heart also sensed the danger in Ay. For he was never quite easy—never his true, happy self—when Ay stood behind him with a hand upon his shoulder.

But though they worked together grudgingly, Horemheb and Ay did guide Tutankhaten well. For the first three years of the young Pharaoh's reign, they united their efforts and unpicked the Aten's lingering influence thread by thread. It was long and tiresome work. Despite the damage Aten-worship had done to Egypt, the distant, faceless god had taken hold of many hearts, and the cult of the sun-disc spread underground like rats through their tunnels.

But by the third year of Tutankhaten's reign, the Aten cult had been sufficiently eradicated that my husband's advisors felt confident in proclaiming the throne's unshakable allegiance to the old gods. We made a grand gesture of commitment to Amun, Mut, and the gods of generations past—a sacrifice I was thoroughly pleased to offer. I shall never forget the joy I felt, the leaping, soaring freedom, when my husband and I stood once more in the darkness of the temple sanctuary, gazing up at the golden statue of Amun, and took our new names. From that day on, he would be known as Tutankhamun. And I, smiling, my eyes welling with tears of faith and relief, cast the last influence of the Aten from my life forever. My new name was Ankhesenamun, and it felt as dear to me as my *ren*, the name written in secret on the walls of my heart.

When the ceremony was over, Tutankhamun and I walked hand in hand through the temple's outer corridors to the great staircase that extended down into the courtyard. There we stood, blinking in the brightness of the sun as thousands of throats shouted our new names. It seemed all of Waset had come to the temple to witness our great feat—the restoration of Amun's righteous supremacy, after the Aten's long and depraved reign. I still remember the sun's warmth on my body, the way it seemed to embrace my whole being. We wore our new identities like cloaks; I could feel the name, and the gods' blessing it conferred, settling over my shoulders, a slight but welcome weight. Never in my life had I felt so good, so pure—so united with *maat*.

For a full week, all of Egypt celebrated our new identities—and the return of Amun's blessing to the Two Lands. The feasts, the processions, the glittering entertainments—I had never known such excitement, nor such *ka*-deep contentment. As the festival stretched on, Tutankhamun and I were free to be giddy and foolish, to play like the young boy he still was—and the child I was never allowed to be. He was nine years old, and I eighteen, but despite the years that separated us we grew closer every day. Tutankhamun was always kind, always thoughtful, and ready with a laugh or a comforting embrace whenever I had the slightest need. He was more than my divinely ordained husband. He was my constant and dearest companion. I loved him more with every beat of my heart.

I look back now on the early years of Tutankhamun's kingship, and they fill me with a great, rending pain. Not because I suffered during those blessed days—far from it!—but because the peace and comfort I felt ended all too soon. Now I understand my sister Meritaten—why her love for Smenkhkare, and her grief at his death, led her down the path of her own destruction. Even today, I cannot say that I would not have done differently. Like Meritaten, I might have struck against my own family if it would have kept Tutankhamun safe.

As my husband grew from a boy to a man, both Ay and Horemheb impressed upon him the importance of siring an heir. We two were the last of the royal bloodline, the sole remaining members of a family that had been bred for generations by the gods themselves. Our line had sprung from the divinely appointed king Ahmose, who, hundreds of years before, drove the invaders from Egyptian soil and restored the true gods to glory. We owed it to our ancestors to bear children—to carry on their legacy. Tutankhaten and I often spoke privately of this sacred duty. We both agreed that we felt our obligation more keenly than his advisors could have guessed, for we longed to instill in our children a piety for the true gods of Egypt, and redeeming our blood in the wake of Akhenaten's heresy.

As soon as his voice began to change and the soft down on his upper lip darkened, we tried to conceive an heir. My husband was fumbling and sweetly inept, for he was still more boy than man. But in time I did fall pregnant, and for five months my joy grew along with the child in my body.

But then the baby ceased to move in my womb. It felt heavy, ominously still, like a dry, dead stone weighing down my body and my *ka*. I had never carried a child before, of course—but still I knew that tragedy had befallen this child, so anticipated, so badly needed. For a week I hardly slept, hardly breathed, and prayed to every god and goddess I could name to make the baby live again, to let me feel the flutter of its movement.

My prayers went unanswered. The pains of birth came upon me four months before my time. I went to the birth bower grieving, knowing my child would be stillborn. Broken-hearted, I forced myself through the terrible task, knowing that when at last my labor was done, I would hear no baby's cry, nor feel the suckling of an infant at my breast.

The midwives let me hold the miniature, unmoving child for as long as I could bear to do so. It was a girl— or would have been, had the gods seen fit to hold the sacred ankh to her nostrils, to let her draw the breath of life. Tutankhamun came to me when it was all over, and together we wept over all we had lost, touching our tiny baby with reverent sorrow, bathing her with our tears.

"I would have named her Nefertiti Tasherit," I told him.

He agreed that it was a good name.

The sad-eyed midwives tried their best to comfort us both. "The Pharaoh is just too young," they said. "Perhaps his seed will not be strong enough to make a healthy child until he is fully grown."

They may have been right. But I knew we could ill afford to wait until Tutankhamun was older. The nobles and the *rekhet* loved us, supported us both on the throne—but Ay was still hungry, keen for his chance to seize power. And as Tutankhamun matured, trusting ever more to his own judgment and strength, Ay surely felt himself pushed farther away from Egypt's seat of power. Tutankhamun's autonomy was Ay's greatest threat. The sooner I could birth a healthy child—the sooner we could form the holy triad of Pharaoh, King's Wife, and son—the sooner we could free ourselves from the shadows of Ay's ambition.

Ankhesenamun

*Year 9 of Tutankhamun
Lord of the Forms of the Sun,
Strong Bull, Perfect
Who Satisfies the Gods*

ANKHESENAMUN GAVE ONE last push, screaming with pain and relief as the child fell heavily from her body into the midwife's arms.

She swayed, her feet nearly slipping off the birthing bricks, panting and heaving with the force of her effort. A cool, damp cloth pressed against her brow, wiped her gently. The garden's breeze, flowing in through the soft linen curtains of the birthing bower, was sweet as praise from a goddess.

But little by little, as the pain slowly receded, Ankhesenamun realized something was amiss. The midwives flurried about the bower, faces tipped low in grim concentration, eyes dark and determined. They moved about their tasks with an urgency she did not yet understand. Yes, this birth had been an early one—but it was not unheard of, for healthy children to come two months before their time. The midwives had all told her so—all of them!—as she labored in fear and pain. And this pregnancy had been different, too. Many times over the past two years, ever since her first disastrous trip to the birthing bower, Ankhesenamun had miscarried early, within weeks of conceiving. But not this time. This child had been mobile throughout, up until the hour of her premature labor—kicking and turning so often, so strongly, that Ankhesenamun had barely slept for more than an hour at a time. And she had said all the correct prayers! She had made all the right sacrifices to the gods and goddesses who protected mothers and children— Tawaret, Lady of the Birth House; Bast, the Mother of the Kittens; the dwarf god Bes who drives away the demons that come for helpless babies. She prayed to Hathor, the gentle cow goddess who loves all mothers; she prayed to Nut, the Night Sky, who birthed the world and the days of the year.

You worry over nothing, she wanted to snap at the women who fluttered around her. *Now help me to my bed and let me hold my child.*

But just as she opened her mouth to speak, she realized that of all the sounds she heard—low, insistent talk, harsh breathing, the clatter of tools and rushing feet—there was one sound she did not hear.

"Why is it not crying?" she gasped. "Tell me—why is my baby not crying?"

They cut the pale cord that snaked from between her legs, then helped her to a pallet strewn with cushions. The women laid her down and pulled a sheet across her body, but none of them would answer her questions.

"Bring me my baby!" Ankhesenamun cried. She tried to rise, but weariness and pain of her torn, bleeding body dropped her back onto the bed.

Finally the leader among them, the chief midwife, looked up from where the women huddled—where they worked over the child. "Too soon," the old woman said, her voice hoarse with sorrow. "The little thing never breathed at all. She was born too soon."

Ankhesenamun's scream was high and sharp and full of rending grief, like an animal struck by a hunter's spear. She sobbed, she tore at her hair; she would have scratched her face with her nails, carving deep gouges of fury and loss into her flesh, but the women held her by the wrists and she could do nothing—nothing. They held a bowl to her lips and made her drink a thick, choking potion of herbs. The bitter stuff contracted her womb all over again, expelling the afterbirth. She shrieked and howled the whole while as she pushed the cursed stuff from her blighted womb, but her cries were not from pain. It was anger that filled her throat, disbelief, and hard, furious denial.

When at last she was exhausted by her body and her screams, she fell back in the bed—silent, eyes open but seeing nothing.

The old midwife bent over her. "Do you want to hold the baby, my lady? Do you want to see her?"

Wordless, Ankhesenamun waved her away.

"My lady, shall we admit the Pharaoh? He waits outside. He is most anxious on your behalf."

"No." Ankhesenamun well remembered the tearful scene when she and Tutankhamun had wept together over their first stillborn daughter. She could not do it again—would not survive it. Not now, while the shock of their shattered hope still lay like a shroud on her *ka*.

She was helpless, utterly alone, abandoned by the gods. They had left to her own devices, isolated her with this cruel blow. Only once before had she felt so abandoned, so callously discarded. She remembered being a small girl on the high wall of Akhet-Aten's palace, listening as her sister Meketaten died in childbirth. *Better that I had died in this birth than face my grief. Better to die than to try to find the strength to go on living.*

She remembered Horemheb, a younger man then, standing with her beneath the stars. She had looked up at him, that girl on the palace wall, and he had towered over her, strong and unshakable—as her poor young husband was not. Suddenly Ankhesenamun wanted Horemheb's protection—his solidity, his unwavering loyalty—almost as much as she wanted her baby to live.

"Send Horemheb to me," she told the midwife calmly. "Horemheb, and no one else."

It seemed to take hours for Horemheb to arrive, though common sense whispered to Ankhesenamun that hardly any time had passed, that he had come running, as always, the moment he received her summons. She lay staring blankly at the bower's ceiling, counting the relentless beats of her heart until he arrived.

"My lady." His voice was hoarse with grief, with pity.

She turned her head and looked at him. She was not weeping now—she was detached, drifting somewhere far away, watching herself and Horemheb placidly, as if they were actors playing out some harmless, make-believe scene.

Horemheb hesitated at the bower's edge, holding back the curtain with a trembling hand. Here he was entirely out of his element, for this was a place of women, a place of the strongest magic known to mortals—the magic of the blood that makes life. *But it does not make life for me.* He picked his way through the foreign territory with hesitant steps, edging around the baskets that held the midwives' tools, taking care not to step in the blood that still spattered the floor. *What does it matter? My woman's blood holds no power. It is as useless, as inert, as fouled as a back-alley puddle.*

Horemheb found one of the midwives' folding stools and sat next to Ankhesenamun's pallet, waiting in silence for her to speak.

She looked up at him—again he was a tower of strength above her, again she was the small child lost and forgotten. Tears blurred her vision, but she could find no words.

Finally he said, "I am sorry, my lady."

"Why?" she demanded. Her heart suddenly unleashed,

the words—the rage, the grief—flowed across her tongue. "Why has this happened again? What have we done to anger the gods? Why would they do this to me, *why?*"

Horemheb shrugged his wide shoulders, a brief, uncomfortable flinch. He was just a soldier, Ankhesenamun knew. He was not a priest, not a king. He didn't have the answers she needed. But she *had* to ask the questions of somebody, had to push them out of her heart... even if she found no answers.

"Perhaps the Pharaoh is too young," Horemheb ventured.

"That's what they said the last time. But he is fifteen years old! How many men have sired healthy children at his age?"

"Many," Horemheb admitted. "You are not wrong, my lady."

"*Why*, then?" She pulled a cool, silk-covered cushion to her face and buried a wordless scream in it, a shriek of anger so pure and vast that she felt it course through her body, a white-hot light, a strike of lightning in the desert. Then she sank her teeth in the cushion and pulled like a leopard rending a gazelle's flesh. But the fabric held, then ripped from her teeth, and the pillow was still intact. She could do nothing—powerless, weak, broken.

Horemheb shifted uncomfortably on his stool, opening and closing his mouth. He was on the point of speaking— Ankhesenamun could see that clearly—but hesitant to do it.

"Speak," she told, marshalling her calm. "Say what you will."

"My lady, forgive me."

"For what?"

"I... Any man who enjoys hunting knows that hounds must be carefully bred."

She stilled, slowing her breath, her heart pounding loud in her ears. She waited. Horemheb's silence stretched for a long time, but at last he resumed.

"And any man who bets on the chariot races knows that horses, too, must be mated with care. It is not good, my lady... to breed animals that are too closely related, or to make close pairings for too many generations."

Ankhesenamun stared at him in disbelief. She could not stop her jaw from falling open. Horemheb hung his head and would not meet her eye.

"We are not horses or dogs!" she finally said, affronted.

"No, but—"

"We are descended of the gods themselves!" She shook her head, stunned at the implication of his words. "We are divinity made flesh!"

Horemheb lapsed into miserable silence.

"You shock me," she told him levelly. "It's a great offense, to compare the Pharaoh and his blood to mere animals."

"My lady, I meant no offense, I swear. I only—"

"I know." Her voice turned so thick in her throat that for a moment she could not speak. She swallowed hard, but that only brought fresh tears to her eyes. "Perhaps you are right. But even if you are, what can we do, Horemheb? Tutankhaten and I—we are the last of our dynasty. If we do not have children—"

"If you *cannot* have children together, my lady... if your blood is too close—"

She squeezed her eyes shut and held up a hand to silence him. Dogs and horses—*their* lines must be tended, *their* blood separated. The gods would not make people that way. The gods would not make *royalty* that way, with a fatal weakness built into their dynasties, their lines doomed to die sooner or later. *It undoes the purpose of royalty. It makes a mockery of the divine.*

And yet Horemheb's words had the bitter taste of *maat*. Even as she rejected his assertion—it was very near blasphemy!—the idea calmed her, cast the demise of so many children, so many pregnancies, in a new light. *If what he says is true, then it all makes sense. At least it makes sense.* Small comfort, but it was the only comfort she had.

She opened her eyes. "Speak on," she said quietly.

"Children will still carry the divine blood—will still be Tutankhamun's heirs—if he fathers them on other women. Perhaps it is time our young king built his own harem."

Ankhesenamun cried out, a long, sobbing wail of loss. Minor wives and concubines were a natural part of royal life, she knew. But still the idea pained her, the image that sprang up in her heart of Tutankhaten smiling and laughing with other women. She hadn't realized until now just how much his affection meant to her. After her childhood of isolation and fear in Akhenaten's court, the simple reliability of Tutankhaten's love was the breath of life to her. But as much as she disliked the idea of sharing him with others, she hated even more the thought of other women doing what she could not.

"What use am I, as King's Great Wife?"

Though it was an audacity to touch her, Horemheb caught her hand as it flailed uselessly at the air. He squeezed it, and her cries subsided into silent, body-shaking sobs.

"You are a comfort to the Pharaoh's heart, my lady," Horemheb said gently. "You are his beloved—*you*, alone among all women. That will never change."

"I hope you are right," Ankhesenamun whispered. "I know I must do this thing—*we* must do it—even though I fear it might kill me. If someone does not give him a child soon, then Ay—"

"I know," Horemheb said. He squeezed her hand again.

"Don't say anymore. Don't upset yourself further—not now. I know."

Ankhesenamun

Year 9 of Tutankhamun
Lord of the Forms of the Sun,
Strong Bull, Perfect
Who Satisfies the Gods

"LADY BENERIB of the House of Ten Vines," Mutnodjmet said in a clear, ringing voice, "and Lady Ka-Nut of the House of the Ibis Pond."

Both young women bowed low as their names were announced, lifting their hands to show their palms in a courtly display of submission. Their obeisance was perfect, well-trained—as one would expect from the daughters of two of the oldest and most revered families in Waset.

But they looked so young—girls, really. Neither one was much older than sixteen, if even that. *And I am already as barren as a grandmother at the age of twenty-four.* Never in her life had Ankhesenamun felt so old, so worn out, fit only for discarding.

"Rise," she said, and she was pleased to hear that her voice betrayed nothing of her bitter thoughts.

Her smile was genuine, too. The fears and pains that plagued her were real—she embraced them, for what else could she do with them? But her hope was real, too. And each new woman who accepted the honor of joining the Pharaoh's harem multiplied the hope of the Two Lands.

Benerib and Ka-Nut straightened, the golden baubles in their wigs swaying and clattering with a fine, alluring music, their embroidered, hundred-pleated gowns shimmering like heat haze around their lovely bodies.

"I am pleased that you and your families have shown such love and support for Tutankhamun, our king," Ankhesenamun said. "You both came highly recommended by the Pharaoh's personal staff. Benerib, I hear that you have many years of training in dance."

The girl bobbed another bow. "That is so, Great Wife."

"Very good. I hope you'll demonstrate your skill for us soon." *I am sure Tutankhamun will find it most fascinating.* She refused to let out the pained sigh that pressed inside her chest. It was not Benerib's fault that she was so very appealing. "And you, Ka-Nut; you play the harp and weave very well, I am told."

Ka-Nut's narrow face flushed. "You flatter me, Great Wife." She was not as pretty as Benerib, but she had a bold intelligence in her eyes that Ankhesenamun appreciated. Beauty wasn't a necessary trait in any woman—it was only an ornament, a thing of little consequence that would one day tarnish and dull. But a bright heart never faded. *Tutankhamun appreciates a sharp wit and good conversation. And I would be pleased if the heir was born to a clever, deep-thinking woman.*

"It isn't flattery," Ankhesenamun said with a soft laugh. "Your father's men sent samples of your weaving when the king inquired about you. I saw it myself; it's some of the finest work I've ever seen. We need that skill in our midst. We hope you'll teach your sister concubines the art; we would love for all of you to have some occupation, to earn your own keep—though of course the Pharaoh will see to all your needs. But it is good—don't you agree?—for any woman to maintain a certain amount of independence, even in the king's service."

"I do agree, Great Wife." But Ka-Nut's eyes lowered and the smile slipped from her face.

Ankhesenamun came to her, took her hand. Ka-Nut

looked up, startled, and Ankhesenamun saw the tears standing in her eyes. "You are valued for much more than your weaving," she said, close to the girl's ear. "It's *you* the king and I chose, not your linen. I know Tutankhamun well. Take my advice: tell him clever stories when you are alone together, and talk to him of great things, important things. He will love you for it. There's nothing the king loves more than good conversation."

Ka-Nut's smile returned. With gratitude shining from her face, she was lovely indeed. "Thank you, Great Wife."

Ankhesenamun let go of the girl's hand. She drifted to her garden window and stood there, staring out across the green, blooming grounds, watching the little birds dive among the hedges and trellises in pursuit of flies. She simply needed to set her eyes on something else—to forget for a few precious moments that the new harem girls existed. They would join three others who had recently moved into the palace—one of whom, Wadjet, was already in the earliest stages of pregnancy. *May the gods give Wadjet better luck and more joy than they ever gave me.*

Six months passed since Ankhesenamun's second and final visit to the birthing bower. Those months had passed slowly, but not unpleasantly, if she disregarded the many clouded days of grief and confusion, of vicious self-blame. Tutankhamun, concerned for her well-being, had encouraged her to spend time away from the rigors of court life. She had spent those days with Nann and Mutnodjmet, taking leisure in the gardens or visiting the upscale marketplaces of Waset. The pain of losing her two daughters never entirely dissipated from her *ka*, but with the help of her two most trusted friends she found a fragile peace.

As the months progressed, she grew used to the idea that Tutankhamun should adopt a harem and try harder to conceive his heir. But even as she accepted the harem's inevitability, she found a hardness settling in her heart, a bleak anger at her circumstances—at the gods, for letting her children die. For allowing Tutankhamun to grow, to change from the boy companion of her happy, younger years into this savvy, politic king—the Pharaoh Egypt needed him to be. It was a foolish, selfish, useless anger—Ankhesenamun knew that. But knowing it did nothing to diminish her rage.

Those glad days—the week of their great celebration, when the whole of the Two Lands celebrated their new names, when she and Tutankhamun were free as children—were gone forever. Their innocent joy had died along with the children they'd conceived. Happiness for Ankhesenamun would never come again—she knew that much, with a blunt conviction that burned in her gut.

But now that there was hope of children from Tutankhamun's concubines, the dynasty might yet continue. And better, she and Tutankhamun could still raise those children to revere the old gods, to erase the shameful scourge of Akhenaten's years. It was a cause she felt ready to commit herself to, no matter how her heart broke over sharing Tutankhamun with other women.

"Great Wife?" Mutnodjmet said uncertainly, breaking into Ankhesenamun's thoughts.

She turned from the window with a warm smile. "My good friend Mutnodjmet will show you to your wing of the palace," she said to the girls. "It's quite a large wing, for the old kings kept many concubines—but none as welcome as the two of you, I am sure. You'll have your choice of rooms—any that aren't already claimed by the other three women. I'll be sure to visit you this evening, to see how you're settling in. If there is anything you need... anything at all—"

Nann cleared her throat from her place beside Ankhesenamun's door. "Great Wife, it is time. You're needed in the throne room."

Ah yes, the throne room. Ay had important business to discuss. The stewards had been most vehement, chattering about Ay's business almost from the moment the sun came up. There was nothing Ankhesenamun wanted less in that moment than to listen to Ay drone. She would even have preferred to spend more time with Tutankhamun's concubines and the pains they sent clenching into her heart. But the sooner Ay was dealt with, the sooner he could be ignored again.

"Yes, all right," she said to Nann. She gave the new concubines a gracious nod. "Until this evening."

W HEN ANKHESENAMUN ARRIVED in the throne room, Tutankhamun rose from his golden seat, offering his hand to help her climb the dais. She sank down on her throne a little uneasily. She hadn't been on the dais for six months, and now it felt like a foreign territory, a place where she was out of her element, clumsy and awkward. But with her husband beside her, the rhythm and ceremony of court began to return.

"I'm glad to have you back with me," Tutankhamun said, grinning. "Especially today. Ay's business is always tedious."

"I'm glad to be back. I've just been greeting two more women, the new additions to your harem. They are both lovely and sweet; I'm sure they will make you very happy."

"No one will ever make me as happy as you do, sister." He kissed her hand, and Ankhesenamun blushed with pleasure and relief, her heart swelling with gratitude.

Ay and Horemheb entered the hall. They strode side by side down the long, malachite floor, neither of them allowing the other to pull ahead by so much as a step. Such subtle challenges had been their habit for nearly nine years, since that tense, frightening morning when

Nefertiti and Meritaten were killed. As the two men drew nearer, Ay seemed serene—even happy, though he did not quite smile. Smiles on Ay's thin-skinned, angular face were as rare as rain clouds in the desert. But Horemheb's countenance was as dark as a Delta storm. The stewards and scribes who always attended court functions actually shrank back from Horemheb, pressing themselves into the shadows between the pillars, so palpable was Horemheb's anger.

"My lord," Ay said when he and Horemheb reached the foot of the dais, "I believe the time has come for you to go on campaign."

Ankhesenamun's heart leaped; she felt cold, stunned—as shocked as the stewards must be, judging by the instant cessation of their whispers and rustlings. "To war?" she blurted.

Tutankhamun chuckled, his wide collar of gold jumping as his shoulders bounced with amusement. "You say this without any preamble, Ay?"

"To *war*?" Ankhesenamun said again, more fiercely this time.

Ay bowed, but only fractionally. "Yes, my lady. It is time."

"I never knew any king to go to war," Tutankhamun said. He sounded thoughtful, wondering—not panicked, as Ankhesenamun felt he ought to be. "Smenkhkare never went on campaign. And he told me Akhenaten never did, either."

"That is so," Ay said. "But the kings before Akhenaten were mighty warriors. It has been a long tradition with Egypt—a tradition reaching all the way back to Ahmose, the Liberator—to subdue enemies of the Two Lands. And after Akhenaten's disastrous reign, there are plenty of foes begging to be chastised. You know, my lord, that the Assyrians in the north invaded many of our outposts, all the way into Mitanni. They have taken root in cities once conquered by the Thutmoses, First and Third—those great warrior-kings who expanded Egypt and built the Two Lands into a true empire."

Ankhesenamun glanced uneasily at her husband. He leaned from the edge of his throne, eyes shining, hanging on Ay's every word. *Young men are always so hungry for stories of war. They think it's so very grand! They never consider the danger, the cost.* Ay had lured Tutankhamun right into his fishing-net with the most obvious but most irresistible bait.

"These louts have taken root," Ay went on, "in domains that belong to Egypt by right of conquest. They will soon press farther south, and take more of your territory unless they are stopped—unless they are rebuked with a firm hand, and driven back into their northern crags where they belong. They should be uprooted like weeds, thrown back across our former borders. You, my lord, can establish Egypt as an empire once more, and—"

"It's madness," Horemheb broke in. "The Pharaoh is young, and has not been trained to fight."

"That is true," Ankhesenamun said, clinging desperately to Horemheb's point. "Tutankhamun hasn't the training. He cannot fight. It would be madness to risk our Pharaoh for a... a *display*."

Tutankhamun sighed and leaned back in his throne. He seemed deflated by Ankhesenamun's words, and looked more a boy than he had in several years. But he did not rebuke her. Surely he knew that Horemheb was right—that *she* was right. "If it must be done," he said, "then I will send the army in my name."

Those words should have calmed Ankhesenamun. But she could hear the doubt and hesitation in her husband's voice. He disliked the thought of sending men to fight for him when Thutmose the Third, the great expansionist—and even their own ancestor, Amunhotep the Third—had actually led their armies themselves. She shot a pleading look at Horemheb, but before either of them could speak up, Ay shrugged and addressed the king.

"It can be as you say—you might send the army. But if you were to go yourself, my lord, then you would remind all the people of Thutmose the Third. You would recall the lost glory of this dynasty, and secure the lands you *do* hold more tightly in your fist."

Horemheb snorted in disgust. "You only want the king to be killed! It's the throne you want, Ay, not glory for Egypt."

"I want no such thing," Ay said calmly. "After all, it is the king's decision. He may make whatever choice he pleases, of course—and I will obey, as his faithful servant."

Ankhesenamun turned quickly to Tutankhamun, reaching out for his hand, unsure what she might say but nevertheless prepared to make a passionate case for his safety.

But she never had the chance. His boyish excitement enflamed by Ay's cunning words, Tutankhamun stood, and Ankhesenamun's hand closed on nothing. He said, "It shall be as you suggest, Ay. You've convinced me of the importance of a campaign, and the value of my participation." Ankhesenamun could have screamed at the confidence in his voice, his certainty, so plain to hear, that no harm could ever befall him because he was young and favored by the gods. "It will make a very fine symbolic gesture if I go to war myself. And you need not fear, Horemheb: the gods will protect me. When I come home again, everyone in the whole reach of the Two Lands will know that our bloodline is stronger than ever—that we have moved past the weakness of Akhenaten's years. Egypt will never go back—only forward!"

Ankhesenamun

Year 9 of Tutankhamun
Lord of the Forms of the Sun,
Strong Bull, Perfect
Who Satisfies the Gods

STEAM PERFUMED WITH ROSEMARY and cedar oil rose from the bath in a gentle cloud. Ankhesenamun breathed in the soothing scent, shutting her eyes— shutting out, just for one brief but welcome moment— her dark thoughts, her gnawing anxieties, the terrible, vast loneliness that seemed to roar through her *ka* like a scouring sand storm in the Red Land. Her maids had prepared the hot bath when she complained of a headache, though in truth she always seemed to have a headache nowadays, whether she admitted it to her servants or not. The dull throb had plagued her nearly every waking moment for the past two months, since Tutankhamun left for his first campaign of war.

He had gone to Pa-Qas to test his mettle. It was a small but hotly contested territory on the eastern edge of the Delta, raided and abused by Assyrian rogues who strayed beyond the larger, more strategically important cities they had already claimed along the northern and eastern borders of the empire. Even knowing that the fighting would be minimal and the Egyptian forces far greater than the Assyrian, Ankhesenamun still feared for her husband—for he had no experience of battle, and had received only a little training from his generals before he'd set sail with his fleet, heading downriver in a brave flourish of horns. Her only comfort was that Horemheb had gone with him—had sworn not to leave his side for a moment. "Not even while he pisses, my lady," he had sworn on the quay, "if you'll forgive a soldier's tongue."

If Horemheb brought her Tut back alive, Ankhesenamun was prepared to forgive him anything.

The evening was purple and cool, almost cold; an hour soaking in the peace and privacy of her sunken, red-tiled tub might very well chase the throbbing pain from her forehead, for all she knew. She was prepared to try it, at least. Anything that remedied her constant, pulsing anxiety would be welcome, and blessed by the gods.

She loosed the tie of her robe and was about to drop it on the marble bench when a frantic shout rang through her apartment.

"My lady!"

Ankhesenamun jumped and pulled her robe tight again, whirling to see what the trouble was. Her bath servants murmured and clustered around the door, peering out into her chambers.

"My lady!"

It was Nann's voice. Nann, shouting in excitement. No wonder Ankhesenamun hadn't recognized her the first time—had actually felt afraid. Nann never shouted, and Ankhesenamun had never heard her friend sound so thrilled about anything.

"It's only Nann," she said to her women. "Move aside; let her in!"

Nann came panting into the bath chamber, but her cheeks were flushed pink and her green eyes glowed with happiness. She held a folded bit of papyrus up in one hand, waving it overhead like a victory banner. "A letter! A letter from the Pharaoh!"

The women murmured with approval; some of them clapped their hands. Ankhesenamun took the letter from

Nann with an undignified grab, so hungry was she for news from Tutankhamun. Nann and the other women drew close as she broke the Pharaoh's seal and scanned his words quickly.

Then, smiling, she read the note aloud for them all to hear.

My most beloved sister and King's Great Wife,

For the past two days we have made our assault on raiders' camps that surround Pa-Qas. The general here is very good, and his fortress has excellent men, but not enough of them to hold back the Assyrians. Our support has made the men of Pa-Qas strong again, and together we broke three raiding parties and utterly destroyed two of their camps. We found another camp abandoned this morning. Let them run back to their Assyrian masters and tell them that Egypt has risen again, and the wrath of the Pharaoh is great!

I find war most agreeable. It is a good adventure, though I have kept my solemn promise to you and have been as cautious as a king may rightfully be. I feel very grand and powerful whenever I take to my war chariot. The gods have made me for this purpose! Ay was right to suggest campaigns; soon we will put Assyria in its place, and then the Kushites who gnaw like rats at our southern border, and then, who can say? Perhaps I will do as our forefather did, Thutmose the Third, and push Egypt's borders farther than they have ever stretched before. Instead of Two Lands, we shall have a hundred lands! I will conquer all the way to Ceres and bring back all the silk and white vessels you could ever desire.

Horemheb has been true to his word, and has not left me alone for a moment. I feel like a child with a nurse all over again. But he has shown me sword fighting and taught me the bow, too. I am already a better shot than he.

I will see you again soon, and will praise Amun for the sight of your beauty.

Your loving brother and king,

Tutankhamun

"Oh!" Muttuya, the eldest and dreamiest of Ankhesenamun's bath maids, clasped her hands beneath her chin and sighed. "Imagine the scene! Our good Pharaoh chasing off those blasted Assyrians. He is the most gallant young man."

The other maids dug their elbows into one another's ribs and giggled.

"I cannot thank the gods enough," Ankhesenamun said, the sudden well of tears nearly choking her. "I'm so relieved he's safe."

"The campaign in Pa-Qas sounds finished," Nann said. "Or nearly so. He will return home soon."

Impulsively, and not caring one bit whether it spawned gossip among the servants, Ankhesenamun grabbed Nann in a tight, giddy hug. "Home! He'll be home soon. And if the gods are good, he won't go off to war again. Not for a very long time."

Ankhesenamun found her headache had dissipated entirely, but still she took her bath, luxuriating in the hot water, feeling the tension that had knotted her muscles for two months ease and drift away with the scented steam. She soaked until the water went cold, alone with her thoughts—with her simple, all-encompassing relief.

Finally she retired to her bed, lulled into pleasant dreams by the cheerful music of frogs and night insects.

But after only a few hours of rest, she found Nann at her side again, shaking her out of sleep, her voice low and urgent.

"My lady, there is trouble. Wadjet's baby—"

Ankhesenamun sat up quickly. She stared at Nann; though only a patch of starlight lit the room, still she could see the pallor of the Hurrian's face, the deep well of sorrow in her eyes. All of her personal horrors flooded into her heart—her own doomed pregnancies with their tragic ends.

She said nothing, but rolled quickly from her bed. She didn't bother with sandals, or even a cape against the night's chill. She took Nann's hand, as much for strength as guidance in the dark palace, and together they ran down star-paled corridors toward the concubines' apartments.

In the weeks since Tutankhamun left, Ankhesenamun had turned her attention to the young harem women. At first they had been a distraction from her fears; seeing to their requests and aiding their settling-in filled her days and kept her thoughts away from Tutankhamun's danger. But very quickly, they became more to Ankhesenamun than just a distraction. They were good, sweet, earnest girls—every one of them—and she grew to like them despite her initial misgivings. They seemed to like her, too, though naturally they were cautious around her, and were always careful to treat her with the deference due the King's Great Wife. But the more she tended to them, the more they seemed to sense her loneliness, her need— and soon they encircled her like sisters, diverting her from sadness with games and gossip, with dinner parties full of laughter and music. She had come to regard them all as friends—and thanked them now, deep in her heart, for the chance they might provide to Tutankhamun and the dynasty's unbroken line.

If Ankhesenamun had been pressed to pick a favorite from among the harem girls, Wadjet would have been her choice. Her delicate good looks and sweet singing voice belied her wicked sense of humor and her propensity for dirty jokes, which often had Ankhesenamun teary-eyed with laughter. But she liked the girl even more for the way she shared her pregnancy so openly. She seemed to understand why Ankhesenamun was so keen to know how the baby fared. Whenever Wadjet let her lay a hand on her belly to feel the first barely detectable fluttering of the child's movement, the girl always looked into her eyes with sympathy—with love. And once she had whispered, "If my child is a boy, Great Wife, I would be honored if you would choose his name." The kindness of the gesture struck Ankhesenamun speechless. She could only wrap the girl tightly in her arms.

So far as Ankhesenamun knew, Wadjet's pregnancy had progressed well. The baby was growing steadily in its fourth month, just beginning to round out the girl's flat belly. And Wadjet seemed so happy, so healthy. *By all the gods, what can the problem be? It's only my womb that is cursed, not the Pharaoh's seed. Please, Amun, let it be so!*

As she and Nann rushed across the central garden, gravel biting into the soles of Ankhesenamun's feet, she nearly convinced herself that all would be well... that this was just some trial from the gods, a false alarm to test the mettle of her heart, as Tutankhamun's strength was tested by battle.

But long before they reached the concubines' rooms, Ankhesenamun could hear weeping and the high ululation that heralded death.

"No!" She sobbed and stumbled to a halt in the garden, pressing both hands tight over her eyes—but she couldn't shut out her own memories. She saw the birth bower, the midwives' useless implements scattered, a trail of blood across the floor. She saw the too-small baby in her own arms, and tears in Tutankhamun's eyes.

"My lady," Nann said gently, "Wadjet needs you."

Ankhesenamun was too weak, too defeated to stop Nann from taking her hand again, leading her on toward the chamber where the wails rose up like altar smoke and poured out into the cold, uncaring night. She was surrendered to her fate, and hadn't the strength to stop Nann from leading her inside the chamber—though she would have spared herself the sight, the vivid resurgence of her most hated memories, if she could have done it.

In the sickly yellow glow of her lamps, Wadjet sat naked and trembling on her bed, rocking, keening, while all around her the other women and their servants stumbled, their faces streaked with tears, their hands tearing at their night dresses in helpless, agonized grief. Wadjet's sheets were soaked in blood, her thighs covered in red.

"I'm sorry!" Wadjet cried when she saw Ankhesenamun standing on her threshold, staring dull-eyed at the scene. "I'm sorry! I'm sorry!"

The girl's misplaced sense of guilt shook Ankhesenamun out of her stupor. She rushed to Wadjet's side, pulling her into her arms. The girl pressed her face against Ankhesenamun's shoulder and shuddered with the force of her sobs.

Ankhesenamun rocked her gently. "Sh—sh. It's not your fault. Poor Wadjet, my sweet Wadjet. You are not to blame."

I'm to blame, she thought darkly as she smoothed the girl's hair, stroked her bare back. *Tutankhamun and I—we are cursed, soiled by our own blood. We are the last. The gods will not let us continue.*

Horemheb

Year 9 of Tutankhaten
Lord of the Forms of the Sun,
Strong Bull, Perfect
Who Satisfies the Gods

ALMOST AS SOON as his magnificent war ship moored at Waset's quay, Tutankhamun pushed past the soldiers and generals who surrounded him and rushed down the ramp to the shore. The Pharaoh nearly made it past Horemheb himself, but the soldier was true to his word and dogged the young king's heels as closely as his own shadow.

The city was one great roaring, waving, clamoring mass, the people thronged along the docks tossing flower petals high into the air, children dancing on the rooftops beneath festive canopies of colored cloth, every weaver and beer-maker, every fisherman and whore hanging from the windows of the nearest buildings, shouting together in one unending cry of victory.

But Tutankhamun seemed to see none of it, hear none of it. His eyes were for one lone figure standing calm and self-possessed within the ring of her palace guards—and even those soldiers raised their fists into the air, chanting the Pharaoh's name. But Ankhesenamun, slender and poised, her dark hands clasped at the breast of her glowing white gown, seemed stricken to stillness by the force of her joy. She watched as Tutankhamun ran down the ship's bouncing ramp—Horemheb faintly sick at the ramp's motion as he followed closely—and when the young king landed on the broad stone quay she held out her arms invitingly, waiting for his embrace.

Horemheb couldn't hold back a laugh of delight—of relief, too—when Tutankhamun reached his Great Wife's arms. He lifted her and spun her around and around, all their dignity forgotten before the eyes of the whole court—the city itself. The crowd roared all the louder. Horemheb did not hold back his own voice. It was good to be home at last, good to deliver Tutankhamun safe into his sister's arms. *May the gods grant he stays right here until he's a much older man. It's where he belongs.*

When Tutankhamun set his wife back on her feet, she looked up at Horemheb, dizzy and laughing. "You *are* a protector," she shouted over the noise of the crowd. "You told me once, long ago, that you couldn't protect me. But you did. You kept my brother safe—my own heart—and brought him back to me."

"Horemheb was by my side the whole time," Tutankhamun told her. "He hired the best teachers to show me how to fight. The battles themselves were frightening—I won't deny it! But the gods were with me. Somehow they made me into a warrior—the gods and Horemheb—though only for a short time. After every battle I vomited everywhere! I couldn't help it; I was so tense and overwrought."

Ankhesenamun kissed him. "I'm glad you're back, even if your stomach is weak."

The Pharaoh and his wife locked their hands together as they walked to the double-throned litter that waited for them. Horemheb fell in beside them as the bearers lifted the great, gilded platform to their shoulders. Loath still to leave Tutankhamun's side, he walked nearby as the royal couple were carried through the cheering crowds.

The victory celebration—perhaps the fighting, too, Horemheb reluctantly admitted—agreed with Tutankhamun. He beamed as he waved to his subjects, as he threw kisses toward the children and salutes to the old soldiers who hailed him with battle cries. There was a force growing inside the young man—quiet but undeniable—a greatness burgeoning in his *ka* that Horemheb had not sensed before. Tutankhamun held himself now with a particularly masculine pride, a maturation that made him seem less like a boy and more like a man—more like a king.

Horemheb felt a stab of longing for the little boy who had once played around his feet, who had once looked to him with the trust a child might show its own father. The dust of the crowd pricked at his eyes; he blinked resolutely and pushed away his sentimentality, replacing it with a pride that was almost as great as a father's would be.

He glanced up at the litter again and saw Ankhesenamun's mouth moving, her pretty face darkened by a frown. Tutankhamun smiled at her, shaking his head—he could not hear her words over the chanting and cheering, the horns and songs. Ankhesenamun subsided, shaking her head in dismissal, and Tutankhamun kissed the back of her hand.

Y OU KNOW YOU DON'T have to stick so close to my side anymore, old fellow." Tutankhamun, collared with lapis lazuli, his strong young arms ringed with gold, clapped Horemheb smartly on the shoulder. "Though of course I'm glad to have your company—always! But I think now that we are back in the palace, even Ankhesenamun will release you from your pledge to watch me like a hawk. Won't you, sister?"

Ankhesenamun looked up from the hand mirror one of her women held. "If I could have my way, Horemheb would sleep in the same bed with you to keep you safe."

"Amun forbid it," Tutankhamun said. "Horemheb snores terribly. Every night I thought lions were roaring outside my tent, but it was only Horemheb, sawing through stones."

Horemheb folded his arms tight across his scarred chest. "You'll snore too when you're my age, my lord. See if you don't."

Ankhesenamun added a touch of red pigment to her lips, then sent her maid away with the basket of cosmetics. She paused, listening to the swell of voices in the great hall beyond the small keeping chamber where the three of them were closeted, making their final preparations for the victory feast. She turned to look at Tutankhamun with a solemn, dark-eyed stare that drove the laughter right out of Horemheb's heart.

Tutankhamun too realized that something was amiss. He went to his wife quickly, squeezing her small hand in both of his own. "What is it? You look so sad all of a sudden—almost fearful. Did something happen while I was on campaign?"

"My love..." Ankhesenamun swallowed hard and hung her head, clearly reluctant to speak.

"I can leave, if you would prefer," Horemheb said. "If you need privacy—"

"No," the Great Wife said, drawing herself up, bracing herself for what was to come. "I think you should hear this too, Horemheb, and no better time than now, while we three are alone."

She gazed into Tutankhamun's face for a long moment, then finally said, "Wadjet miscarried her child. I tried to tell you sooner, while we were on the litter. But you couldn't hear me, and... and it wasn't the best time, anyhow."

The Pharaoh sighed and reached up as if to rub his eyes. But he remembered the kohl that painted them and let his hand fall again. "Now isn't the best time, either, my love. They'll call us in to the feast at any moment."

"I know, and I'm sorry for it. But I didn't want you to hurt Wadjet inadvertently. If you saw her at the feast and asked about the child—"

"It's better that you told me now, after all." He turned his back, stood staring at the small room's mural of men hunting a hippopotamus, but he seemed to look beyond the painting, to a place far away. Out in the feast hall, reedy pipes rose in a whining tune and a great, joyful gust of laughter blew through the crowd. But Tutankhamun did not move, did not turn away from his own thoughts. At length he said, "I wonder if there is a curse upon us."

Ankhesenamun was beside him with two quick steps. She took his arm. "I have often asked myself the same question. But I..." She trailed off and shook her head, wrestling with the decision to speak up or keep her silence. "I wonder if perhaps this was a deliberate act."

"Would Wadjet truly do such a thing?"

"No, not she," Ankhesenamun said. "One of your enemies."

"Who is my enemy?" Tutankhamun gestured through the wall, toward the crowd that cheered him even now, when he was hidden from their gaze. "Waset loves me, especially now that I have set the Assyrian raiders to running. Who could hate me so, to strike against my child still in his mother's womb?"

"Ay has always hungered after power," she said darkly. "He has never stopped lusting after your throne. I wouldn't put it past him to kill your heir—the younger, the better, even before the child is born! With no child to inherit your power, he'll come after you next. You are the last barrier between Ay and his power."

Tutankhamun tossed his head; the high, white tip of the Double Crown flashed in the lamplight. "Don't be ridiculous! Ay hasn't steered me wrong yet. He was right to send me on this campaign—look what it's done for me, for all of Egypt!—and he was right about the next campaign, too."

Ankhesenamun's face fell. "The next?"

"Yes." His eyes slid away from her own and he blushed, sheepish. "Now it's my turn to apologize—this isn't the time or place to tell you, but out it came, all the same. We are going to Kush next. Ay says—and I agree—that it's best to strike again while the army is still riding high on its victory. It will keep the men strong and fierce, and a second victory will make our other enemies much more fearful."

"You can't!" She stepped back in horror.

"But look what this first expedition has brought us! Reclaimed territory, and the love of the people. When I have another triumph, they will be certain to support us even more—to forgive our family for Akhenaten's blundering."

"But you'll be killed!"

Cheers rang from the feast, a counterpoint to Ankhesenamun's fear that seemed a mockery from the gods themselves. She flinched, and Horemheb nearly reached for her to offer his comfort.

But Tutankhamun got there first. He kissed his wife's cheek tenderly, holding her by her shoulders. "I must do it, my love. It's for Egypt's sake."

"You can't press the gods like this, Tut. You can't tempt them so! They were merciful once, but again?"

"I'll be back before you know it, and then all these fears will be forgotten."

She wiped her eyes with careful fingers, but the paint around her eyes still smeared. "When will you leave?"

The young king hesitated before he answered. Horemheb didn't blame him. She wouldn't like the answer.

"In three weeks' time."

Ankhesenamun gasped, pressing a hand to her stomach as if seized by a great pain. Tutankhamun reached for her again, but she turned away—and looked to Horemheb instead. "You must go with him again. You *must*. I can trust no one but you to keep him safe."

Horemheb felt the Great Wife's pain in his own belly. He wondered at it while it swelled inside him, making his breath turn shallow and cold. Finally he identified it: fear. The skirmishes in Pa-Qas were nothing—children's games, compared to what they would surely face in the more organized and populous southern realms of Kush. And it had nearly frozen his heart a hundred times, watching over the Pharaoh on his first campaign.

He wasn't sure how much longer he could protect the young king from the rigors of war. But he nodded. What choice did he have, but to accept the Great Wife's charge?

"Of course, my lady. I will do my best."

Horemheb

*Year 9 of Tutankhaten
Lord of the Forms of the Sun,
Strong Bull, Perfect
Who Satisfies the Gods*

M Y LORD," Horemheb said, doing his best to banish his exhaustion and impatience from his words, "I implore you to sleep. Look; your servants have set up your cot already." *And it looks inviting enough that I'll crawl into it myself, if you don't.*

Tutankhamun laughed, pounding Horemheb's back. "Sleep? But it's just past noon!"

"I know, my lord, but there will be precious little time tonight. You know as much; you heard General Inti's plan. We launch our attack tonight, just after sunset."

The general had laid out his vision for the campaign while Tutankhamun's war ship eased to its mooring. The moon would be dark that night, but with the river at their backs, the Egyptian forces should have just enough reflected starlight to find their way into the deep-gouged ravines that led from the Iteru's western bank into Kushite territory. Thrilled by the prospect of a daring night attack, Tutankhamun had barely been able to maintain his dignity while still aboard the ship. Now, in the privacy of his campaign tent, pitched in the midst of the Egyptian encampment, the king couldn't stop himself from bouncing with eagerness. *Watch him on his throne and he seems as wise and staid as any king who has ever ruled before. But give him the prospect of adventure, and he reminds you in a heartbeat that he's still a boy—still very much a child.*

Horemheb sighed and sank onto one of the folding, leather-seated stools that waited beside Tutankhamun's small table. Maps had been placed upon the table, ready for more of General Inti's strategizing, but they hadn't yet been unrolled. If they had, Horemheb would nearly have expected to see Tutankhamun spreading toy soldiers and model chariots over the maps' bright surfaces.

Well, it could be worse. Better to have an eager but untrained king than a coward.

Tutankhamun was certainly no coward. The boy had an aptitude for war, even if his instincts were as yet unrefined, his body and heart still largely untested. He was growing stronger every day—his body was of slight build, but his muscles had plenty of wiry definition. In another year or two he'd be strong enough to throw Horemheb in a wrestling match. And his enthusiasm for these early campaigns proved that he was a natural fighter, channeling with ease the warrior blood of his expansionist ancestors. What did it matter if that conquering spirit had lain dormant in recent generations? The fighters who had made the dynasty great had resurrected in Tutankhamun. Day by day his burgeoning might emerged.

But the king wasn't yet the wise warrior he hoped to be. The boy still needed plenty of guidance.

"My lord, you'll be no good on the field tonight if you don't get some rest."

Tutankhamun threw his arms wide, spinning to take in the interior of his campaign tent—trampled earth floor, uncomfortable cots with their inadequate wool bedding, the trunks and chests full of weapons and armor, hastily deposited by the servants who unloaded the war ships, and all of it dimly lit by sun that strained to penetrate the thick, coarse linen of the tent's peaked roof and gently flapping walls. It must have seemed as grand as a palace to Tutankhamun.

"How can I sleep when there's so much to think about, so much to plan? Kush! The southern border! And tonight we'll push even farther south, make the Kushites swear on their knees to be my loyal subjects."

Horemheb rolled his eyes. "One battle won't do the trick. You know that—or you should. Tonight will be the first strike of many. This will be a long and difficult campaign—nothing like Pa-Qas. You should conserve your energy. And your enthusiasm."

The boy flipped open one of his trunks with the toe of his sandal. "Ah!" He sighed in admiration, reached into the straw packing, and lifted out his Khepresh crown. It was the war helmet worn only by the king, high and rounded, the brilliant blue of polished lapis, and shining like a beetle's shell. Tutankhamun eased the war crown onto his brow. "This is what the gods meant for me."

"The gods meant for you to sleep."

"Not while the sun's up. That goes against the nature of men and beasts."

Horemheb groaned, leaning his head on his fist and his elbow on the map table. The final stretch of their sailing journey had been long and harrowing—the fleet had passed through the rapids of the upper Iteru, and Horemheb had never been able to stomach choppy water. He needed sleep, even if Tutankhamun didn't. But he wasn't about to let the boy out of his sight.

"Let's go out into the valley," Tutankhamun said. "The ships with the horses got here hours before we did. They're out there now, warming the animals up, checking the chariots' wheels and axles. Come on, old fellow! Let's go and have a look."

"War is serious business, my lord. This isn't a festival day. We aren't at the race track, betting on our favorites.

Leave the charioteers to their business. We'll need them sorely tonight, and it's dangerous to drive in poor light; they must be sure of their horses and their carts."

Tutankhamun's sigh would have been the envy of a whole troop of actors. He sagged where he stood, as if all the bones in his body had gone limp at once. "Sometimes I think you're as old as Ay," he said. "When did you forget how to have a good time?"

"You'll have all the good times you can *stomach* tonight."

The allusion to Tutankhamun's unfortunate habit of sicking up after all his previous battles took some of the wind out of his sails. "You don't fight fair, old fellow. Why, sometimes I think—"

The Pharaoh paused. The sounds of the camp's bustle had risen in pitch. The low hum of conversation broke and rose in harsh shouts; the shuffle of men going about their business turned to the urgent pounding of many running feet. Sudden tension was in the air—a sensation Horemheb didn't like one bit.

Tutankhamun tilted his head. "What is it, do you suppose?"

Horemheb rose slowly from his stool. He tested the change in atmosphere like a hound scenting the wind, deliberate, sensitive, sharply alert. "Armor," he said quietly to Tutankhamun.

"What? I—"

"Get your armor on," Horemheb snapped, grabbing up a spear that stood propped beside the table. "Now!"

Then he heard what he most feared—a faint call from the high hills that surrounded their encampment. *Ambush!*

"The enemy is here already!" Tutankhamun darted for the tent's flap. Horemheb made a grab for him but he wasn't quick enough; the king bowled past him and out of the tent before Horemheb could do anything more than curse. Tutankhamun had nothing on but his kilt and sandals—and the Khepresh crown, as bold and obvious as a painted target in the archery butts.

Horemheb shoved through the jostling, shouting crowd, yelling after Tutankhamun, struggling to reach him. But men and horses wove between them, and though the Khepresh crown taunted him as it bobbed rapidly through the camp, Horemheb couldn't catch up to his king.

"Wait!" he yelled. Useless to shout—the whole damn place was in an uproar. But there was nothing else he could do. "Wait, damn you! You haven't got your armor!"

Horemheb shoved through a contingent of foot soldiers armed with short spears and round shields. Tutankhamun was beyond the last of the tents now, jogging steadily toward the charioteers and their rearing, shying horses. Horemheb spat in anger and pelted after the king, catching him by the arm just as he was about to jump into a chariot.

"Get back to the tent," Horemheb growled.

"Hide while my men fight for me? Never!"

"This isn't Pa-Qas, boy. The Kushites are—"

"I'm not your boy," Tutankhamun said coldly. "I'm your king, Horemheb. You mustn't forget that."

He bobbed a quick bow of apology, then squinted up at the sere brown hills that loomed above the valley floor. Dark arrowheads of chariots in formation, pulled by the Kushites' small but indefatigable horses, flew down the slopes toward the encampment. The Kushites would be in their midst soon. There was little time now to wrangle Tutankhamun back to the tent and into his armor. "If you survive this ambush, do remember to rebuke me later for my disrespect."

"I'll come through the battle just fine," the boy said, laughing. "The gods are on our side!"

Tutankhamun sprang into his chariot. The man who'd

held the horses released them; Tutankhamun clutched he reins tightly in his fist. "Come on, Horemheb! You must be my driver. I want to fight, not drive!"

"Oh, by Set's balls," Horemheb muttered. He climbed up beside the king and swiped the reins from his hands. The two war horses screamed, throwing their heads high. They backed and swiveled the chariot, fighting one another, fighting Horemheb in their eagerness to charge. "This isn't a game, Tutankhamun! I have to keep you safe—and that means keeping you away from the battle. We'll let the other chariots lead."

"I will lead the attack, or else I am no king." He lifted Horemheb's spear high above his head. When they saw him there, conspicuous in his great blue crown and waving the damn fool spear in the air, the men who still clambered into the Egyptian chariots cheered and howled their challenges to the Kushites.

"Will you listen to me?" Horemheb pleaded. "Stop being so... so blasted *young*!"

Tutankhamun thrust his spear forward; the chariots thundered past, surging to meet the ambush. Horemheb waited for his chance—for the last of the Egyptian drivers to pass him. Then he would grab the boy and toss him out of the cart, leap out after him and wrestle him back to the camp, back to the boat where the Kushites couldn't reach him. But Tutankhamun wasn't about to let the battle move on without him. He leaned over the chariot's rail, shouted, "Ha!" to the dancing horses, and they lunged toward the fray, galloping after their mates.

"Damn you!" Horemheb yelled, fighting the reins. He had no idea whether his curse was meant for the king, the horses, or himself.

They crashed into the fight like the river bursting over the black stones of its rapids. All around them sand and curses flew; spears whistled as they slashed through the air. A spray of blood hit Horemheb across his chest, as hot as the sun overhead. The valley was a confusion of carts, of men knocked from chariots struggling in the sand, of horses' hooves pounding and kicking as spears rang loud against shields and arrows hissed into the fray.

Damnable arrows! Horemheb struggled to wheel his horses about while Tutankhamun stabbed and parried with his spear. *If I can just keep him out of the bows' range!* He would have knocked that foolish Khepresh crown right off the king's head—it was nothing but a target for archers and spearmen alike—but he didn't dare drop one of his reins.

"Look out!" Tutankhamun pointed to the left, across Horemheb's body, and stabbed to the right with his spear. A Kushite soldier, knocked from his own cart, made a mad swipe at Horemheb's horses with his sword. Horemheb pulled hard on the reins to turn his animals—too hard. The horses veered away sharply; the chariot rocked up onto one wheel. He and Tutankhamun shouted in alarm with one voice, both of them grabbing tight to the rail, leaning hard to keep their cart from tipping. It rocked back onto both its wheels, but the jar was tremendous. Tutankhamun let out a hoarse, wordless howl as he lost his grip on the rail. A moment later his slight, thin body lifted into the air and... was gone from the chariot. Gone, knocked from the platform and out there, onto the hard earth, amid the trampling hooves and the arrows punching into the ground.

Horemheb's scream of rage carried even over the din of battle. He leaned, hauled on the reins, shouted furious commands at the horses—and finally turned the beasts around. He swung back, ready to plunge into the fight to find the king, no matter how many arrows he took, no matter how many spears stabbed into his guts. He prayed the boy had the wits to draw his sword. *Lord Amun, mighty Horus, Lady Sekhmet who loves war... let the boy rise. Let him defend himself as I've shown him how to do!*

Through the rush and chaos of the fight, through the blur of brown bodies and black hooves, the dull ochre of dust, the mist of red, Horemheb caught sight of a flash of blue, brilliant as the purest turquoise. *The Khepresh crown!*

"Go!" Horemheb shouted desperately to his horses, pointing them toward the place where Tutankhamun had fallen.

As he thundered toward the king, Horemheb saw Tutankhamun pick himself up slowly, painfully, rising from where he lay sprawled on his back. The boy rolled onto his hands and knees, struggling, hesitating, as if the wind were knocked clean from his lungs.

"Draw your sword," Horemheb yelled—though at this distance the Pharaoh could not hear. "Draw your sword, Tut, and fight!"

The horses raced on; Horemheb beat them with the reins, shouting in helpless, wordless agony as they seemed to gallop in place, coming no closer to the king—not fast enough, at least, to be of any use.

Tutankhamun looked up suddenly, his eyes searching the brawling crowd, as if perhaps he had caught Horemheb's cry. He struggled to his knees, and his hand went to his sword hilt.

Yes! Horemheb thought. *He remembers. Now draw it, boy! Draw your sword and fight!*

A bright flash of white and red darted toward the king—an unmanned chariot pulled by two spotted horses, careening through the fight in a panic. The boy seemed to stare at it dully as it bore down on him. The horses dodged aside just before their hooves could pound him into the dust, and for a heartbeat Horemheb dared to hope. But in the next moment the chariot collided with Tutankhamun's body. The wheel caught him in the center of his chest, and Horemheb seemed to feel the impact in his own body—the loud, final snap of bones breaking, the life inside him fracturing like the fragile shell of an egg.

Horemheb jerked his horses to a halt beside the king's motionless body. "Help me, damn you," he shouted to the handful of Egyptians who fought nearby. Together they held the Kushites at bay as two of them lifted the Pharaoh into Horemheb's chariot.

He galloped back to the encampment—to the boats that waited on the river, beyond the reach of the Kushites. But what good were boats now? Still he urged the horses on with desperate speed, even though he knew all hope had fled. Every time looked down at Tutankhamun, he could see how still the boy lay, how utterly empty that poor, brave, broken vessel was.

The king was dead. So quickly, so decisively—a promising young life gone like a lamp's flame in a stiff breeze.

Just as Ay had hoped.

Ay, who waited in Waset with one hand on the empty throne... and with Ankhesenamun, the last of the dynasty's pure and sacred blood.

Ankhesenamun

Year 1 of Ay
Everlasting is the Sun,
Righteous Born,
Making the Staff of Two Lands

ANKHESENAMUN HADN'T HAD a letter from her husband in several days—and his most recent note had been hasty, written just before his war ship arrived at the plain in Kush where his southern campaign would begin. The note had been full of a young man's bravado. Tutankhamun's faith in a victory—in the continued favor of the gods—was unshaken.

But Ankhesenamun's was not. In truth, she'd had no faith at all in the Kushite campaign. The water of her bath had gone cold around her as she lay back, lost in her darkest thoughts. She shivered, but whether from the chill or from her own fears, she couldn't say.

"My lady?" Muttuya, her bath maid, bent over the sunken red tub to peer at Ankhesenamun in concern. "Are you well? You have been in so long."

"I'm well."

The words sounded distant, distracted, even to her own ears. Tutankhamun had promised to write as often as he could, for he knew Ankhesenamun would be wracked with anxiety for the duration of this campaign. She knew there was nothing to fear—letters from the southmost provinces were often delayed, for not every boat could navigate the rough waters of the upper Iteru easily. And yet she also knew, far down in the fluttering heart of her *ka*, that there was everything to fear. The silence from Tutankhamun—the vast, stretching distance between them—had the feeling of finality. She wanted to weep, but knew there would be no point, that there was no cause. Yet still she felt a stab of mourning in her heart, and could barely hold back her senseless tears.

"I'm well," she said again. "I'll get out now, and then have my supper."

"Yes, my lady."

Muttuya fetched a long, soft towel of well-worn linen as Ankhesenamun stood, her muscles stiff and knotted from the cold water. But just as she stepped out of the bath, the door of her outer chamber crashed open. The maids who had been tidying her apartment shrieked in alarm; Ankhesenamun heard the pounding of men's feet and the subtle metallic clinks and clatters of belts laden with heavy weapons. Men—soldiers—coming to apprehend her.

All at once, she knew exactly why she had felt on the verge of tears. She knew she had reason to mourn.

Ay appeared on the threshold of her bath room. His small, dark eyes flicked dismissively down the length of Ankhesenamun's body. Muttuya shouted a wordless protest and lunged with the towel, trying to cover Ankhesenamun's nakedness from the old man's gaze. But Ankhesenamun brushed the towel aside, let it fall to the cold, slick tiles.

"Tutankhamun?" she said to Ay. The level calm of her own voice shocked her. How could she be so placid, so accepting, when she knew... she *knew*...

Ay's mouth tightened, a subtle, small movement. But she realized he was holding back a triumphant smile. "He is dead. Killed in battle, the brave boy."

A silent roar shuddered through Ankhesenamun's body, her *ka* itself crying, howling in its ineffable grief. She hunched over the pain in her heart, clutching her roiling stomach. She would be sick in another moment, and didn't care who saw.

Muttuya's soft, plump arms encircled her, and through the loud, fierce buzzing in her ears Ankhesenamun could hear the woman murmuring meaningless comforts, cooing away her pain. But the pain did not recede.

Mutnodjmet shoved into the room, past Ay and his men.

"Gods' sake," she scolded, "get out of here, Ay, and take these brutes with you! Have you no shame, no sense of propriety?"

Mutnodjmet too wrapped Ankhesenamun in her arms. The two women were the only strength she seemed to have. A hard, dark weight was pulling at her, dragging her down, insisting she fall, that she collapse on the cold tile floor and scream out her loss and fear. But somehow the women kept her standing.

"Pull her together," Ay snapped at her women, his voice quiet with disgust. "Does dignity mean nothing to any of you?"

Fighting that harrowing weight, Ankhesenamun struggled out of her women's arms. She could stand after all—could stand and face her enemy. "You did this!" she cried. "His death suited your purposes, and so you arranged it!"

Ay huffed a sigh, a display of tolerance for female weakness. He said slowly, as if explaining to a young and particularly dim-witted child, "My lady. No one can arrange a death in battle."

"I'm not fool enough to believe that, Ay." She stalked toward him, her body shaking with the force of her rage. "No one can arrange a death in battle, you say? Would you make the same claim about the death of a child in the womb?"

Ay exchanged quick, confused glances with his soldiers. "What is all this?" he said.

Ankhesenamun flung each word at him like a stone. "Can no one arrange for a woman to miscarry?"

She advanced still closer, and Ay shrank back at the hateful fire in her eyes. It was no more than the merest flinch, but his flicker of misgiving spurred her on. Her voice rose to a hysterical shriek, but she didn't care.

"Wadjet's baby, Ay! You killed Wadjet's baby before it was even born! Did you poison the children in my womb, too? Tell me!"

She thrust out a hand to seize him, to rend him like the goddess Pakhet with her lion's claws. But one of the soldiers batted her hand away and pressed Ay back, out of her reach.

"Get the King's Wife dressed," Ay said to her women, "before she does something she'll later regret. She is wanted at the Temple of Amun."

"The temple?" Her teeth were clenched, her breath coming harsh and fast. Every bit of her flesh, every bone shook with the need to reach Ay, to hurt him, to destroy him. "The temple? The temple?" She went on screaming the question, gnashing her teeth, until Mutnodjmet pulled her away from Ay, whispering pleas for self-control into Ankhesenamun's ear.

"Yes," Ay said coolly. "You have a marriage to attend."

Ankhesenamun stilled on the instant. She understood his words, read all too clearly the meaning in the gleam in his eyes, their light of mockery and self-congratulation. Disgust surged in her gut, so strong she choked back a renewed urge to vomit.

But as she stood there, watching Ay's slow, pleased smile curl across his face, her horror and disbelief fled, replaced by a sense of perfect strength that spread like the tingle of strong wine along her veins. Her shaking stopped. Her spine straightened until she stood as tall and poised as a goddess in a shrine.

Ankhesenamun went to Ay and his soldiers with three quick, decisive steps. She held his stare for a moment in affronted silence. Then she spat full in his face.

Ay jerked away from her—and this time there was nothing subtle about his flinch. Grimacing in disgust, he wiped the spittle away with his bony fingers.

"You will marry me," he said, hoarse with anger, "whether you like it or not. I will not play at regent any longer, Ankhesenamun. The throne will be mine now. And you are the last royal woman remaining."

"But I will never marry you." She didn't scream the words. She was beyond that panic now, beyond hysteria. Ankhesenamun spoke clearly, slowly, so there could be no doubt in Ay's mind that she denied him—would always deny him. "You are a murderer. And a king-killer. Your *ka* is cursed forever. I will not soil my own spirit by indulging you in these fantasies of power. You will have nothing from me, you low-born, scheming, vile, black-hearted *murderer*."

Ay slapped Ankhesenamun, so hard he nearly knocked her to the floor. She staggered, caught herself against Mutnodjmet's shoulder, gasped in shock at the pain and the fierce, hate-filled force of his blow. She held a hand to her burning cheek and stared at him, silent, watching.

"I will hold Egypt together no matter what the cost," Ay said quietly. "Get used to that notion. I will have your cooperation, one way or another. You can give me your aid willingly, or I will take it from you by force. The choice is yours, Ankhesenamun."

"This has nothing to do with Egypt," she answered calmly. But she still held her cheek; it burned like a torch under her hand. "This is about your own selfish whims.

You will do anything—kill any person, even children in their mothers' wombs—to obtain power. And for what? So you can look in your mirror and say, 'There stands the mightiest man in all the world'?"

Ay flipped one hand toward her women, an impatient and dismissive gesture. "Dress her now. The High Priest is waiting."

Ankhesenamun raised her voice. "You cannot make me marry you against my will."

Ay watched her with brows raised. *Can I not?* his expression said.

"And anyway, I will tell the High Priest that Tutankhamun is not dead. In fact, I will not believe it myself—and neither will the priest—until I see my husband's body."

Those words nearly brought a fresh tide of tears to her eyes, and more sobs to her throat. But she couldn't afford such a display of sorrow now. She needed her strength, her composure—all the skills of a Great Wife that Nefertiti taught her. She needed to wear her power like a cloak, wrapping her, concealing her true heart from Ay's gaze. She forced herself to lower her hand from her stinging cheek, and stared defiantly at her grandfather.

Ay narrowed his eyes. His thin lips twisted with spite. Ankhesenamun had his back against the wall—she could tell that much. And Ay knew it, too.

Finally he shrugged. "The wedding can wait until Tutankhamun's corpse is brought back on his boat. It is all one to me. The boy is not the god Waser; he won't resurrect on the way here."

The harsh words were like a blow to her gut, but outwardly she remained unshaken. She had no doubt that Ay's grim news was true—*Would that I could change it! I would give anything, Amun!*—but she had bought herself some time, and she might yet find a way to beat Ay at his own deadly game.

"In the meantime," Ay said, gesturing to his guardsmen, turning away, "you are not to leave these apartments. I won't have you slipping off to plot with some noble in the city, or the High Priest of Amun. You can't evade your fate, Ankhesenamun. You will marry me, and the throne will be mine."

NEVER BEFORE IN HER LIFE had Ankhesenamun felt so trapped—not even as a child in Akhet-Aten, leaning out over the palace wall, watching as her mother vanished like a white-shrouded spirit among the streets of the City of the Sun. Throughout that long, grief-laden day she paced among her women in the confines of her chambers, as restless and helpless as a lion in a bronze-barred cage. She did not weep for Tutankhamun anymore. She had no doubt that he was dead—the gods told her so, instilling her heart with a cold, brutal certainty. There would be time enough for tears when she found some way to defeat Ay, to turn the tables of his game. Then she would weep for months, for years. Then she would spend the rest of her life rocking and keening in grief for the loss of the only person who had ever truly loved her, who had never once looked at her and asked himself, *What can I get from this woman? How can I use Ankhesenamun to further my own ends?*

She would mourn Tutankhamun properly as soon as she found a way to free herself. And she would not rest until she had made a suitable plan. She had only seventy days, more or less—the length of the ceremonial embalming—until Tutankhamun's war ship returned to Waset's quay, carrying his wrapped and blessed body home to meet his eternity. It wasn't much time... but it was a respite from Ay's machinations, and Ankhesenamun was determined to make the most of the time she had been granted.

But her heart was clouded by the despair she tried to keep at bay, and after a day of pacing, of praying, of pounding her fists in frustration against the walls of her prison, she had nothing to show for her efforts but an aching back, skinned knuckles, and the ominous silence of the gods.

Finally she collapsed across her bed, staring dully out the window into the garden beyond.

Mutnodjmet came to her, fanning her gently with a spread of plumes. "My lady, you've worn yourself out with all this restless walking."

"What else am I to do? Ay hopes that if he just keeps me here, shut up in my rooms, I'll become desperate and lonely enough to give in. At least walking helps me think."

"And has all your walking and thinking gained you anything?"

She sighed. "No. I can't see a way out of this mess. Unless it's to..." She trailed off darkly, unable to meet Mutnodjmet's eye.

"Not that," Nann called. The Hurrian lounged against the chamber wall, leaning casually on the window sill. A breeze from the garden stirred her bronze-colored hair as she saluted Ankhesenamun with a slow, deliberate blink. "You won't take your own life."

Ankhesenamun sat up, laughing bitterly. "Oh? What makes you think that?"

"Ishtar isn't done with you. She has told me as much."

"Ishtar isn't my goddess," Ankhesenamun rejoined. But even so, she couldn't hold back a superstitious shiver.

"Perhaps she ought to be your goddess. She has taken a liking to you."

She was suddenly angry at Nann—at her unconcerned attitude, at the tears she did not shed for the king. "So you are a priestess now?"

"Of course not. I don't need to be. Mitanni's gods are not like Egypt's."

Mutnodjmet held up a hand to silence them both. "Listen!"

None of the women spoke. Ankhesenamun strained to hear whatever had caught her friend's attention; even Nann stood up straight, peering around the chamber with a cautious air.

Then she heard it: a faint scratching at the garden door, so low down its frame it might have come from the ground outside.

"A rat?" Ankhesenamun whispered.

Nann waved her to silence, then crept to the door on her toes. She paused, gathering herself, then jerked the door open with such sudden force that a gust of garden air was sucked inside, tumbling dried leaves, bits of grass, and an errant moth into the room.

A man came with it, scuttling in a low crouch. Ankhesenamun started up in fear, her nerves worn so thin by the long day of sorrow and anxiety that she nearly screamed. But Mutnodjmet cried out and ran to the man, throwing herself into his arms with a desperate sob.

"By the teats of Iset!" Nann's coarse oath hardly registered in Ankhesenamun's heart. She was too stunned by the sight of the man, ragged and dirty, his dark eyes infinitely tired. "It's Horemheb!"

Horemheb kissed Mutnodjmet, long and deep. Ankhesenamun felt a wave of bitterness rise in her stomach; she turned away from the sight.

"I tried to get back sooner," Horemheb said. "I tried to make it back to Waset before word arrived of... well, you know of the tragedy by now, I suspect."

"Yes," Ankhesenamun whispered. "We know."

He disentangled himself from Mutnodjmet's clinging arms and rushed to Ankhesenamun's side. There he fell on his knees, staring up at her with pained, pleading eyes. "I took the fastest boat I could find, my lady. But it wasn't fast enough. I'm sorry."

"No," she said, the words thin and quavering. "Not fast enough. Ay heard the news this morning. I'm trapped here, Horemheb—locked in my own chambers."

"Guards all through the garden, watching for our lady to escape." Nann arched one light eyebrow. "How you managed to get through without being seen is a mystery to me."

"A mystery to me, too," Horemheb said. He struggled to his feet, groaning. "Hobbling through the flower beds bent-backed might have had something to do with it. But it was the gods who protected me. I heard talk in the city, before I even reached the palace, that Ay was to marry the King's Great Wife. I knew he wouldn't like to see me—no doubt he'd hoped I would be killed in battle, too... begging your pardon, my lady," he added with a guilty glance at Ankhesenamun. "I expected to be captured at any moment as I slipped through the palace grounds, but the gods were my shield. They wanted me to find you... wanted me to tell you what I know."

Ankhesenamun braced herself. "And what do you know?"

"I know how the Pharaoh died."

Tears burned as they gathered, raising the taste of salt in her throat. She closed her eyes. "So it is true." She hadn't doubted it, hadn't hoped for anything different. But still the knowledge cut her—cleaved her *ka* in two.

"It is true," Horemheb said gently. "I wish it were not."

She nodded, still refusing to look at him—to look at anything in this blighted, gods-damned world. "Tell me," she said, and sank back on her bed to hear the tale.

Horemheb recounted the events quickly—Tutankhamun's eagerness for battle, the ambush in the hills, how the king refused his counsel and would not be persuaded to leave the fighting to better-trained men. He spared her the details, and for that she was grateful. All too vivid images rose in her heart's eye without the need for embellishment. She would never forget the hard, heavy feel of those awful words—*Hit by a chariot's wheel.* She had no need for details. She could see her husband's death, *feel* it with more force than she could stand, through Horemheb's spare words.

When he fell silent, Ankhesenamun opened her eyes. The walls of her bed chamber seemed closer than ever before, the space between them narrow and confining—and shrinking every moment, a trap tightening around her. "I have to get out of here," she said, wiping her running nose on the back of her hand. "Ay will marry me and take the throne."

"That is what I feared."

"I don't know if I can stop him, Horemheb! The gods know I've tried to find a way."

"You still have time," Mutnodjmet said, stroking her hair. "Until the Pharaoh's embalming is finished... until they bring him home."

Ankhesenamun clutched Horemheb's hand. Desperate for his aid—for anyone who might help her—she kissed his palm to bless him, to bind him to her. Rough calluses scratched her lips. "Tell me you can help me, Horemheb. Tell me you can free me. Please!"

In the garden a soldier's call rang out. "Horemheb has been spotted around the palace gate!"

Another man answered, "Come on; be quick!"

Mutnodjmet sucked in a sharp breath and held it, trembling as she stared up at her husband.

Nann edged to the window again and watched the garden. "They're running toward the corridors," she reported. "But they won't be gone long. Ay has them all under strict orders to keep a close watch on these chambers."

"You'll have to go now," Ankhesenamun told her soldier—perhaps the only loyal man she had left in the world. "Be quick, or they'll catch you."

Mutnodjmet embraced her husband quickly, but then pushed him toward the door. "My lady is right; you must go now. Get out of the palace, out of the city—you must hide! Ay will kill you if he finds you. And he will search for you, now that he knows you've survived the campaign."

"I know." He kissed his wife one last time, then nodded stoically at Ankhesenamun. "I will be back, Mutnodjmet, and you, my lady... if I can. I won't leave either of you here in Ay's hands. I promise you that. And if there's any way I can help you, I will. Wait for me to return."

"There won't be anything left of you for the gods to bless if you don't go now," Nann said.

Without another word, without a backward glance, Horemheb slipped through the door, out into the wide expanse of the garden. The sound of his pounding feet faded long before the guards returned to their posts.

Mutnodjmet exhaled a long, weary sigh.

"May the gods bless Horemheb, and keep him safe." Ankhesenamun took Mutnodjmet's hand. "Your brave husband may be our only hope."

Ankhesenamun

Year 1 of Ay
Everlasting is the Sun,
Righteous Born,
Making the Staff of Two Lands

ANKHESENAMUN STEPPED BACK, hanging her head meekly as the door to her apartments opened. The guards outside raised their voices.

"All right, set the basket down and let us have a look."

Mutnodjmet, returned from her trip to the kitchens and store rooms, coolly did as the guards commanded. Her large reed basket was piled high with all the accoutrements any royal captive would need: flat discs of bread, ripe fruit, clean sheets for Ankhesenamun's bed.

"Just my lady's necessities," Mutnodjmet said.

The guards pawed through the basket all the same, examining each piece of citrus and every fold of linen as if it might conceal weapons or vials of poison.

"Don't crumble the bread!" Mutnodjmet snapped. "You stupid, blundering oxen!"

One of the guards pulled up the long snake of a woven belt. The thing dangled a few frayed linen ties. "What's this? I've never seen anything like it. Explain yourself, woman!"

Mutnodjmet snatched it out of his hand. "It's a belt for cloths."

"Cloths?"

"*Women's* cloths," she said, rolling her eyes. "For my

339

lady's monthly flux."

The guards rocked back on their heels, glancing uneasily between Mutnodjmet and the basket. Most men had a superstitious fear of a woman's blood, for it carried the potential for magic not even the strongest male priests could use. But whether Mutnodjmet's blundering oxen could be manipulated by that fear remained to be seen.

Mutnodjmet reached into the bottom of the basket and pulled up a folded piece of white linen. "And here, one of the cloths to catch the blood itself. Shall I show you how it works?" She began fiddling with the ties of the menstrual belt, preparing a matter-of-fact demonstration.

The guards stood quickly and backed away. "All right, all right," one of them said. "You're clear to go in with the prisoner."

"Oh, how very kind of you." Mutnodjmet dropped belt and cloth back into the basket, then quickly heaped the rest of the strewn supplies on top. She hefted the load up to her hip with only a small grunt to indicate its weight. "Good day, men."

As soon as the door was safely closed behind her, Mutnodjmet's stern mask cracked. Her shoulders shook as she tried to stifle her laughter, but it forced its way out as a rough snort.

"It worked!" Ankhesenamun whispered.

She rushed to help her friend with the heavy basket. Together they eased it down beside Ankhesenamun's couch, then they dug through its contents almost as roughly as the guards had. They piled the food on the nearby table, set jars of oil for washing carefully on the floor, tossed the linen sheets over the back of the couch. Ankhesenamun threw the monthly cloths out of the basket by the handful, finally uncovering her true prize. The dark brown, inch-thick plank of hard wax rested at the bottom of the basket. The writing stylus had pressed lightly into the tablet. She stared at it for a moment, face to face at last with the only plan for her own salvation she had been able to devise. It was such a small thing, that slender instrument with its plain wooden handle and copper point. But it was the only weapon Ankhesenamun had. She plucked the stylus up. It came loose from the wax with faint click.

Ankhesenamun closed the stylus in her fist and paused, sending up a prayer to any gods that might be near. *Guide my hand and my words, I beg of thee. Let my plea land in sympathetic hands.*

She trusted Horemheb—how not, after all he had done in her service? But Ankhesenamun had learned better than to leave her trust with only one man. Horemheb might be the most loyal creature the gods ever made, but he was one man alone against Ay's faction—and Ay's followers grew by the day as the nobles and priests of Waset learned of Ankhesenamun's captivity and her all-but-inevitable marriage to Tutankhamun's former regent. For all she knew, Ay's allies might already have spread a net of eyes and ears across the city, and trapped Horemheb somewhere in the maze of Waset's alleys. For Mutnodjmet's sake as well as her own, she hoped that was not the case—prayed that Horemheb was still free. But she knew by now that she couldn't trust to any god's mercy.

"Do you think this will work, my lady?" Mutnodjmet pulled the heavy tablet out of the basket and setting it on the tabletop.

"I don't know. But we must try. How much longer do we have until the Pharaoh's ship returns to the city? Sixty-five days... or less? Then I will no longer be able to deny that Tutankhamun is dead." How those words still burned in her throat!

"But why did you send me out to get this tablet? I don't understand what you're planning."

Ankhesenamun tossed the stylus, bouncing it in the palm of her hand. "As a royal woman of Egypt, I have a strength no one else possesses. I can offer something of great value, too—something no one else in all the world can give. If the gods are with me, I may be able to build my own powerful alliance against Ay."

Mutnodjmet shook her head vaguely. "I don't follow you, my lady. What can you offer?"

"Myself. I am going to offer my hand in marriage to a foreign king."

Mutnodjmet gaped at her. "You can't! In all the thousands of years of Egypt's history, no King's Daughter has ever gone to a foreign land as a wife. It... it simply *isn't done!*"

"I am not asking to be sent to a foreign land. What good would I do in another country, leaving Ay uncontested with the Horus Throne? No, Mutnodjmet: I intend to bring someone here—someone who controls great armies, who holds more power than Ay can ever hope to muster. Someone whom Ay will fear to cross."

"A new husband," Mutnodjmet said, furrowing her brow. "But will your subjects accept a foreigner as their king?"

"Perhaps not," Ankhesenamun said lightly, bending over the tablet, pressing the stylus into its firm, dark surface. "But we shall handle that problem when it arises. For now, it's time I went courting."

The words came to her quickly, flowing from her heart to her hand, embedding themselves in the wax with elegant phrases that pleased. *Djehuty, god of wisdom, guides my hand. And if the gods love me, Hathor will guide my heart.*

When she had written all she could think to say—all she felt was dignified, without resorting to desperate pleas for succor—she sat back calmly on her couch and read her letter.

Ankhesenamun, King's Great Wife of the Two Lands, to Suppiluliuma, mighty king of all the Hittites, saying thus:

The Pharaoh, he who was my husband, has died. I am left with no son; Egypt has no heir. But I still remain, and through marriage to me may a man rule Egypt as its rightful king.

Never shall I take a subject and make him my husband. A man who is like a servant to me is not worthy of Egypt's throne. But a King's Son of a powerful nation is not like a servant. They say you have many sons; send one to me. To me he will be husband, and to Egypt he will be king.

You know that from time immemorial, no daughter of the Pharaoh has been given to any other king. I have written to no other land: only to you do I turn.

Ankhesenamun drew a shaky breath. It was such a small thing on which to stake her hopes—her life. One tablet of wax, a few lines of writing. *But I must send it now— today. Time is running short, and it is a long way to the court of Suppiluliuma.*

"Very well," she finally said. But she couldn't seem to drop the stylus now that it was in her grip. "Wrap it well, for I won't have any word of it damaged. Deliver it to Nann. She has a man she trusts in the city, a Hurrian who trades with Hatti. He is prepared to carry the letter to the king."

"Can he get there fast enough?"

"The gods alone know." Ankhesenamun sighed. "But Nann thinks so, and I trust her judgment. It's a costly trip, though, and all the more so for making it in haste. But I'll gladly pay any price. I cannot let Ay win. Now take the letter to Nann, quickly."

"I will, my lady."

Mutnodjmet shook out a long cloth and folded it, ready to wrap the precious tablet for transport. Ankhesenamun's fingers twitched against the stylus.

"Wait," she said. "Don't wrap it yet."

She had more yet to say, more words for the king of Hatti, her final hope for salvation.

Mutnodjmet laid the wax back on the table, but Ankhesenamun stared at it for a long moment, all the words in her heart clamoring together at once, crying out to be said, wringing her body with their urgency.

She pressed the point of the stylus against the wax and left it there, hesitating.

The only one who ever loved me is dead, she longed to write.

And then, *My heart is a shadow.*

She let her hand move of its own accord, and when it stopped she stared down at the new marks incised in the thick, dark wax. Tears blurred her vision, but not before she saw with brutal clarity the words she had written: *I am afraid.*

T HE TENSION OF WAITING settled so completely into Ankhesenamun's gut that she hardly noticed it anymore. She went about the small routines of her captive life with that tightness coiled perpetually inside her, bathing, dressing, eating, waiting—all with the quiet acceptance of a horse finally broken to its harness. Days passed. Then weeks passed, while she and her friends waited for word—from Horemheb or from Hatti; either would have pleased her, would have brought her some relief. By day she paced her chambers, and offered a portion of every meal to the small gods who watched her quietly from her room's private shrine. By night she prayed in her bed, watching moonlight creep across her floor, sending up as many prayers for Tutankhamun's *ka* as she did for her letter to find a welcome reception in Hatti.

As the seventy days of the embalming ceremony sped by, Ay had the decency not to harass her. But though he was content to leave her alone—for now—still Ankhesenamun could feel him waiting, gloating, somewhere in the depths of the palace.

In her optimistic moments, Ankhesenamun would turn toward him—toward that quiet pulse of victory she could feel beyond her chamber walls. *You think you have won*, she thought. *You think you have me cornered. But I know better.* She had been loyal to the true gods of Egypt since her marriage to Tutankhamun. She had every faith that they would sustain her—that they would answer her prayers as the Aten never did.

But not all her hours were spent in optimism. Just as often—more often—all control and faith would slide away from her and she would plunge into a sinkhole of despair. Weeping, tearing at her hair, she would be inconsolable in the face of her fate, sensing like some small, frightened animal the approach of a predator in the dark.

When the seventy days were almost past, Ankhesenamun's hope dried up like a desert well. Why had she not heard from anyone yet? Surely by now King Suppiluliuma would have made some response if he had received the letter... if he believed the unbelievable, that Egypt was willing to give its throne to a Hittite king.

But early one morning, when she was sure the seventy days had passed, when the light through her garden window was thin and weak, a flourish of horns woke her from a fitful sleep with dark, haunting dreams.

Horns. Has Tutankhamun's ship returned, then? Was his body finally here, the final proof of Ay's victory?

But no—the horns were too close. They came from within the palace itself, not from the quay. She sat up in her bed, straining to listen.

The sound was coming from the great courtyard just

inside the palace's gate. The place where an important visitor might announce himself... an ambassador, perhaps. Or a King's Son, come to claim his throne.

"Nann! Mutnodjmet!" She scrambled from her bed and stooped down to their pallets to shake her women awake, to pull them to their feet.

But her outer door crashed open, just as it had on that bleak day when Ay told her of Tutankhamun's death. *No.* She covered her mouth with her hand, fighting for breath, stunned that the gods she had come to love could be so monstrously cruel.

Nann and Mutnodjmet were on their feet by the time Ay and his soldiers stormed into her bed chamber. They tried to shield her, to hold the guards back, but Ay's men shoved the two women aside.

"Take her," Ay said coldly.

The guards seized Ankhesenamun, one on each side, clamping her thin arms in their unbreakable grips. They dragged her roughly from the apartments she hadn't left for more than two months.

Long before they reached the palace's great outer courtyard, Ankhesenamun knew she wouldn't like what was waiting there. She jerked in the guards' grip, planted her feet against the corridors' slick stone floors and tried to stop them from hauling her out into the morning light, out to face the consequences of her actions. But they dragged her along as easily as if she were a child, or a lifeless sack of grain. All the while Ay strode before her, never looking back, intent on his grim business but his *ka* fairly glowing with satisfaction.

At last they reached the courtyard. A troop of soldiers were gathered there, dusty and stained from a long march but their eyes keen and darting, each of them as riled and dangerous as a dog ready for a fight.

A chariot rolled between the soldiers' ranks. It halted in front of Ay and Ankhesenamun where she hung, helpless, between the towering guards.

"What is this?" she demanded, gasping, cringing back from the hard, hot eyes of the gathered soldiers.

But the cold smile Ay gave her made her still more fearful. "It is the answer to your letter, my lady."

Ankhesenamun's heart turned to stone in her chest. So Ay had intercepted the missive after all... or its response.

She threw herself against the guards' restraints again, kicking until the hem of her night dress tore. "Damn you, Ay! May the gods drown your *ka*!"

Ay ignored her tirade, nodding to the chariot driver, who stooped, reaching into the depths of his cart. She heard the sound of a basket being untied, the *snick* of its lid lifting. And she knew with sudden terror that she didn't want to see what was in the driver's basket. There was a sudden buzzing of flies and a great, choking stench; the man lifted the corpse-blue head of a Hittite man by its long, dark hair.

"Zennanza," Ay hissed in Ankhesenamun's ear. "His name is Zennanza—*was*. Your husband, sent to claim the throne of Egypt in Hatti's name. You promised a foreigner the Horus Throne, you treacherous bitch!"

Ankhesenamun bent double and retched, but even as she thrashed and gagged, she couldn't lower her eyes, couldn't look away from the Hittite's head, its staring, empty gaze.

"My men intercepted Hatti's response to your kind offer," Ay went on. "So I knew what was coming. My force laid in wait to greet Zennanza and his entourage as he came across the border. Really, Ankhesenamun. You would rather have a foreign dog on the throne than a man of true Egyptian blood?"

She retched again. Then, weeping, trembling, she said,

"You are no true Egyptian!"

But Ankhesenamun knew it was hopeless to resist. Ay had won.

Ankhesenamun

Year 1 of Ay
Everlasting is the Sun,
Righteous Born,
Making the Staff of Two Lands

ANKHESENAMUN TORE OFF her wedding finery the moment the door shut on her cold, confining chamber. She had suffered through the marriage ceremony at Amun's temple, weeping openly before the whole court—before the god himself. But she had no care for who saw her despair, who noted her weakness and shame. Let all the world know, and the gods above and below it, that Ankhesenamun did not consent to this marriage. Ay could force her to stand at his side in Amun's temple. He could even force the words of the ceremony from her mouth—and what dark power he had employed to make her speak those hated words, Ankhesenamun couldn't begin to guess. But he could not make her believe in her heart that she was truly his wife. Let the court see her desperation and know the truth: that Ay was treacherous, Ay was cold. He would brutalize the Two Lands with the same hard hand he used to force his granddaughter to do his bidding.

After the marriage, Ay's guards bundled Ankhesenamun onto the royal processional litter with its two gleaming thrones—the very one she had ridden so many times, glorying in her happiness with Tutankhamun high above the heads of cheering throngs. This time she sat stiff and unsmiling, her hands in her lap, as the court paraded back through the city of temples and along the wide, hot avenue of the Royal Road. Tears streaked her cheeks, the skin tightening as her ruined kohl dried in two long tracks below her eyes. But she didn't wipe at her face, didn't look at Ay when he spoke to her or at the women in the crowd who called out to her in sympathy.

Ankhesenamun sat as unfeeling as a woman carved from stone, and would have held herself in that quiet, impenetrable dignity all the way back to the palace had she not seen, as the litter swung down toward Waset's quay, the bright blue hull and fiercely pointed prow of Tutankhamun's war ship returning. She stared, disbelieving, as the boat turned in the current and nosed toward the docks, its oars lightly treading the river.

His body has returned. Ay would waste no time performing the Opening of the Mouth—and then he would be the king in truth. *He has a Great Wife of royal blood—has me in his fist, to wield like an insensate tool. And now he has Tutankhamun's body. We are both Ay's prisoners, both his to use.*

Fresh tears flowed, though she tried to hold them back. They wetted the streaks of kohl and dripped in dirty-gray splatters on the pure white linen of her gown.

I'm sorry, my Tut. Ankhesenamun hoped his *ka* could hear—and hoped just as fervently that he was far away, that he saw nothing of the spectacle playing out in the streets of Waset.

Now, shut up once more in her chamber, she ripped the gold bracelets from her arms and threw them down atop her dress and the tangled locks of her discarded wig.

"I won't stand by and watch as Ay performs the rites on Tutankhamun's body." Ankhesenamun kicked off her sandals. Then, not content to leave them where they lay, she picked them up and hurled them as hard as she could at the chamber door. Each sandal struck the wood with a clap like thunder. "Ay isn't fit to touch Tutankhamun, living or dead!"

"You'll get no argument from me," Nann said drily. "Ay isn't fit to touch a ball of dung."

Mutnodjmet rolled her eyes at Nann's useless commentary. "But he *will* perform the rites, my lady. There is nothing to stop him now—*no one* to stop him."

She turned her back on Ankhesenamun, gazing forlornly out the window into the sunlit garden. It was the place where Mutnodjmet had last seen Horemheb—where anyone had last seen the man, so far as Ankhesenamun knew. *If only Horemheb had returned to us... if only he had brought some strength to aid us. We might have kept Ay at bay; the Hittites might have gotten through. If only.*

"Ay has wedded me, and shown all the court, even all the *rekhet* of the city, that I am his wife." Calm and unhurried, resigned to her fate, Ankhesenamun crossed to her cosmetics table. She soaked a clean cloth in oil and began wiping away the dark mess of her kohl. "I've served my purpose. I have justified his place on the throne. He has no need of me now. He still intends to keep me locked here in my apartments as a prisoner. But once the Opening of the Mouth is done, he will have me killed."

"We won't let him kill you," Nann said levelly.

"I think you'll have little choice in the matter. I know I won't have my say. Ay has so many powerful men under his employ now. And now that Waset has seen me, presented as his Great Wife, he'll gain even more allies. All those who would have doubted his right to the throne—him, an upjumped charioteer, of no particular blood!—they will doubt no longer. I have given my consent to his reign, or so they will believe. If I have consented, then the gods have consented, and no one will stop Ay from doing whatever he pleases. That includes getting rid of me, and anyone who tries to protect me."

Nann edged closer to Ankhesenamun. The Hurrian's face appeared beside her own in the tall, narrow mirror of bright electrum. "Perhaps *you* might stop him, my lady."

Slowly, Ankhesenamun's hand fell away from her face. She had cleaned only one cheek; the other was still scored by the tracks of her tears. She gazed into her own dark eyes, studying her own reflection as she tested Nann's suggestion in her heart.

Kill Ay? Could she truly do it? Certainly she could not live with herself as Ay's wife—*would* not. The very thought revolted her, chilling her down to the marrow of her bones. But could she take his life in an act of vengeance?

It's what your mother would do, a voice whispered distantly in her heart. *What anyone of your dynasty would do—Nefertiti, Meritaten, Tiy. Or Akhenaten. Your own father. Him most of all.*

"I've never killed anyone before," she said. "If I do it, what will it mean for me—for my *ka*? Will I be condemned in the afterlife?" For her afterlife was near, her *ba* tugging to break free of her body. Ankhesenamun could feel it. She knew her death was coming.

"Ay is no innocent." Nann held her gaze sternly in the mirror. "If you are right, then he sent Tutankhamun to war knowing he would die—or hoping it, at least. Killing him will restore the balance of *maat*."

Ankhesenamun turned to Mutnodjmet, raising her brows in a silent question.

She expected Mutnodjmet to object, to raise some sensible caution. Instead, she too came to stand at Ankhesenamun's side. She took the cloth from her fingers and wiped gently at Ankhesenamun's other cheek, erasing all evidence of her tears.

"And if you kill Ay before he can perform the Opening of the Mouth ceremony," Mutnodjmet said, "then you will not be killing a Pharaoh. Not a full-fledged king, anyway. He won't be the king in the eyes of the gods until Tutankhamun is laid in his tomb."

"I can't see how that will make a difference." Ankhesenamun turned her face so that Mutnodjmet could reach the last of the kohl. "The people recognize Ay as king already. And why should they not, when I didn't even fight him over the marriage?"

"You fought him with all the strength you had. Your gamble with the Hittites was a good one; it would have come off, if the gods had willed it."

If the gods had willed it.

By that reckoning, didn't the gods now will that Ay should be king? Yet even if they didn't—even if Ankhesenamun could hope to avoid Ammit's jaws on timing and particulars—murder was still murder. Ankhesenamun doubted the specifics of the act, the loopholes through which she might wriggle, would make much difference when she stood before the gods in her hour of eternal judgment.

And restoring the balance of *maat*... was it so? Even if a murder righted many wrongs, was it still *maat* if it was done to gratify a wounded, bitter *ka*? Ankhesenamun didn't know whether her desire to spill out Ay's life blood— to feel it pouring hot and final through her hands—was legitimate or merely self-serving.

But as she turned again to consider her own face in the mirror, she knew she didn't care. She was willing to take the chance, whether or not it would end in her eternal damnation. If Ankhesenamun didn't kill Ay, then he would kill her. And she would rather try to set *some* of his wrongs right—or even just comfort her bruised *ka* with base vengeance—before she left this world forever.

The kohl was gone from her face, and all her tears had dried. Ankhesenamun was ready.

EATER OF HEARTS

ANKHESENAMUN SAT VERY STILL upon the tall, jeweled dais, staring down the length of the feast hall as unmoved and unfeeling as she had been on the litter. The music and murmurs of the feast rippled about her, below her, like the Iteru's waves lapping at its shore, a force unconnected to her and unaware of her pain—or the vengeance she brooded in her heart.

The wedding celebrations had only just begun. The hall filled moment by moment with wealthy men in the long, pleated kilts of nobility, their wives and concubines wrapped in robes of the brightest, cheeriest hues. But Ankhesenamun could see how most of the women cast surreptitious glances up to where she sat on her lonely throne. Their faces were pale with sympathy, their whispers behind their hands affronted and urgent. Many of the men also seemed to understand that this wedding was not what it should be—not a union the gods were likely to bless. They huddled together in wary groups, speaking into one another's ears and cutting sly looks at the throne that still sat empty beside Ankhesenamun.

She brushed the tight, wide sash at her waist with an eager hand. Nann and Mutnodjmet had dressed her carefully, binding the sash of green silk with a knot that hid the small blade perfectly. Nann had tucked the knife in with an air of expert concentration. The weapon of *maat* was tiny, its blade barely as long as Ankhesenamun's finger. But it was sharp as Sekhmet's fang—sharp enough to open the vein in Ay's neck and let his blood pour down the steps of the dais.

She would do it right in front of everyone—strike him down in Tutankhamun's name. She shivered with impatience—not with fear. She had no concern for the hundreds of eyes that watched her, for the witnesses packed into the hall like olives in a jug of oil.

Let everyone see. Let them see the knife in my fist, the blood on

354

my hands. Let the whole world know what I do.

The guards would seize her when it was over—as soon as the women stopped screaming, the men stopped shouting. They would strike her down right away, maybe run her through with their swords there on her throne. *Let them do with me whatever they will.* All that mattered now was that Ay would perish.

The doors at the hall's far end—how very far away they seemed!—opened smoothly, their groans unheard over the din of the feasting guests. But Ankhesenamun couldn't take her eyes off that great square of darkness, the black that opened to admit Ay into the hall's honest light. Ankhesenamun's mouth twisted when she saw that he wore the fine, embroidered robe of a Pharaoh and balanced on his withered old head the proud Double Crown of Egypt. She had last seen it on Tutankhamun, her love—and now the sight of it on Ay's brow, its flat-topped red base and its high, proud peak of white—turned her stomach like the worst of blasphemies.

The people cheered as Ay entered, as he made his way slowly down the hall's vast length. He seemed to savor every step he took, every moment of his long-sought victory. The cheers of his new subjects sounded dutiful to Ankhesenamun—not loving. But she knew it made no difference to Ay. He didn't require love—not from his family, and certainly not from Egypt. All he had ever required was obedience, and the acknowledgement of his ultimate, undeniable power.

They don't love him, but even so, they won't understand why I do it. She prayed the gods would understand her reason, her sacred purpose—even if they condemned her for it. That would be enough for her.

At last, Ay reached the dais and climbed up to his throne with the same ponderous, luxuriating slowness. His hard eyes narrowed with suspicion as they met her own.

Ankhesenamun's lips quirked; arrayed in his ostentatious finery, Ay looked older and feebler than ever before. But despite his age, he sat with natural ease on the throne, settling with the contentedness, the surety of *maat*, that any young man of the royal blood might have shown.

"I see you have dried your tears," he told her shortly.

"I am resigned to my fate."

"I doubt that," he said. "You were always the quiet one, but even so, there is too much of Nefertiti in you. You will make trouble for me, I think."

"What does it matter?" she said lightly, almost gaily. "Once you've performed the Opening of the Mouth, you won't need me anymore."

Ay turned to her with a long, assessing stare.

You heard no fear in my voice, Grandfather—no pleading. And there is no fear in my heart.

"Perhaps you *are* accepting of your fate," Ay said, raising a hand to signal for the first course.

And are you? Ankhesenamun watched him coolly from the tail of her eye. *Do you know what the gods have in store for you?*

The musicians played their love ballads as stewed fruit and roasted fowl were carried into the hall, hundreds of great carved-wood or gold-plated dishes borne on the shoulders of servants dressed in blue kilts—blue, the color of victory. They set steaming figs in honey sauce before Ankhesenamun, and placed a choice cut of goose's breast in her bowl. But she couldn't eat a bite. Nann's hard-eyed stares from among the servants told her she ought to try, ought to act naturally so that Ay would suspect nothing. But he already suspected her, was already on his guard. Those dark eyes darted, the old head turned, his gaze catching every one of her movements—even, she felt sure, the leap of her pulse at her throat.

For his part, Ay ate heartily while she suffered fresh pangs of doubt beside him. His appetite disgusted and frightened her—how readily he packed away the rich food, how he grabbed just as readily for power. And Ay's hunger for power was a gluttony that could never be sated. Even now, with the Double Crown on his head, seated in Tutankhamun's throne, she could feel his appetite growing, feel him searching for more... ever more.

How could the gods have allowed this? Tears prickled her eyes, but Ankhesenamun blinked them away. She forbade them from pooling, refused to let her heart ache. She had work to do, a moment to watch for. And her time was coming soon.

The music played on; an hour whiled away, and Ankhesenamun's food remained untouched. The first course was cleared away, and then, with a flourish from the musicians, a huge side of roasted beef, perfumed with herbs and crusted with salt, was carried into the hall. The kitchen staff paraded it down the aisle on its huge, smoke-blackened spit. They halted before the Pharaoh apparent; Ay laughed in delight.

But when the servers carved into the beef, Ankhesenamun saw that it was rare on the inside. Red and tender, the flesh parting easily under the carving knife, the bloody sight turned her stomach. She felt Nann watching her from within the crowd below; she could hear her friend's voice as clearly as if Nann stood behind the throne. *You must be strong. You must strike this righteous blow—here and now, where Ay will expect it the least, with all the eyes of the court on him, to witness* maat *done.*

Ankhesenamun's hand scrabbled at the knife in her sash. But she couldn't make herself draw it. She squeezed her eyes shut and turned her face away when a strip of bloody beef dropped into her bowl.

Death frightened her. She knew that now. Death... and

all the uncertainties that came after.

With her eyes tightly shut, she could see the scene of her imagination as vividly as a mural on a wall. She would stand before the old gods, whom she hardly knew but whose power she certainly did not doubt. Mut with her white wings, Amun whose skin was gold. Anupu, the black jackal, bending his graceful neck to stare down at her, to watch with cold, white eyes as she stretched out her hand to place her beating heart upon his scale. The white feather of *maat* in the scale's opposite pan— the feather gently curved, light enough that the merest breath would blow it away. And behind them, concealed in darkness, Ammit with his maw gaping wide, Ammit with a thousand teeth for rending.

Even with her eyes closed, Ankhesenamun's head spun. She stood abruptly.

"Where are you going?" Ay snapped.

"Outside… to the garden. I want fresh air." She clung to the back of her throne, steadying her legs.

Ay pressed his lips together; his gaze skated to the pillars of the portico, the blue dusk in the garden beyond. She thought for a moment that he would deny her. But no doubt the place was surrounded by soldiers, alert for any attempt the Great Wife might make to run from the palace, to evade her fate.

He settled back in his throne, flicking one hand in permission or dismissal. "Don't be long."

Ankhesenamun hurried down the steps of the dais. Even her flowing skirt felt tight and restrictive. As she passed the feast's guests, Nann and Mutnodjmet looked up from their places, concern evident in their furrowed brows. But Ankhesenamun waved their worries away, and they subsided in their seats, albeit reluctantly.

The cool air of night embraced her the moment she was

clear of the hall. Its touch was a relief, and sent a poignant stab through her heart, for she knew the night's kiss was the last kindness she would ever know. She walked alone through the dark garden, her steps slow and dragging, tears of despair stinging her eyes.

She couldn't do it—couldn't muster the strength or the courage to strike Ay down. And yet she must. She *must!* She had only a few days left until the Opening of the Mouth. And then, once Ay was the Pharaoh in truth, Ankhesenamun would meet an abrupt and callous end.

She rounded a grove of shade trees and found a secluded stone bench. She dropped heavily onto the seat, feeling the cold of the stone bite up into her flesh. She dropped her face in her hands and wept, the sobs of despair shaking her body and choking her breath, until the force of her fear and sorrow dulled a bit. The tears flowed silently now, leaking out one by one between her fingers.

A sustained rustle in the grove of shade trees made her spring up from the bench, her heart climbing into her throat. No bird or small night creature made such a sound. *Has Ay sent one of his soldiers after me? Will he do the deed tonight?* She stared around wildly at the blue-black shadows of night, their alien shapes, their slow, encroaching cold. *Or has Anupu come already to claim my ka?* Would he drag her down now, into the black depths of the Duat to face the judgment scales?

But a familiar voice called softly from inside the ring of trees: "Ankhesenamun!"

She gasped, her palms and the soles of her feet tingling with sudden excitement. She didn't dare speak his name. She looked cautiously up and down the garden path, then, when she was sure none of Ay's guards were close enough to see, she pushed her way into the screen of vines and leaves that concealed him from her view.

There he stood in the blue twilight. He wore a perfect

disguise for a night of privileged revelry: the long, formal kilt and ornate wig of a Waset nobleman. Without his soldier's garb, she might have mistaken him for one of the revelers. But his face was even more familiar to her than his broad shoulders, his scarred chest.

Shaking with gratitude, she whispered his name. "Horemheb!"

Horemheb

*Year 2 of Ay
Everlasting is the Sun,
Righteous Born,
Making the Staff of Two Lands*

W HAT ARE YOU DOING HERE?" Ankhesenamun
asked him. "Here... in the garden?"

"I know the Opening of the Mouth must happen soon,"
he murmured, darting his head like a curious bird as he
listened for guards on the pathway. "I've come back to
prevent Ay from taking the throne, if the gods will let
me."

"No," she said. "It's I who will do it. I who *must* do it."

The fear and sorrow that had wrung tears from her
only moments before seemed to vanish. She slid her hand
inside her wide sash, just behind its ornate knot... and
pulled out a tiny knife.

Horemheb laughed, struggling to stay quiet. He
couldn't help it. The blade was absurdly small, even in
Ankhesenamun's hand. "What, with that? That knife isn't
big enough to slice a fig, let alone kill a man!"

"It's no laughing matter!" Her eyes glittered at him in
what little starlight filtered down through the trees. "Ay
as good as told me that he'll get rid of me as soon as
Tutankhamun is in his tomb. I'm no use to him anymore—
or won't be, once the Horus Throne is his. Should I go
meekly to an unjust death?"

"You're a fool," he said, affection and admiration welling

up in his chest. "But a very brave one."

"Do you think I can't do it—can't kill that treacherous creature who calls himself the king?"

Horemheb steadied her with a hand on her shoulder. "My lady, I wouldn't put it past anyone of your bloodline to commit any shocking deed. But I will do this task for you—when the time is right."

"The time is right now," she hissed. "It must be now, for once Tutankhamun's funeral is done, Ay will be the king by all rights... and anyone who kills him *then* will be cursed forever!"

Horemheb nodded. He couldn't speak for one long, painful moment. He remembered holding Baketaten in his arms as the last of her blood drained, as the warmth faded from her body. "That is why it should be me," he said soberly, "why it can only be me. I am already so cursed. I have struck down one king. What's another added to my tally?"

But still Ankhesenamun persisted. "It should be a person from my own dynasty, Horemheb. And who is left but me? Perhaps if *I* kill Ay, and rid the world of his evil, then my family's wrongs will be set right. Then I can go on living for Egypt. I can find a new king, have sons who will be righteous and true. My blood will be redeemed."

Horemheb took the knife from Ankhesenamun's hand. It was easy to do; she surrendered it without complaint, her fingers going limp, trembling as he brushed them with his own. "My lady," he said softly, "the time has come to end your dynasty's reign. Let Egypt suffer no more under your bloodline."

Tears filled her eyes. "What do you mean? The throne is ours by right."

"'Ours?'" How he longed to comfort her, to wrap her in his arms and beg forgiveness for what he soon would do.

But he couldn't do it. In the many long days of his exile, Horemheb had come to understand what must be done for Egypt's sake, what part he must play in this strange drama, even with the curse of king-slaying staining his *ka*. "There is only you, Ankhesenamun. Only you who still carries the divine blood." *And all the corruption that flows with it.*

"If I had a new husband," she said, blinking, "I might bear him living children."

"No," Horemheb said, pitying her. "The sun has set on your kin. Your line grew too corrupted; Egypt suffered too much. The gods will not allow it to go on." Unworthy as he was, Horemheb had seen that much. "It's time we gave the Two Lands a fresh start. Let's not draw out this curse forever."

"I am no curse," she said. But she wept, her face contorted with the pain of surrender. "Gods, Horemheb, I am the last! The very last! I must try to preserve my family's legacy. They weren't all treacherous. Tutankhamun was good, and Smenkhkare. For their sakes—"

"They are dead and buried," he said, "or will be soon."

"You cannot think to let Ay reign. He is far more treacherous than my family ever was."

"No," he agreed. "Ay will not reign. I will not allow it. It's time for a new king, a new dynasty."

She stared up at him, searching his face. In the faint starlight he could see her features still, the stunned comprehension that widened her eyes, that left her mouth to hang mutely open.

"I have friends now," he said, explaining it, justifying. "Supporters. These seventy days I've been away, but I haven't been idle. My men wait outside the palace walls even now. We've surrounded the palace, and have spread all through the city, too. Waset is full of my men now, while all of Ay's supporters are gathered here for the feast."

"Trapped," she said, "like goats in a pen."

"So you see, Ay's reign will not last long. In fact, I should think it will be breathtakingly short."

"When will you do it?" Her voice trembled.

"Soon—very soon. I would get to a place of safety if I were you. I will make this coup as bloodless as I can; I don't want innocent people harmed. But I will not tolerate Ay's rule—Egypt will only suffer under his power—and if it comes down to hard choices, I will do what I must to break Ay's hold. He and his loyal men will certainly resist; there will be at least a little violence. You will be better off away from the feast, the dais—as far as you can get from Ay's side."

She glanced down at the sword on his hip. Then she turned quickly, heading back toward the hall. "Nann and Mutnodjmet—"

Horemheb caught her by the arm. "I will have one of my friends warn them before the fighting begins. They will have a chance to get to safety. Believe me, Ankhesenamun; I wouldn't endanger my own wife."

She paused, still turned toward the feast hall, staring off into the night with that strange way she had of watching, of seeing. Music, distant and thin, rose gaily up to meet the stars. Ankhesenamun listened. A tiny smile stirred her features; sorrow loosed its hold on her heart, for a moment at least. Then she faced Horemheb resolutely once more.

"When it's over," she said, "will I be gotten rid of too? After all, I am the last of my family's line—the last part of the dynasty you think to unmake. What will be *my* fate, Horemheb?"

He sighed raggedly and shuffled his feet. In the two months while he plucked at Waset's secret strings, consolidating his power and planning his attack, Horemheb had thought often of Ankhesenamun. He had thought up a dozen different ways to heal this torn and suffering land. But he had not yet solved the problem of Ankhesenamun.

Sense told him he ought to kill her. She was, as she said, of the old royal blood. If she could bear living children, they might be a threat to his power. But he liked her— respected her. There were times when he even thought he loved her, with a protective, brotherly fondness. Recalling her vulnerability as a child in Akhet-Aten, and later, her astonishing grief at the loss of her children, Horemheb pitied her. He wished her no harm, would cause her no harm if the gods were merciful to them both. But Ankhesenamun was his enemy now... even if she had long been his friend. Egypt needed Horemheb more than she did. Egypt needed them both to be brave, self-sacrificing. Ankhesenamun—or any children she might produce— could plunge the country into a battle for rightful inheritance, a war the Two Lands had no more resources left to fight.

"I don't know," he finally admitted. "I don't know what's to become of you, and that is the honest truth. I want to believe there is goodness in you, Ankhesenamun. I want to believe that you can rise above your family's evils—that you have already, that you are safe for me and for Egypt. I want to believe you're different from all those others who shared your blood. But you are what you are. The same blood runs in you that ran in Akhenaten—and that runs still in Ay."

"You believed in Tutankhamun," she said. "You trusted him. And he was of my blood."

"Indeed I did trust him, and believe in him, too. But he was young. Perhaps in time the corruption that darkened your family's hearts would have fallen over him, too." He closed his eyes briefly, listening to the music and laughter of the feast, the rhythmic song of insects in the garden. The last moments of peace before the palace would erupt into chaos. "Perhaps there is no escaping our fates," he said softly.

She flared up at him in anger. "And is it your fate, to usurp the throne that rightfully belongs to me?"

Horemheb laid one gentle hand on her shoulder. "Take your throne back from me if you can."

"You won't even let me try."

As she said the words, Horemheb knew they were true. And it pained his heart to know it. "Go off to your chamber," he said. "Shut yourself in. Bar the door and stay quiet inside."

"My chamber?" She laughed bitterly and jerked out from under his hand. "You mean my prison."

"Don't unbar your door until you hear from me. I'll send you word when it's safe to come out."

She held his eye a moment longer. Her dark stare was full of challenge, the desperate, brave, furious fight a leopard gives when it knows it is treed by the hounds— when it knows there is no escape from the hunter's spear.

Forgive me, Horemheb wanted to say. *My friend, forgive me.*

But for Egypt's sake he held his tongue. With all the quiet dignity of a King's Great Wife—with the regal grace of the divine blood—Ankhesenamun walked away.

Ankhesenamun

Year 1 of Horemheb
Holy Are the Manifestations,
Chosen of Re

ALTHOUGH ANKHESENAMUN went straight to her apartments, just as Horemheb bade her, she did not bar the door. Instead she left it open and sat wrapped in a heavy blanket, huddled on her blue silk couch, listening as the fighting raged through the palace. Though harsh, angry shouts and the clashing of blades rang down corridors and through the courtyards—even spilling out into the gardens as night gave way to dawn— no one approached the Great Wife's chambers. The door hung open, a tacit invitation for anyone to come and take her, to dispose of her however they would—Ay's men or Horemheb's, or Anupu with his slender neck and piercing eyes. But no one ever came. Ankhesenamun was forgotten in the fury of the coup. Left entirely alone.

In the morning she rose stiffly from her couch and found a few scraps of bread, a quarter of a jar of wine left over from the breakfast she could barely eat before her wedding to Ay. She stuffed the food in her mouth, though the bread had gone stale and the wine sour. She slept through the heat of the day, curled on her rumpled bed, her fitful dreams plagued by the ringing of blades against shields and the hoarse screams of men.

She did not wake until moonrise. Whether she had slept one day away or two—or more; a whole year, perhaps— Ankhesenamun couldn't say. Her chamber was still as empty as her stomach, the door still thrown wide in a mute appeal for mercy, for an end to the waiting, the not knowing.

She stood in the garden door, leaning against its stone frame, watching as a violet-gray dusk gave way to the silver flush of starlight. The garden was at peace, if the rest of the palace was not. Now and then she still heard an occasional skirmish from some distant wall, or a chorus of curses from the roof of a nearby wing. But insects trilled among the flower beds and bats dipped low to brush with their wingtips the luminescent surface of the lake.

I could walk away now, she realized. *Ay's men, Horemheb's... they are so intent on one another that no one will think about me. No one will stop me. No one will see me.* She would go straight out the palace gate, into the streets of Waset, and would keep on walking wherever her feet led. Just as Nefertiti walked from Akhet-Aten, calm and quiet, surrendered utterly to the gods.

But Ankhesenamun didn't move. Though her belly ached with hunger and she was dizzy with the need for water, she remained at her garden door as the full moon climbed higher in the sky. She stayed and watched, stayed and listened. That had ever been her way.

After an hour or more, she heard a soft rustle in her apartments. She turned, staring into the unlit rooms, the shrouds of shadows that hung about their dark corners. She recognized Mutnodjmet at once, even without her lamps lit. The woman didn't run to Ankhesenamun, wasn't solicitous as a servant ought to be. Mutnodjmet stood still, holding herself at a deliberate distance while she and Ankhesenamun regarded each other in silence.

A change had come over Mutnodjmet; Ankhesenamun saw it clearly. Though she still wore the simple linen smock of a servant—and even that was splashed with the foulness of vomit—she looked as haughty as Nefertiti ever had. Finally she lifted her chin and approached

Ankhesenamun slowly, head held high.

"You're safe," Ankhesenamun said. "I am relieved to know. Is Nann safe as well?"

"Nann and I have been attending the Pharaoh apparent," Mutnodjmet said. She sounded coyly amused, but she did not lower her chin. She looked down her nose at Ankhesenamun. "I'm sorry to report that he has died."

"Ay is dead?" Ankhesenamun perked up, a new energy rattling through her. The quick movement was a mistake, given the emptiness of her stomach. A wave of dizziness swept her, and she clung to the garden door.

Mutnodjmet's shrug was eloquent. "Ay was an old man. Old men have sudden maladies. He overindulged at the feast, I suppose. A terrible pain in his belly. Nann and I gave him potions all night to ease his discomfort, but alas, he was too ill even to rise from his bed and rally his men. When the forces from Waset flooded into the palace, Ay could do nothing."

"You poisoned him?" She glanced again at the stains on Mutnodjmet's dress.

The woman smiled coolly. "Nann was most insistent that she should care for Ay in his unfortunate sickness. She often leaned close to him and spoke in his ear. I couldn't make out much of what she said, but I did hear her whisper a certain name now and again."

"Tadukhepa," Ankhesenamun guessed.

"Our Nann was always a remarkably patient woman. And terribly loyal."

"But Ay had nothing to do with Lady Tadukhepa's death."

"That makes no matter to Nann. He was a patriarch of your foul line, and so he was responsible—for Tadukhepa and every other evil your dynasty ever committed."

Ankhesenamun narrowed her eyes, assessing

Mutnodjmet more sharply. "And you think *your* dynasty will be less terrible than mine. Is that the way of it? You think your husband, your blood, will resist the lure of power?"

"I don't know what you're talking about," Mutnodjmet said lightly.

"Don't play the fool with me. You were my servant. I thought once that you were my friend. I spoke to Horemheb on the night of the feast. I know what he planned. I know what he's doing even now—setting himself on the throne." Her fists clenched of their own accord; she stumbled toward Mutnodjmet despite the quivering of her legs. "My throne! While I still live! I, in whose blood the divine right flows!"

Mutnodjmet sniffed. "It's not the right of blood that should determine who rules. The right of strength is *maat*—the right of justice and good intent."

"That is not how the gods have made the world," Ankhesenamun said. She felt the last surge of her power rise, the last throb of her dynasty's heart beating deep in her body. "Horemheb cannot be king unless he marries me. It is my gift to bestow—not yours, or your husband's, to take."

"That was the old way," Mutnodjmet said. "What is old passes away, sooner or later." She looked down pointedly at her stained tunic.

"You don't know how to be a King's Wife," Ankhesenamun said. She said it harshly, desperately, trying to wound her former friend with a sudden, childish venom.

But Mutnodjmet stood in a place beyond Ankhesenamun's wrath, and it was she who did the wounding. Her careless shrug cut deep into Ankhesenamun's heart. "That hardly matters," Mutnodjmet said. "I will be King's Wife—Great Wife—whether you like it or not." She swallowed hard; her pretty face turned down to stare at her own feet.

"Whether I like it or not. I did consider you a friend, Ankhesenamun. I did love you, I swear it. And I don't wish to hurt you."

Ankhesenamun's body had gone very cold. "Leave me."

Mutnodjmet did leave, but paused on the door's threshold. All her sudden, alarming haughtiness returned. She said over her shoulder, "You aren't needed anymore. Horemheb will be king without you—with me by his side. But there are still some in the palace and the city who will resist the destruction of the old ways. There will be more fighting, and you would be wise to leave the city now—this very hour, while you still can."

"I will not leave!" Ankhesenamun's voice rose very near a scream, though she didn't will it—tried to hold it back. "This palace is mine, while I still live—my birthright! It is the only thing I have to show for all the ways I've suffered. I will not abandon what is mine!"

"Please yourself," Mutnodjmet said, and vanished through the open door.

As Mutnodjmet predicted, throughout the night more fighting rolled through the palace as factions regrouped and threw themselves at Horemheb again. But Ankhesenamun could hear by the triumphant cheers of Horemheb's name that the usurper was winning. It was true, what Horemheb had told her: the people of the land had no love for her family. They had suffered too much under the rule of her dynasty. They were ready for a change—starving for it— even if it meant tearing down tradition and embracing a brash, irreverent new way.

Nann came with the dawn. She stood over Ankhesenamun's bed, her green eyes gazing down with mild curiosity while Ankhesenamun stared back in a daze of hunger and defeat.

"Up," the Hurrian said.

Dull, uncaring, Ankhesenamun struggled up to sit on her bed.

Nann pushed a covered basket across the bed toward Ankhesenamun. The latter lifted the lid warily, but when she saw the flat discs of bread, the boiled eggs and long, green melons nestled inside she threw the lid aside and tore ravenously into the bread.

"Water," Nann said, passing her a full, heavy skin.

She was dimly aware that Nann might have poisoned the food—used, perhaps, the very same potions she had given to Ay, in a bid to do away with the final member of the family that had tormented her beloved mistress Kiya—that had meant Tadukhepa's death. But she couldn't make herself stop eating, and didn't care anyway if she swallowed a river of poison as great as the Iteru. She had eaten almost nothing for three days, and her body, still bent on survival despite her *ka*'s fatalistic desire to wait for whatever might come, insisted that she eat.

After she had eaten three rounds of bread, five eggs, and half a melon, Ankhesenamun's stomach protested. She sat back and pushed the basket away. For a long moment she held Nann's calm, level gaze. Then she wept. The tears poured down her cheeks, stinging her skin with their salt.

"Will I die now?" she asked between her shuddering sobs.

Nann stroked her hair gently. "Not by my hand."

"Even though I am one of them—the dynasty that hurt your mistress?"

Nann hummed in sympathy. "My lady, you were as much an innocent in your family's schemes as Tadukhepa ever was."

"What will become of me now, Nann? Tell me, if you know. Horemheb... will he...?"

"I respect Horemheb," Nann said decisively. "He will be

a strong Pharaoh."

"I respect him, too." Ankhesenamun was surprised to feel the truth of those words, the power of *maat* ringing deep inside her *ka*.

"He will put Egypt to rights."

"But I—"

"I cannot tell you what will come." Nann stood and gathered up her things—the basket of food, mostly empty now; the half-drained water skin. "My duty has been discharged; Ishtar has no use for me anymore. I cannot see your fate, my lady, any more than I can see my own."

"Won't you stay with me?" Ankhesenamun reached for Nann's hand, but the Hurrian stepped back, out of her reach. "Where are you going?"

"Back to Mitanni. There is nothing left for me in Egypt. I'm going home now—at last, after so many years. I will leave offerings to Ishtar at all the shrines in Mitanni, and I will pray that the goddess guides Tadukhepa home."

"Please don't leave me." Ankhesenamun's voice was small. Its frailty made her shudder.

But Nann turned away without another word, and walked out the garden door.

Ankhesenamun

Year 1 of Horemheb
Holy Are the Manifestations,
Chosen of Re

HOREMHEB FINALLY walked through Ankhesenamun's open door, just as the heat of midday was rising. A thick bandage wrapped one forearm and he moved with a slight limp, but he seemed whole and strong, buoyed up by his decisive victory.

Ankhesenamun watched him approach, but said nothing. He stood before her for a long time, holding her gaze. Then, abruptly, with an uncomfortable twitch of his shoulders, he dropped his head and turned away.

But he spoke to her: "I am glad to see you survived the fighting."

Ankhesenamun only looked at him, seeing the terrible triumph that shone from his body, knowing the moment of her judgment had come.

"Now that the palace is secured," Horemheb said, examining the mural on her chamber wall, "we will finally be able to carry Tutankhamun's body to his tomb. His well-deserved rest is at hand."

"You'll open his mouth, then," Ankhesenamun said dully. "You will be Pharaoh now."

"Yes."

She sighed. "Will you allow me to come to see his burial? Will you let me stand in my husband's tomb for the rites of death?"

"You must remain here a while longer, I'm afraid," Horemheb said gently, sadly. "Your doors and the garden will be heavily guarded. Please don't try to escape. I don't want you harmed, if I can help it."

She let that sink into her bones—the awful knowledge that she would not be with Tutankhamun when his *ka* stood at the doorway to the Duat. "And what will you do with me after?" she finally asked.

"Once I've claimed the throne I will be able to decide. I want you to live, Ankhesenamun—you must believe me about that. But I will do whatever I must, for Egypt's sake."

"Can you tell me nothing? Can you not give me some idea?"

Reluctantly, Horemheb shook his head. "I simply don't know—not yet. But I will keep you as comfortably as I can until I've had time to consult with the gods as well as my priests and advisors. Whatever fate they decide for you, I will carry out faithfully."

"Will you?" she said bitterly. "Even if it means you must kill a woman who was once your mistress and your friend?"

"You will always be my friend," he said. "Always a brave, admirable fool. Do you need anything?"

I need help, she thought hopelessly. *I need gods who aren't heartless and cold. I need courage that won't abandon me. I need Tutankhamun—the only one who ever loved me.*

"Papyrus," she finally said. "Plenty of it. And ink, and a brush to write with."

Horemheb tilted his head, a wary look. "I've heard all about the damage you can do with a letter, Ankhesenamun. I won't allow you to send for help."

"There is no one for me to write to now, no one who might give me aid. And no one cares for my story but the gods."

Still he hesitated, and seemed about to deny her request. Ankhesenamun said softly, "Horemheb..."

He nodded. "All right. I'll see to it." He limped closer, lifted her chin in his rough, conqueror's hand. Then he bent and kissed her cheek. "I will pray to Amun to grant you mercy. Let us hope my prayers are heard."

He left, pulling her door shut behind him. Ankhesenamun heard the stamping of the guards as they saluted at their post—and heard Horemheb's unsteady gait as he made his way slowly down the hall.

Shortly a servant came, bearing a fat roll of papyrus, a pot of ink, and several good brushes. Ankhesenamun thanked the man, but after he had gone she sat at her table, staring at the blank paper in desolation. The sun spilled down the narrow throat of her chamber's wind catcher. The square of bright, hot fire crept inexorably across the floor.

Soon the sun would set. Another night would pass, silver and cool, quiet and private as a tomb. In the morning the sun would rise again, its featureless face cast down to watch a new Egypt unfolding, a new empire building itself, brick by brick, from the rubble of a broken dynasty.

And by the morning, the gods would give their answer. Horemheb would return with Ankhesenamun's fate in his hands.

Ankhesenamun unrolled the first hand's breadth of the scroll. It lay waiting for her words—her confession— truth that was *maat*. She dipped her brush in the ink pot, listening to the clamor of voices in her heart: all the ones she had called her family, the ones in whose image the gods had seen fit to make her. Their voices were a chorus in her *ka*, and though their singing was discordant, still she knew the hymn.

Ankhesenamun laid her brush to the scroll and began to write.

ABOUT THE AUTHOR

Libbie Hawker writes historical and literary fiction featuring complex characters and rich details of time and place. In her free time she enjoys hiking, sailing, road-tripping through the American West, and working on her podcast about Jem and the Holograms.

She lives in the San Juan Islands with her husband Paul. Between her two pen names, she is the author of more than twenty books.

Find more, including contact information and updates about future releases, on her web site: LibbieHawker.com